CRITICS' PRAISE

AMERICA - EARLY REVIEWS

"The writing of author Mike Bond features lovely descriptions of nature and the scenes in the book. Each of the main characters are well-developed and engaging. Many of the adventures and events in the books are exciting to read about...America reminded me of James Michener's book *The Drifters*." - Jean, Goodreads

"America was the book I needed to read in high school to really understand American History. Mike Bond wrote characters that you instantly fall in love with and desperately need to know what happens next. Bond made events in American history interesting and wrote about them so well you felt like you were there yourself." - Niki Mackedanz, Goodreads

"Mike Bond has the most beautiful prose I have ever read...The style of writing is very elegant and the book reflects the ideas of our times. Maybe our knowledge today can help new readers learn how the government can lead others to kill and be killed. The author does not tell how others should think, but the beautiful story will help others to think. Each new book from Mike Bond seems to become better." - Jay Williams, NetGalley

"America is a spell-binding story of three young people who meet in the 1950s and disconnect and reconnect in the 60s. The author touches on many of the themes of the decade but majors on the assassination of President Kennedy, the Vietnam War, the Civil Rights Movement, and the sexual revolution. The characters are well developed and the story is enthralling. I recommend this book." - Irene L., NetGalley

"This novel is a saga that reminded me of a John Jakes series. The characters are compelling and I love how we follow them through growing up in the 1960s and see how they react to and are affected by all of the major historical events of their time. I can't wait to read the second book in the series." - Educator, NetGalley

"It's an ambitiously conceived saga and when the last chapter ended, I found myself hooked......there's no question that I'm eager to read the next book in the series. And for anyone afraid to take on an epic like this, I can only say that I found Mike Bond's writing swift, accessible and filled with knowing observations and viewpoints on those monumental times." Scott C., NetGalley

"This is the first book in a series that has captured the feelings and turmoil of the 1950-1960s. The characters reminded me of people I grew up with. The conflicts of that time had faded for me but this story brought back a lot of memories- both good and bad. I could not put it down- looking forward to book 2." - Helen J., NetGalley

---

SNOW

"A captivating story of three friends on opposing sides of a betrayal... Bond tells his story in a crisp, propulsive prose that darts from sentence to sentence... He also has a sharp ear for dialogue and a knack for character development... Themes of the destructiveness of greed, both private and corporate; the sacredness of nature; and the primeval ways of mankind lend weight to a well-paced tale with intricate storylines." – *Kirkus*

"An action-packed adventure, but also a morality tale of what happens when two men who should know better get entangled in a crime from which they can't escape. " –*Denver Post*

"More than just a thriller, *Snow* lights up the complexities of American culture, the tensions of morality and obligation and the human search for love and freedom, all of which makes it clear Bond is a masterful storyteller." –*Sacramento Bee*

"A complex inter play of fascinating characters." –*Culture Buzz*

"Exploring the psyche and the depths of human reasoning and drive, *Snow* is a captivating story." –*BookTrib*

"An action-packed thriller that wouldn't let go. The heart-pounding scenes kept me on the edge of my seat." –*Goodreads*

"A simple story at its heart that warps into a splendid morality tale." –*Providence Sunday Journal*

GOODBYE PARIS
Pono Hawkins Book 3

"There's tension, turmoil and drama on every page that's hot enough to singe your fingers." – *New York Times* Bestseller, Steve Berry

"A rip-roaring page-turner , edgy and brilliantly realistic." – *Culture Buzz*

"Exhilarating ." – *Kirkus*

"Another non-stop thriller of a novel by a master of the genre." – *Midwest Book Review*

"A stunning thriller, entrancing love story and exciting account of anti-terror operations." – *BookTrib*

"Doesn't stop until it has delivered every possible ounce of intelligent excitement." – *Miami Times*

"Fast and twisty, and you don't know how it's going to end." – *Arizona Sun*

"Mike Bond is my favorite author... and his books are nothing short of works of art... I could not put this book down once I started reading it." – *Goodreads*

"A great book with normal special forces action and thrills, but what makes it great is the integration of Islamic terrorism." – *Basingtone Reviews*

"An action-packed story culminates in an exciting ending." – *The Bookworm*

"Thrills... crisp writing and intelligence." – *St. Louis Today*

ASSASSINS

"An exhilarating spy novel that offers equal amounts of ingenuity and intrigue." – *Kirkus*

"Bond is one of America's best thriller writers ... You need to get this book... It's an eye-opener, a page-turner... very strongly based in reality." – *Culture Buzz*

"An epic spy story... Bond often writes with a staccato beat, in sentence fragments with the effect of bullet fire. His dialogue is sharp and his description of combat is tactical and detached, professional as a soldier's debriefing. Yet this terseness is rife with tension and feeling... A cohesive and compelling story of political intrigue, religious fanaticism, love, brotherhood and the ultimate pursuit of peace." – *Honolulu Star Advertiser*

"Packs one thrilling punch after the other... A first-rate thriller." – *Book Chase*

"Powerful, true to life, and explosive ... A story that could be ripped right out of the headlines." – *Just Reviews*

"Riveting, thrilling... so realistic and fast-paced that the reader felt as if they were actually there." – *NetGalley*

"The action is outstanding and realistic. The suspense flows from page to page... The background is provided by recent events we have all lived through. The flow of the writing is almost musical as romance and horrors share equal billing... I wish everyone could read and understand this book." – *Goodreads*

KILLING MAINE
Pono Hawkins Book 2

FIRST PRIZE FOR FICTION, 2016, *New England Book Festival*: "A gripping tale of murders, manhunts and other crimes set amidst today's dirty politics and corporate graft, an unforgettable hero facing enormous dangers as he tries to save a friend, protect the women he loves, and defend a beautiful, endangered place."

"Another terrifically entertaining read from a master of the storytelling craft... A work of compelling fiction... Very highly recommended." – *Midwest Book Review*

"Quite a ride for those who love good crime thrillers... I can't recommend this one strongly enough." – *Book Chase*

"Bond returns with another winner in *Killing Maine*. Bond's ability to infuse his real-world experiences into a fast-paced story is unequaled." – *Culture Buzz*

"A twisting mystery with enough suspicious characters and red herrings to keep you guessing. It's also a dire warning about the power of big industry and a commentary on our modern ecological responsibilities. A great read for the socially and environmentally conscious mystery lover." – *Honolulu Star-Advertiser*

"Sucks in the reader and makes it difficult to put the book down until the very last page... A winner of a thriller." – *Mystery Maven*

"Another stellar ride from Bond; checking out Pono's first adventure isn't a prerequisite, but this will make readers want to." – *Kirkus*

SAVING PARADISE
Pono Hawkins Book 1

"Bond is one of the 21 Century's most exciting authors... An action-packed, must read novel ... taking readers behind the alluring façade of Hawaii's pristine beaches and tourist traps into a festering underworld of murder, intrigue and corruption." – *Washington Times*

"A complex, entertaining ... lusciously convoluted story." – *Kirkus*

"Highly recommended." – *Midwest Book Review*

"A rousing crime thriller – but it is so much more... a highly atmospheric thriller focusing on a side of Hawaiian life that tourists seldom see." – *Book Chase*

"An intersection of fiction and real life." – *Hawaii Public Radio*

"An absolute page-turner." – *Ecotopia Radio*

"An unusual thriller and a must-read." – *Fresh Fiction*

"A complex murder mystery about political and corporate greed and corruption... Bond's vivid descriptions of Hawaii bring *Saving Paradise* vibrantly to life." – *Book Reviews and More*

"*Saving Paradise* will change you... It will call into question what little you really know, what people want you to believe you know and then hit you with a deep wave of dangerous truths." – *Where Truth Meets Fiction*

THE LAST SAVANNA

FIRST PRIZE FOR FICTION, 2016, *Los Angeles Book Festival* : "One of the best books yet on Africa, a stunning tale of love and loss amid a magnificent wilderness and its myriad animals, and a deadly manhunt through savage jungles, steep mountains and fierce deserts as an SAS commando tries to save the elephants, the woman he loves and the soul of Africa itself."

"A gripping thriller." – *Liverpool Daily Post (UK)*

"One of the most realistic portrayals of Africa yet... Dynamic, heart -breaking and timely to current events ... a must-read." – *Yahoo Reviews*

"Sheer intensity, depicting the immense, arid land and never-ending scenes... but it's the volatile nature of nature itself that gives the story its greatest distinction." – *Kirkus*

"One of the most darkly beautiful books you will ever read." – *WordDreams*

"Exciting, action-packed ... A nightmarish vision of Africa." – Manchester Evening *News (UK)*

"A powerful love story set in the savage jungles and deserts of East Africa." – *Daily Examiner (UK)*

"The central figure is not human; it is the barren, terrifying landscape of Northern Kenya and the deadly creatures who inhabit it." – *Daily Telegraph (UK)*

"An entrancing, terrifying vision of Africa." – *BBC*

"The action is exciting, and a surprise awaits over each new page." – *NetGalley*

HOLY WAR

"Action-filled thriller. " – *Manchester Evening News (UK)*

"This suspense-laden novel has a never-ending sense of impending doom... An unyielding tension leaves a lasting impression." – *Kirkus*

"A profound tale of war ... Impossible to stop reading. " – *British Armed Forces Broadcasting*

"A terrific book ... The smells, taste, noise, dust, and fear are communicated so clearly." – *Great Book Escapes*

"A super charged thriller ... A story to chill and haunt you." – *Peterborough Evening Telegraph (UK)*

"A tale of fear , hatred, revenge, and desire, flicking between bloody Beirut and the lesser battles of London and Paris." – *Evening Herald (UK)*

"If you are looking to get a driver's seat look at the landscape of modern conflict, holy wars, and the Middle East then this is the perfect book to do so." – *Masterful Book Reviews*

"A gripping tale of passion, hostage- taking and war, set against a war- ravaged Beirut." – *Evening News (UK)*

"A stunning novel of love and loss, good and evil, of real people who live in our hearts after the last page is done...Unusual and profound. " – *Greater London Radio*

————

HOUSE OF JAGUAR

"A riveting thriller of murder, politics, and lies. " – *London Broadcasting*

"Tough and tense thriller." – *Manchester Evening News (UK)*

"A high-octane story rife with action, from U.S. streets to Guatemalan jungles." – *Kirkus*

"A terrifying depiction of one man's battle against the CIA and Latin American death squads." – *BBC*

"Vicious thriller of drugs and revolution in the wilds of Guatemala." – *Liverpool Daily Post (UK)*

"With detailed descriptions of actual jungle battles and manhunts, vanishing rain forests and the ferocity of guerrilla war, *House of Jaguar* also reveals the CIA's role in both death squads and drug running, twin scourges of Central America. " – *Newton Chronicle (UK)*

"Grips the reader from the very first page. An ideal thriller for the beach, but be prepared to be there when the sun goes down." – *Herald Express (UK)*

———

TIBETAN CROSS

"Bond's deft thriller will reinforce your worst fears… A taut, tense tale of pursuit through exotic and unsavory locales. " – *Publishers Weekly*

"Grips the reader from the very first chapter until the climactic ending." – *UPI*

"One of the most exciting in recent fiction… An astonishing thriller." – *San Francisco Examiner*

"A tautly written study of one man's descent into living hell… a mood of near claustrophobic intensity." – *Spokane Chronicle*

"It *is* a thriller … Incredible, but also believable." – *Associated Press*

"A thriller that everyone should go out and buy right away. The writing is wonderful throughout… Bond working that fatalistic margin where life and death are one and the existential reality leaves one caring only to survive." – *Sunday Oregonian*

"Murderous intensity … A tense and graphically written story." – *Richmond Times*

"The most jaundiced adventure fan will be held by *Tibetan Cross*." – *Sacramento Bee*

"Grips the reader from the opening chapter and never lets go." – *Miami Herald*

———

THE DRUM THAT BEATS WITHIN US
Poetry

"Passionately felt emotional connections, particularly to Western landscapes and Native American culture… compellingly linking the great cycles of stars with little, common lives… to create a powerful sense of loss… a muscular poignancy." – *Kirkus*

"The poetry is sometimes raw, painful, exquisite but there is always the sense that it was written from the heart." – *LibraryThing*

"A collection of poetry that explores the elements of nature, what nature can provide, what nature can take away, and how humans are connected to it all." – *Book Review Bin*

"An exploration of self and nature... that asks us to look at our environment through the eyes of animals... and the poetry that has been with us since the dawn of time... comforting, challenging, and thought provoking." – *Bound2Books*

"His poetry courses, rhythmic and true through his works. His words serve as an important alarm for readers to wake from their contented slumber of self-absorbed thought and notice the changes around them. Eye-opening and a joy to read, the master of the existential thriller can add another winning title to his accolades." – *BookTrib*

"The language is beautiful, heartbreaking, romantic, sad, savvy, and nostalgic all at once. From longer poems to very short, thought-provoking poems, the lines of each take the reader to a world the poet has experienced or given much thought to. Truly beautiful." – *Goodreads*

"This is such a beautiful book of poetry ... the imagery is vibrant, devastating, and haunting... A thoroughly modern 21st century collection that revisits and revises classic themes. Highly recommended." – *NetGalley*

"The poems are beautiful and range from the long lyrical expressions of love and nature to the brief expressions of a moments insight into a sudden feeling, expressed with a few words that capture the moment and the feeling perfectly. " – *Metapsychology Reviews*

"*The Drum That Beats Within Us* presents us with a world gone awry, a world in which the warrior poet has fought, and a world in which only love survives." – *Vine Reviews*

AMERICA

Published in the United States by Big City Press, New York.

ISBN paperback: 978-1-949751-20-8

ISBN ebook: 978-1-949751-21-5

Cover Design by Alan Dingman

Author photo by © PF Bentley/PFPix.com

https://mikebondbooks.com

PUBLISHER'S CATALOGING-IN-PUBLICATION DATA
Names: Bond, Mike, author.
Title: America : volume 1 / Mike Bond.
Series: America.
Description: New York, NY: Big City Press, 2021.
Identifiers: ISBN: 9781949751208 (pbk.) | 9781949751215 (ebook)
Subjects: LCSH Friendship--Fiction. | United States--History--1961-1969--Fiction. | United States--Social conditions--1960-1980--Fiction. | United States--Social life and customs--1945-1970--Fiction. | United States--History--20th century--Fiction. | Bildungsroman. | BISAC FICTION / General | FICTION / Historical / General | FICTION / Coming of Age
Classification: LCC PS3619.O54 A64 v.1 | DDC 813.6--dc23

to
Jude

It is the consistent choice of the path with heart which makes a warrior different from the average man. He knows that a path has heart when he is one with it, when he experiences a great peace and pleasure traversing its length.

– Carlos Castaneda

MIKE BOND

AMERICA

BIG CITY PRESS

CONTENTS

FOREWORD

AFTER THE KOREAN WAR ended in 1953, for nearly a decade America was at peace. Despite the fear of communism there was little active war. People flourished, ideas expanded. Cities, roads and suburbs grew, rural and wild lands diminished. These were the last gentle years before America killed its president and collapsed into a war it could not win, antiwar and civil rights revolutions, a bewildering new world of altered perceptions, and a chaotic tsunami of sexual and social evolutions.

By 1965, Vietnam had shocked America with its horror, anguish and brutality. A vast divide grew between those who supported the War and those against it. At the same time the evils of segregation and the economic disparities within America were leading to a cosmic clash of riots and burning cities. Into this seismic rift marijuana crashed its hedonic way, enticing people to doubt many beliefs previously accepted, to have fun, be kind, and follow the path with heart. And even worse, to challenge authority by teaching that the individual has the right to decide how to live.

Along with marijuana arrived other psychotropics that teased the mind into altered states of perception and wisdom, with profound results on morality and behavior. At the same time the pill began to change the sex lives of young Americans – for the first time it was possible to make love with no fear of pregnancy. And as more and more people enjoyed more sex and the pleasures of marijuana, young men became less and less willing to go off to war and die.

And into this primal upheaval erupted music – a *new* music – raw, nasty, sexy, sardonic, loud, sometimes based on ancient melodies and often very beautiful, music that bypassed the mind and grabbed the heart. And with lyrics that replaced schmaltz with naked, dirty truths.

It was earth-shaking, the profoundest upheaval to strike America since the Civil War. A tragic and unpopular war plus racial conflict, mind-enhancing drugs, powerful music, and tons of wild sex – the Sixties shook America to its foundation, with worldwide ripple effects. They framed the end of the 20th Century and where we are today.

This first book of the *America* series covers nearly a decade in the lives of four young people – Mick, Tara, Daisy and Troy – and of many others who with them experienced the joys and miseries of the time. It opens in the shadows of World War II and Korea and ends as the US is sinking deeper into the horror of Vietnam. This first book begins and ends with a quest. For love, for safety, for brotherhood, for hope, and for freedom. It's about the leap that must be taken before you land; the fear that must be surpassed before you can grow and become whole; and the distance that must be traveled before the house lights beckon you back to whatever it is you now call home.

FREEDOM

THE BOY STARED through the cyclone fence at the dirt road, golden meadow and forested hills beyond. He listened a moment more to the din of other boys playing in the concrete yard behind him, scrambled up the cyclone fence ripping his shirt on the barbed wire top and dashed across the meadow uphill into the cool shadowed forest.

Minutes later he glanced down from the hilltop at the hostile brick walls and barred windows of the orphanage. A black Ford police car with white doors had stopped at the gate, its yellow roof globe flashing. Two priests and a cop were walking along the road, one priest gesturing at the forest.

He imagined them catching him, hitting him, wished he'd never run away, turned uphill through the dark trees then down a wooded valley to a stream. He knelt in the wet moss, his reflection rising toward him – dirty and skinny, tan hair askew – and drank the icy water tasting of rock and mud. *So this is what it's like to drink from a stream.*

He followed the valley for a long time till he saw a dirt road ahead through the trees. A big red car was there. Afraid he'd been seen, he pulled back into the trees. From the car's open windows came voices, a man and woman. If he moved back up the hill they'd surely see him. He'd be taken back to the Boys' Home, the Fathers would whup him.

A warm breeze stirred the leaves. His heart hammered, his knees shook with fear and fatigue. Soon the car would leave and he could cross the road.

The woman was moaning. Holding his breath he listened. The man must be hurting her. She cried out; the boy glanced round but there was no one who could help.

Shivering with fear, he worried what to do. If the man killed her and he had done nothing to help, it was a terrible sin. But if he tried to help her he'd get sent back to the Boys' Home. Standing, he tried to see better. The man was pushing the woman down in the back seat, maybe strangling her.

The boy dashed across the road and banged on the car. "You leave her alone Mister!" he yelled, voice shaking, "I'll call the cops!"

They were naked from the waist down. "Get him out of here!" the woman screamed. The man threw open the back door shouting, "You little shit!" and slapped the boy hard across the head. The boy tumbled into the ditch and scrambled through brambles uphill. The man wasn't following but the boy kept running, gasping for wind, legs weak with fear that the man would circle somehow and get him. He ran till he could run no more, stumbled, fell, and ran again.

After a while he stopped and bent over panting, watching behind him. He couldn't stop shivering but wasn't cold. He tried to talk to himself and his voice trembled. His head spun, his ears whined. If the man wasn't killing her what was he doing? Why had she said get him out of here? Why were they naked like that?

Confused and terribly lonely, the boy moved on through the forest, jumping in terror at the crash of an animal running away, a flash of tawny fur. Even the Boys' Home was better than this.

In late afternoon he came to a big place of empty, run-down tarpaper-covered buildings, some of their windows broken, tall grass spiking up from their concrete yards. He felt hungry and afraid, then angry at himself for feeling it. He snuck along one building and looked in a window hoping for something to eat, but there were only empty concrete floors, yellowed newspapers, rusty cans, torn tarpaper, and a broken toilet lying on its side. He slipped through a half-open door and stepped silently from room to room around broken bottles, boards with nails sticking up and chunks of fallen ceiling.

A window shattered overhead and he ducked into a closet, broken glass in his hair, deafened by his pounding heart, hoping whoever it was hadn't seen him.

Maybe it was a bird hit that window. Stupid bird.

He tiptoed from the closet toward the door. Another window crashed. He ran stumbling over cans and bottles. Someone was shooting at him. At the door he halted, fearing what to do. Blood ran down his cheek onto his shirt. They were going to kill him.

Steps scuffed outside in the concrete courtyard. A kid. The kid picked up a rock and slung it. Glass shattered and the rock hopped across the floor inside.

The boy ran at the kid, fists clenched, stopped. "What the hell you doin?"

The kid tossed a stone in his palm. A slingshot hung from his back pocket. "You shouldn' swear like thet."

"You better look, 'fore you throw rocks."

The kid pointed at a sign on the wall. "You ain't supposed to be in there."

The boy punched at the kid who ducked aside and punched him back in the nose, a stinging blindness, then in the gut, and he swung at him again and missed. The kid stepped back grinning. "No point in fightin. I kin whup you easy."

The boy swung again, missing. "I can beat anybody."

"Not me you kin't. Anyways I weren't tryin to hurt you." The kid tossed him a stone. "Try breakin winders. It's fun."

Angrily the boy slung the rock but it bounced off the wall. He kicked another out of the ground, threw it and it sailed through the empty space where a window had been.

"You're tryin too hard," the kid said. He threw another that punched a perfect hole in the center of a high window. *"There – I saved you the big window in the middle."*

The boy found a rock, threw carefully and missed. "I got to get going."

The kid eyed him. "Your Ma ain't gonna be happy about thet shirt."

He looked down at his wire-torn, blooded shirt, said nothing.

"Where you from?" the kid said.

"Over by Orangeburg."

"On the way to New York City?"

The boy shrugged. "Don't know."

"I'm from Shanks Village. Near Tappan, the Jersey line. What's your name?"

"Troy."

"Mine's Mick. How old're you?"

"Eleven this March. So what?"

"Wow me too – what day?"

"Twenty-nine."

Mick squinted at him. "You jokin?"

Troy threw a rock at a locust tree making the slender trunk quiver and cutting a white wound on the bark. "Why would I joke?"

"Me too, March twenty-nine. You're making it up!"

"March 29, 1943, that's what they told me."

"Wow, me too. We're like twins... You got a bike?"

Troy shook his head.

"Me neither. Why you come so far?"

"Just walkin." Troy turned away.

"You can't get out thet way. This's abandoned Army barracks. From the War. We got to go down front."

Troy glanced back at the wooded hills. "Going back how I came."

"Thet's all forest. Like when the Algonkins had it. We kin follow the railroad tracks."

"Algonkins?"

"The Indians we kilt and stole it from." Mick tugged a slingshot from his back pocket, put a rock in it, pulled back and hit a narrow pipe atop a building. "They could shoot arrows like thet."

"No one ain't there, on the railroad tracks?"

"Nobody never ain't. Why, what you 'fraid of?"

Troy tightened his fists. "Nothin."

The sky cracked apart as two jets roared over. "F-86's," Mick yelled. "Saber jets. They shot down tons of MiGs in Korea."

They walked along the tracks, Mick on a rail, Troy stepping unevenly between the ties. "Toilets in them trains dump in the middle," Mick said. "So I walk on the rails."

Troy tried a rail but couldn't keep his balance so kept walking on the splintery ties, their creosote stinging his nose. Mick nodded far down the tracks where they converged and vanished into forest. "Down there's Florida. Palm trees'n beaches. You kin go swimmin every day."

"Where's that?"

"*Flor*-ida. I tol' you."

The forest opened into a ravine with a flashing river below. The tracks crossed it on a long wooden trestle. Walking on the trestle ties was harder because there was no gravel between, just fast-moving white-blue water far beneath.

Keeping to the middle of the rails and short-stepping from tie to tie, Troy tried not to look over the edge or between the ties down at the frothing river. But if he didn't look at the ties it was easy to stumble and fall between them.

"Where's this go?" he said nervously.

"It's a short cut. Or you hafta swim the river'n climb the other side."

The rail creaked. "What's that?"

"Don't know." Mick glanced back. "Just keep goin."

Troy could hear it now, a dull shudder above the river's roar. "Behind us!" Mick yelled, snatched Troy's arm and ran along the ties as a black locomotive rumbled out of the forest across the trestle at them, headlight coming fast.

Its whistle screamed, its steel wheels screeched as the locomotive braked. Troy tripped and fell, his ribs smashed a tie, his breath knocked out, the train's black cowcatcher plowing toward them. Mick ran back, the train howling closer as he yanked Troy free, shoved him off the edge and leaped after him. The river came up fast and crashed over them and Troy sank deep, choking, knew he'd die.

2

HOME

MICK PULLED Troy to the surface. "Gotta get away!" he yelled over the crashing water, pointed at the two men from the locomotive scrambling toward them down the ravine. "They'll whup us!"

Troy glanced up at the trestle and the black underside of the train, the two men. He dogpaddled after Mick with the current and around a bend and followed him up the bank into the willows. "Damn!" Mick whispered. "Lost my slingshot."

Troy tried to stop shivering. "You came back for me."

Mick looked at him. "So?"

Troy checked his bruised ribs. "Nothin."

The train chugged away. They climbed to the track and walked along it to a road dappled in late sun. *"Look at them!"* Mick pointed at a broad swath of green between rows of bright-leaved trees.

"Them what?"

*"Straw*berries! Can't you *see?"*

Troy squinted but could see no berries.

"Don't you want some?" Mick said. "The Widder Clough, she grows the best in the valley... ripenin' already..."

They climbed over a wooden fence and crawled uphill through tall grass and newly-leaved trees to the garden where Troy could see bright red berries cascading over the tangled plants. Mick slid forward on his belly and picked a handful, squirmed back and gave half to Troy.

Troy sucked them in, juice down his chin and neck. "Jesus!"

"Shouldn't swear!"

"The Fathers do."

"What fathers?"

Troy wiped a sleeve across his mouth. "Can I have more?"

"Go get your own."

Troy squirmed to the berry plants and picked handfuls soft and heavy in his fingers, their taste entrancing, slivers of bright sweetness across his lips and tongue and down his throat. He stood, stunned and alive with their flavor, this taste he'd never known, that pleasure like this could exist.

Something snapped past his head – a bee or something. He grabbed a last handful and tucked them in his shirt. *Bang!* a loud noise – *Bang Bang* – as he ran back across the grass with bees whistling round him, whacked his head on a bough and dove into the grass, forehead stinging, the strawberries squashed on his belly.

"What'ya do thet for?" Mick hissed.

Troy scraped red juice off his stomach. Blood and sweat down his forehead stung his eyes. "Do what?"

"Squish them berries. Plus you got us shot at."

"Shot at?"

"Just rock salt. But now thet old Widder's gonna tell Ma and I'll catch heck."

They walked along the road through lengthening shadows. "What's that noise!" Troy said.

"Owls. And them's nightingales. Don't you know nothin?"

"T'ain't dinosaurs?"

Mick laughed. "Be neat seein' a Taranasorus right now."

Troy glanced at the sky. "Gettin dark."

"See thet streetlight there?" Mick picked a rock from the dirt and whipped it in an arrow line that never hit the reflector, just passed through the bulb and kept going. The bulb hissed, flickered and died.

"So what," Troy said.

"Gonna be late when you get home to Orangeburg. Your Dad's gonna whup you."

"Don't got a Dad."

"You don't got no Dad? Your Mom'll whup you then."

"Don't got a Mom neither."

Mick glanced at him. "Who hits you then, when you do bad?"

"The Fathers. They hit me all the time."

"You said you don' *have* a Dad. How many you got?"

"Twelve, I think. Fathers, not Dads."

"How come's that?"

"My Dad was a Marine. He died fighting Japs. Then my Momma died. That's how come I have to live with the Fathers."

"I wouldn't wanna be you."

Troy glanced at the hills, worried about the Tyrannosaur. "I'm okay."

Mick turned off the road. "You thirsty? I'll show you somethin' neat." He turned up a path to a low dark pool under huge trees with prickly needles. "This's Washington's Spring."

"Washington?"

"The guy what won the Revolution? This's the spring they used for water when his army was camped here in Shanks for the winter. Hadn't been for this spring, Dad says, we might not a won the Revolution. Might be English still."

Troy knelt, realizing how thirsty he was. The icy water made his lips sting and his teeth ache. He raised up wiping his face. "Too cold."

Mick shrugged. "Cold water's good for you."

Troy felt safer when they'd regained the road in the gathering dusk.

"Hey!" Mick said, "what's this?"

Troy backed away from a lump at the edge of the road. "It's movin'!"

"It's a pigeon. He's bleedin'!"

9

Huddled on its side, the pigeon weakly flapped one wing. Mick knelt and carefully turned it over, its red feet quivering. "He's been shot." He lifted it in both palms, nodding down at the red hole in the pigeon's breast. "How kin anybody shoot a poor bird thet never hurt nobody?"

Troy watched blood trickle down Mick's arm. "Now what you gonna do?"

"We'll take him home. My Dad kin fix anythin."

They left the road and followed a path through the trees, Mick holding the pigeon to his chest. "We got a tel'phone – my Dad can call up your house, tell your Dads you're at our place. You got a tel'phone don't you?"

"I dunno."

"Anyways we got a car, too. My Dad'll drive you home –" he pointed at a white farmhouse and red barn under tall trees atop a knoll. "After dinner."

Troy glanced at the pigeon. "What kinda dinner?"

"Don't you know nothin? Cowburger and 'tatoes and peas and soup and apple pie – no, Mom made peach today – you shouldn'a squished them berries –"

Troy's mouth filled with saliva. "Don't tell your folks..."

"Don't tell them what?"

"That I don't have no Mom and Dad."

THE WHITE FARMHOUSE stood on a grassy hill under wide elm trees. Black and white cows wandered in bunches by the red barn whose tin roof glinted in the afterglow of the sun. Beyond the house the hill drifted down to a valley with a stream and a white church whose steeple glimmered against the darkening forest. A narrow road curved down the hill and along the valley past the church.

"You wait here." Mick pointed to the fence where the cows were.

"I ain't goin by them."

"Sissy, they won't hurt you." Mick carried the pigeon up the path to the house. A brown and white dog came out of the barn, leaped up on Mick and ran beside him, tail wagging. The screen door clacked shut. Eyeing the cows, Troy backed away from the fence. One watched him, grass in its mouth, switching its tail.

Beyond the house a hammock hung between two huge elm trees. Robins flitted along the grass that looked almost red in the dying light. *Shoulda stayed in the woods,* Troy decided. *Where you was safe.*

Big white and red chickens were scratching at dirt by the barn. The biggest one ran at him flapping its wings and jabbed its beak into his shin. "Get out, you!" he yelled, kicking at it and backing away.

"Heavens, he won't hurt you!" It was a tall, raven-haired woman in a white apron.

Troy backed away. "Who're you?"

"I'm Mick's Ma. And you're Troy. Come inside and have dinner."

Wanting to run away he followed her into a warm bright kitchen smelling of fruit and cinnamon and other delicious scents that made him want to weep. The red and white dog sniffed him and sat in the corner. "I got to go," Troy said.

She hooked a warm arm around him. "Wash your hands for dinner. Goodness, what happened to your forehead?"

Troy touched his head, tried to remember. "Bonked it on a tree."

"We'll wash it up good now, won't we?"

"Where's Mick at?"

"Showing his Dad that poor pigeon."

"He can make it better?"

She moved him toward the sink. "I don't think so."

A strange sorrow stung him. Wordlessly he soaped his hands. A big dark-haired man in a red shirt came into the kitchen holding the pigeon. "So you're Troy."

Troy wiped his hands on his shirt. "I was just leavin' –"

"No you're not. You're havin' dinner."

The pigeon was just a ball of fluff in the man's hand. "You saved him?"

"He's been shot through the chest. I'm going to put him out of his pain. Real good of you boys though, trying to save him."

"Mick did it. Not me."

11

The man patted Troy's head with a heavy hard palm. "Go sit down."

Mick came in looking different and Troy realized he'd washed his face and combed his hair. Like you had to do at the orphanage before dinner. Mick's Ma went into the corridor. "Tara!" she yelled, "get down here!"

The wood table had a red and white cloth. Troy sat on his chair edge ready to run, gulped the spit filling his mouth from the smell of everything so good.

Footsteps came downstairs into the kitchen, a girl with dark pigtails and glasses on a freckled pug nose. "Who're you?" she said.

"This's Mick's friend Troy," Mick's Ma said.

"How come he's sittin' at my place?"

"He ain't, Tara," Mick's Dad said. "Mind your manners'n git over here."

"So," Mick's Ma said to Troy, "Mick said you don't have a phone."

"No Maam."

"What was you doin way out in the woods over here from Orangeburg?"

Troy had an urge to ask her about what the man and woman had been doing half-naked in the red car. "Jes' walkin', Maam."

"Good for you," Mick's Dad said. "A boy can learn a lot in the woods."

"After dinner we'll take you home," she said. "Your folks'll be worried."

Troy glanced at Mick who shook his head slightly. "They don't, Maam."

The food was so good Troy's hands shook when he ate. "Slow down, son," Mick's Dad said, "fore you choke to death."

"I was wrong about the pie," Mick said. "It's strawberry rhubarb."

It was sweet and juicy and exciting. In all his life Troy had never tasted anything like it. "It's like Heav'n, Maam," he said.

Mick's Dad smiled. "So you been there?"

Troy swallowed. "Like it might be..."

"So who tol' you about Heaven?"

"Well, the Fathers – I mean –"

Mick's Dad drank down his coffee and stood brushing crumbs. "Mick, you go clean the buckets, since your Mom did your milking, and hay up the stalls while Tara does the dishes, and I'll start the car and take Troy back to his folks."

Troy stood. "I kin go by myself."

"I did the dishes last night," Tara said. "It's Mick's turn."

"Troy can help me do the chores," Mick said.

"Yeah, I kin –"

Mick's Dad's big hand dropped on Troy's shoulder. "Let's go."

Headlights flashed across the window; a car rumbled up and stopped. The dog leaped up barking, nose thumping the door. Mick's Dad tugged the dog aside. "Well hullo, Pete," he called. "Whatcha doin here? Come on in and have a cup."

A tall skinny-faced man with a big jaw came in taking off his policeman's cap. Troy slid behind Mick's Ma. "That durnt Widow Clough," the cop said, "raisin hell again. Some kids stealin' her strawberries."

"What's she care?" Mick's Dad said. "Lets half a them rot on the ground."

"Shame," Mick's Ma said. "Good food goin to waste –"

The cop scratched at his thin hair. "Yeah but it's her land, now ain't it?"

"Goin to do my chores." Mick moved toward the door. "C'mon Troy."

The cop glanced at Troy. "Well I'll be durnt. C'mere."

Troy sidled away. "I said git over here!" the cop said.

"Better do as he says, son," Mick's Dad said.

"I been lookin all day fer you!" The cop turned to Mick's Dad. "Why's he here?"

"He's a good boy. We just fed him dinner."

"He ex-caped from the Boys' Home. They'll be real happy ta git him back."

"Oh my!" Mick's Ma said. "Is that true?"

Troy nodded. "I don' wanta go back, Maam."

The policeman snatched him by the neck. "They all say that."

"They hit us!" Troy begged. "Sometimes they don't even give us food!"

"These kids," the cop said, "they'll say anythin'." Fingers deep in Troy's neck, he yanked him out to the black-and-white Ford with the yellow roof globe and shoved him in the back. "You move one inch," he whispered, "and I'll whup yer durnt ass so bad you'll wisht you *was* in Hell."

3

NUMBERS

S TREETLIGHTS FLED past the police car's windows against the dark hills. Silently Troy twisted the door handle but it wouldn't open. His wrists and knees would not stop trembling. He swallowed hard to keep dinner down.

The cyclone and barbed wire orphanage fence glinted in the car's headlights. The cop honked the horn and Father Damon came bustling across the yard and unlocked the gate and locked it behind them and the cop drove up to the door.

The cop grabbed Troy's wrist and yanked him out. "Our lost lamb!" Father Damon said. "Thanks so much, Pete."

"He was way over by Shanks Village, the O'Brien farm."

"*My* what a long way." The Father snatched Troy's wrist. "There's more joy in one returned than all the ones we have –"

"You have a marvelous gift, Father."

"We must suffer the little children..."

Troy pulled free and sprinted for the fence. "*Hey!*" the cop yelled, his big feet clattering behind Troy as the boy leaped the fence over the barbed wire, but the cop caught his ankle and dragged him by the hair to the orphanage.

"My *my*," Father Damon said. "You'd think we beat him!"

"You do, you hit us all!" Troy yelled, his voice muffled by the cop's arm.

"No gratitude, this one," the cop said.

Father Damon hustled Troy down metal stairs. "Little bastard!" he puffed, "shaming us like this!" He yanked a cord and the basement's dark walls shone damply. He swung open a metal door and shoved Troy into a cold cell with a wood bench and concrete walls and floor. "Drop them!" he seethed, flicking a willow switch.

Troy backed into the corner, eyeing the door. "No you don't!" Father Damon slammed the door, the switch catching Troy on the arm. The Father knocked him down across the bench and whipped him till he could count no more, throat ripped apart by screams, and the whip stopped and slowly the cold little cell reappeared around him, the hard wet floor, the thick dank air, the Father blocking the door's sallow light.

"Better pray," he panted. "On your knees praying all the time. That the good Lord Jesus forgives your many sins. We'll be watching, and if you don't you'll stay down here forever. Maybe you won't sin so much if you have a taste of Hell." The door screeched shut, the bolt thunked down, and his heavy feet scrunched up the stairs.

MICK WATCHED the green branches rise and fall in the breeze beyond the dusty homeroom window. The calendar on the wall had a red circle around April 25, 1954, so that must be today. Not really, because in here each day took forever.

Though it was warm outside, Mrs. Purdy kept the windows shut to avoid what she called "dangerous drafts." In front of Mick, Cathy Gringold's two blonde braids hung down her back; her pink elbows and the fine hairs on her arms were disgusting. She always crooked her wrist funny, left-handed, when she wrote. In front of her Mabel Strain, plump and placid, wiping her snot on the bottom of her desk, made Mick worry he might some day be moved there. Ahead of her Billy Wylie, always getting A's and making the teacher smile, a kid who'd hit you when your back was turned then run to Mrs. Purdy and say you'd hit *him.*

The homeroom clock had a long hand that you could watch for minutes but never moved. The short hand that took all morning to move an inch. *Why does time go so slow here, but so fast outside?*

"Mick!"

He squelched a yawn, realized he'd dozed and forced his eyes open.

"Mick O'*Brien!*"

Cathy Gringold turned and stared at him with round blue eyes. Billy Wylie sneered.

"Yes'm?"

"Where were you, boy!"

He swallowed, tried to think. "Right here, Maam."

"Six times nine?"

He took a breath. Across the room Daisy Moran mouthed something to him but he couldn't be sure. "Sixty-four?"

"No! Seven times eight?"

This was trouble, the high numbers. Mabel Strain's pumpkin face staring, Billy Wylie's snicker. Mrs. Purdy slapped a ruler on her desk. "Boy –"

"Well, it depends, Maam."

She smiled. "On what, pray tell?"

"On your system." Dad had told him this... "We use ten, because we have ten fingers, but if we had eight, our number system'd be all different..."

"We don't have ten fingers, boy."

He looked down at his hands. "We don't?"

"Can anyone tell the class?"

"I can!" Cathy Gringold waved her hand. "We've got eight fingers, and two thumbs!"

"Of course," Mrs. Purdy smiled again. "But it seems Mick's math is *all* thumbs –"

Jeering laughter. His face hot, Mick sank into his seat. He didn't dare look at Daisy Moran – she'd be laughing too –

. . .

A SMALL WINDOW near the ceiling of Troy's cell cast a sick light down the sweating cold walls, the metal door. He lay in the corner on his side with arms wrapped around his knees, the position that hurt the least.

Why couldn't he get along? What was wrong with him? Shame heated the back of his neck. His whole life was going to be like this. One failure after another.

The plate with a slice of white bread sat untouched before him, the cup of water. His stomach lurched when he thought of yesterday's dinner and pie at Mick's house. He hadn't deserved it.

Feet slippered down the stairs; the bolt slid up; the door inched open casting a dirty glow across the floor. Troy stood, his back to the corner, hissing against the pain.

The plump cassocked form of Father Loudy slipped into the cell. "How are you, dear boy?" Father Loudy slid the bench to himself, sat and crossed his legs. "Come here."

Arms crossed against his chest Troy inched from the wall.

"Closer, boy!"

Troy stood his ground.

"I feel sorry for you," Father Loudy said softly, "but you must understand, dear boy – the pain you feel now is nothing next to the pain of Hell, where you're headed unless you change. Do you understand?"

"Yes."

"Yes what?"

"Yes Father –"

Father Loudy beckoned. "Now come here."

Troy inched closer. "It's so sad," Father Loudy sighed, "you won't accept love, you won't accept forgiveness... All the Lord wants is to soften your heart."

Tears dampened Troy's eyes; he bit his lip; he would not cry. Father Loudy pulled him to his chest into the itch and stink of cassock, kissed his head. "There," he whispered, "dear boy. Isn't that better?"

Troy knew he had to answer, nodded his head against the scratchy wool. "Would you like to go back to the dormitory?" Father Loudy said. "With the other boys?"

He didn't care, didn't want to go anywhere, but nodded, to please Father Loudy.

"This is called the Prayer Cell." Father Loudy rumpled Troy's hair, "because here you can pray and your prayers will be answered. You can become a better person just by praying. By going down on your knees and asking the Good Lord Jesus for forgiveness." He kissed Troy's temple, his hand sliding along Troy's thigh, between his thighs, and Troy leaped free and backed into the corner, teeth clenched, hands up like claws.

"Evil boy!" Father Loudy smacked him hard across the face and hustled from the cell. The bolt dropped into place; Troy rocked back and forth in his dark corner, hand against his burning cheek, tears choking his throat.

SCREECHING TIRES and a thunderous crash of metal and glass behind Mick made him jump from home plate and drop his bat. Beyond the school's ballfield fence was a stoplight where the New York and New Jersey roads crossed, where a black Studebaker had just been crushed sideways by a dump truck. Two people lay face-down by the curb, a chubby gray-haired woman in a blue and white print dress and a gray-haired man in brown trousers and a check shirt.

They had been thrown through the air from the car a hundred feet away. The dump truck driver was slumped in his seat not moving. The stoplight over the crossing turned from red to green to yellow then red again, cars easing round the dump truck and shattered Studebaker, their drivers staring at the man and woman lying at the side of the road.

"They're killt," Tommy Spears said.

"Nah," someone said. "Jest knocked out."

"How come they ain't wakin up, then?"

A cop car came flashing its yellow dome, then an ambulance hooting its horn. A man in a brown wool suit with a little black bag got out of the ambulance. He knelt by the two people, not looking at the boys lined up along the fence. He pulled open the man's eyelid, then the woman's, turned and shook his head at the cop who stood silently, cap in hand. Only then Mick noticed an eyeball, strangely blue and white, lying on the curb.

Stomach queasy, Mick walked home slapping his glove against his thigh. A meadowlark was singing by the convent wall; little puffy clouds chased each other single file across the blue sky.

Either the two old people had gone through the red light or the truck had. Had the truck driver fallen asleep?

One moment those two old people had been sitting beside each other, talking maybe, thinking of what they were doing next, the next instant knocked out of the car flying across the highway smashing their heads against the curb.

His gut burned with sorrow for them. Death was a huge black tent over the world. Nothing he could do would ever help those poor people. He imagined their families, the cop who had to stand at their door with the news, the ravaging sorrow... And the truck driver sitting motionless at the wheel? If it was him who'd gone through the red light then his soul was crushed forever.

To stay alive you couldn't trust stoplights. Even when they were green someone could be coming through the red.

It was fine that people made rules, but you couldn't bet your life on them.

Don't trust nothin you ain't seen yourself.

4

PARADISE

DAISY MORAN lived over the next valley on a dirt road that went down a hill across a cornfield with a white farmhouse and red barn. There were Holsteins and Guernseys on the back pasture and Rhode Island Reds in the front yard and an old red Ford tractor covered with hay in the barn. The paint was peeling off the barn and the whitewash off the house and raspberries were growing out of the well.

She was tall, rangy and tough, green-eyed with auburn hair in a curly halo round her freckled face, and when her broad lips rounded into a smile she was even lovelier. She had dirty fingernails, ran like a deer, climbed trees, hit like a boy, and knew how to use her teeth too, and Mick loved her deeply. She loved history and math and biology and books.

"That's sissy stuff," he told her, jealous of anything that could take her away from him.

"Not big and tough like football, huh?"

He shrugged, pleased she'd recognized the difference.

"Any moron with two arms and legs can play football."

. . .

BUT HE HATED Daisy the cow who'd wait when he milked her till the pail was full then kick it over or put her dung-caked hoof in it and he'd have to dump the pail outside on the dirt, the chickens clucking and running over to peck out the drowning bugs, and back in the stall Daisy switching her tail and coating him with her grassy sour breath.

"Damn it, son!" his father said, "you learn to manage that cow!"

"She just does it to me, Dad. Tara milks her fine."

His father grinned. "Your sister ain't doin *your* milkin'."

In the yellow dawn Mick finished the milking and let the cows into the back pasture, their empty udders swinging, flies hovering round their tails. He cleaned the pails and pitchforked the new dung out of the barn. "Mick!" his mother called from the porch. "Seven-twenty!"

From the tool shed he took a torn tractor inner tube and cut four thin strips eight inches long, put the inner tube back on a nail and found his father attaching the harrow to the tractor. "I'll lift it up," his father grunted, "you drop it on the pin."

His father lifted the harrow's heavy frame and swung it back and forth over the hitch till Mick could guide it down on the pin and shove the bent nail through it that kept it from slipping out. He ripped a knuckle on the hitch and sucked the blood off, liking its metallic taste mixed with grease from the pin. "I need a piece of leather."

His father slapped a horsefly, straightened up wiping hands on his pants. "You break your slingshot?"

"Lost it."

"Try looking in Widow Clough's field."

"Thet kid –"

"The one who came here? Troy?"

"Never had strawberries before. Didn't know what they was."

"He sure loved your Ma's cooking."

"Wisht he didn't go back."

"They take good care of kids, the Boys' Home."

"No they don't." Mick sucked his bleeding knuckle. "He never had a Dad."

His father squeezed Mick's shoulder. "Let's get some leather."

From the wall of the milking shed he took down a worn leather apron, flicked out his knife and sliced off a square. "You got an awl on your knife, don't you?"

"Sure." He watched his Dad. "Troy's father was a Marine too."

His father stopped. "He said?"

"Got kilt by the Japs. Then his Ma died. That's how come he's an orphan."

"I didn't know that," his father said. "About his dad."

"Maybe you knew him, even –"

His father smiled softly, as if coming back from somewhere. "There was plenty Marines, son. And plenty got killed."

"Mick!" his mother called. "Mick!"

"Coming!"

"Tara wants to leave."

"So tell her go!"

"Stop that," his father said. "She likes to walk with you."

"She's ten. Can go on her own."

"She's the only sister you'll ever have."

"She complains at me all the time, Dad. Besides, I got to find a forked stick and make my slingshot."

His father smiled down at him. "You go with Tara."

Mick shoved the leather square and pieces of inner tube in his pocket, crossed the yard to the kitchen and picked up his lunch bag. "I made you chocolate milk," his mother said.

"We're going to be late," Tara said, twisting the edge of her skirt between thumb and finger. "Because of you."

"I was helpin Dad hitch the harrow." He set off across the yard, turned to make sure she was coming, whistled for Rusty. "C'mon, you silly dog!"

Dew glowed on the tall grass in the first rays of the rising sun. They followed the path through the upper meadow under the elms where the hammock hung and past the old chicken shed into a wide field, the dog gamboling ahead, the grass wetting their knees, flies rising like myriad diamonds as chittering swallows darted among them.

After a mile the meadow sloped toward a derelict farmhouse where the swallows had built mud houses under the eaves. "Wanta see somethin' neat?" Mick said.

"I don't like it here," she said. "It's haunted."

"Miss Purdy says some famous guy lived here."

"General Lafayette. Don't you know anything?"

"Who cares?"

"He helped George Washington. The father of our country."

"Yeah, the one who stole it from the Algonkins."

"That wasn't him. Are you just dumb by accident, or do you try to be?"

"Being a smart sissy ain't good for nothing. I'm going to be like Dad."

"A cow farmer?"

He turned on her. "What's wrong with thet?"

She peered at him. "Is that what you really want to be?"

"I'm going to be a Marine. Just like Dad was."

"And kill people?"

"Look over here." He led her to the front porch, the steps caved in, the broken door ajar. He threw a rock that cracked loudly as it hit the porch.

"So, you can hit the house? Big deal."

He threw another, harder. A hiss came from under the porch. "I'm getting out of here!" she said.

He threw another; the hiss grew louder and a long gold-red snake slipped from under the porch, casting its raised head back and forth, flicking its tongue. Rusty barked at it, backed away.

"Kill it!" she snapped. "Quick!"

"I ain't hurtin her. It's just a momma copperhead, protecting her kids." He moved toward the snake, knelt down two feet away. "Don't worry, momma. I just wanted to show you to my sister..."

The snake wavered before him on its tall muscular body. Feeling brave he stretched a hand slowly toward her. She watched it, flicking her tongue. "Mick!" Tara screamed. "*Stop* that!"

Feeling relieved he backed away. "See, she didn't hurt me."

Tara gripped his arm. "Don't *do* stuff like that!" A tear ran down her cheek.

His throat caught. "Didn' mean to scare you."

She stomped to the path. "I wasn't scared for me, dummy. I was scared for *you*."

Chagrined, he followed her down the meadow another mile to the edge of Tappan. They walked along the dirt road under the wide oaks, a white horse following them along the other side of a fence, Rusty trotting ahead.

"Got to find an ash tree," Mick said. "Make a forked stick."

"That snake had a forked tongue."

"When we get to the bridge I'm cutting an ash by the crick. You can go up to school by yourself."

"Waiting for Daisy Moran, aren't you?"

"Daisy *who?*"

"You love her, ha-ha!" Tara skipped ahead. "My brother's getting married, ha-ha."

"Tara will you stop it?"

"Eleven years old he's getting *married*. Just like the kids in India..."

He looked crossly at the dog. "You go home now, Rusty! Go home!" The dog looked up at him sadly, dropped back a little.

They came to the bridge over Sparkill Creek. Tara crossed it swinging her lunch bag in her hand. He watched her ascend the lane under the double row of elms and cross into the schoolyard. Then he went down to the ash saplings along the Creek and cut an inch-thick forked stick. Sitting with his back against the huge oak by the 1776 House he squared the ends of the stick and cut slots in the forks to tie the inner tube through. Rusty came up tentatively and Mick waved at him, "I mean it! Go home!"

Daisy Moran came down the alley by the feed store carrying a blue lunchbox. She wore a blue dress with a white blouse and black shoes. "It's bad luck," she said, "to be sitting under that tree they hung Major André on."

Mick nodded at the wide façade of the 1776 House. "My Uncle Hal owns this place. He kin cut thet tree down if he wants."

"My Pa says he just runs the bar."

"So? Maybe your Pa shouldn't spend so much time there."

She glanced down. "Whatcha makin'?"

"Slingshot. Want it?"

She giggled making his heart leap. "What'd I do with a slingshot?" she said.

"I'll make you somethin' else. What you want?"

She dug a shiny black shoe in the dirt. "Nothin."

He wiped sap off his knife and shut it. "Let's play hooky."

"Pa'll whup me."

"He ever whups you again I'll kill him."

She looked at him darkly. "Don't *say* that."

"I'll write a note. Like I was him. You can give it to Miss Purdy tomorrow."

She tossed her head. "Let's go. I don't wanta be late."

Dizzied by her nearness he walked with her onto the bridge. "You laugh at me yesterday?"

"In class? No. I *hate* that Miss Purdy."

He noticed the rail of the bridge. "Wanna see something neat?"

"We're late!"

He handed her his lunch bag and leaped onto the rail, lost his balance and caught it, stood carefully, wavering, and started walking the rail, the bridge on his left, the creek frothing below on his right. "Git *down* from there!" she called.

As he turned to grin at her his feet slipped and he fell smashing his ribs on the rail and down ten feet into the creek. "Silly!" Daisy called. "Now you're all wet!"

Furious and hurting he clambered up the bank and grabbed his lunch bag.

"You shouldna done that," she said. "You'll get in trouble again."

"Ain't my fault," he breathed shallowly against the rib pain. "Was a accident."

"Yeah, Miss Purdy's gonna believe that –"

. . .

"YOU'LL CATCH YOUR DEATH," Mrs. Purdy said.

He grinned, looked at the puddles round his feet. "I better go home."

"You are *not* missing another day of school." She led him down to a basement closet with racks of clothing along the walls. "Drop those wet trousers and we'll change you into something dry."

He slipped off his soggy shoes, with a shock remembered he hadn't worn underpants. "I'm near dry."

She tugged an outfit off the rack. "These are from class plays. Older grades, nothing your size. Here's one seems right." She stopped at the door. "Hurry – we've got a geography test in ten minutes."

He waited till her footsteps climbed the stairs then looked at the outfit she'd chosen. Flappy white pants with vertical purple stripes. Orange jacket with blue polka dots and big pink flower buttons. Clown suit.

He sat disconsolately on the floor, imagined Cathy Gringold's laughing eyes, Mabel Strain's grinning pumpkin face... even Daisy'd laugh, this time.

He yanked on his shoes, crept upstairs, darted into the morning sun and across the schoolyard down the lane. At the Sparkill Creek bridge he took a deep breath, seeing the wide blue sky, the green trees, loving the spring breeze on his face.

Free.

THE LOCK TURNED. Father Loudy carried a plate with a slice of bread and a jug of water into the dark cell. Troy knocked him aside and raced upstairs down the corridor across the yard over the fence up the field, voices yelling behind him, into the forest, ran till the voices vanished and he fell down at the stream and drank, pushed himself upwards and kept running deeper into the forest till there was nothing but birdsongs and wind in the leaves.

When he reached the army barracks the sun had sunk into the treetops. The barracks' stink of mold and emptiness made him feel lonelier. His stomach sore with hunger, he tried to think what to do next. *Even dying's better than going back. Even being eat by a tarranasor.*

He took the tracks to the trestle, descended the ravine, dogpaddled across the river and followed the road to the field where strawberries gleamed like tiny fires in the dying sun. He ate all he could, tucked more into his shirt, and returned to the road. The sweetness of the berries made him sick; he sat against the streetlight Mick had broken, thinking that when he was here before how much better everything had been.

Strange to have a mother, a father. A sister. On the trestle Mick had run back to save him from the train. Would *he* have done that too? Did he have no Mom and Dad because he was evil, like the Fathers said, or had it just happened?

A car was coming; he scrambled into the brush. It passed clattering the gravel. The cop car.

If they got him now they'd really beat him. Maybe kill him.

Mick had talked about a place you could swim in the ocean. Palm trees – he'd seen a picture once, big leaves hanging down. Coconuts, you could eat them and not starve.

The farther away the safer he'd be. Paradise. Was it what the Fathers said – if you suffer in this world you can get to Paradise in the next? Or can you find Paradise here?

MICK FOUND A BABY RACCOON in a hemlock grove and put it high on a branch where foxes couldn't get it. Crows followed him cawing; he called back but they wouldn't come down. In quicksand he lost a shoe and spent a half hour kneeling on the bank digging in the slime before he found it, washed it in a stream and put it on and sat watching the water spiders skitter back and forth. He broke open fresh bear scat to see what the bear was eating – mostly berries, the bones of a squirrel – but backed away when he saw the little prints of a cub next to the larger tracks. For a while he followed deer sign, then a bobcat who finally took to the trees, then the slithery trace of a water moccasin. *This is so much fun I'm never goin back to school.*

School made no sense. Okay for girls like Cathy Gringold and Mabel Strain and brown nosers like Billy Wylie. Even Daisy seemed to like it. But nobody who hated school should have to go. How could they make you go if you didn't want to? How was thet freedom?

Stretched out in skunk cabbage by a stream he watched water spiders race round a pool where crayfish strutted across the bottom. He picked up a crayfish, saw it was afraid, waving its tiny claws. *I'd like to be you for a day,* he told it, *see what it's like. Wanna be me?* He put it back and it scuttled under a rock, after a while stuck out an eye for a quick look and finally wandered off across the muddy bottom, its fears seemingly forgotten. *I could pick you up again,* he told it. *I could cook you and you don't even know.*

So how do I look out for things thet could get me? Thet I don't even know?

It was getting dark and he was miles from home. *The milking.* He checked the tree trunks for the sunset side and ran through the woods, saplings lashing his face, mud splashing, snakes hissing, deer crashing away through down timber.

Clothes torn and muddy, shoes squeaking, he reached the hayfield that smelled so good from Dad's first cutting today, the stubs prickly as he ran up the long slope and across the chicken yard, the house lights making him feel even more guilty, yanked open the screen door and stood muddy and dripping in the hard light.

"I'll be damned," Dad said. "The Prodigal Son."

"Got lost in the woods."

"Hell you did. When'd you *ever* get lost in the woods?"

"I was havin so much fun, forgot the time."

A grin spread across Dad's face. "Hungry?"

"I'm *not* doing his chores," Tara said.

"I'm so happy," he told her, "I'll do all mine and yours too."

TROY DIDN'T KNOW how to get away from the mosquitoes. Lying on the ground he covered himself with leaves but they found a way in, and something else in the leaves bit too. Worse, they bit where Father Damon had whipped him and that itched double bad.

He ate more strawberries, wondered how Mick had known about all this. Mick seemed to always know what to do. Cause he had a Mom'n Dad?

He wiped leaves from his face and through wide high branches saw the stars. A warm flush filled him. *I can go out there in the stars. If I get away I can go anywhere.*

He snuggled down in the dirt and leaves and tucking the last of his strawberries to his chest fell asleep. Once something tickled his cheek, a spider maybe; he brushed it aside carefully, not wanting to hurt it, for all the world was magical and good.

In the morning he'd go where you could swim in the ocean and eat the coconuts that fall from the trees.

The first few drops pattered softly; he settled deeper into the leaves telling himself this was just dew maybe, then the drops were spattering the ground bouncing into his face then raining hard and he wished he was back in the orphanage dormitory in his bed with the tucked sheets and the blanket itchy like Father Loudy's cassock then he didn't want to be there anymore, telling himself *no matter what this is it's better.*

In the place with the ocean and palm trees he'd have a hut, and rain wouldn't touch him.

5

THE PURSUIT OF HAPPINESS

T HE RAIN STOPPED; grass glinted in dawn light. Troy's clothes were soaked and stiff with cold. He ate the last strawberries, brushed off leaves and dirt and stood trying to get warm in the first silver rays of the sun.

He should light a fire but had no matches. Remembering something he'd read, he crouched in the wet grass rubbing two sticks till his arms ached but nothing happened. He felt warmer but the hunger in his stomach had grown.

If he could get matches and some food and a rain jacket that'd be enough. Could take the railroad tracks, like Mick said, to the place with palm trees.

Just cause you never done it don't mean you can't.

But that was just talk; last night he'd looked up at the stars and felt good, but then it rained and he'd been cold and wet all night and wanted to be back in the Boys' Home.

If he went back they'd beat him, but he could promise to pray a lot and after a while they'd leave him alone and it would be like before. Why did he leave? He knelt on cold-stiff knees but could not pray. If I don't like God, what right do I have to pray?

Wasn't so hard, really, to find food and someplace dry. Like

Robinson Crusoe did on that desert island, in a book he'd found in the Fathers' attic.

That place had palm trees.

But Robinson Crusoe had the ship to take stuff off of.

Here there were farms. He could find food. The thought warmed him. He looked down at the steam rising off his clothes. Not so bad, this life. Just had to get used to it.

MICK POURED the milking bucket into the vat watching the cream swirl to the top and wondering should he ask Ma to write a note. Without a note he couldn't go to school. Ma and Dad didn't know he'd played hooky yesterday. Didn't know about the clown suit.

He cupped his hands into the vat and drank a handful of sweet warm cream. What if he never went back to school? In the forest there was so much to do, always new things over the next hill, down the next valley. Better than school could ever be. But if he quit school Dad'd kill him.

Better to go to school today. Maybe Miss Purdy'd forgit about the note. If she said something he'd say he forgot it, bring it tomorrow. Tonight he'd ask Ma.

Licking the cream off his fingers he felt better. You could always figure stuff out if you thought hard. He wiped his hands on his shirt, ducked into the chicken coop and filled the water in the round trays and topped up the mash feeders and tossed corn to the pullets clucking and pecking each other which was foolish because there was plenty of corn. Are we like thet, he wondered, fighting over stuff when there's plenty to go around?

"I did your chickens," he told Tara at breakfast.

"Don't talk through your food, Mick," Ma said.

"I ain't. I swallowed first."

"Not supposed to say *ain't*," Tara interposed.

"You say it, I heard you talkin' to your teeny weeny friends –"

"Oh *really?* What about Daisy Moran – *that* spoiled baby – you follow her like a pet hamster!"

"I do *not.*" Feeling his face redden made him blush more. He slammed the screen door and ran across the meadow, stopped to kick the hammock and hurt his ankle.

"*Mick!*" Ma called. "Come get your lunch and wait for Tara!"

He ran down the dew-bright meadow, larks fluttering up before him, past Lafayette's house to the dirt road to town, past the Sparkill Creek bridge, climbed into the ancient oak by the 1776 House and sat on a bough pretending he was a bomber, spitting on the ants far below.

When Daisy came down the alley he whistled. She stopped, looked round. "Daisy!" he whispered; she couldn't tell from where.

He slithered down and wiped bark off his clothes. "You're in trouble," she said.

"What for?"

"Miss Purdy was looking all over for you. We had the Civil Defense alert. Had to stand outside for a long time with the sirens going."

He told her about the clown suit. "That's awful," she said. "I'd a gone home too." He told her about the forest, the baby raccoon, the other neat stuff. "Wish I'd went with you," she said. When they crossed the bridge he smiled at how stupid he'd been yesterday, falling off the rail because he'd looked at her. "Today's my last day," she said quietly.

"Last day for what?"

She looked at him strong, biting her lip. "We're movin' to Nyack."

His insides turned weak. "Why?"

"The farm won't break even, Pa says –"

"That's cause he don't run it right."

"He got a job at the lumber yard in Nyack. He rented a house'n all, never said till last night. We're leavin' tomorrow."

He looked at the trees across the road, couldn't breathe. "You can't..."

She shook her head, face clenched. "Hafta."

He grabbed her arm, starched gingham and slender muscle beneath, everything so precious. "Daisy let's get married –"

She giggled, tears in her eyes. "Silly – we're eleven..."

33

"He can't just take you. We'll run away..."

"They'd ketch us, put us in jail. Pa'd whup me."

"He *been* whuppin' you?"

She smiled crooked. "Not like he does Ma."

"Please Daisy come live with us –"

"Pa hates Ma and me but he won't give us up." She glanced up the lane, kissed him and backed away. "We'll be late."

He tasted her blood from where she'd bit her lip. "I don't give a damn!"

"Hush, Mick!" She started up the lane and he followed, remembered Tara saying *you follow her like a pet hamster,* slung a rock at a streetlight and missed. Daisy turned back. "You can't be late. Not after yesterday."

In class he stared at the map of the world with the countries brown and green and the oceans blue. The evil black clock on the wall was going fast now, Daisy's last day. Mrs. Purdy's chalk squeaked on the blackboard as she wrote out stuff about history. "Who can tell me," she called out, "what caused the American Revolution?"

Billy Wylie jumped up waving his hand. "We wanted to be a free country."

"We didn't want tea laws," Cathy Gringold said, sitting very straight with elbows wide and palms overlapping on her desk, "or hafta pay taxes to a king."

"In our *Declaration of Independence,*" Mrs. Purdy said, "it says everyone's created equal and given by their Creator life, liberty and the pursuit of happiness."

"Before that people were serfs," called a squirrelly girl named Barbara Trueblood.

"That's true. In some places they were. Billy Wylie?"

"America invented freedom?"

"We certainly increased it, yes. In many places people still aren't free... Who can name some of those places?"

Cathy Gringold waved her hand wildly. "The Communists!"

"Absolutely... Daisy, what are some of the Communist *countries?*"

Daisy jumped, faraway. "Japan?"

"No, Daisy, Japan is a free country. Since we conquered them in the War. Wake up, girl. Give me a better answer."

"Germany?"

"What's with you, girl? You'll stay after school and write down the names of the Communist countries. Mick O'Brien's going to tell us some of them, aren't you, Mick?"

"We may of won the Revolution, Maam, but America still ain't free."

She stood a little straighter. "Now that's just plain *wrong*."

"How kin it be free if Daisy has to stay after for not namin' a country? If we *have* to go to school?"

"I thought most young people *wanted* to be in school." She looked around. "Don't you, children?"

They all nodded except Mick and Daisy. "Yes'm," Billy Wylie called.

"Back when we lived like Indians," Mick said, "everybody was free. Nobody worked for anybody except themself."

"Them*selves*. And we weren't Indians." She smiled. "At least not most of us."

Mick ignored the giggles. "Back in history we all lived in tribes and shot arrows. Just like Indians. Thet's what I meant."

"No one *has* to go to school," she said primly. "People do it because they care about their future. They want to have a good job when they grow up."

"But," he struggled with the thought, "if we have to go to school so we can grow up and work for somebody, when are we free? How's thet liberty and happiness? So why'd we fight the Revolution?"

The bell rang. Mick looked across at Daisy facing down at her desk.

"Mick!" Mrs. Purdy called, "come up here."

He stood before her. "Maam?"

"You're going to change your attitude young man. I can't believe you just ran off yesterday."

"But –"

"No *buts* about it! You bring that note tomorrow. Or you'll be a sorry boy."

He said it, knowing he shouldn't: "How is thet freedom?"

"You wait right there!" She went to her desk, wrote a quick note, sealed it in an envelope and handed it to him. "I'm telling your folks I want to see them. And I want their answer back tomorrow!" She pinched his ear hard.

He yanked his head aside and walked out. "Mick!" she called, but he kept going, down the front stairs to the playground to wait for Daisy.

"Commie lover," Billy Wylie called. "Waitin' for little Daisy. Maybe she's a Commie too..."

The punch came from deep inside him up his legs and guts into his shoulder and out his arm smashing his fist into Billy's round nose and pig eye and Billy went down like a tree, books and pencils scattering.

"Ohhh," Billy wailed, "oooh I'm dying, *oooh help oooh Help!*" The kids clustered around him as he lay sprawled with blood pouring from his nose through his fingers onto the dirt.

"Mick!" yelled Mr. Schneider, the principal, striding fast at him, bald head gleaming. Mick ran across the playground through the junipers where the girls peed and over the rock wall, splashed through Sparkill Creek and up the back streets into the cool shadowed forest where Washington's army had come forth to win the Revolution.

6

WALKABOUT

TROY HID in the Lafayette house when a police car turned onto the road below. "What *you* doin here?" a voice said.

He jumped, peered into the shadows. "Who's that?"

"Thought you was back to the Boys' Home," Mick said.

"Ex-caped," Troy panted. "What you doin here?"

"Don't like school."

Through the broken-paned window Troy watched the police car take the county road toward Orangeburg. "That place you said? Palm trees?"

"Florida? It's a long ways. On the map... I was thinkin' maybe go out West, become an Indian."

"How far's that?"

"More'n Florida."

"It rained all night. I got real cold."

"Go south."

"Where's that?"

"Jeez you still don't know nothin."

"On them railroad tracks?"

"They go all over the country. Hafta know which ones to take."

Troy glanced out the window. "You know where there's more a them strawberries?"

"Up to the Widow's. But we can steal better food. Then I'll show you south."

FROM THE FOREST EDGE they watched the Olsen farm. Old Man Olsen was haying the lower pasture; it'd take him ten minutes to drive the tractor up here. Missus Olsen had gone off in the blue Hudson fifteen minutes ago. "C'mon," Mick said, keeping the barn between them and Old Man Olsen as they crossed the chicken run to the coop, Troy nervous behind him, chickens clucking and darting about.

"Don't keep their coop clean," Mick said. "Deserve to lose some eggs."

"Won't they know?"

"Think the coons got them. Gimme thet rag over there, we'll wrap eggs in it."

Outside the coop Mick pulled red-stalked plants from the garden then a cucumber, stopped to stare at the house. "Oh Lordy!"

Troy braced to run. "They comin' back?"

"Lookit thet pie!"

Troy squinted, seeing no pie.

"Thet coolin' rack under the kitchen window!" Mick ran to the house and came back with the pie, scooping some in his fingers. "Cherry – the best!"

Knees weak with hunger Troy gulped it down listening to the tractor mowing in the pasture below, for a car coming up the road. "We'll put the dish back." Mick wiped cherry off his face. "They'll think the crows ate it."

Troy thought of the pigeon they'd tried to save. "They won't shoot the crows?"

"People always shoot at crows. But crows is too smart."

Back in the woods Mick showed Troy how to eat rhubarb. "It's sour!" Troy spit.

"Better'n dyin' a hunger. Ma puts sugar with it." For a moment

Mick said nothing, then, "Better save thet cucumber. Eat it tomorrow."

THE TRAIN TRACKS curved past the brick buildings of Old Tappan, their back porches tilted and peeling, roof shingles gray with moss, abandoned rear gardens of apple trees ablaze with blossoms. Robins were singing in the sumacs and blackbirds in the cattails by the ditch along the tracks. Ahead a few cars trundled over the loose ties of a street crossing. A bell started dinging; the crossing gates dropped.

"Git in here!" Mick ducked into the sumacs. "If he's slow you jump aboard –"

"I ain't sure –"

A locomotive and coal car then boxcars, some empty with their doors open, clickclacked round the bend. "He's slowed for town –" Mick shoved him. "Run alongside and jump in – thet way's south!"

Troy stumbled up the gravel railbed cradling the sack of eggs trying to run as fast as the train, fearing to fall under the huge grinding wheels, the rumble and squeal of rails terrifying, grabbed for the sill of a boxcar's open door thinking *Let go or die*, threw the eggs in, gripped the sill in both hands running sideways, tripped on a tie and stumbled, dragged along, the train gaining speed, didn't dare let go or he'd be crushed, ties whacking his feet as they fled past then Mick was running beside him, leaped into the boxcar and pulled him in.

"Shoot!" Mick panted. "You broke the eggs."

The train clicketyclacked faster; the crossing flitted past, cars in a line like patient toads; the town slid away behind them, spring wind through the boxcar door, fields of new corn and flowering orchards and a line of trees and a pond glinting in the sun.

With his teeth Troy pulled splinters from his palms. "Where's this go?"

"South. I tol' you."

"You comin'?"

Mick scanned the green hills and puffy white clouds. "I got bad trouble in school, can't go back. If I go home I'm in bad trouble too."

He reached into his pocket. "I got two nickels. Kin call my folks, tell em I'll be back soon."

"They ain't gonna want that..."

"We kin do a walkabout –"

"What's that?"

"It's like a quest. You just start out walkin', go wherever you want."

The timbers of a trestle flashed past and Troy saw it was where they'd jumped into the river and it seemed the world went round in circles but now maybe he could get free. The locomotive's whistle echoed through the hills; coal smoke eddied on the sidings and in a singsong of rails and quickening chug the train stretched out and gained speed.

BEYOND THE FLITTING TREES and marshes and slow-moving gloomy hills the sun went down; cold wind cut through the door that was too heavy to shut.

"Anyways," Mick said, "they'd notice if it was closed –"

"Who?"

"Train guards." He rubbed his arms. "Let's et thet cucumber and the eggs we kin scrape off thet rag."

Now and again the locomotive howled three times and a crossing flashed past, dinging bells and a gate with blinking lights, and the train rumbled on into the night, the cold wind whistling, rails crying. As the stars brightened over the far hills Troy thought of the night he'd lain in the leaves and seeing the stars through the branches and how the world had seemed wonderful and good. A town crept past, bare streetlights, a car's taillights fading away, and he wondered who was in that car and where were they going.

A house near the tracks slid by, a bright room with an oval rug and couch and chair, a kitchen with a wooden table and red-white curtains, a man in a white undershirt stepping from the sink, a pale glow in an upstairs room. What was it like to live in that world? Why would Mick give it up? Was it no better than the Boys' Home, only different?

Huddled against the cold they woke as the train slowed, rails shrieking, boxcars lurching, couplings grinding. It shuddered to a stop on a single track, dark forest beyond, distant signal lights turning from yellow to red, a white lantern swinging down the siding. "They're checking the cars!" Mick whispered.

They scrambled over the sill into the forest, crunching gravel and tripping over branches, stopped where the ground was soft needles and the air smelled like resin. "Let's wait here," Mick said. "See if it starts movin'."

"How come it's so cold? If we're headed to this palm tree place?"

"Ain't there yet." Mick fished matches from his pocket. "Find some a them pine needles, dry ones, any branches that break easy, not ones what jest bend."

A tiny flame climbed the teepee of needles and twigs Mick had built; Troy tried to warm his hands and knocked it over. "Dummy!" Mick pushed the coals together and blew softly till they glowed and pale fire slipped up the twigs again.

"First make a teepee," Mick said, "then lay down twigs around it like a log house." As the fire grew they hunched closer, blood returning to their hands and feet, their stinging ears and fingers.

The tracks began to creak, an engine thundered toward them and a freight train roared past. "Goin north," Mick said.

"Ain't you scared?"

"You're supposed to be scared when you do a quest."

"Them palm trees. What they like?"

"They's tall, and you got to stay out from under them 'cept to get coconuts. If one falls on your head it'll kill you."

Troy tried to imagine a coconut, how it could hurt you. "It's like a peanut?"

Mick snickered. "Like a big rock."

For a while Troy said nothing. "How you know all this?"

"My Dad and Ma tell me stuff. Or from books. When my Dad was a Marine he had to fight the Japs on islands with coconut trees."

"There's Japs in Florida?"

"Nope. My Dad and his buddies kilt em all." Mick sat up. "Hush!"

41

Sudden footsteps crunched through the brush. A flashlight flared, a man's huge shape lunged at them, grabbed Mick as Troy tore free. "Run!" Mick yelled.

"Goddamit!" the man grunted. "Stop fightin'! I'm takin you in!"

In fire-jagged darkness the man dragged Mick toward the train. Troy snatched a burning bough and shoved it into the man's face; he screamed and knocked it away and Mick broke free and they ran through the forest, night-blinded tripping over roots and rocks till the man's yells grew faint behind them.

"Lordy!" Mick gasped, catching his breath. "Lordy."

"He still comin?"

"Too far. But now we can't ride the trains. Not for a while." Mick grabbed Troy's arm. "You saved me."

Troy said nothing, then, "You came back for me on that trestle."

"We watch out for each other, ain't nothin kin stop us."

Troy was shivering. "Can we make another fire?"

"See up there," Mick started walking, "that's the Big Bear, points to the North Star. We keep thet to the right. Soon's we hit a road we head south agin."

They reached the road and walked fast along it in the biting cold, and Troy decided if Mick knew all these things then he could learn them too, could know the world, make his way. The Fathers said he'd always be evil and fail everything unless he prayed. They made the world scary and unhappy. But maybe it wasn't really like that. *You made yourself ex-cape. Maybe you don't have to do what don't feel right.*

"When we get to Florida we can work," he said. "Buy lotsa food."

Ahead a few houses slept under pale streetlights, a stop sign stood lonely at a crossroads. "Lordy lookit thet!" Mick said, pointing to white shapes on a line outside a little house with dark shutters. "Lazy folks left out the washin' –"

They climbed the picket fence and crossed the crinkly dew-frozen lawn to the clothesline, found two shirts not too large, two pairs of socks and two towels. "What we need these towels for?" Troy whispered.

"For sleepin'." A dog started barking inside the house and they ran down the road and put on the damp shirts, stuffing the long tails into their pants, the socks in their pockets and the towels round their necks.

"Hey," Mick said. "Lookit this!" Behind a corner store stood a stack of wooden crates filled with empty soda bottles. "We'll take some bottles and sell 'em."

The town petered out into dark forest. Even walking fast Troy got colder. Hunger chewed his stomach, his legs weak from walking and no food.

The stars faded, another town, houses and paved streets, street-lights flickering out. At the sound of an engine they hid behind a hedge as a truck trundled past and halted at the next house.

A man stepped from it carrying a wooden box on a handle. He set it down on the house steps and took out bottles that clinked as he put them on the steps. He picked up two empty bottles and put them in the wooden box and took it back to the truck, drove to the next house and did the same thing. "Thet's what they do," Mick said. "When my Dad sells our milk they take it to people's houses, people what don' have cows."

When the truck turned the corner they grabbed two bottles and went into a field and drank them down, the sweet thick cream on top then the lovely cold milk. Mick took up his towel full of empty soda bottles. "Soon's a store opens we kin sell these."

"We gonna walk all the way to Florida?"

They started walking again. "We could. If we have to."

"Yeah," Troy said, "We stick together, we can do anything."

"HOW COME YOU BOYS aren't in school," the man in the store said.

"Our folks is visitin'," Mick said quickly. "So we got the day off."

"Who they visiting?"

"My Dad's buddy from the War. Up on Maple Avenue." Mick nodded at Troy. "We been out collectin' bottles. Crazy how folks jest throw em in the ditches."

The man counted out forty-two cents on the counter, looked at

Troy. "You guys brothers?"

"Yeah," Troy shrugged. "Twins."

"You sure don't look it."

"Them kind what's not 'dentical," Mick said.

"Fraternal."

"Yeah. How much is thet bread?"

"Ten cents."

"And some peanut butter?"

"Thirty-seven cents, a little jar. You'll be a nickel short."

Mick dug into his pocket and took out the two nickels. "Take one a these."

The man got the bread and peanut butter and put it on the counter. "What's your Dad's friend's name?"

Mick looked at Troy. "You 'member?"

Troy shook his head. "George somethin'."

"Okay, boys," the man smiled. "Get out of here."

In the forest they spread the peanut butter on the bread and ate it all, bellies full. Mick took a chocolate bar from under his shirt and gave Troy half.

"Where'd you get this?"

"When he was getting the peanut butter I grabbed it off the stand."

"That's stealin'."

Mick shrugged. "To make it to Florida we gotta steal."

"He was a nice man."

"Knew we was tellin' lies. Didn't care."

"How'd you know about that Maple Avenue?"

"Saw it on the way into town. Always gotta know where you are, that's what my Dad says. If you want to be a Marine."

"I don't wanta be a Marine." To Troy it seemed insane to risk death. What had killed *his* Dad.

"Sometimes you hafta be. When people attack your country you hafta protect it."

Troy looked up at the golden sun clearing the treetops bringing light and warmth to the world. "I don't wanta get kilt."

"That's a long time away. We don' hafta think about it yet."

7

NEVER TRUST NOBODY

M EADOW GROVE, the sign said. *Butter Capital of Maryland.* "Where's Maryland?" Troy said.

Mick wished he'd paid more attention to the map on the wall in Mrs. Purdy's home room. "Somewheres under New Jersey."

They walked through the midmorning shadows of tall elms. White houses with huge barns sat back from the road. "They's rich," Mick said, "havin' barns like thet. Those brown cows, that's Guernseys, give the best milk, lots of cream. Makes the best butter."

"For Christmas we got butter," Troy said. "A whole piece of toast with butter. Then I had it at your house."

"Got to find a telephone," Mick said. "Let my folks know I'm doing a walkabout."

"They ain't gonna be happy."

"My Dad run away lots when he was a kid. He got no right to argue."

A gray-haired woman was taking letters from a mailbox. She put in more letters and pushed up a little red flag. "Mornin, Maam," Mick said. "Kin you tell us where there's a outside tel'phone?"

"Here in Meadow Grove? There isn't one." She looked at them over narrow glasses. "Where you boys from?"

Mick nodded over his shoulder. "Up in Ravensdale."

She pursed her lips. "You should be in school."

"Teacher's sick, we got the whole day free." Mick glanced at the spreading white barn, the whitewashed fences and peaceful cows. "Do you have any work for the day? Shovelin' manure, loadin' hay, paintin' fences, we work real hard –"

A smile touched her face. "No I don't need help."

"Your husband does everythin'?"

"My husband's dead."

"Then we kin help you. One dollar for the whole day." Mick looked around. "Who does your milkin'?"

She chewed her lip. "The hired man."

"Lots a jobs he don' wanna do. We'll do em. We're the best."

She smiled now, hand on her hip. "The coop hasn't been cleaned since last winter. You want to do that?"

"We're special good at chicken coops," Troy said.

"Okay, a dollar it is."

"A dollar each," Mick said. "Thet's what I meant."

It was a wide low building stinking of dried chicken manure, old feathers and dry infestations of poultry lice. She handed them two pitchforks. "The chickens all died of flu last winter. I was waiting on cleaning it before I got new ones."

Each forkful of the foot-deep manure they dumped in the wheelbarrow raised a filthy dust that fogged the light and clogged their throats and lungs. It was dry on top but lower down it was soggy and stank of ammonia and rot. Troy's hands began to sting with blisters from the pitchfork and the wheelbarrow's cracked wooden handles.

They drank from the pump outside, taking turns pumping while the other stuck his head under the icy water. "We'll have two whole dollars," Mick said.

Troy tried to imagine it. "In Boys' Home you don't get money."

Mick wiped water off his face. "You didn' have no uncles or aunts? Or a Grandma and Grandad?"

"Not that was livin'."

Mick looked at the sun. "We got to keep workin, to finish today."

"Maybe she'll let us work tomorrow too. Make two dollars more."

"She'd wonder how come we ain't in school."

Troy rubbed blistered palms. "People's sure crazy about school. Same as the Fathers, whup you if you don' study."

"Grownups want us to be like them – all worried and busy."

"Like the Fathers, sayin you gotta pray and be misrable to get to Heaven. But it ain't sure there's Heaven, is there?"

"My Dad says we got to live in this world, not plan on some 'maginary one."

At noon the woman brought them fresh cold milk and ham and cheese sandwiches on thick brown bread. They ate in the shade of the hayloft, the milk washing down the manure dust. Golden dust motes danced in the sun, like stars at night, too many to count.

Troy thought of asking Mick was he going to call his folks. But Mick might decide to go home and Troy couldn't find Florida by himself. Though if Mick wanted to go home, how was it fair to argue him against it? He looked at his sore hands. Mick's hands weren't bleeding – he was used to this. So if Troy worked like Mick he'd be tough too.

When they finished the sinking sun gilded the meadows and the cows were coming in, lowing, their udders swollen. "Here's your two dollars," the woman said. "You boys earned it."

Mick handed one to Troy. "Maybe we could work some other time..."

"That'd be fine."

Troy shrugged. "How 'bout tomorrow?"

She watched them. "What about school?"

Mick shook his head at Troy. "The teacher'll still be sick –"

She smiled. "How convenient."

"Guess we'll be goin home," Mick said.

Her lips tightened. "You should rest a bit. Soon's the hired man comes back I'll drive you to Ravensdale, so you don't have to walk..."

"Oh no Maam – we couldn't do that." Mick backed away. "We'd rather walk."

"Heavens no. I'll get you a root beer and then you can sit out on the front porch." She started toward the house, walking fast, turned round. "Come on now!"

The front porch was wide and cool under the long shadows of the trees. "This is wonderful!" Troy said.

"Ain't you never had root beer afore?" Mick seemed angry, nervous.

In a distant room they could hear the woman talking. Mick moved to the screen door, listening. "Who's she talkin' to?" Troy said.

"Tel'phone."

"Maybe you could use hers, call your Mom 'n Dad."

Mick motioned to be quiet, stepped across the parlor toward the sound of the phone, came back fast. "She's talkin' to the cops."

Troy stood. All around were wide empty fields, no place to run. He saw Father Damon's whip coming down, the high wire fences. This time he'd never get out.

The woman's footsteps crossed the parlor toward them. They jumped over the porch rail into bushes and ran along the side of the house to the barn up into the towering cool bales. "She'll think we run off." Troy crawled across the prickly bales and peered through a crack in the siding. "Jeez, look at this –"

A blue police car stopped at the gate. The woman leaned to the driver's window, pointed at the house, the barn, the road and distant meadows. The policeman got out and looked around, got back in and drove slowly down the road. The woman returned to the house; the screen door clacked shut.

"We wait till dark we can git away," Mick said.

"You boys havin' a good time?" a man's voice said. He was a short, slender and thin-faced, an amused smile across the stalk of hay in his mouth.

"We wasn't doin nothin," Mick said.

"That won't keep you out of trouble."

"You gonna turn us in?"

"What for – you kill somebody?"

"Don' wanta go to school, that's all."

"Hell I wisht I'd stayed in school. Wouldn't be doin' this work now." The man turned away. "But I'm just doing the milking. Never saw you boys at all."

They listened to the shuffling cows downstairs, the spatter of milk into pails, the slosh of pails into the tank, the man whistling a familiar song that Mick couldn't place.

"I don' believe 'im," Troy whispered.

"Never trust nobody. That way we can keep safe."

Troy turned back from the crack in the siding. "She's goin."

After the woman's car had left they ran across the road down a long meadow to a string of trees along a brook. "Let's git back to the train," Mick said.

"Which way's that?"

Mick looked at him. "You tell me."

Troy thought. "Well, we went west then south. So now we go east."

"Which way's thet?"

Troy looked up. "Stars ain't out yet. Can't tell."

"Which way the sun set?"

"Oh yeah," Troy grinned. "Let's go."

IT WAS DARK when they reached the tracks and turned south. "Hafta find a place where the trains slow down," Mick said, "so we can jump on."

Troy thought of the crushing steel wheels and hard rails. "What if we can find one on a siding, like when we got off?"

Wind came up, gusting coal dust. Drops hit their faces and spattered on the ties. "Shoulda found raincoats." Mick said. "Hafta walk all night."

"Less we find a town."

On they walked into the sullen night. The rain fell in sheets making the rails too slippery to walk on. It invaded Troy's skin, a sodden shivering cold. "This ain't no palm trees," he kept saying, pretending it was a joke.

A faint tang of smoke stopped them. They crept closer, rain hailing on their heads and shoulders. Ahead in the windblown gusty night a fire flickered beneath a road overpass, a man's shape hunched over it. "Quiet," Mick whispered, "let's git around him."

Troy tugged his soaked collar up his neck. "Who is it?"

"Tramp. They ride the rails too. Kill you and eat your heart."

"I'm so cold..."

"Come on in, then, loveys," a woman's voice behind them, "'n get warm."

Mick jumped so fast he tripped and fell. "Run!" he yelled, scrambling up.

"Hey sweethurt!" she called as Troy backed away. "You're all wet."

Troy kept his distance. "Where'd you come from?"

"Here I was out takin a tinkle and you boys almost walked right over me. A girl's got to have some privacy –"

Troy glanced toward the fire. "Who's that?"

"That's Joe, sweethurt. We're Molly'n Joe. Been everywhere the rails go – 'Laska to Mexico and back – ainta gonna hurt you." She took his arm. "Now you come outta the rain'n get warm by the fire, loveys, and Joe'll put on a nice warm cup a tea."

A rough-faced man in a tan hat looked up from the fire. He had deepset eyes, a round nose, a missing front tooth and silver whiskers. "Here, Pal," he patted a log, "have a seat."

"I'll stay back," Mick called to Troy. "You git warm then we change places –"

"Now you don' needta be like that," Molly said.

"People try to turn us in," Troy said, jumping back when he saw her face.

"S'amatter, boy," Joe chuckled, "ain't never seen a Negro afore?"

In the yellowish firelight her face was glossy black, wide-nosed and thick-lipped, her tight curls half-covered by a yellow kerchief. "Make the puur boy some tea, Joe."

"S'right here." Joe gave Troy a tin can hot in his hands, delicious nectar sliding down his throat shivering him all warm inside.

"Puur boy." She slipped off her jacket and slid it over his shoulders, pushed him down on the log and beckoned at Mick. "You git here right now!"

Mick edged closer. "Joe," she said, "make these boys a jelly somewich. Lotsa that plum jelly –"

A distant rumble shook the tracks. "Git in here," Joe yelled at Mick. They huddled against the embankment as a passenger train roared by knocking the fire sideways and scattering sparks. There was a car of people eating on white tablecloths, half-lit sleepers with white sheets and gray blankets folded down.

"Which way you boys goin?" Joe said.

"Florida," Mick said.

"And what on God's green earth'll ya do when ya gets there?"

Troy shivered with new warmth. "Eat coconuts."

"Give ya the shits, boy. Too much coconuts'n you'll be runnin' all night."

The vulgarity bothered Troy. "We'll eat fish too," he said. "Lotsa stuff."

RAIN FELL like a cold gray curtain, pouring off the overpass. A freight train shook Troy from a dream of holding hands with Mick's sister and she said, "You don't *have* to be like this," and he woke not knowing what she meant or where he was, found himself with his head on Molly's lap, covered by her coat. He was warm and the rain had stopped and sun was shiny on the rails and mist was rising from the tracks.

He jumped up. "Sorry!"

She looked at him surprised. "For what, lovey?"

"I been sleepin' on you –"

"Your friend been sleepin' on my other side. S'okay."

Joe came down the embankment with an armload of sticks. "They're wet but we'll get'er goin." He laid them one by one on the coals, puffing gently.

Troy crouched beside him. "S'posed to put them in a box, like a little log house."

Joe chuckled, showing the missing tooth. "You boys want breakfast?"

Mick came down the embankment with more sticks. "We'll pay you."

"For what, lovey?" Molly said. "Gets lonely wit only Joe to keep comp'ny wit."

They had bread with plum jelly and hot tea, Mick and Troy standing by the fire with steam rising from their clothes. "Hafta find another train," Mick said.

"You'll be walkin' halfway to Washintun," Joe said, "'fore ya catch one."

"Where's thet?" Mick said.

"They're too dang young, Joe," Molly said. "Oughtta go home."

"We're on a walkabout." Troy glanced at Mick. "I ain't got no home."

"Me neither," Mick said.

"Better watch out the man don't git ya," Joe said. Troy thought of the man he'd hit with the burning stick. Joe bundled the tin cooking cans and bread and jelly in a blue sack he slung over his shoulder. "Ain't gonna git ta Floridy standin' here."

They trudged all day south along the tracks, Molly singing in a deep sweet voice that made Troy feel sad and happy. They drank from streams and ate jelly and bread and when trains came they hid in the woods. Dusk was falling when Joe turned up a hill. "A shack here somewheres, I 'member."

Molly stood on the tracks, arms akimbo. "That was further on, lovey," she called.

"Not the tin-roof one... I'm considerin' a early Thanksgivin' dinner." Brush thrashed as Joe climbed over the top, came back. "Come on up – there's room at the inn!"

8

THE SECRET

I T WAS A SHED open on one side, a dirt floor with a stone firepit circled by log seats, empty windows and wooden hayricks along the sides. *"Heaven!"* Molly said, glancing up at the underside of the shingled roof. "Last time never even leaked."

"C'mon, boys!" Joe led them through the edge of the woods to a field with a farmhouse and barns on a far ridge. "I figgered!" He crossed the cropped field toward a haystack, cut a bale and broke off sections. "Gotta take the whole bale'n leave no scraps, or he'll see we been here and tear down the shed and then folks won't have it."

They carried the sweet-smelling new hay to the shed and spread it over the wooden hayricks. "Softer'n a feather bed." Joe nodded to Mick. "Come with me."

Mick followed Joe across the field, the stubble crunching under-foot. Swallows were swooping in the early darkness, owls and nighthawks called. "Young turkeys is awful sweet," Joe said softly. "Trouble is dogs. Turkey farmers keep big dogs to kill coons."

"So how we gonna git one?"

"See that, it's the turkey barn. Ya go 'long these here trees an when ya git near to the house ya start whackin' a stick on a tree. That'll start the dogs barkin' in their pen'n in all that ruckus I'll sneak down to the turkey barn'n fish one out. When I got 'im back in the woods I'll make a crow call and ya come quietlike."

The house lights were mellow and soft like his own when Mick had come from the forest across a new-mown pasture, knowing it was home, warm and full of love and food. Shutting out the thought he banged a stick against a maple and deep baying erupted behind the house. The back porch light flashed on, a man's dark silhouette under it, his voice indistinct. After a moment he went inside and the dogs quieted.

A crow called. Mick slipped through the woods to Joe sitting on the dewy grass, a white body beside him. "Ya did great, Pal."

In the shed the fire was warm and bright, the smell of new hay and oak smoke delicious. "We'll put the feathers in a bag," Joe said to Troy. "An drop em in a stream."

"Why?" Troy said.

"So that farmer'll never know." Joe began yanking feathers from the turkey. "Be invisible, Pal. That's the secret... Come'n go an nobody knows you ain' never been there 'tall." He stuffed feathers into the bag. "Jes' like Korea. We useta cross into the Chinese lines at night. Cut throats'n leave witout nobody seein'. Made em somethin' fearful, it did. Yes it did."

When he'd pulled off all the feathers, Joe gutted the turkey and cut off the head and feet. "These go in the stream too." Molly drove a pointed stick through the turkey and turned it slowly on two forked sticks. After a while, fat began to sizzle on the coals.

All was darkness outside their little circle of fire. With his huge knife Joe cut slices from the outside. Mick felt a happiness like his last day in the woods before the trouble at school, before Daisy had gone. "This's great." He pushed at his stomach to make room for more.

"Life on th' road," Molly said, wiping her mouth.

"But how come you're out here?" Mick said, feeling ashamed for being so forward. "You could have jobs'n all."

Joe spit; it hissed in the fire. "Why'n God's green earth'd we want that?"

"Everbody does. That's what happens when you grow up."

Joe tore a scrap from the end of the paper bag, dug into his bag for some tobacco that he rolled in the scrap and lit with a twig from the fire. "Who says?"

"In school. That's what they tell you."

Joe puffed deeply and lay back with his head on a log. "Ya believe that crap?"

"Now Joe," Molly said, "you be good."

"Do you see me workin?" Joe said. "Why should I work when I got my Molly and my freedom, don't have to get up when I don't want, or go where I don't want?"

"But you don' have any money," Mick said. "Do you?"

"So that's the choice – money or freedom. Which ya gonna take, Pal?"

Mick thought. "Can't you have enough money an keep your freedom too –"

Joe emitted a rough cackle. "Ya think that, do ya?"

MICK WATCHED THE COALS DIE, trying to stay awake, nestling into the savory soft hay and thinking of the galaxies in the universe Dad had told him about, how they were dying too, over billions of years. It made him hungry to live as long as those galaxies, watch tyrannosaurs and pterodactyls and the great forests in his dinosaur books, see what was going to happen a million years from now.

It made no sense that Joe had been a Marine and now was riding the rails, with no money. Dad'd been a Marine and they gave him money for college, so why didn't they for Joe? It was okay to ride the rails while you were a kid, but not for your whole life. Maybe Molly'n Joe would get a house somewheres and settle down... *Settle down*, like mud to the bottom of a pond – is that what it meant?

He was being tough, though, when he wanted to run home, see Dad and Ma, even Tara, have Ma's food every day. Even his chores were okay, really. But once you gave your word you had to keep it and pretty soon it didn't matter what you wanted.

And what about school? He couldn't breathe just thinking of it.

What they didn't tell you about a walkabout was how lonely and afraid you get. He looked at Troy asleep in the hay. Maybe tomorrow he'd bring up going home. But how could they?

He drifted, half-wakened by Joe and Molly snuffling and snickering in the rustling hay, Molly moaning softly, and he wondered what they were doing but fell asleep before he could think about it.

THEY CAUGHT a freight next morning at the switching yard and rode it all day, the forest turning to fields and farms, a warm grass-scented breeze through the door, then to roads and houses, then more houses then dirty brick buildings blotting out the sky, the air stinking of burnt rubber and other foul odors, Joe sitting back from the door scratching at bug bites, Molly singing in her low deep voice, *"Nobody know the trouble I see –"*

"When the train starts to slow down," Joe said, "we jump out and run like Hail, 'n you two boys stick with me'n Molly –"

"Where are we?" Troy said, awakening from a doze and staring at the jagged bleak landscape clicking past.

"Hail, son, we're in Washintun.'"

THE TRAIN WAS MOVING FAST when Joe leaped out tumbling on the tracks and got up running. "Jump!" he yelled. *"Jump!"*

Molly swung over the side then Mick falling face down in gravel. Troy hung on till he saw Joe's angry wave and leaped. They crawled across the greasy gravel after Joe and Molly, under a freight car then a passenger car, Troy thinking what Mick had said about the toilets dumping on the tracks.

They crouched under a flatcar. It shook with a huge clang of couplings and inched forward; they ducked under an oil car on the next line as the flatcars pulled away, wheels grinding, rails groaning. They darted over an open track and under the next cars to a cyclone fence with rusty prongs on top, through a hole in the fence over broken bottles and metal scraps, and walked fast down a dirty street where trash cans lay on their sides, corroded fire escapes hung from grim brick buildings, dark-skinned men watched them from doors, a tin can rattled back and forth in the wind over oily cobbles where water gathered blackly. "Is this a city?" Troy said, panting to keep up.

"Ain't Heaven," Molly answered, wiping a torn hand on her shirt.

"What we gonna do?"

She looked at him sharply. "Find some friends, lovey."

"Stop staring," Mick snapped at Troy.

"Ain't never seen people like this," Troy said. "Cept for Molly."

They came to a broad avenue of stained buildings, shops, faded billboards, skinny children loitering by broken-down cars. A gritty sheen coated streets and buildings; loud strange music rattled from doorways and windows; a tainted orange sun sank beyond the sagging wires and dirty facades. Voices called in strange accents; tall gangly boys were tossing a basketball through a broken sign that hung off a wall.

They climbed crumbly steps past men sitting with paper-bagged bottles, into a gloomy corridor stinking of old food and some foul chemical that stung their nostrils, up creaky stairs down a hall yellowed by a single bulb on a cord, past splintered doors into a room painted orange by the last sun, couches sagging against the walls.

"I don' like it here," Troy said.

"It's Molly's cousin's place." Joe patted his shoulder. "Ya can bunk here tonight wit us and tomorra we'll find ya a train goin south."

"Ain' noplace to steal food," Mick said.

"We hafta go out a whiles," Joe said, stopping at the door.

"But you lovelys don't go anywhere," Molly said.

There was a bedroom with mattresses on the floor, a blanket askew over the window, a bathroom stinking of urine and mold, a broken-seated toilet and rusty tub piled with trash, a kitchen with a formica table and three wooden chairs, an icebox half-open, a sink with a dripping faucet and dirty dishes on which masses of dark bugs crawled.

Molly and Joe came back with a loaf of bread and gave them each two pieces and left again. The room darkened; Mick tried a light switch but nothing happened.

The building grew loud with voices, laughter, radio music, the blare of passing cars. Troy tried to not think of the Boys' Home. Its bright dining room, warm food and familiar faces, worn benches and polished floor, the dormitory with his little bed, Clarence Dillaway in the next bed who cried in his sleep, Tommy Pruitt snoring on the other side, even harsh Father Loudy with his willow switch – did he hit you only when you deserved it? It all seemed remarkable and nearly good, a comforting dream from which he'd awoken and wanted to return.

"You 'member how to get back to the train?" Mick said.

"How we gonna find Florida?"

Again Mick tried to remember the map on the schoolroom wall. "There's Washington... then nothin maybe, to Florida... Wisht I could 'member..."

"If we go back to Shanks Village we can live in that old broken house –"

"Lafayette's –"

Heavy footsteps crunched down the hall; the door banged open and a big shape stumbled in. "Joe!" Mick called. "That you?"

The shape swung on them. "Who the hell're you!"

The voice was impossibly deep and dangerous. "We're friends a Molly'n Joe," Troy whispered, then said it louder.

The man grabbed him. "They here?"

"Gone out," Mick said. "Said they'll be back."

"Better fockin' not!" The man threw him against the wall. "Git outta here!"

They scrambled into the hall downstairs into the reeking night, fast music, harsh laughter, the tantalizing smells of fried food. "Gotta wait for Molly'n Joe," Mick said.

"Maybe we can steal some food," Troy said.

Further down the sidewalk stood a cart lit by a single bulb. "Dogs five cents!" A grizzled old man limped round the cart toward them. "You whiteboys come git some!"

"Kin we have two?" Mick said.

"Mustud? Pickalilli?"

"We can run faster'n he can," Mick whispered.

Troy glanced round the sidewalk crowded with black faces. "Don' do it."

Mick fished out the nickel. "This's all I got. Musta lost the other one."

The man inspected him, handed them the two dogs. "You boys can sure use'em."

"You don' have any work?" Troy said fearfully. "We kin do anythin' –"

He tilted his head back in a great laugh of black teeth. "Better split 'fore you get all beat up."

They turned down the dark side street, the hot dog a sweet memory in the back of Troy's throat. After a few blocks he heard the puff of a locomotive, the rumble of a diesel engine and the slow clickety-click of wheels. "Which way we goin?" he said.

"South," Mick answered. "Ain thet what we 'greed on?"

Shapes closed round them, from nowhere. "Now whair you whiteboys think *yu're* goin?" A mellow smiling voice.

"Catchin' a train," Mick said quickly.

"Hair that, Twig? Whiteboy he catchin' a *train* –"

"I don' think he right," another voice said.

Troy tried to see how many but could only make out tall shapes closing in. "We're Molly's friends. She said go this way."

"Hear that, guys? Molly said go *this*away."

Troy looked back up the dark street. A long way to the lights. "Guess we'll go back'n see her."

A hand knocked him down. "Ain goin nowhere whiteboy. You stayin' *rait* here."

"Take they money first," another voice said.

"We don have no money," Mick said.

There was a whack and Mick fell, feet kicking his head. Troy rolled over him, covering him, the feet smashing his ribs. "Gotta run," he gasped, and swung up hitting a groin, the kid screaming and falling, Troy punched another and a great crushing pain fell down on his head exploding lightning inside it, his mouth in bloody dirt, trying to get up for if he didn't they'd kill Mick, kicks crushing his ribs, as he faded hearing the thunk of feet into Mick's body, Mick swearing and kicking, then a sharp agony in his arm swept him away thinking nobody could hurt him now.

Anything better than pain. Lie unmoving, begging the pain to slow, wondered what is that whine, realized it was his breathing, trying not to breathe made it no better.

"Well look a this." A faraway voice.

"Don't kick me," Mick moaned.

"Better call them ambalents," another said.

"You go up that street," a woman said, "find a tel'phone."

"Not *me*," someone laughed.

"Shit," the woman said, "who gonna arrest *you?*"

Let them talk, Troy decided. Just lie here not moving, begging the pain to stop but it just kept filling his body with agony making him hope to die just to stop it. He turned over so he could breathe through the blood in his throat. If he could get up they could get away. "Mick where are you?"

Mick gripped his hand. "You'all lie still," the woman said. Her hand caressed Troy's shoulder.

"Oh God don't touch me!" Everything faded again, the street soft and warm. It's okay if a car came, it could run him over. A car *was* coming but stopped and the woman was gone and new people came from the car. "Holy Jesus!" a man said.

"Hit by a car," another said.

"Get the stretchers you two –"

"Got beat up!" Mick coughed. "Get them!"

"You ain't getting anybody, kid. Lucky you're alive."

SOFT LIGHT. Mick heard voices in the distance, slowly understood he *was*. He opened his mouth; it hurt; he moved and that hurt horribly. If he breathed real gentle it hurt less. That's the secret, he told himself: be quiet.

"Mick!" a hoarse voice but he couldn't place it. "Get up!"

He twisted sideways, saw he was in bed. Someone in another bed, head bandaged, arm in a thick cast. *We got hurt*, he remembered. "Troy?"

"Kin you git up?"

Mick tried, gasped. "Hurts too much. Where's this?"

"Hospital I think. Cops'll take me back to Boys' Home. I gotta go!"

"Wait!" Mick took a breath. "I'll go with you." *I don' wanta. Wanta go home.*

Something clicked open, then a swishing sound. "So my munchkins woke up!"

Black woman in white, uniform rustling, cool fingers on his forehead. "Lie down." She turned on Troy. "You too, munchkin!"

"What's gonna happen to us?" Troy said.

"Your Daddy's comin'," she said. "All the way from New York state. He was one happy fella when we tole him."

Mick saw his father's agonized face. "You *tol'* him? How'd you *know?*"

"You said it, honey. When you were under the ether..."

"I don' wanna go back," Troy said.

"Now that's silly. Your Daddy's comin' to get you both."

Troy took a breath, lay back. "I don' have a Daddy."

She looked at him. "You sure do."

Tears dampened the corners of Mick's eyes, ran down his cheeks. *Damn*, he thought, tried to stop them. "He's my brother. We're twins."

"That's what your Daddy said. He's comin' to get you both."

Mick dreamt his Dad was sitting beside him, hand on his arm. "Son, what the hell were you doing?"

"On a walkabout, Dad. Like you once done. I'm fine."

His father clasped both hands to his face, wiped under his eyes. "Oh Jesus son."

Mick smiled, unutterably happy. "Come on, Dad. Everythin's fine."

His father broke down in great lurching sobs, leaning over Mick as

61

if to protect him from what had happened. "I'm so sorry, Dad," Mick said. "I love you so much. I love Ma and I love Tara. I even love the cows, even that Daisy cow."

His father laughed through his tears, wiped his eyes. "Nobody can milk her like you do."

"I can't leave Troy. Twice he saved me. They beat him at the Boys' Home..."

Dad sat back. "Well you always wanted a brother."

"He's my best friend. Two times he saved my life."

"Jesus son I don't want to hear about it. I just want you home. Your Ma's been crazy. Tara cries every night, says you ran away because she teased you about a girl."

Tears choked him; he couldn't speak. "No Dad she didn't do nothin."

His Dad smiled. "Didn't do *anything*..."

"Yeah, I'm gonna learn to talk better. And study in school –"

"Not too hard."

"And we kin bring Troy?"

Dad went to Troy's bed. "Hello, son."

Troy looked up. "Please don't send me back. I promise I'll be a good kid. I'll be a good friend to Mick'n Tara, 'n work hard. I promise I will."

9

THE WOODLOT

TROY LINED UP the furrow of new dirt exactly with the vertical exhaust pipe on the front of the tractor as Mick had shown him, so the harrow on each side and behind it cut a new straight line next to the last. From the corner of his eye he could see the line of trees at the end of the field, the furrows already harrowed on his right, the mown stubble on his left that had not yet been turned.

He liked the smell of the exhaust through the tin can muffler though it burned his throat. Loved the deep engine rumble, the calluses on his palms from gripping the iron wheel and yanking the levers to raise and drop the harrows, the swinging feeling in his hips from sitting straight while the tractor tilted between furrows, loved most the perfect lines he plowed up and down the field so that Dad said, "You did a mighty fine job." And the red and yellow trees alongside the field, the breeze chasing fallen leaves across the furrows, the first bite of winter and the earthy new dirt and dry, crushed stubble.

Even when he'd tipped the tractor over in a furrow and bent the exhaust pipe, all Dad had cared about was if he was hurt. "I'll work extra hard to pay for it," Troy had said.

Dad had pulled the tractor upright with the pickup. "Come on," he patted Troy's shoulder. "I'll show you how to fix that pipe."

Though four months had passed, it seemed he hadn't really been alive till the day he ran away from the Boys' Home. As if he'd always lived with the O'Briens, always had a Brittany Spaniel named Rusty and a paint named Apache and growed up on a farm.

School was different, nearly exciting, not all prayer and religion classes like at the Boys' Home. Even though he was the same age as Mick, this school had placed him a year younger, in the same class as Tara. "This boy's very bright," the teachers told Dad and Ma, "but there's so much he's never learned." He didn't mind, the homework was easy. And sometimes he got an excited feeling, just watching Tara in class.

At home after dinner the family sat talking around the maple table that had been made by Dad's great granddad. It had a side leaf that jiggled if you leaned your elbows on it. Dad made everyone drinks, Shirley Temples with a cherry for the boys and Tara, whisky and ginger ale for him and Ma. Some weekend nights they talked till the cherry grandfather clock bonged one or two, about a man in a plaid overcoat Ma'd seen down to the market, or Charlemagne trying to unite France long ago, Roland and Oliver at Roncevalles, the C.S. Lewis story about life on Venus, Tara talking about Mozart, always talking about Mozart, Ma and Dad remembering people from when they grew up in the valley, Dad on this farm, his family from way back before the great-grandfolks to the days when you hid in the safe place between the two fireplaces when the Mohawks attacked, 'cause even if they burned the house down you might survive.

Ma's family was Vandemeers, from way back too, Dutch, on another farm "up the valley" where Sparkill Creek comes out of the hills and where now the town of Orangeburg with its two-block long main street, the school and post office were. She and Dad got married when she was eighteen before he went to fight the Japs, and they made Mick the same time Troy's Pa and Ma made him. But this Dad survived and came home and they took over the farm when Grandpa got hurt a few years later.

When Ma's own Ma and Pa died from the lung fever, the Vandemeer farm was bought for nothing by the strange disease of new little houses that seemed to be taking over up there. Though thank God not down here.

Once Doc Rasmussen said although Ma never finished high school she was the best-read person in the county. And you could believe it, the way she'd tell you neat stories out of books, stories that made you want to read everything.

Sunday afternoons often lots of neighbors showed up, folks Troy didn't know. Dad'd put chairs out on the lawn and do cowburgers and fresh corn and lots of whisky, the men talking about cattle diseases and milk and feed prices and other dull things, the women about kids and making clothes and how to cook a rooster and if you chop up alfalfa in your chicken feed you get yellower eggs, and if you grind in some beef bones it makes the shells stronger.

The Boys' Home now seemed unreal, its weary dormitory dawns, the chilled showers of numb silent boys, the mean ones, the broken ones, those half-dead of loneliness, harsh meals at wooden benches, dishes to wash and floors to scrub... Once because he'd sneezed in church he'd had to spend a weekend polishing all the banisters and rails of the stairway from the Fathers' quarters on the third floor down to the dorms on the second and the dining hall and classrooms on the first – perhaps that too was a dream.

Chapel every dawn kneeling on icy concrete, the priests' endless mumble. Prayers morning, noon and before bed, prayers at every meal, extra chapel – could God really want people to spend so much time on their knees adoring Him – was He really that *needy*, as Ma would say? In all this vastness of stars and space didn't He have better stuff to do? Even He must notice that the folks who spent a lot of time adoring Him seemed to be the ones with the least love and kindness. The least like God.

Not that Dad and Ma had much truck for religion, never even went to church. "Sunday's for sleepin' in and big family dinners and fixin' tractors and takin long walks," Ma said. "That's enough religion for me."

"Religion causes war," Dad declared. "A disease of the soul."

"But," Tara needled, "religion reminds us we *have* a soul." She was always pushing, never satisfied with anything you said. Thought she was smarter than anyone.

She's your sister now.

Another row done, he looked down the valley with the white steeple and the forest beyond, thinking as he often did of the first time he'd seen them, and how different it had been. Why was he picked out to be so *lucky*?

Prayers at the Boys' Home, wasn't that what Commies did to our soldiers in Korea – brainwashing? Didn't the Fathers do that to the kids? If kids grew up in a family like the O'Briens with no religion they wouldn't have no religion neither. He shook his head fast trying to feel his brain inside his skull – how do you wash *that*?

He realized he was smiling and couldn't remember ever smiling at the Boys' Home. *Without light there is no darkness,* Dad said one night when they were camped out, the fire dancing, mosquitoes biting... So without God how could there be evil?

The Fathers had told him over and over again that he'd lost his parents because he was evil. But how had he, a baby, been evil? If God made a baby evil, how could He be a loving God? Ma said a baby can't even speak, doesn't really think – "eats, shits, and sleeps." How was that evil?

When the next row was done he cut the engine and sat on the metal seat hearing the cooling tick of the engine, tasting the harsh exhaust and hay and dust in his throat, feeling his heart beat. Maybe everything happens at the same time – that everything's *simultanerous,* Dad's word for it – the Boys' Home and now this. If that was true, then wasn't the future, what he *would* be, wasn't that happening now too?

"Troy!"

He snapped out of it. "Yes, Ma?"

"You going to sit there all day? Or you want lunch?"

"Where's Mick?"

"Up to the woodlot splitting."

"Can I do that too?"

"You can go get him."

He walked across the stubble he hadn't yet harrowed, legs stiff from the tractor's vibration. When they loosened he ran across the hayfield and behind the barn and chicken coop, took a shortcut into the woods along a path grown over with maple saplings, stopped to listen for the thunk of an axe, broke through the undergrowth and across the brook and into the birches and beeches and ahead there were trees down, their branches all pointing along the ground, leaves already wilting.

Mick stood astride a downed trunk swinging the axe steadily side to side, cutting off branches as he backed down the trunk from bottom to top. Troy stood watching how to do it and waiting for him to stop so not to startle him. "Hey you!"

Mick buried the axe in the trunk. "We shoulda gone to Florida."

"I could eat a whole cow. Even that bitch Daisy."

"How much you do?"

"All the back hayfield 'cept for maybe twenty rows."

They stepped over cut branches to Grampy's '28 Ford pickup. "You drive," Mick said. Nervously Troy swung onto the worn seat with the sharp horsehair sticking up. He stretched his foot to shove in the clutch and jostled the stick, pushed his foot on the starter. It ground and yowled but the engine didn't catch.

"Gotta turn on the key," Mick grinned.

"Oh yeah." The engine caught and Troy slid the stick down to first and let out the clutch and the truck lurched forward and died.

"Slower," Mick said. "Let thet clutch out slower."

This time he eased it out and the truck stuttered forward, engine growling as he pushed the gas pedal. "Shift it!" Mick said. Troy shoved in the clutch and shifted and the gears snarled, the stick banging his hand. "No!" Mick yelled, "that's reverse!"

Troy slipped it into neutral and sat angry and embarrassed on the prickly seat, the engine idling erratically. "You drive. We're late for lunch."

"Just keep tryin."

He got it going again in first, bumping down the woodlot track over rocks and boughs half-buried in mud, then into second, the truck going faster, split birch logs rattling in the back, now on higher ground along the woodlot road, shoved in the clutch and slung the stick down to third, the old truck jumping ahead.

"Downshift now," Mick yelled, "into second for the brook!"

He clutched again and splashed across the brook downshifting to second and quick up the other side, rear tires slithering, and the truck slid sideways and whanged into a birch tree, the fender ripping, split logs whamming against the back of the cab as he yanked the steering wheel left and the truck jerked to a stop.

"Holy shit," Mick said. "We're screwed now."

Troy got out and went round the front. The right front fender was torn back where it had hit the tree. "I'll leave." He fought back tears. "I'll go away right now."

"I DONE IT," Mick said.

"That true?" Dad looked at Troy.

"No sir, I did." Troy flinched as Dad reached out but Dad just patted him on the shoulder. "You're a good boy." He nodded at Mick. "You are too, son. I'm mighty proud how you stand up for each other. But I don't want anybody lying."

"It's okay to lie, you once said," Mick answered, "to 'tect somebody else."

"Never to me." Dad got up, folded his napkin and laid it beside his placemat. "Tonight when I get back from Nyack we'll get the welder and I'll show you boys how to mend that fender."

"I'll stop by the feed store tomorrow," Troy said, "and tell Grampy."

"He'd rather you had an accident in his truck, learning how to drive, than out on the road."

"What's Dad goin all the way to Nyack for?" Tara asked after he'd left.

"To see if there's work in the plastic factry," Ma said.

"What about the farm?"

"He's gonna do that too... him'n us. Just till the price of milk comes back up."

"He never had to do that before." Tara glanced at Troy.

"Instead a worryin' about it you kin start mendin' the sheets and git out the clothes for tomorrow and clean out the woodshed so we can lay in the new wood –"

"How come I don't get to drive Grampy's old truck? Bet *I* wouldn't wreck it..."

"You kin't even drive, Tara," Mick said.

"I can drive the tractor." Again she stared at Troy. "Better than him."

NOMADS

MICK HAD PROMISED himself to pay attention in school, trying to pretend that Mrs. Magruder was like God or something. Promised himself to be more like Troy, walking to school in his starched plaid shirt Ma had made, his sleeves rolled down and buttoned like a parson's, in clean jeans when his other ones hadn't even been real dirty.

But Mrs. Magruder certainly weren't God unless God had a fat chin with a big old wart on it and hairs sticking out. Why din't she shave off the hair anyways? Why do people let themself be ugly?

He opened the geography book, liking its paper and ink smell. Why couldn't you just read what you want, instead of what they tell you? Wouldn't you learn more going your own way? It's when you quit the trail and wander the forest that you learn about animals'n things.

"Page two forty-nine," Mrs. Magruder called out. "Let's review what we learned about New York City. Clark Kinnell, what can you tell me? No, you don't have to stand up, boy. Just be seated and tell me what you know..."

Mick flipped to the page, a photo of the Vampire State Building. That's what Daisy used to call it, always making fun with words. Fun if there *was* vampires in't. He flipped more pages, to a photo of white sands stretching in huge dunes toward dark peaks. *The Sahara Desert is filled with nomads called Bedouins.*

"Very good, Clark," Mrs. Magruder was saying. "Mick, what can you add to what Clark has said about New York being the business capital of the world?"

He started to stand then remembered he wasn't sposed to. "Well, it's got city people in't. It ain't the desert, where there's lotsa nomads..."

Across the room Cathy Gringold giggled. "You oughta have to ride a camel," he called to her. "Git a little dirty sometime –"

"That's enough!" Mrs. Magruder snapped.

"I was jest makin' a joke."

"Making jokes at other people's never good."

"She was laughin' at *me* –"

"You stay after school. We'll discuss it then."

A siren on the wall screamed stridently, an awful clashing sound. Hands over her ears she jumped up and down yelling, "Atomic Bomb Alarm! *Atomic Bomb Alarm!* Under the desks! Quick! Quick!"

She paced the aisles, checking they were all curled tight beneath their desks. Mick lay there enjoying the dry dust-bunny odors, the old floor wax fragrance and the rusty smell of the desk's iron feet, grinned at Mrs. Magruder's swollen shoes clunking past. This was much better than class. The alarm siren ceased; his ears kept ringing.

"Okay, children, back to your desks." Mrs. Magruder strutted back and forth, head high, a hen who'd just laid an egg. "I want you all to know," she began, "how important, how essential, it is to curl up in a tight ball when you're under your desk."

Mick raised his hand. "But we've all seen pictures of Hiroshima and Nagasaki – it wouldn't have done those kids any good, to crawl under their desks –"

"Sometimes, Mick, you just have to do what you're told. And stop challenging things."

"I'm not challenging, Maam. I'm just trying to understand."

. . .

TROY SHOT ROCKS at light poles with his slingshot waiting for Mick. They walked for a while saying nothing, over the bridge where Mick fell off the rail for that girl named Daisy last year and had to wear the clown suit and got in trouble 'cause he wouldn't.

"When people make fun of you, you gotta inore them," Troy said when Mick told him what had happened. "I learnt that in Boys' Home. Kids always laugh. You have to pay no 'tension."

Mick kicked a rock. "How come you know all about numbers'n stuff?"

"It's easy. Just study, then you know."

"I hate numbers. What good are they?"

"Some day I'm gonna be a pilot, go out into space, hafta measure how far to go and how high you are, all that stuff..."

"What you wanta be that for?"

"Wouldn't it be neat way up in the clouds? Looking down at the world?"

"You kin do that climbin mountains."

"Ain't the same."

"Anyways I'm going to be a herpatolagist."

"What's that."

"Studies insex. Bugs and spiders and worms and stuff."

"That's disgusting." Troy shot a rock at the big oak by the 1776 House.

"That's the tree they hung Major André on."

"Weren't he a bandit? It's okay to hang bandits."

"He was a famous English spy. My great-great-grandad – *our* great-great-granddad – guarded him all night before he was hung. Said he was a brave young guy, the perfect gentlement excep a need for frequent mictarations."

"What's that?"

"Mictaration? Means to spit." Mick groaned. "Don't you know nothin?"

They crossed under the old oak's vast boughs of new green leaves to the 1776 House and into the cool beery shadows of Uncle Hal's bar. A few men stood at the counter, two more on stools, a man and a woman in a booth at the back. Mick ducked under the bar flap, took down two Coke glasses, dropped in some ice and filled them from the root beer tap.

"One time this big drunk guy wouldn' leave," he said, "and Uncle Hal pulled that stool there right outta the floor with the guy sitting on it, ripped the bolts right out like anythin and threw it outside onto the street with the guy still on't."

Troy sipped at the frothy sweet root beer. "Ain't possible."

"I was right here, havin' a root beer like now. Five foot six, Uncle Hal is."

"We're almost that tall."

"He told the guy, 'When I say you go, you *Go!'"* Mick slapped his palm with a leather truncheon that hung beside the cash register. "Metal inside it. Can crack a skull."

The cellar door thumped open and Uncle Hal came up with a beer barrel over one shoulder. He clicked off the cellar light, shut the door and put the barrel down with a great thunk behind the bar. "How was school?"

"Same's ever," Mick said.

"You see your cousin Johnny?"

"At recess. Couldn't find him at lunch."

Hal tapped his Camels on the bar, pulled one out. "Been to see your granddad?"

"We stopped by the feed store yesterday, but he was loading hay."

"You guys want a sandwich?"

"Oh no, thanks Uncle Hal –"

"How 'bout a hot dog?" Hal turned to Troy. "With mustard and ketchup?" He popped two dogs on the grill, buttered the insides of the buns and slapped them down on the grill, pulled three beers for the men down the bar and mixed two Old Fashioneds for the couple in the back and snatched two packs of Kools and one Chesterfield for people off the street, tossed the hot dogs into the buns and refilled their root beers. "You see Johnny tomorrow get him to play sports, participate a little for Chrissake."

"He don't like sports," Mick said.

"So talk to him about beatnik poetry or something." Hal rang up two tabs and made two more Old Fashioneds and pulled more beers and more people came in, Ray the town cop slapping down his hard-brimmed cap, two guys with greasy hands and a painter named Barney smelling of turpentine. Troy thought about the cop who had arrested him the first night he'd fled the orphanage, of the nice cops who'd talked to them after they'd got beat up in Washington, this cop Ray who was a friend of Uncle Hal's and got free beers and nobody parked in front of Hal's ever got a ticket.

"We must see to it," the voice on the radio on the shelf behind the bar was saying, "that the small family farmer gets a fair share of the national prosperity."

"That him?" Ray the cop said.

"Yeah, Stevenson," Hal said.

"Hell," Ray said, "all our farms are going under. Look at your brother –"

"He ain't under yet," Hal said.

"And we must face the grim fact," Stevenson went on, "that today thirty million Americans live in families trying to make ends meet on less than two thousand dollars a year."

"Shit," Ray said, "that's no news."

"It is to Ike," Barney said.

"I'll tell you about Ike," Uncle Hal said to him. "After the War, I was assigned to Westmoreland's staff. Westmoreland was a Colonel – a pail of dishwater even back then – and since I was on his staff I had to go to his meetings with Ike. He's a fraud, Ike. A big affable fraud. A political general. Talks about principles but never lives by them."

"He says we all must be dedicated to peace," Ray added, "that without it there's no future. Hell, everybody knows that. Question is, how we gonna get there?"

"Bomb ourselves back to the Stone Age," Barney rasped.

Troy and Mick took their glasses into the kitchen and washed them and the other glasses that were there. "You didn' have to do that," Hal said.

They took the sun-dappled road out of town, the white horse

following them along the white fence, belly-deep in new grass. "You hear what that cop said," Mick said. "About Dad losing the farm?"

"You think it's true?"

"When Dad and Hal got the farm," Mick said, "Dad paid Hal half the value and that's how Hal bought the bar."

"Then he married Sylvia?"

"They was already married, in Germany when he was a paratrooper killing Nazis. He saved her; she's Jewish. When you go to the library she helps you find books."

"Librarian," Troy said, trying out the word.

"Says I should be a doctor."

"Why anybody'd want to do that?"

"She says to save lives and make the world a better place. Her family all got kilt in the concentrated camps."

Troy set a rock in his slingshot. "See that ol' Mercury in that field? Bet I can hit the back window."

"From here? No you kin't."

"What you bet?"

"You do it I'll bring in the cows tonight myself."

Troy pulled his slingshot way back, aiming upwards. The rock sailed across the field and whacked into the Mercury's rear window exploding a spiderweb of cracks.

"I kin't believe you done that," Mick said. "From here."

Troy grinned. "Me neither." He dug out a rock and handed it to Mick. "This's a good one."

Mick missed, found another rock and hit the car's roof. "Wow. You did good."

They walked along the sunny shadowy road shooting at trees and poles. "Hear this car comin?" Troy said. "Bet I can tell what it is without lookin... It's a Hudson."

It passed, low-slung, two-toned. "Ain't so," Mick said. "Was a Kaiser."

Troy shrugged. "Same engine."

"How'd you tell?"

"Just listen to the engine. Every engine sounds different."

They cut across the meadow to the Lafayette house. "Ever see a picture of this guy?" Mick said. "Had a wig and fluffy clothes. How you gonna fight like thet?"

"Maybe he was a gen'ral. Made other guys fight."

"Like Eisenhower, Dad says. He got 'lected first time by being a General, but he never did any combat, always made other guys do the fighting –"

"But he's gonna beat that guy Stevenson again, your Ma says."

"Dad says it's a crime. Why 'lect a stupid guy instead of a smart one?"

"You handing out Stevenson leaflets all over Tappan ain't going to get him 'lected."

Mick halted. "If we don't do something..." he hunted for the words, raised his hands, "then what?"

"Eisenhower's gonna win anyway. Why waste your time?"

They went on, Mick thinking it through. "What we want is what's best for America..."

Troy smiled. "Who decides what's best?"

Mick shrugged. "The people."

"Well why do they need your help deciding what they want?"

"Heck," Mick said, "It's impossible to talk to you."

For a while Troy said nothing, then, "Think we can do all your Dad's work now he's at the plastic factry?"

"And all our chores too. 'Cept now you don' hafta bring in the cows."

"Let's do it both of us, like always."

At Washington's Spring they sat on a sun-warm grassy bank dangling toes in the bone-chilling water. "Every time I'm here," Mick said, "I wonder what if America didn't win the Revolution."

Troy glanced up at the dark hemlocks across the little pool, the brighter leafy trees beyond, the golden meadow. "Like if this spring wasn't here, that last winter when they needed water? When everbody thought they were gonna lose, but they came out and won? That's what your Dad says."

"Yeah, or we'd still be speaking British and saluting the Queen."

"British's the same as English."

"No it's not. You kin't hardly understand it."

"Not so. Think of Marilyn Monroe in that movie."

"Yeah, but she's English. Why are you so stubborn when you're wrong?"

"Because I ain't."

Mick dug his feet into the mud. "This's like squeezin' meadow pies in your toes."

"It's best when your feet're cold'n the meadow pies're hot from the sun –"

"Think of the poor kids in New York City, don't ever git to squish their toes in meadow pies. No woods neither, no wild animals..."

"No nomads neither. You said Mrs. Magruder din't like it when you said that."

"Grownups don't like what you think. Till you grow up and think like them."

Troy shivered from the pleasant memory of warm cow dung between cold toes. "Can't be that bad. Or there wouldn' be no reason to grow up, would there?"

11

ANGELS AND CLOWNS

"**I**F THE BOMB was gonna hit in an hour," Mick said, "what would you do?"

Tara flipped a page of her piano book, flexed her fingers. "Be with you'n Dad'n Mom."

"And Troy?"

"Not him. I can never tell what he's thinking –"

"Why don' you ask him? What he's thinkin'."

"I don't *want* to. I don't want to know *any*thing about him."

"Think what it's like to be him."

"It's horrible but I can't help that. I just want to be me." She ran her fingers down the piano keys, a lovely tinkling sound. "You heard me play this?"

"I don' see how you like thet stuff –"

"It's Haydn. It's really hard but I'm getting it."

"I'd rather be in the woods..."

She smiled, drifting into the rapture of the sound. "This is *my* woods."

In the kitchen he cut a piece of new warm bread, stuck it in his pocket and went out letting the screen door slap. Saturday, no school – why couldn' he just be happy?

Grampy's old Ford pickup stood in the shade beside the barn with two pairs of feet sticking out from under it. "What you guys findin?" Mick said.

"Troy's got the transmission down," Grampy called. "Git under here'n help him."

Angrily Mick slid under the truck. Troy grinned, black grease on his nose. "Grampy's gonna show me how to shim the gears."

"Was runnin' fine before," Mick said.

"Gears been grindin'," Grampy said.

Mick raised the transmission off the ground and swung it from under the engine, mashing a hand on the running board, squirmed free and stood. "There."

Troy slid out. "I'd a helped you."

Grampy stood dusting his sleeves, his long white hair disheveled, grease on his pants. "This's stuff you should know, Mick."

Mick sucked his bleeding fist. "Can't know everthing."

Grampy squinted at him. "Should always know how to break down a tranny."

Mick walked away. *If I was a bear I'd live in the woods and never git troubled by nothin. Everbody I didn like I'd bite.*

Maybe it woulda been better if they'd got to Florida. But he'd made the whole family worry. He was mean, didn't care about people. He sat on the jack fence by the woods watching the green boughs through the fence rails and wondered why he liked trees and forest more than human stuff.

A catbird landed on the top rail and called its feline cry and he broke off a piece of bread and tossed it by the fence. The bird cocked its head and looked down sideways at the bread with one black glowing eye then the other, then straight down with both eyes, and he tried to imagine its fear of danger, of cats, wondered how long it would live and marveled at the power and strength and mystery of its life.

That was *it*. The miracle of life, of wanting to live. *The importance of life.*

He'd brought Troy home but it didn't matter that everbody liked Troy more than him.

He tried swinging in the hammock between the elms, but it was boring; he took ants from different anthills and held them together in his fingertips till they began to fight, gripping each other in hard mandibles. He put them down and more ants came over and started fighting and he tossed acorns like bombs among them.

He thought of going into the woods for a yew stalk to make a bow. At the Lafayette house he threw rocks but the copperhead didn't come out. Back in the Revolution everybody fought the British so they could live like they wanted, but were they happy afterwards? Did it make any difference? Did a lot of them die for nothing?

He climbed through a window of the Lafayette house and sat on the pale brick hearth of a ruined fireplace trying to imagine the people coming in and out, planning battles, taking care of wounded and counting up the dead. If then was 1779, that made a hundred years to 1879 – all the Indians was killed by then – and 21 more years made it 1900. So 121 plus the 55 years of this century made it 176 years since Lafayette and the French helped us win the Revolution. But what if like Troy said, if all time was happening now?

He tried to remember what things had been like before Troy; it had faded like an old movie. *I don't want you boys to ever fight*, Dad said once when they had a fistfight. *All your lives you're going to be each other's best friend.*

At the 1776 House he threw a rock at the old oak where they'd hung Major André. A young brave guy and they took away his life... He tried to imagine what it was like, falling and the shooting pain as the rope jerked hard snapping your neck bones. Weren't humans the evil ones, even though they spent so much time talkin' about God? And if the Revolution was so good how come it killed lots of neat guys like André?

Beyond town he went down Larch Avenue to the last house on the left, green field and orchards beyond. The silver Packard was gone from the driveway and white curtains fluffed through the upstairs window. He wanted to run away but instead climbed the wide steps with curling gray paint and rang the doorbell, listening through the screen door.

Footsteps came slapping lightly downstairs and across the living room.

"Hiya Libby. Whatcha doin?"

She watched him through the screen. "Studying."

"Studyin'? It's Saturday. Kin I come in?"

"Just for a minute." She swung it open. "What happened to your hand?"

"Banged it on the pickup." He glanced round the cool shadowed living room, the wide rugs and soft chairs, the white curtains and polished tables. "Your folks here?"

"Gone shopping." She backed away. "They don't like you here."

"I ain't." He took her hand. "You said I could have a kiss."

She tossed back the long brown hair framing her ivory face. "Didn't say when."

He watched her, trying to breathe steady. "You said if I come by sometime." He leaned forward and pushed his lips against hers, they were slender and cool and warm and soft and a little wet and made him dizzy and scared and he could feel the skin of her cheek and taste her breath and the silkiness of her hair against his face.

She broke away. "There – you had your kiss!"

Her face was flushed and he kissed her again and she pushed her mouth at his, teeth bumping, her nose squishing his till he turned his face and they fit together better and he put his arms round her noticing her little breasts against his chest and her square hips against his and again she broke away.

"I gotta breathe," she said.

"Wow, this's fun."

"You never kissed anybody before?"

"No. Never."

"I kissed Tommy Swann. Behind the baseball field."

"He's a cretin with zits. What you kiss him for?"

"He asked me. Just like you."

"Open your mouth a little when you kiss. That's how grownups do it."

"Yuck. I don't want your spit."

"It ain't like that, Libby. Try it. Just once..." He kissed her again, her soft hair down his arms as he pulled her head toward him and she opened her mouth just a little so he could push his tongue between her lips and she snapped her teeth shut biting his tongue. "Ow!" he said. "That hurts."

"Don't go sticking in your tongue then."

He sucked at his tongue. "Kin I see your fish?"

She retreated. "They're up in my room."

"What kind you got?"

"Angels and clowns."

The stair carpet made no noise. A breeze billowed her lacy curtains. The teddy bear on her bed had a red ribbon round its neck that made him think of Major André.

"This one's Fanny." She pointed to a fish. "And this one's –"

He kissed her again, steady now, her body coming against his and it was the most amazing feeling how everything fit together, not just the bodies but the wanting and excitement, and he realized *she* liked it too, they were sharing, giving it to each other.

Like in the movies he picked her up – "Hey what you doing?" – and lay beside her on the bed. She pushed up. "What if my folks come?"

"We'll hear them," he kissed her.

Gripping his hair she pulled his mouth against hers, opening a little, the tip of her tongue to his, opening more, pushing her body against him. He pushed his hand up her pleated skirt along the back of her leg to the softness behind her knee. "Stop that Mick O'Brien!" she snapped but kept kissing him and he slid his hand up her thigh, astonished at its cool smoothness and she pushed away. "I said *stop it!*"

"Ain' nothing wrong... Let me see your underpants –"

She smiled kissing him. "What you want to see *them* for?"

"Jest do." He took her hand and pulled it down to his crotch. "Feel this –"

"It's weird. What is it?"

"It's what you do. Make me all big." She yanked her hand away and he put it back, slid up the woolly fabric of her skirt till he could feel her cotton underpants. "Kin I show you?"

She kept her hand there. "Don't want to see."

Through her underpants he felt the groove of her buttocks and she opened her thighs a little so he could feel deeper. "Unzip me," he whispered.

"Don't want to."

He reached round and unzipped his jeans, put her hand inside. It was the most amazing feeling, her cool hand. They were panting now; he raised her skirt to see her white underpants and the darkness beneath, a few little curls alongsides, his hand covering her and she sighed and somewhere a door slammed; she jerked up banging his mouth with an elbow and jumped off the bed yanking down her skirt, "My folks!"

He rolled off the bed jamming himself into his jeans. Something thudded up the stairs and thundered into the room – her stupid white sheepdog – and skidded to a stop growling at him. "It's okay Rex!" she whispered.

"Libby!" her mother called. "We're home!"

"Hi Mom! Be right down!" She opened the closet. "Get in here!"

"What if they look?"

"My dad finds you he'll shoot you... Coming, Mom!" She smoothed the bed. "Quick!"

He scrambled in among the dresses and puffy blankets, imagining Libby's father – bald, tall, severe. "C'mon Rex," Libby called.

The dog sniffed at the door and growled. Zipping his fly Mick caught his prick; the zipper broke as he jerked it free. The dog snuffled at the crack under the door. "Go 'way, Rex!" he hissed, gripping his wounded prick.

The light through the crack under the door dimmed; food smells sifted through it. He tried to figure if he could climb out Libby's window and slide down a drainpipe without being seen. Or he'd be late for his chores. Dad'd be mad. But if her folks saw him, he didn't never need to go home again.

The memory of the darkness beneath her white underpants and the few black curls alongside drove him crazy; that place *there* between her legs seemed divine.

The door squeaked open. "You in there?" Libby whispered.

"Where else I gonna be?"

"They're goin to Aunt Mabel's. I said I got to study. Just stay a whiles longer."

Her steps descended the stairs. He remembered her on the bed, her slender thighs, the white underpants, her hard kisses and slim twisting body. His chest tightened, hard to breathe. She'd let him kiss her more, lie on the bed with him... What did you do next?

Later he'd figure out what to tell his folks. That he got lost in the woods? No, Dad never went for that. Troy'd help him. He'd have to do Tara's chores forever.

A sound of engine backing away. Troy'd know if it was the Packard. Her steps pounded up the stairs; the door flew open. "Get out! Get out!"

He stood blinking under her bedroom light. "Hurry!" she said. "You got to go."

He laughed with relief. "They're gone – we can kiss some more."

She slapped him. "You almost got me kilt. I don't like you anymore."

He ran all the way home, stopping just twice to put out streetlights but that didn't make him feel better. He'd risked his life for her and now she didn't like him. He hated girls. If he was a pirate he'd make them walk the plank.

Dad'n Ma were so nice to him and all he did was make them feel bad.

The kitchen light was on. Softly he climbed the back porch stairs. Dad was sitting in half-darkness at the kitchen table. "Thought it might be you," he said.

"Sorry, Dad. I –"

"Don't say a word."

He stood watching his father's huge hard hands, hairy thick fore-arms with the sleeves rolled up to the *USMC* tattoo on the left bicep, the broad shoulders, the long legs and worn boots, the whisky bottle and half-filled glass on the checkered table.

"You know, son, life is damn hard," his father said.

"I know, Dad. I'm sorry I –"

"I said *Shut* up!"

He bit his upper lip, looking at the floor, watching his father too. "When I was a kid," his father said, "I didn't understand a damn thing. Your grandfather ran the farm and your Grandma did the house and clothes and cooking and garden and all the other chores 'n I thought everything was easy. I didn't know how hard they worked, didn't understand there was never enough money, got mad when they wouldn't give me a nickel to go to a show." He looked up at Mick. "So I figure it's the same with you."

Mick half-shook his head, saying nothing.

"Price of milk's down again. We have to sell off half the herd for hamburger. All the milk's coming by truck now from down south. You wanted me to take Troy into the family. Your Ma's made his clothes and I fixed up a room for him and we been feeding him just like our own blood. He's a good boy – I don't regret him. But I can't worry 'bout you anymore, son. I need you to be grown up."

"I'll go to work, Dad."

His father tossed back the half glass of whisky, looked at him and smiled. "So now tell me. Where you been. No lies."

"I went down to Lafayette's house, then to town."

"Town ain't so far away that you don't get home till nine-twenty."

"Went to this girl's house –"

"And?"

"We was upstairs... she was showin me her fish then her folks come home and she made me stay in her closet till they went out, after dinner, and I run straight home."

"Why'd she put you in that closet, son?"

"Said if her dad found me he'd shoot me."

"Shit, then I'd have to shoot him. See all the trouble you cause?"

"Sorry, Dad."

His father nodded at the other chair. "Sit." He poured more whisky. "You gotta be careful with girls. You're almost twelve now... You seen how the bull covers the cows – we're the same way... You stick your pecker in some girl and she's gonna have a baby then what're you gonna do?"

If he married Libby he could kiss her all the time. And see the place between her legs. But marriage would be like school, always having to be there. "I was just lookin at her fish."

His father snickered, caught himself. "Afore you get all heated up with some girl, come see me an' I'll tell you how to make sure it don't cause trouble."

"I kin quit school, work on other farms. Soon as I'm eighteen I'm goin in the Marines... Please don't sell the cows, Dad."

His father knocked the glass aside. "You stay in school goddamit! Goddamit you learn something! Don't you grow up like me, workin a dairy farm that's goin broke and sweatin' in a factory for some rich prick in a big house who won't even speak to the men who make his money for him!"

His father set up the glass and filled it with whisky. "You quit school, son, and I'll shoot you myself."

12

THE LONG WALK HOME

THE BASEBALL CAME LEAPING across the grass, took a bad bounce and smashed into Mick's stomach before he could catch it. He rolled on the ground clutching his gut, couldn't breathe.

People surrounded him. "Mick!" Troy pleaded, *"Mick!"*

He sucked in air, pain shooting through him, sat up. "Okay."

"Got the wind knocked out," someone said.

He stood, bent over with the pain in his stomach. "Who scored?"

"Just Ryan," Tommy Conlan said. "I stopped at second. When I saw you was hurt."

He walked back and forth trying to suck in air. "Ain't hurt."

The world took shape, the far trees, a white fence, the rush of tires on the road, rooftops in the sun.

"I'm up next," Billy Wylie said.

The pain surged through his gut. He forced himself straight, couldn't find his glove. *There it was*, on the ground. How could he bend down and get it? "Still one out," he said. "Tommy on second."

He could reach the glove. He pulled it over his left hand, punched it with his right; pain shot into his belly. Billy Wylie stood at the plate whipping his bat back and forth. "Don't hit nothing this way," Mick

89

begged him silently. Billy swung the bat one more time, pointing it at him. "Come on," he called. "Throw that thing."

Mick tightened his fingers on the seams, swung up and back and kicking out his left foot threw the ball at the distant tiny hole in Troy's catcher's mitt. The ball hit the dirt and bounced over the plate smacking Troy in the chest, Troy running after it and Tommy Conlan sprinting for third.

Mick ran to cover the plate, Troy grabbed the ball and gunned it to him; Tommy slid past him over the plate. "Four to two." Billy Wylie pointed the bat at him. "'N I'm gonna hit a home run."

Lightning pain darted up his middle; Mick crumpled to his knees, forced himself to stand. "I gotta stop a whiles."

"You're coppin' out," Billy said. "Know we're gonna beat you."

"Fuck you," Troy said. "Can't you see he's hurt?"

"Shit I got hit like that, kept playin." Billy looked at Mick. "You a sissy?"

Troy threw down his mitt. "I'll break your face you little turd."

"I think we should stop," Tommy Conlan said.

"Who's callin' who a turd?" Billy said.

Mick walked away, the horizon weaving before him, the trees a nauseous green, the ground rising and falling in waves, each step jarring his gut. Biting his lip he crossed the outfield then the playground and out the schoolyard toward town. Troy came up behind him. "You forgot your glove."

"Go back'n play."

Troy looped Mick's glove over the bat on his shoulder beside his catcher's mitt. "We'll kick their ass next time."

All that mattered was to find some way to walk all the way to town across Sparkill Creek then past the 1776 House and up the long meadow past the Lafayette house and over the top and then it'd be downhill to the farm and up the stairs to his bed. *Only a couple miles. You can do it.*

. . .

THE PAIN WAS HUGE. There was nothing *but* pain. Mick lay shivering under the down comforter trying not to move his stomach. The sky beyond the calico curtains had gone from orange to dark as if the world were ending. He didn't care, anything to make the pain to go away.

Ma's kitchen noises below – footsteps across the linoleum, cupboards shutting, an iron pan clattering on the stove. The cows mooing as they came in for milking; he wondered was Tara helping Troy the way she did with lots of stuff now? Wondered when Dad would get home, rolled a bit on his side, moaned and moaned again, for the low vibration of his voice almost eased the pain.

His sweaty pillow and t-shirt stuck to him. Heat thudded in his brain; his blood ebbed sluggishly; breath seared his nostrils and hissed in his throat. "Please come," he begged Dad. "Please soon."

"Mick!" Tara whispered, silhouetted in the door. "You comin' down for dinner?"

"Where's Dad?"

"Has to work late. You havin' dinner?"

"Ain't hungry."

His mother's steps; she touched his brow. "You're fevered, son."

"Got cold, comin' home."

She tugged back the comforter and touched his belly. "No!" he screamed, panting.

"My God, son!"

"Sorry, Ma. Didn't know it hurt so much." Red and yellow light cascaded before his eyes. "Do I have to go to school tomorrow?"

She vanished; he lay whimpering. The world didn't matter, life didn't matter. All that counted was stopping this pain.

The doctor put his little black case on the floor. His hand on Mick's brow smelled of soap. He rolled back the comforter. "Tell me when it hurts."

"Don't touch me –"

The thermometer choked him. The room grew distant, the people strange, their voices hollow. They put him in a white van with a flashing light... Streetlamps blinked past – no, they were stars – the

Hunter with Betelgeuse at his head, the Dog Star, the North Star toward which the Iroquois traveled on the long night road after death. The ambulance howled on, an ancient beast screaming to kill, survive.

TROY TRIED TO PRAY. Hunched over on the Nyack hospital bench he said the words over and over silently. *Dear Lord please save Mick. I'm sorry I sinned, left the Boys' Home. Please Jesus don't let him die.* But all he saw was Father Loudy's bitter smile, all he could feel was the sharp willow switch or Father Damon's soft palm on his thigh.

If he hadn't escaped the Boys' Home to live with the O'Briens, he and Mick wouldn't have been playing ball this afternoon. Mick wouldn't have taught him to catch the amazing fastballs that Mick could throw for hour after hour and never lose control. *It's from throwin' rocks*, Mick'd say, *since I was a little kid...*

A nurse rolled a gurney past, cigarette in her hand, the wheels hissing, her rubber soles squeaking. Ma sat beside him, hands on her knees, facing the far wall with its round clock like the one in the classroom that Mick always said ran so slow. Beyond her Tara sat sucking in sniffles, her fists bunched in front of her chest as if Mick's death was an enemy she could fight off.

The door slammed open and Dad came racing in from work, Ma running to him, Tara grabbing him like a tree that would keep her from falling.

Troy sat still, looking at the wall. *Please Jesus I'm sorry I sinned. I'll go back to the Boys' Home if you let Mick live. Or I'll die in his place.*

"Where's the doctors?" Dad said.

"Inside," Ma said.

He shoved through the yellow doors where they had Mick. "Stop!" a nurse called.

"I want to see the doctors!" Dad yelled.

"They're operating, sir. On your son –"

"Please tell me –"

"I'm sorry, sir, we'll know soon... someone will come out and talk to you..."

Troy bit his lip till blood slid down his throat. *Jesus sacrificed himself to save us. If I die maybe Mick can live. Please Lord tell me...*

A rough warm hand on his head. He looked up. Dad. "How are you, son?"

He tried to speak, tears pouring out of his eyes. "It's my fault."

Dad sat beside him, hand on his arm. "What do you mean?"

"If I wasn't here we wouldna been playin ball. He wouldna got hurt..."

Dad's huge hand squeezed his shoulder. "Don't be silly. Mick loves you. You're the best friend he's got." Dad glanced at Tara. "'cept for Tara, of course."

Dad paced, sat beside Ma, held Tara and Troy to his great hard knees, paced again. Ma was pushing away tears with the side of her finger, wiping them on her dress.

Please, Jesus. If you let him live I'll love you all my life.

"**KIN I STILL** be a Marine?" Talking hurt Mick's throat. He'd come out of a gray nowhere. Hadn't known where or who he was, fire inside, this horrible burn in his throat.

His father half-smiled. "You don't need an appendix to be a Marine."

"Kin I play ball?"

"Not for a while."

"And football in the fall?"

"Everybody's in the waitin' room, sends their love. Ma and Tara and Troy and Grampy. Uncle Hal's here, and Johnny and Cordelia. Room's full of O'Briens and Vandemeers."

How warm and lovely to be cared for. "Grampy likes Troy too."

Dad grinned and ruffled his hair. "Not like you, son. Blood's blood. Grampy likes Troy plenty though, and wants to see he has a good life. What counts now is getting you back on your feet."

Mick eased back into his pillows. When he got better he'd find a yew tree in the woods and make a longbow and willow arrows with green chert arrowheads like you could chip at the place on Rocky

Hill where the Iroquois used to make them. Tied on with real buckskin.

"TELL-A-VISION is what they call it." Dad eased the big black box onto the living room table. "We were gonna get it for you kids for Christmas but decided on now, so Mick can watch it while he's getting better."

Mick wanted to sleep but that wouldn't be nice since they'd gone to this trouble. It was a huge ugly box. Dad plugged it into the wall and snapped a switch. After a while gray lines raced across the front then a picture like a little black and white movie flickered on. Dad turned the dials; faces came and went, a man riding a horse, others chasing him. "Wait!" Mick said. "Keep that!"

He soon got to know them all, Howdy Doody – how silly for a grownup to be talkin' to a wooden doll, Captain Kangaroo that was for little kids, Roy Rogers a little better but silly too with its happy endings and stupid girls. Gene Autry and Dale Evans – what a pair of idiots... Lone Ranger was like it was on the radio, but the man's voice was different. And why would Tonto be so stupid as to always take care of this white man when he could be an Indian and have the whole world to himself?

Almost as silly as the newspaper comics. The only good one was Pogo. Mark Trail wasn't like a real guy though he lived in the woods and smoked a pipe and had a plaid shirt and a canoe but never got dirty and never got hurt. The worst was Archie with his idiotic grin and bow tie and stupid friends who all always acted the same... Or the ones in Gasoline Alley who were even dumber, and who could believe Rex Morgan MD or Dick Tracy with his wrist radio? Were people so bored by the jail they'd locked themselves in that anything was a distraction?

Sometimes the tell-a-vision had Laurel and Hardy movies from the old days: they made Mick laugh so hard he had to stop watching because it hurt his stitches too much. And you could watch baseball, they even had the World Series, but who wanted to watch other guys do what you wanted to do? Don Larsen's perfect game was exciting, you kept wondering *is he going to make it*, but for the rest if you couldn't play ball why waste time watching it? Didn't folks have anything better to do?

Everything had gone different. His house looked smaller, older, the paint peeling. Beyond the front pasture the white church in the valley was closer, its steeple shorter. Even the road that snaked off through the hills toward the army barracks, the road he and Troy had taken home that first night, seemed nearer, the trees and trestle smaller. Even the sweet lonely whistle of the train coming up the valley no longer called to him.

The darting orange flames in the stone fireplace told how the sun went into a tree and the tree made fire, but where had these round gray hearthstones come from, and who had collected them so long ago and built this fireplace? Dad said the house was here when Washington and Lafayette led their American and French soldiers against the Germans and British. Those ancient days felt very near now, in this house full of spirits of the people who once lived here.

Everyone came, uncles and aunts holding his hand talking softly, Grampy patting his shoulder and blinking pale eyes, the Cormers from the next farm peering down at him like some strange thing found in their barnyard. People from farms all around, friends of Ma's and Dad's, come to squeeze his hand and tell him they're happy he made it, the Olsens where he and Troy stole that cherry pie – even Widow Clough sayin he could have all the strawberries he wanted anytime. And all the farmers were going broke, Dad said, because the government made a law to bring milk from far away, but nobody'd be that stupid. The farmers were awful nice and the fear they were going broke made him unhappy.

Not that it was hard to understand the world. Everything seemed clear, revealed. He used to think grownups knew stuff but most of them really didn't, like cows munching grass and coming to be milked when their udders were full. And once they stopped giving milk you took them to the slaughterhouse.

Ma making hand gestures when she talks to Aunt Gracie on the phone. Why – Aunt Gracie couldn't see her? Dad had to have all three clocks bonging the same time, the cherry grandfather one that come down in the family since before the Revolution, that marble clock over the fireplace and the wooden one on the kitchen wall like the horrible one in school with the hands that always go so slow. Why'd he care so much what time it was?

The best part of being hurt was not having to go to school. The trouble with school was that none of it mattered, silly stuff you forgot soon as you learnt. He thought of Libby Walsh leaning over the desk in front of him, her tongue aslant her lips, pushing back her hair in hurried strokes, writing away *squeak squeak* like it was some contest she could win just for telling them back what they'd told her.

What was it you won in life? If he figured real hard maybe he could make it out.

Since the day on her bed she'd acted like it never happened. Was that how you win in life? By pretending?

The doctor came and pulled the last black ugly threads out of his red swollen flesh. "Feared we might lose you, Mick. You had the highest white blood count – that means infection – in the history of Nyack hospital."

Mick felt a dizzy pride. "You were lucky we had these new drugs," the doctor went on, "or we'd a lost you. *Aunty Biotics*, they're called."

He'd lost the sense he'd had when near death of being able to be anywhere, in any time. "When I was in that place I could see everything how it really is – how come now I'm back seeing it the wrong way again?"

"What place? The hospital?"

"No." It tired him, so hard to explain. "When I almost died."

"That's just imagination," the doctor smiled wearily. "Not real life."

IN THE FALL he returned to school. Winter soon came, the land bare and white. Snowdrifts whorled in the hollows and dead grass crunched underfoot. Walking to school their breath froze on the collars of the plaid coats Ma had made. The deer had yarded in the forest, chewing bark off the young birches and digging in the frozen earth for roots and leaves. At night the owls called and through his cracked-open window Mick could hear the tree trunks booming as they froze.

It got so cold Ma shut Rusty in the kitchen so he wouldn't follow them to school and come limping home with his paws froze. Once Mick glanced through the class window and saw Rusty sitting outside holding one paw off the concrete. He got permission to bring him in, the dog racing across the hallways to greet Troy while Mr. Fellows the science teacher tried to act stern but gave up and let everyone play with Rusty till the bell rang for second class and Mick locked Rusty in the principal's office.

Sometimes he woke at night feeling cramped then realized his legs were bent to make room for Rusty, who had spread out across the bottom of his bed, his legs twitching as if he were chasing rabbits in his dreams. Rusty's life seemed a bounteous variety of good times, fun, food, and games; he wondered what the dog thought of death – was he just living as hard as he could while life lasted?

Mick's scar still hurt, and sometimes splitting wood or plowing snow with the tractor it sent a sharp crescent of pain through his belly. He thought a lot about death, if it was really the end or could you go on into other dimensions. In school Mr. Fellows told them how Einstein said time was the fourth dimension, but how many more dimensions were there?

When you died could you still have your own body, go walking in cool crinkly snow and eat hot dogs and hamburgers and go fishing once the ice broke on the stream, dropping your worm into little pools between the rocks and fallen trees?

As the snow rose to the windows the house grew warmer, closer; the crackling birch in the fireplace and its dancing glow was a reminder of times they'd lived but couldn't remember. There was no school or open roads; the chores were easy, leaving hours to read by the fire or to sit in your room, lost in the whirl of snowflakes beyond the frigid glass, how they veiled the fields and woods, turned every-thing gray.

Then spring came, and soon June and early summer, and he had finished eighth grade and in the fall would go to Nyack High, nine miles away. He'd been to Nyack once and didn't like it, too many streets and cars, no quiet.

One Friday night Dad and Ma took the bus to New York City because she wanted to see a movie and go up the Vampire State Building. After chores Tara came down from her room with a pack of Lucky Strikes. "Where'd you get those?" Mick said.

"None of your beeswax." She lit one, raised it casually in her fingertips like women did on the television. "You should try it – they're cool."

"We're not supposed to smoke," Troy said.

Tara blew a lopsided smoke ring. "One won't hurt you."

Mick and Troy lit them, trying not to cough. After a while Mick went to the storeroom and came back with Grampy's whisky jug and they each took a swig, choking down the burn in their throats. They drank half the bottle and filled it up with water and brown Karo syrup and Troy went outside and threw up.

"It ain't so neat," Mick said. "This stuff."

"Don't see why grownups like it." Troy wiped his mouth. It wasn't right that he was drinking whisky they'd stolen from Grampy, for when Mick had near died he'd promised to love Jesus always.

Tara flicked ash, tossed back her whisky, sighed and licked her lips. "What a pair of pussies you two," and Mick wondered where she'd ever learned to talk like that.

13

BLOOD ON THE LEAVES

AT FIVE-TWENTY Troy woke and stretched out warm under the feather comforter till five-thirty, slipped on wool socks and stood toe-curled on the icy floor, dressed and went down to the kitchen and restarted the fire in the woodstove, then down to the basement to shove new birch logs onto last night's coals in the barrel stove, hearing Ma's slippers to and fro on the linoleum upstairs as she filled the coffee pot and put new biscuits in the woodstove oven.

He couldn't believe Dad had let him take over starting the morning fires and wondered why Mick would give it up. At the back door he pulled on his coat and stocking hat and hustled into the stinging November darkness, flipped on the barn light and stepped into the thick warm cow odor, the urine and dung and hay smells, then into the milking room where the clean pails were stacked upside down. Grabbing a stool he sat beside Annie, the first cow, warm milk sliding through his fingers and spattering into the shiny pail then gurgling deeply as the pail filled, then sloshing as he poured the creamy liquid like warm smooth paint into the milk tank.

"You do Daisy?" Mick came in hair askew, spit in the hay and snatched two pails.

"Not yet. But she don't give me no trouble."

Mick began to milk another cow. "Maybe she's in love with you."

When the cows were milked they drove them out to pasture, the frozen dew crinkling underfoot, ice crunching on the puddles, and came back to pitchfork last night's soiled straw into the wheelbarrow and trundle it out to the manure pile then hosed down the milking room floor "till it's clean enough to lick the water off" as Ma would say.

Troy heard the chickens squawk and flutter in the coop as Tara went from nest to nest collecting eggs. Almost five hundred hens that made three hundred eggs a day that Ma boxed up and Dad dropped off in Nyack on his way to the plastic factory. And the family joke was *what kinda chicken we havin' for dinner, Ma?* To which she'd answer, "O'Brien chicken."

Back in the kitchen smelling of new biscuits and bacon and coffee, fresh butter in the biscuits and raspberry jam and new eggs so yellow on top like sunrise when you busted them on top of the whites and soaked it up in your biscuits. "Deer season starts Saturday," Dad said. "With you two boys maybe we can fill three tags."

"No more O'Brien chicken?" Tara said.

"Not likely," Ma said.

"Coon got in last night," Tara said. "There was feathers."

"Damn!" Dad said. "How many?"

"Just one hen. That I saw."

"He comes back I'll call Clem Hays and get his dogs over here." Dad gulped the last of his coffee and grabbed his lunch bag, leaned over Ma and kissed her cheek. "Guys," he called as he went out, "when you get home from school check the chicken run, find where that coon got in."

As the car rumbled away Troy noticed the first yellow traces of day through the kitchen window. Dad didn't like the plastic factory but said he was lucky to have work to take care of the family and that was all the happiness anybody needed. He and Ma worried about the 'lection but the government was so far away Troy didn't see how it mattered if Stevenson wasn't President or Eisenhower wasn't a real soldier just a desk man.

"You should wear mittens," Tara said as they went up the meadow past the hammock and headed down toward the Lafayette house and school. "My piano teacher says you don't keep your fingers warm they get 'thritis and don't bend."

"My hands is plenty warm," Troy said.

"We're not girls," Mick said.

"Girls are tough as boys," she answered. "We just don't act stupid."

"It's stupid just sayin that."

"Mick you're mean all the time now. Isn't he, Troy?"

"He ain't mean. He's just fine like he is."

"I don't need nobody likin me," Mick snapped.

"If we get a deer," Troy said, "it'll make your folks happy." He'd wanted to say *Dad'n Ma* the way Tara and Mick did, but couldn't in front of them, only said it alone sometimes to make himself feel good.

He'd seen the deer bounding away with their white tails held high – how do you hit somethin movin that fast? Dad made him and Mick practice shooting till their shoulders ached and their ears rang and they could knock a tin can off the fence at a hundred yards. "Not that I want you takin a shot at that distance," Dad had added. "Just want you to be that good."

Not that Mick ever missed a shot.

Once when they'd had a combined class he'd glanced across at Mick who'd been scowling out the window, then dragging his finger-nails down the blackboard beside him to annoy that girl Libby who sat in front of him. Now he was reading a book about dinosaurs that he kept hidden on his lap while Mrs. Magruder was explaining long division or how to find a square root.

Maybe because Mick'd never had to live at the Boys' Home he didn't know how lucky he was, how easy this life was.

GRAMPY HAD A 30.30 WINCHESTER lever action with an octag-onal barrel that he'd gotten for his fourteenth birthday "back in 1888, if you kin believe that." Now he was 83, tall and straight with sparse white hair, fast on his feet, a rugged red face with a sharp blade nose and deep blue eyes piercing you from under thick white brows, and knotty gnarled hands with hard red knuckles and thick white-haired wrists.

He always wore a green work shirt and gray trousers with a worn leather belt, and had a bone-handled pocket knife with a large and small blade, a regular and Phillips screwdrivers, a beer bottle opener and a saw he'd once used to cut all the way down a buck's spine. He'd been a Marine in World War One and after a few whiskies would tell them about the *madamoyselles* in Paris and the battle of Belleau Wood. "We took that place from the Germans and lost it again six times. Almost two thousand Marines were killed and another eight thousand wounded. And still to this day I don't know for what."

"Soon's I get eighteen I'm goin in the Marines," Mick said.

"Not if your folks have anything to say. Or me neither."

Back when Mick was three years old Grampy bust his leg on the plow and that was when Dad and Ma took over the farm and paid Uncle Hal for half. When Grampy's leg got better he moved to town to work in the feed store, but Ma always said he moved to be closer to Sadie Armstrong, and he was foolish if he thought people didn't know.

Two years ago when Grampy broke his arm he said it happened cutting down a birch tree, but Dad said he broke it falling out of bed while he was doing it with Sadie. "After all," Dad had said at the time, "the poor man's only eighty-one."

"So what happened to your Granma?" Troy asked Mick, fascinated by so much family.

"She died before I was born. She used to make whisky durin' Inhibition."

Troy walked quietly beside Mick, aching to be part of this blood clan and wishing he could of known his own.

THE NIGHT BEFORE deer season started Troy lay awake till dawn smelling gun oil on his hands and on Grampy's Winchester standing in the corner, the bacon in the sandwiches Ma had made, the worn wool of his red plaid jacket on the bedpost and the sharp cold forest through the cracked-open window. His heart thudded in his ears, his muscles tense to get up, start moving. He imagined a buck leaping a stone wall and darting through the apple orchard or slinking away through the underbrush. Imagined that he raised the Winchester, sighted down the barrel at the place on the buck's chest where the heart was, the punch of the recoil, the huge crack of the shot.

They'd given him a home; he'd kill a deer, bring food on the table. *No more O'Brien chicken.*

Finally he slept, woken by Dad's hand on his leg. "Don't sleep all day!"

Fire crackling in the woodstove, coffee burning his gut, toast gulped whole, out the door across the barnyard and pasture, the stars sharp and icy. Dad laying his rifle against the jack fence and climbing over, Mick handing him the three rifles one by one then he and Troy climbing over, the path in the woods, frozen dew hissing on their boots, across the ice-covered stream deeper into dark forest, Orion's knife glimmering through bare treetops, Dad moving fast now, Troy trotting to keep sight of his flitting dark form, Mick's rapid steps behind him like an animal closing in.

Ahead a lighter darkness: the old orchard. Dad gripped Troy's arm. "Like we said, you set up by those trees. It's all overgrown so you'll have to look for the buck's horns above the undergrowth, or for his legs under the low branches. Mick's going to be on the other side of me." Dad licked his finger and raised it. "Wind should stay in our face."

Troy nodded, trying to remember everything. "When I whistle like a blackbird," Dad said, "you look at me. If I raise my gun you can load yours but keep the chamber empty and the safety on. When I wave us forward we move together into the orchard, in a line across. Don't jack one into the chamber till you see a buck. Shoot only straight ahead or to your right, never to my side... Remember: forked horns or better..."

Pulse thundered in his brain; his stomach swirled. The gun felt heavy and weightless. Tired of standing he knelt to watch through the low brush.

The sky had lightened. He could barely breathe. *There* – beyond the crisscrossed web of low branches a sapling had moved. No, he'd been fooled, it was still.

Easing to his feet he scanned over the branches and winter-red blackberry leaves, crouched again, couldn't find the place he'd seen the sapling move. It hadn't moved, really, he'd just imagined.

It vanished. He blinked, squinted: nothing. It came back. No, a different one. He turned toward Dad, waved his hand forward, made a forked sign for a buck, shrugged.

Dad nodded, whistled toward Mick, waved them forward. Stomach tight, wrists shaking, Troy moved into the orchard. Dead grass tugged at his ankles, his knees felt weak. Step at a time he parted the raspberry branches rasping at his clothes. Coffee boiled in his stomach; he needed to throw up. *There* – horns bobbing across the orchard, angling away.

He sighted toward them, just below the horns, pulled the trigger. *Click.* He levered a round into the chamber, couldn't see the horns… no, *there* they were, halted now, swinging toward him. He sighted on the shoulder, squeezed slowly. *Click.* The horns swung toward him. Hand shaking, he eased the safety off.

The buck stepped forward, head visible now, black eyes searching: *Is there something? What are you?* Troy sighted again on the shoulder and slowly squeezed the trigger.

Cataclysmic roar knocking him back and booming away through the trees. Excitement and great sorrow filled him; he started to rush forward then remembered, looked at Dad who pointed down meaning *Wait there*, and eased silently through the woods to him. "What'd you see?"

Troy told him. "We wait ten minutes," Dad said. "So if you hit him he'll tighten up." Mick came up, gun on his shoulder, a question in his eyes.

They moved forward, red fallen leaves of the blackberry bushes and red maple and yellow birch leaves underfoot. "Here!" Dad whispered.

A hoof print deep in the soil, then another. Where the buck had turned and jumped away. "Go first," Dad said. "Keep it on safety till you see him."

Watching the ground Troy mistook the reddened birch leaf for a maple then came back to it, knelt to touch it, red wet on his finger, pain and excitement in his heart. Dad nodded: *Go forward.*

Blood on the branches chest-high. Troy's heart thundered. Dad came up beside him. "Lung shot."

A bright blood trail now. He wished it and wished against it, gut sick. They passed through the thick brush beyond the orchard into the darkness of the tall trees. A rock ahead became the buck on his side, head tilted by the horns.

Chest heaving, the buck was coughing blood in a pool at his mouth. "Shoot him again," Dad said, "just behind the head." He touched Troy's arm. "First you thank him. And tell him you're sorry for taking his life. Go ahead. Do it."

The buck looked at him with dark wet eyes: *You the evil, dark universe, enemy of life, taker of all that is good.* Troy raised the gun. The buck watched him. He fired. The buck jerked, the eyes turned to stone.

Dad's hand on his shoulder. "You did good. Now we have meat."

Troy looked at Mick who looked back with envy and delight. "Get out your knives, guys," Dad said. "I'll show you how to gut and dress this guy."

When it was done he and Mick took one end of a sapling with Dad on the other and the gutted buck between them, its horns on Dad's shoulder. The sapling was heavy and he stumbled on the wet ground, the rifle heavy in his other hand. The sun rose higher, dew falling from the leaves in a steady patter. It had been a different universe when the three of them had come through the dark forest and he'd never had blood on his hands.

He'd killed meat for the family. They would love him now.

Why did he have to kill to feel good about himself?

. . .

ON THEIR 13th birthday Ma made a big dinner with lots of deer-burgers and whisky. Grampy came, and the aunts and uncles on Ma's side from Orangeburg and Nyack and far away as Teaneck. Uncle Hal and Aunt Sylvia brought Cousin Johnny and three bottles of Canadian Club. Aunt Gracie with her dolloped hair and shy curving smile and her husband Uncle Howard chuckling and stuttering and pulling his watch out of his pocket on the gold chain and blinking at it, Uncle Ted who had a thin moustache and wore a red plaid shirt and had once fought off a black bear with his hands when it attacked his dog, his wife Cordelia who laughed in great bursts and hugged Troy to her scrawny bosom banging his ear, Uncle Jim who had no wife, austere and unsmiling till he had a few whiskies then talked all the time.

Uncle Phil pumped gas at the Cities Service and washed the wind-shield till it squeaked and when you had a flat he fixed it. When Phil was twenty, Ma said, he'd whupped just about every other man in Rockland County and the only person he was afraid of was his wife, Aunt Wilma. Five inches shorter than he, she'd once been cheery and beautiful, Ma said, but now was all wiry and mean. Even Mick was leery of her irascible tongue and small red fists.

Aunt Sin had no husband, just bobbed hair and bangs and a pinched mouth, talking like they were old friends – "Now Troy make sure I only have one drink," then after that one she'd started laughing with Ma and having more, finally mixing her own "martoonees" in a Mason jar in the kitchen sink. There were other uncles and aunts, maybe fourteen in all, and Grampy rocking in the living room chair with his whisky neat, long white hair and pale eyes shining with firelight.

Johnny came up amid the din and nodded to them, said something but nobody could hear. The noise was more than anyone could stand – the laughing and singing, Tara playing the piano too loud.

After the deerburgers and ice cream Dad put more planks in the kitchen table and the boys brought down all the chairs from upstairs and Ma got cards and Grampy came out crotchety from the living room and filled up his glass with whisky neat and shuffled the cards with a sputtering noise and called, "Git over here," at Troy, slapping the chair beside him. "Got any money?"

"Just my chore money."

"Go git ten cents."

"I was savin' for a model plane."

"Hell you kin buy your own real F-86 when I'm done wit ya."

"How come you don't teach *me?*" Tara called.

"I already did. You're a better crook'n I am." He ground his teeth. "Johnny git in here. I'm going to make you a rich man."

Johnny sat with that dreamy uncertain smile of his, the one that made you figure he disagreed with everything you said but was too bored to say so.

When Troy came back with two nickels Grampy was dealing the cards. "Five card flush. Ante up a penny, all you victims." He took Troy's nickels and gave him ten pennies, leaned over to scan Troy's cards. "Play that one."

"Dad kin I have a beer?" Mick said.

"Hell no," Ma said.

Grampy looked up. "How'm I gonna win any money les'n you git these boys drunk? C'mon, Maude – one won't hurt'em."

Dad grinned. "Okay Mick, you boys can split a bottle."

"What about me?" Tara said.

"Nah, honey, you're too young –"

"They're going to be fourteen next year. And I'll be thirteen. We're *teen*agers." She looked down the table at Johnny. "And he is too –"

"Alright, Mick, a shot glass of beer for your sister. And another half for Johnny."

With Grampy showing him what to play Troy won four cents. He could already see the model, the sleek F-86 Saberjet the American pilots had used to shoot down Communist MiGs in Korea. He took a sip of beer and it went up his nose, stinging and bubbly. The next hand Uncle Howard won, and Troy was down to nine cents. Then Cordelia won and he had only five cents, then Tara won big and Troy had a penny.

"Don't worry," Grampy said. "I'll make you a loan."

"J-J-Jesus he'll r-rob the k-kid blind," Uncle Howard said.

"This's a private business arrangement," Grampy said. "You keep outta it."

When it was over and Grampy had given Mick, Tara, Troy and Johnny all his winnings and the uncles and aunts had gone out the back door, Uncle Ted singing "Rose of Tralee" at the same time Cordelia was singing "Come back to Erin, Mavourneen Mavourneen", and dizzy with the beer Troy went up to his room with twenty-two cents heavy in his pocket.

Forty-nine more cents and he'd have the Saberjet, American flag decals on the fuselage and raked-back wings, a transparent canopy with the pilot inside. He'd hang on it fishing leader like the others, the B-25 Jimmy Doolittle had flown over Tokyo, the beautiful gull-winged Corsair that could land on a carrier, the Hawker Sea Hawk with its straight wings. On his bookcase a black P-38 stood with flaps down; he looked in the tiny window where the tiny plastic pilot sat and could feel the stick in his hands, the machine gun's red trigger button at the top, the joy of soaring above the clouds into the darkening blue.

THE QUEST

A **BEAUTIFUL GIRL** came down the corridor on Mick's first freshman day at Nyack High, someone he remembered, talking with another girl, her books cradled against her breasts. Mick halted. *"Daisy?"*

She turned to him, eyes wide, her face lit up and she started to hug him but pulled back. "It's *you!*" She'd grown tall and very slender, a lovely young woman in a red cardigan, white blouse and gray plaid skirt, wide green eyes, a freckled little nose and full lips, her hair down one shoulder like an auburn waterfall.

Other students bumped past them. He backed against a locker. "You look wonderful."

She touched his arm. "You do too."

He couldn't think what to say. "So you still live here? In Nyack?"

She shrugged. "Pa's still workin at the lumber yard." She gave him a quick smile. "And I still miss the farm."

And me, he wanted to say, *like I miss you?* The bell rang. "Where you going now?"

"Latin Three."

"You're in *there?* As a freshman?"

"I did One and Two this summer."

"On your own?"

She shrugged. "I like it. Miss Quinn tested me and put me in Three."

The idea stunned him; why would anyone want to take harder classes? The bell rang again. "What's your home room?"

"202. Mr. Marshall. The chemistry teacher."

"Can I see you after school?"

"I have to be at work at two-thirty."

"What kinda work?"

"Whitman's soda fountain. Every day till six."

"I've got freshman football after class. But I'll come to your home room for a few minutes."

She was waiting when he got there. Sun through the high multi-paned windows flashed in her hair; the room had a heady scent of chemicals. This time she took his arm. "I'll go with you as far as the gym."

He felt stunned and nervous having her walk beside him. A freshman girl could even date seniors, all the guys would be after her. "When can I come see you?"

"You are seeing me."

"No, I mean let's go somewhere." The hunger to kiss her, hold her, inhale her, was too great, he had to force himself not to do it now.

"Come to Whitman's after practice. I'll make you a soda for free."

Practice passed in a dream, the other grunting sweating guys all seemed stupid and aimless. He led his receivers perfectly and they all caught his passes up close to the chest. Coach was teaching blocking, how to let your opponent spend his force in an initial push then deflect him; it was ridiculously easy, as if Mick already knew the other guys' moves before they made them.

At the fountain three guys were talking to her at one end of the counter; he sat at the other. She kept talking as if he weren't there, then came quickly. "What you want?"

The word rushed out. "You."

She smiled. "What kinda soda?"

"Cherry Coke."

It tasted fantastic sliding down his throat after the hot dry exhaustion of practice. When she turned to pull the tap down on the soda nozzles he could see the outline of her breasts under her white blouse and he ached to touch them. He thought of Libby Walsh's white underpants and the little hairs curling out the sides, wondered if Daisy wore white underpants too, if her thighs were cool and smooth like Libby's, imagined her taking a pee then tucking her underpants up under her skirt like he'd seen Tara do. His prick got hard the way it always did now, at night in bed till he rubbed it and it felt so amazingly good then the warm sticky stuff squirted out and he felt strangely guilty, wiped it on his dirty football socks hoping Ma wouldn't see.

He put his freshman algebra book on his lap. "You, studying?" she laughed.

More people came in and she got busy serving them and it was time for chores so he tucked his books under his arm and waited for her at the cash register. "I'll come back tomorrow."

She smiled and he smiled and it was like they'd never been apart three years, never missed a day of seeing each other. "I'll be here."

"PA THINKS it's neat," she'd said one day the following week outside homeroom, her books tucked against her breasts. "That you're a football star."

"I don't care what he thinks."

Now sitting in homeroom remembering her made his body ache. He glanced at the clock – in three minutes they would change class; he held his breath to see if that would make his prick stop being hard, thought of the girls giggling at it tented out the front of his chinos. He could hold his books in front of him but that was how girls held them.

Everything about Daisy entranced him – her ironed skirts and pliant cashmeres, the turquoise bracelet loose on her wrist, her slender fingers and transparent tapered nails, the startling cascade of her hair, her upturned nose and knowing eyes, the way she ran not like a girl but straight-footed like a boy.

These feelings he kept from her as best he could, nonchalant and confident walking beside her, her books under his arm, barely noticing the world around him – new grass in a sidewalk crack, a fallen beech twig, random red and yellow flowers around an old white house... He couldn't breathe, his legs trembled; he said foolish things he instantly regretted. "Why do *you* think we're here?" she said one day.

"Here? It's the way to your house."

She gave him an affectionate smile. "No, life!"

He shrugged. "Cause we got put here."

"By whom? What?"

He felt distant. "I don't worry about such things."

She snatched his hand. "Why do you try so hard to *not* think? Is that supposed to be brave?"

"I think about stuff."

"Stuff? What stuff?"

"I think about football. And Troy and I are fixing a stock car for the fair. I think a lot about that. I think about why animals do things or why trees are all different. You can learn a lot just watching water, how it flows..."

"Don't you ever wonder what *life* is? What all this means?"

"What good does that do?"

She gritted her teeth. "You're just stubborn."

He had a sudden sense he *did* care, was being stupid on purpose. Maybe the doctors who discovered aunty-biotics had hated school too. But there were so many bad things in the world, could you improve them if you learned things? "After I almost died last year everything was clear. Then I came back and it all got foolish again."

"*That's* what I'm saying." She walked faster. "School and work and talking about silly things – life shouldn't be just that –" She tugged his hand – "For a while Pa kept rabbits in a fence. They do nothing, just eat and sleep and make babies, and when he wanted one he grabbed it and cut its throat... Most people live like that but *I* won't."

For an instant he felt empty, like a weary traveler who reaches his destination only to learn he must go on. "I don't want to either."

"You're so smart. Why don't you study?"

"It's boring –"

"Not if you study hard. The more you study, the more it's fun."

The idea was comical. She studied too much as it was. As if *he* didn't matter. "I won't study just to make you like me."

She slapped his arm. "Of course I like you."

They stood in the oak shade outside her house. "Friday night I can get the pickup. You want to see *April Love* with Pat Boone?"

"You'll study till then?" she grinned.

"Remember Guinevere? I'll be like Lancelot, the guy she sends on a quest."

Her eyes turned hard. "I know I'm very smart. I understand things other people don't even know about. It's a gift and I won't waste it." She shook his arm. "And I know you're very smart too. So why do you pretend you're not? Why do you waste it?"

FOR THE FIRST TIME humans had sent a satellite into space. Troy grabbed the newspaper every day after school to read the latest on Sputnik and how the Russians were pulling ahead of America in the space race. He alternated between excitement that somebody had done it and despair that it had been the Communists, the enemies of freedom, who got there first.

For three months he stood in the back pasture every night with Dad's Marine binoculars seeking the tiny flit of light across the night. It was only 180 pounds but was sending back information on everything from meteoroids to radio signals and atmospheric density. Even more amazing, it circled the earth every 96 minutes at an inconceivable speed of 17,900 miles per hour.

But now the Soviets could soon shoot atom bombs down from space. There'd be no way to stop them.

. . .

A GUY NAMED SAMSON was named freshman quarterback but couldn't shoot straight, though he was bigger than Mick. "Hey Coach," Mick stopped on the sideline. "I can throw better'n that."

Coach Louie glanced at Samson standing ham-fisted in the middle of the field. "Okay, next set a downs is yours."

When Mick's turn came he flubbed the first handoff; the center, Al Goodman, was Samson's friend and kept giving Mick bad snaps. But he got into a rhythm, gunning fast passes downfield, leading his receivers perfectly; after the last run-through he fired the ball fifty yards through the goalposts and Coach Louie called him over. "Stop showboating."

Mick grinned. "I ain't, Coach. Just wanted to see if I could do it."

"You knew you could do it. You don't got an arm, you got a bazooka. But you're throwin too fast. These guys can't catch them."

Freshman games were on Saturday mornings, before the varsity ones. Mick started the first against Teaneck; Coach Louie made Samson into a tight end and he became Mick's best receiver, not fast but solid, his big meaty hands dragging in the ball, his shoulder and helmet down into the opponent's faces, driving for yards.

The fields turned muddy with the November rains; after the seventh game against Rockland when Mick threw three touchdowns Coach said, "I want you and Samson to practice with the varsity for the Ashland game."

"Ashland?" Mick was incredulous; it was the Thanksgiving Game, last of the season, a deadly rivalry; Ashland had won the last three.

"Maybe I'll play you a little toward the end. Depends how the score goes."

Mick walked to Whitman's in a dream; the Thanksgiving Game packed the stadium every year, and he as a fourteen-year-old freshman might play in it. "That's wonderful," Daisy said, hesitated.

"What's the matter?"

"You could get hurt. Danny Malone broke his arm last week. How many other guys're hurt, and out for the season?"

It dizzied him that she cared. "Working a farm all your life makes you tough. Don't worry for me."

Coach Louie brought him in with ten minutes to go, Nyack behind 23 to 3; Coach sent in two handoff plays then a crossing pattern for Samson and Mick nailed him for a 14-yard gain. First down at their own 48. Coach sent in a deep corner pattern but Mick overthrew McGillicuddy, a senior who came panting back to the huddle and gave Mick an angry glance. Vernal Jones the tailback came in with a new play. "Coach says the same play, but keep your dick in your pants."

Everyone snickered and suddenly the fear of losing was gone. Mick grinned at them, all dirty, blooded and weary. "This is so much fuckin fun." He stared down McGillicuddy. "I'll hit you this time. Perfect."

Hands on knees, still breathing hard, McGillicuddy looked up at him. "I'll juke him then go deep. Be there."

"On one." They slapped hands and trotted to the ball. The Ashland line was ragged, weary too. Their nose tackle, a big kid with a duck's ass haircut sneaking out under his helmet, spit blood into the mud. Mick's center forgot the count and snapped it late; it fell in the mud and Mick knew he should dive on it but seeing McGillicuddy's run in his mind he snatched it up slippery stepping backwards looking for McGillicuddy and ducking their left tackle coming around the side, stepped forward and gunned it to the perfect place McGillicuddy was going to be, the ball soaring through the blue November sky and McGillicuddy's hands gathering it in for the touchdown.

The extra point bounced off the upright and it was 9 to 23. Four downs later they got the ball back. *Six minutes.*

He was breathing too fast. The crowd was roaring; he couldn't hear. He'd been knocked down after throwing the touchdown and the guy'd stamped his cleats into his hand. When he handed it off on first down Vernal Jones snatched it hard banging his hand, and made seven yards. Second down he tossed to Samson for four and a new first down.

McGillicuddy was lined up on the right, arms swinging loose, the Ashland defense watching him nervously. Mick nodded to him, crouched over center, took the snap and darted back four steps. The Ashland backfield was swinging toward McGillicuddy as he cut in then out and slanted deep, raised his hand and Mick found Jones alone going fast down the other sideline and dropped it into his hands for six more points. The kick was good and the score was 16 to 23.

People in the stands were screaming and yelling, the rhythmic thunder of feet on the planks deafening. A fight broke out between the stands, another. Ashland took the kick deep and made a first down, then went four and out. Nyack had the ball on their own thirty-one. *Two minutes twenty-six seconds.* "Set it up for McGillicuddy to run a post," Coach said, "then hand it off to Vernal, let him pound out some yards."

"We're running out of time."

"I can see the clock, son."

He couldn't catch his breath. They slapped hands and went to the ball; he handed off to Vernal who got clobbered. Second and twelve. He caught Samson on a slant for nine, a handoff to Vernal for two, and a quarterback sneak and new first down. *A minute twenty-eight.*

He threw behind McGillicuddy on a post, then over Samson and was almost intercepted. Shit. *Fifty-nine seconds.* Forty-one yards to go. Coach sent in the same play for Samson and he hit him and as he was tackled he lost the ball but scrambled on it. *Thirty-eight seconds.* Twenty-eight yards.

The noise was insane. When the fullback brought out the play he couldn't hear him. They bent close in the huddle, cupping hands over earholes. The play was a standard fullback crunch up the middle but McGillicuddy was to run a deep cross and Mick was to hit him in the end zone.

He darted back from the snap, swung to fake-hand it to Jones but he turned the wrong way and Jones missed it and Ashland's nose tackle broke through so Mick gunned it early down the sideline under McGillicuddy who tried to cut back and slipped in the mud and the ball dropped free and easy into the hands of an Ashland cornerback who cut past Samson and Mick couldn't catch him before he trotted into the end zone holding the ball high.

The Ashland stands were screaming, roaring. Half-blinded by tears of rage he walked to the bench. "Nice try, kid," Vernal Jones said wearily.

"I'm sorry, guys," Mick mumbled, fighting back the tears.

McGillicuddy came up huffing, threw down his helmet. "Little prick!"

THAT NIGHT Dad let him have the DeSoto, a red and brown '51 two-door with the stick on the steering column and a radio in the middle of the chrome dashboard.

It was their third date. Daisy wore a blue cashmere with a white blouse and a Scotch plaid pleated skirt with a long golden safety pin down one side. "You two be careful now," her Mom said as they stood in the kitchen with the white and red linoleum and the jiggling floor.

"If I ever thought of driving fast I just remember that Daisy's in the car. She's far more important, Maam, than I am."

"You're one of the nicest people, Mick," she smiled her gentle, sad smile, "I've ever known."

"Don't tell him that, Mom. He'll be so stuck up. He already *is...*"

He grinned at her mom. "She tells me all the time how to improve."

"I do *not!*"

Inside the car felt intimate and private, grown up and free. They were adults, independent and together. Her perfume thrilled him, her oval, sharp-chinned face and lovely smile. Wrists shaking, he started the car; it stalled. He restarted it and drove through town to Orangeburg, the radio playing one of Billy Vaughan's haunting melodies, the kind that made you feel your body all the way through.

Black and white patterns flitted across the drive-in screen; it was a movie about somewhere called Peyton Place, but he paid it no attention; staticky voices rattled through the speaker hung on his window. She kissed him hard, her lips cool and her mouth hot, her taste intoxicating, then everything was gone except this, the softness of her sweater, hair, and skin, her ardent thrusting mouth and sharp-nailed fingers, the strength of her body pressing into his.

He kissed the warm curl of her ear and down the long line of her neck and the scented hollow of her throat, her breast in his hand like a perfect fruit, and when he fumbled at the buttons of her blouse she pushed his hand aside and undid them, biting through his kisses.

The movie voices faraway, his hand behind her knee, the taut smoothness of her thigh as she opened it to him, nor did she stop him when he reached her center, only bit his lip and licked his tongue faster, teeth to teeth. "Wait," she pulled aside. "Let's go somewhere."

He drove back through Shanks wondering where to go, her hand on the inside of his thigh as if they had been together like this for years. He turned right on the road past the Widow Clough's farm where he and Troy had stolen strawberries, past the railroad bridge and right over the river to the old army barracks, weeds lashing the car, gravel crackling under the tires.

She placed his hand over her and showed him how to move it, then slid down her underpants and took him into her, and all that was incomplete became complete, nothing had ever happened but this moment, no world, no universe, just she.

15

CALL IT

THE STOCK CAR RACES at Nyack Fairgrounds started in the spring and ran till fall. Troy loved the odors of grease and oil and brake pads and worn steel and metal and muffler and paint and tires and hot engine – that was the best, the sear of superheated oil, of the clean shiny block, the pulsing cylinders and throbbing clutch – the hunger of this machine to go out and kill something.

Every race night he sat on the grass outside the fence just to hear the engines waiting for the start, their thunderous patience. One day he pushed his way inside among the cars to Ray Laguerre's low-nosed fifty-one Ford, *Blue Sue*. "That's a beautiful car."

Ray smiled. "Thanks kid."

"On the warm-up laps I listened to the engine when you come out of the back curve, by the light pole? I don't see how you get so much power in the middle range –"

"All in the gears and carbs, kid." Ray flicked down his cigarette. "Hey listen I gotta get ready –"

"Mr. Laguerre, do you maybe ever have work to be done? My Grandpa's a good mechanic – he's taught me how to work on engines and trannies, even body work –"

Ray reached into a cardboard box beside *Blue Sue*, pulled out two

Narragansetts, popped the beers open on *Sue*'s front fender and handed one to Troy. "I win tonight, kid, I take you on."

Ray tossed down three more quick ones while adjusting idle, carbs, and listening to the sewing machine flutter of the valves. He cut the engine and pulled out the dipstick and sniffed it.

"Why you doin that?"

"Head gasket's leakin'. So water from the cooling system's gettin in the oil."

Troy looked painfully down at the Ford's gorgeous V-eight. "Oh Lordy."

"S'allright. I'll push her hard tonight and work on it tomorrow."

At the starting gate the cars thundered and bucked waiting for the flag to fall, then screamed with tires howling down the first straight, *Blue Sue* outside and cutting into third position. Round and round they went under the yellow lights, snarling and thrashing, rubber screeching and wailing, engines gunning, metal whanging and crunching as the cars came together and spun apart tumbling into the field or smashing sideways or headlong into the wall sending splintered timbers flying. The noise and din and thunder was awesome and magnificent and Troy felt an elation he could not remember ever feeling before, that throbbed his prick, choked his throat and dampened his eyes.

Ray led for half the race then cut sputtering and steaming onto the field. "What's wrong!" Troy yelled. "You were ahead!"

"Too much water in the oil. She's overheating." He cut the engine and opened the hood, the engine steaming and ticking.

"Is it cooked?"

"Hell no, just pissed off."

Troy looked with sorrow down on the seething engine. "Sorry, Sir. Guess I don't get to…"

Ray wiped at sweat and grease over one eye. "Come tomorrow after school. First thing you're gonna learn is how to change a goddamn head gasket."

. . .

AFTER SCHOOL Mick walked with Daisy to Whitman's then had baseball practice so there wasn't time for anything but a quick kiss in the sumacs. After practice he worked two hours at McGinnis Hardware till six then chores till seven-thirty, dinner and homework and up at five-thirty for chores before taking the school bus to Nyack.

It was easy to get good grades, he'd learned. Just take careful notes in class then read them before sleeping and before chores next morning and again before a test. And always do your homework right away; even though you hate it, don't let it pile up.

In class if he didn't pay attention Daisy'd snap at him and sometimes wouldn't go in the back seat of the DeSoto on weekend nights even if he had a rubber, which she made him use depending on when it was between her periods. He hated the rubber because it deadened the feeling and beauty and magic of being skin to skin inside her, and hated asking at the Rexall and Mr. Anslow would grin and wink and Mick wanted to punch him but had to smile like they shared some dirty secret.

"GUN IT!" Troy yelled. He cupped his hands over the Mercury's valve intakes till the engine yowled. "Stop!" He leaned out from under the hood and Mick backed off the gas.

"How high?" Troy called.

"Forty-eight –"

"Nice!" Forty-eight hundred on the tach meant the engine would run lean, could hit full output despite the dust-choked low-oxygen air it would be sucking at the track.

Mick killed the engine. "She'll be the hottest car on the track," Troy said. With a clump of grass he wiped grease off his hands.

"They *had* to put us in the back," Mick said. "Because we're new. But she's so fast we can gain ground inside. Every time a car slides wide."

"We can take them on the corners too. The shocks're harder than before, so you can lean into the corners more, there's no roll. These other guys, they don't know nothing about the *science* of mechanics.

They think all you need's a bigger engine and beat up your car and you'll win. Ain't like that. They got to think about weight and steering response and maximum gearing and all that stuff."

Mick caressed the Mercury's shiny black roof. They'd stripped every ounce of nonessential weight: the back seat, carpets and upholstery, the fenders, bumpers, chrome, hubcaps, side and back windows, trunk lid, lights, even the sleek-winged hood ornament. There was nothing left but pure metal and power. Tara stopped on her way from the barn. "Why'd you call it *Bad Dog?*"

Mick shrugged. "Wanted to," Troy said, to annoy her.

"So who drives first?"

"We flip a coin," Mick said.

"One of us does the first race," Troy said, "the other the next."

"*You* rebuilt the engine."

Troy shrugged. "*You* bought the car."

Mick thought of the long sweaty hours digging ditches last summer for McCarthy Construction. "Forty-two bucks of mine plus nineteen of yours."

"And you paid for the parts. Most of them."

"We do well we get to race at Albany, the Labor Day Fair."

Troy glanced at Tara, took a penny from his pocket. "Catch this?" He spun it high and she snatched it out of the sky. "Call it," he said to Mick.

"Tails."

Tara glanced at the penny in her palm, at Troy. "Heads."

DAISY WOKE TO THE CRASH of dishes, her father's yell and her mother's snappy return. "Don't do it, Mom," she begged silently. "Don't answer him back." Then it came, the loud slap and her mother's outraged scream.

"You pig!" her mother wailed. "I hate you!"

"I hate you more, you slut. You whoring bitch!"

Why did people live together if they hated each other? Was hate stronger than love? Daisy put on her bathrobe and turned on the stairwell light and barefooted down to the kitchen. Pa stood unshaven with his suspenders drooping, belly pushing out his undershirt, big flabby white arms. Ma sat on the floor among broken white dinner plates with her back against the icebox, holding her jaw. "Pa you can't hurt Ma. It ain't right."

He gave her an unfocused stare. "Get the fuck out."

Daisy stood taller. "Hit her again and you'll go to Hell."

He stamped across the room and gave her a horrible whack on her temple and the room swooned and she knew she was lying in the broken dishes but there was no way she could move.

Pa was gone. Ma pulled her close and they lay together on the broken dishes, Ma crying and saying "My poor little girl, my poor little girl," Daisy lying there waiting for the night to end.

BURNT EXHAUST stung the air and clouded the lights shining on the track. Troy shivered at the urgent engines and snarling mufflers, the throaty idle of cars hungry to race. He tried to smile at Mick standing by the side of the car, gave him a thumbs up.

He nestled his shoulders into the seat, reached down and notched it forward and tugged his helmet tighter, liking its grip on his head, how it made him feel implacable and pure. The race boss came between the cars flicking his flag for each to pull out on the track. He seemed huge to Troy in the dancing lights and the sweat in his eyes and the acrid nacreous smoke.

He gunned it and eased the clutch to pull out behind a dirty dark blue Plymouth with *Silver Bullet* scrawled in white across its trunk. Clicked it in and out of first then let it rattle loose in neutral, right foot trembling on the brake, tugged at his chest belt, checked that the fire extinguisher was clamped tight on the transmission housing and the angle of the mirrors and the temp gauge and tach was true when he goosed it up to forty and let it back off rumbling.

The flag dropped and like a suddenly awakened beast the crowd of cars snarled forward raging, swerving and screaming. *Silver Bullet* was gone. Sliding in front of him was an orange Barracuda and he gunned *Bad Dog* inside and passed it.

Seven times they circled the track, Troy passing the slower cars and the ones with engine or tire trouble, then two that crashed, then *Kiss Mine* cut inside *Charlie's Towing* and knocked him into a slow upside spin nosing into the boards then whirling wildly and cutting through four cars sliding sideways fenders shrieking tires howling crunching banging into the boards, planks splintering, exploding paint and glass, chunks of flying metal and the shock of steel on steel and he was back on the track again.

Engine roaring, tires screeching, gears screaming he swung half sideways out of the curve and stomped on it in high second then hard into third; the four-barrel snarling as he blew past *Kiss Mine* and rode tight into the turn ducked a spinning car then a bounding tire then a door cartwheeling down the track.

Then it was over and he stood quivering, hand on *Bad Dog's* hot fender, his stomach lurching and bile in his mouth.

"You were fantastic," Mick said, grinning as Grampy came up and slapped Troy on the back.

"You did it!" Tara ran up and hugged him. "You came in third! You made it to the Labor Day Fair!"

"I was scared." He felt angry, alone, looked at her. "Scared the whole time."

FEAR'S NORMAL, Tara wanted to tell him. A hundred twenty miles an hour in a jalopy with crazy people all around trying to knock you off the track – so *what* if you're afraid?

But why did boys always *want* to be afraid? And then act tough and pretend they never were? But Troy had *said* he was. She liked that: not that he was afraid – any sane person would be. But that he dared to say it.

Once Mick had shown her a cottonmouth under Lafayette's house, was going to pick it up if she said to. Why? And why was there something in her that had wanted him to?

Some day she'd have kids and all that. Some strong kind capable guy with muscular forearms and a crewcut. Probably uses Vitalis. Brylcreem even. *Yuck.*

Brylcreem, the gals'll all pursue ya,
they'll love to run their fingers through your hair,

Imagine men put their peter up inside you. Mick does it to that snob Daisy. Once Tara'd found the rubber things he hid in a drawer under his football socks. Should know to hide things better. So the seeds don't come out of him and grow a baby in her.

Not in me they won't. That thing they pee with. I'm not some cow a bull can climb on. I don't want any one man. I'll have them all then throw them away.

THE BRUISE on Daisy's neck was large and blue-black. "Ouch!" she said when Mick touched it.

"He hit you?"

"He was whackin Ma so I told him to stop. He just hit me once. Not hard. Ma went to Doc Sprague but he can't do anything and Chief Logan's a friend of Pa's."

Every day Percy Moran finished work at the lumber yard at five and walked down Lawn Avenue with his black lunchbox in his hand. He stopped at Langley's Grocery for a sixpack and a cheap pint and then at Hal's Place for a pick-me-up. He'd told Daisy he wasn't a drinker but a man had a right to relax after work, particularly after *his* work, and for sure when he was going to be shut up for the next twelve hours with two fuckin crazy females, he'd told her one night, "So shut up you little slut before I knock your head off."

"Don't you *dare* call her that," her mother yelled.

"Hell," he turned on her jovially, "you did'n know your little whore's been spreadin her legs for Mick? Christ, in the back seat of Ned O'Brien's DeSoto... Hell, even up in her goddamn room when they thought we weren't here –"

Mick stopped him next evening as he came out of Hal's Place, the sixpack and pint in his left hand and the lunchbox in his right.

"What *you* want?" Percy Moran belched.

"I want you to keep your hands off Daisy'n her Mom."

The lunchbox came around fast and whacked Mick's forehead with a flashing pain; he couldn't see, Percy Moran's big fist smashed into his teeth snapping his head back. Moran grabbed at him, pummeling his ribs, and drove him backward into the oak. "Little prick!" Moran grunted, spit into his face, punched him low and spun away and punched him in the temple and Mick backed away, couldn't see to hit or to defend himself. "Little prick!" Moran snatched up his lunchbox, pint and sixpack and headed up the alley toward home.

"Who the hell you fight with?" Dad said when he got home.

"Don't matter."

"You got beat?"

"Sort of."

"Jesus go see your Ma. Hey Maude!" Dad called upstairs. "Get down here."

She came slippering down and made Mick sit down by the light. "Lord Jesus. We're taking you to the hospital."

"No we're not." Mick stood. "I'm gonna put ice on it. Dad kin I have some whisky, just to knock me out?"

Dad got out the jug and the ice. "Whisky and aspirin, that's the best thing."

Mick's one eye was black and blue, his lip was split and two teeth hurt. Talking with a lisp infuriated him. Four days later he waited under Major André's oak till Percy Moran came up. "I told you!" Moran said.

Mick swung with all his might and Moran tried to duck it but it caught him full on the cheek and he went down and kicked Mick in the knee and got up smashing his forehead into Mick's face and kicked him in the gut sending a sword of pain through his appendix scar. He grunted to his feet. "I'm gonna kill you kid," and walked away.

"You got to stop this fighting," Dad said. "Is it over Daisy?"

"No," Mick lied. "Let it be."

"You look like shit on a brick," Troy said. "Let's get this guy together."

"This's my deal."

"You ain't winning."

"I'm going to stay with it till I do."

The fourth time Mick waited under the oak Percy Moran saw him and turned up the alley. Mick ran and grabbed him by the back of the collar and tried to throw him against a wall but Moran was too strong. They stood facing each other, panting, looking for an opening. "You sick fuck," Moran hissed. "Don't you learn?"

"Sooner or later you're gonna get tired of being hurt. I'm going to keep fighting you till you do."

"You'll die first."

"You're getting older and slower. I'm getting bigger and stronger. Some day I'm going to beat the shit out of you. Over and over. So it hurts you to breathe for the rest of your life."

Moran snickered, spit at Mick's feet. "You're wasting your time, punk. I don't hit those women. Even if I should." He faced him. "If I ever did I don't no more."

MICK WAS WAITING for Daisy outside Whitman's when Uncle Hal pulled his blue Buick with its fat whitewalls up to the curb and pushed the button that made the window go down. "Percy Moran's complainin' on you. Says you keep startin' fights." Hal chewed on his toothpick. "I says *shit no* my nephew'd never do that. Cause he knows if he loses I'll kill the man who whupped him. Since then Percy ain't come in the bar."

Mick sucked a sore tooth. "He was beatin' on Daisy'n her Mom."

"Jesus then next time I see him I *will* whup him." Hal nodded at Mick. "So how you been?"

"Can't get my fastball down. Or when I do, it's in the dirt."

Hal turned serious. "Your arm sore?"

Mick nodded. "All the time."

"So you're tensing on your pullback so you come forward crooked and screw your release." Hal shrugged. "Any dumbass knows you gotta stop throwing, let it heal."

"I'm starting Friday night."

"Tell Louie you can't. Tell him what I said. Take a week off and start the next game."

"I've got the chance to start and you want me to duck out?"

"If your arm's sore Goddamit *yes!* You won't do yourself or the team any good." Hal slid up the window, dropped it back down. "You see Percy, slug him for me."

THE LABOR DAY FAIR was, as Troy put it, a whole different deal. Instead of beat-up racing jalopies built by men who worked full-time as mechanics or truck drivers, the cars that lined up at the Fair were built by men with the time to do it right: hot, well-built, and very fast. Mick drove *Bad Dog* in the first heat, a wild dangerous howling mass of cars fighting each other for first or second place, because only those two would go on to the semi-final race.

Fighting out of the last lap Mick eased in behind two cars locked in a spinout and accelerated past them, finishing just ahead, in second place. Two hours later Troy came in third in the semi-final, out of the final, and they silently drove *Bad Dog* up on the trailer Dad had made out of an old pickup truck body and towed it all the way back to Tappan behind Grampy's pickup. "Next year," Troy said mournfully, "we'll make her even hotter."

"Ain't no reason for us to lose," Mick said. "Not ever."

On Monday after baseball practice Daisy came out of Whitman's in the red jacket she'd made. With her fiery auburn braids down her breasts she was a magical Teutonic princess. Then he saw her face. "What is it?"

She bit her lip, looked away, at him. "Pa says in the winter we're movin' again. This time to Iowa."

16

ROLL OVER BEETHOVEN

WHEN TARA thought of life before Troy it was vague and misty. Some things stood out – the wool bunny Ma made her that she lost in the woods, a frying pan on fire, a blue dress, the winter snowdrifts came up to the second story windows, her first day of school with all those strangers, the time when blood started coming out of her and Ma said that was good, she was becoming a woman, old musty clothes and books, lost things.

Five years ago on her ninth birthday she got Cyrus. She could still feel his velvety black fur, his purring warm flesh, his soft breath and pulsing heart. Tiny in her cupped hands. Never had she known such closeness, cared so intensely. Then itchy red circles appeared on her face and stomach; she scratched them and blood got on her yellow dress.

Ringworm, Dad said. They gave us a cat with ringworm. I'm sorry, the vet said, there's no way to save him. Dad took Cyrus out to the barn to kill him and she buried him under the lilac outside her bedroom window. Never had she felt such emptiness, a sorrow so vast and complete. Often she crouched beside his tiny grave speaking silently to him and felt his warm response inside her.

"Everything dies," Ma had told her. "We do, the birds, the trees – remember old Greenie, that brindle cow, how she fell down one day and didn't move? All our ancestors who've ever lived have died. Some day our descendants – people who aren't even born yet – they'll die too."

"Is there nothing afterwards?"

"No one knows, darling. Lots of people believe in heaven, in something that comes after. But there's no proof – they're just afraid of dying so they make it up –"

"Make what up?"

"The idea of heaven. So they don't have to face the truth of death. That's it's the end."

"I hate it. I don't want to die."

"We don't get a choice, love. That's why we have to live deeply and truly every day. The way the birds do, animals in the forest. With as much love as we can. And not let our hopes of heaven cheat us into not living now."

At the orphanage they'd told Troy all about God. But he didn't believe it either. Pretty hard to believe people who say one thing and do another. Like Dad says, preaching Christianity and starting wars.

Tara had promised herself to do better with Troy. At first she'd hated his scruffy hardness, his *outside*ness, his distance that seemed both hostile and afraid. But how else could he be? And she'd hated him for Ma and Dad bringing him into the house, breaking up the family. But told herself *Don't be jealous,* he's a poor kid who never had any chances. Imagine growing up like that with no parents. How can we be free and happy when others aren't?

Or are we not that good? Like when she'd told Ma about that fat girl in school. "Dorothy Marshal's chubby, not fat," Ma said. "She just could lose twenty pounds."

"Well she's the only one of four hundred kids who's *chubby.*"

"Don't you go lookin down on folks. Not till you've walked in their shoes."

Now walking to Tappan to catch the school bus to Nyack it wasn't just her and Mick, Troy was there too, he and Mick always talking about football and cars and hunting, hardly caring if she was there or not. And they played baseball and football, and war games in the forest, shooting BB guns at everything – why did boys always want to *shoot* things? Because of that little twig that lets them pee standing up instead of squatting down so it splashes your ankles?

She'd lost her brother, simple as that. You could argue she'd gained another brother but that was the kind of thing adults say when they want you to believe something that's not true. Doesn't matter, she told herself, walking alone across the dew-glinting meadow down past Lafayette's house into the leafy shadows of town. I don't care.

Each morning on the way into Tappan for the school bus to Nyack, and each evening going home she passed the brick convent amid its wide fields where a white horse grazed. Strange the nuns had that horse because none of them ever rode it. Maybe one day she'd ask go ask if she could.

Maybe one day she'd be a nun. Live in that big building and do what you want. They were supposed to be praying but that was just another word for thinking your own thoughts. And even though Ma said there was no heaven maybe there was, and if you were a nun you were likelier to get in.

When she played the piano sometimes these thoughts bothered her and then she'd miss notes and her fingers wouldn't move right. When she had her lesson, Mrs. Zytomirski, who lived in two furnished rooms above the 1776 House, would rap the piano with gristly knuckles saying *"You're not trying good! How you ever play at Carnegie Hall if you don't try good?"*

It was true you had to focus on every tiny note and the spaces between them but you also had to let your mind free like the bird rising into the blue heavens and white clouds, and if she could see the bird yet also listen to each tiny step between the notes then the music flowed and she felt proud and emptied and full at the same time.

And Mrs. Zytomirski would say, *"Some day you will make records people put on the Victrola and all this time will be worth it."* But it's already worth it Tara would think. To soar free like that white bird in the white and blue sky, in the cold brightness that goes on forever.

How to explain to people what this was, music. Like what Elvis did, how he changed this world with his deep hunger for body connection – he wants you and he makes you want him.

What Chuck Berry did, *Maybellene, Johnny B. Goode...* How can anyone *do* this? Where is this deep reservoir of beauty waiting to erupt inside us?

But Mrs. Zytomirski didn't understand about Elvis. Or about Chuck Berry, his new song *Roll Over Beethoven* wasn't just a magical journey into the joyous possibilities of sound; it was also a slap in the face: *Get out of my way, old man, I'm the new dog in town.*

She loved the old dog too. Loved them both.

Because they touched you in the same deep place with their mastery and pure beauty.

Beethoven would've loved Chuck Berry.

TROY HAD BEEN HERE more than three years after he and Mick had run away and now it was almost Christmas vacation and Tara kept wondering what presents she might get. She'd been practicing the same Handel piece for weeks but kept making the same mistakes – sometimes her fingers just wouldn't move right – she put down the keyboard cover hard and went into the kitchen fragrant with cooking apples and acorn squash.

"You shouldn't slam it like that," Ma said.

"I *didn't.*" It made her angry that she was angry and that Ma knew it.

Her hands wet, Ma caressed Tara's cheek with the back of her wrist. "You can't play perfectly all the time, darling. Mistakes is how we learn."

"Not by making the same damn mistake over and over."

Ma turned on her. "Hush that!"

Tara tucked aside a curtain to look at the snow slanting across the barn light, her finger against the cold glass. "I hate winter."

Ma handed her a knife. "Peel these potatoes will you?"

Tara sat at the table cutting so each peel went round and round the potato unbroken in a long crooked strip. Troy came home from cross country practice, hung his coat and set his books down hard on the table. "Damn!" Tara said, her peel broken.

"I *told* you," Ma snapped, "don't use that word."

"*You* do," Tara answered. She glowered at Troy. "You do too. Even worse."

"*I* better not hear it," Ma said.

Troy flipped through his math book till he found the page he wanted. "All the guys say stuff."

"It's okay for *you*," Tara said. "But not for girls?"

He pulled his slide rule out of its green leather case. "I never said that."

Ma turned on him. "You finish the milking?"

He glanced up from the book. "Sure did."

"And you," Ma said to Tara, "the chickens?"

"I'll *do* them." Tara glanced at the snow falling faster now across the barn light.

"You better before your father comes home and Mick's back from the woodlot."

Tara felt hot flush of irritation, stabbed at the last potato, the knife burned across her palm. "Damn!"

Her mother rounded on her. "You'll go to bed without supper!"

"I cut my hand!" She went to the sink and washed blood off the potato, slapped it down on the chopping block and began to quarter it.

"Let me see that," Ma said.

"It's nothing!" Tara shook her head, fighting tears.

Her mother gripped her hand. "You'll live. We'll bandage it."

"No *we* won't!" She finished the potatoes, stalked into the hall, pulled on her boots, yanked down her coat from its hook and tried to slam the door behind her but it wouldn't shut. "I'll come with you," Troy said, blocking it.

"I don't *want* you."

He shrugged on his coat. "I'm coming anyways."

Heads down against the snow they crossed the yard, boots squeaking. The chicken coop was icy despite the two lights hanging from the ceiling. "We'll have to leave them on all night," Troy said.

Wordlessly she yanked the corn and millet sacks from the feed closet, dragged them across the dung and straw floor and filled the feeders with a dented aluminum pot. The chickens ran to the feeders, others in their nests clucking irritably as Troy gathered the day's eggs into a pail. "We should turn the electric heater on in here," he said.

"It's not that cold!"

"It sure is." He put the pail down and took her hand. "Feel how cold you are. Wow, that's quite a cut."

She yanked her hand away. "I don't like you."

He tucked back his Yankees cap, pain flashing across his face. "Why?"

She slapped her hands down at her sides, making her palm sting more. "Oh I don't know – it's not true – I'm just mad, that's all."

"Don't be mad at me. I didn't do nothin."

"I didn't do *anything*! When are you going to learn to talk right?"

"Talk *correctly?*" he grinned.

"Stop mimicking me." She wanted to cry.

He took her hand again, held the cut palm under the light. "Then stop picking on me for no reason."

She saw the blood still trickling from the cut, gritted her teeth furiously. "See, now I won't be able to play my recital!"

"Sure you will."

She slapped his hand away. "How would you know?"

He turned toward the door. "I'll start the heater."

She went after him, wanting to hit him, anything so he'd turn back. "I *said* we didn't need it."

He smiled down at her, his head in shadow haloed by the ceiling light, and for an instant she sensed how much bigger he was and this made her angrier. "You'll be able to play your recital just fine." He leaned down and kissed her, his warm lips making hers feel cold.

"Hey," she said. "Don't do that."

He kissed her again, lips gently touching. It felt good.

"Sorry," he said. "I don't know why I did it." He plugged in the heater, lifted the corn and feed sacks into the closet and shut it, picked up the pail of eggs and stepped out before her into the howling night.

17

TWO UNKNOWNS

W HY *HAD* he done it? Troy felt ashamed, furious, wanted to scream or punch himself. He went to his room, angry at the plastic jet fighter models, the quilt Ma made strewn over his bed. *She's not your Ma anyway. You don't even have a Ma.*

Over and over he relived bending down to kiss Tara, and each time cringed with shock and regret. When he'd done it there'd been this instant of confidence, of doing something more powerful than himself. But *why?* Like the Fathers had said, was he *evil?*

It was so hard to see yourself, because you *were* yourself. He should go away in shame. Where? What was this craziness that made his body ache for her? So he could barely breathe, his knees shaking. They'd taken him into their home, treated him like a son. She was like a sister. Now he'd done this.

Never would he make up for it. He *was* evil. The Fathers were right.

WHEN MICK came in covered in wood chips and snow melting off his clothes the kitchen was silent, Ma rolling out bread and Tara, her hair tossed back over one shoulder, chopping onions for the deer-burgers. "Where's Dad?"

"Not home yet," Ma said as if isn't that obvious because the DeSoto isn't in the yard?

He nodded at the snow building up on the window mullions. "Bad roads."

No one spoke. He sat on the stairs to tug off his boots and went up past Troy's closed door to his own room. It had two windows on the snow-filled furrows of the back field down to the vast black forest. He thought of the deer yarding up under the trees, their fur thick with snow. The books and papers piled on his desk, homework for tomorrow, made him nauseous and sad. Out in the woods, cutting and splitting the birch logs, he'd felt good and competent – now facing these books he felt weary and defeated.

The smell of Daisy's hair, her little ear cold when he kissed it, her cheek cold too, her nose red and sniffly, the red-checked scarf around her neck, her body strong and slim under the green loden coat as she hugged him. He held his hands to his face to catch her odor – her hair, her skin, the coat – all of her. If she was really going, what would he do?

Maybe he'd take his savings and his hardware store money and hitch out to Iowa, imagined her shock and joy when she opened the door and saw him. He and Troy had ridden the rails – if he could do that he could maybe get there. You could do anything you really wanted.

Probably her Pa'd get some other job here and it wouldn't happen.

Disconsolately he flipped through tonight's homework. A biology chapter on invertebrates – who gave a shit? Three poems by Pope – a squirrelly little person. Conjugations in French – *je vois, il voit, nous verrons* – why couldn't they talk like Americans? Another chapter of Caesar, easy to translate:

The Helvetii had by now led their forces up and through the narrow defile and the territories of the Sequani, and had arrived at the territories of the Aedui, and were ravaging their lands...

Caesar was sickening, exulting over his massacres of these tribes he first befriended then turned against each other then conquered. Massacred a million people and wrote a best-seller about it. The Gauls just like the American tribes – if they'd united against the invaders instead of letting them pick them off one by one while they fought with each other they'd have won more, saved more...

His shoulders wearied at the thought. And then goddamn algebra... something about two unknowns – Troy would know about that.

Where *was* Troy? The barn lights were out so milking was done. And Troy never kept his door closed when he was in his room.

Mick changed his snow-soaked jeans and went down the corridor, the pine boards squeaking, to Troy's room. He started to open the door, hesitated and knocked.

"Yeah?" Troy said.

Mick opened it. "What you want?" Troy's voice from the dark by the window.

"Wonderin' where you was." Mick realized he was speaking the way they had *when we was kids*. "Time for eats."

"Ain't hungry."

Troy was talking that way too. Mick sat on the bed, Troy's face silhouetted against the snowy night. I should say something, Mick thought. Count to sixty then talk.

When sixty came he still said nothing. But that was fine, better not to speak. He felt his breathing, regular and fast, felt like a vessel that was empty but would be filled.

"What's double unknowns?" he said finally.

Troy snickered. "What's two plus two?"

"Just cause you're so fuckin' smart in math don't make you no better, does it? So shut the fuck up."

Again Troy snickered. "How can I tell you if you tell me shut up?"

Mick wanted to punch him, thought back to the time when the train was coming and he'd grabbed Troy and jumped off the trestle. "Daisy's moving away. I don't know what to do. I'm going crazy." He never told Troy his sorrows but had to talk now. "Wanna ride the rails to Iowa?"

Again the hoarse laugh. "Remember Molly'n Joe?" Troy said

quietly out of the dark. "Molly used to sing *Nobody know, the trouble I seen...*"

There was so much to Troy, Mick realized, he didn't know. *"Nobody know but Jesus –"*

"And?"

The stairway door far below clattered open. "Dinner!" Tara yelled.

Troy's F-86 Saberjet on its transparent leader was outlined against the snowstorm as if coming in for the kill. "I hate math."

"When you invited me to come here, you didn't know what I was like –"

"Sure I did. You saved me from that railroad cop. Remember?"

"Yeah, but you invited me before that."

"Yeah, because you were my brother." Not knowing why he did it he reached out and patted Troy's shoulder, feeling infinite love. "Let's go eat. Or else you stupid shit you won't know how to help me with two unknowns."

"Yeah," Troy said. "Isn't there always two unknowns?"

"YOU WON'T BELIEVE the ice." Dad rolled up his sleeves and sat down at the table. "That old car was slippin' and slidin' all over the road..."

"You should get better tires," Tara said sharply.

He stared at her, fork raised halfway. "What'd you say, girl?"

"You should get new tires. They're bald, you said so. Of course they slide."

Mick watched his father's face. "That's right, Dad. Like when the track's wet at the Fair, and Troy'n I have worn tires we can't make the curves, have to slow down."

Dad put down his fork. "Well I'll be. Told what to do by my own kids."

"I don't have no right to speak," Troy said, "but she's right. I 'member when you said that."

"Of course you do." Dad dropped an affectionate hand on Troy's shoulder. "Never to old to learn, am I?"

Mick felt a sting of jealousy. "So why don't you get them? New tires, I mean."

Dad chewed. "Never get nothing new till the old gives out, like Grampy says. Never was a thing on this farm he replaced till the old one couldn't be fixed."

"The same with himself," Mom said. "Never go a doctor till you die, he always says. So's not to waste time and money. Then when you're dead you don't need one."

"He certainly doesn't seem to need one," Tara said.

"And never borrow money," Dad added. "And never tell a lie – just say nothing if you can't tell the truth –"

"Grampy lies," Tara snapped. "That's how he taught me to play poker."

"Me too," Troy said.

"Poker's different," Dad said. "You're supposed to lie."

Troy took the dishes to the sink. "Mick and me's got homework."

"Mick and *I*," Tara chided.

He turned on her. "I know that."

"Why don't you *say* it, then?"

He bit his lip, saying nothing as he rinsed the plates. Tara came to the sink and elbowed him. "You go help Mick with algebra. I'll do the dishes."

Mick watched them, conscious of being an outsider. *Je vois.* But what do I see?

How many unknowns can there be?

IN DAISY'S LAST DAYS Mick grew frantic to be with her. Just to see her across the classroom or when she passed with other girls in the hall socked him with pain. "You don't even care you're leaving," he said one night in the DeSoto's back seat as she was tugging on her underpants.

"Of course I do," she said, stopping to kiss him.

"You don't show it." Saying this made him feel a child, a fool, but he said it anyway, sensing something more solid in her than him.

"Does showing make it true?" She slung her bra over her shoulders and turned her back so he could clip it. "People can feel things and not show them all the time, not try to prove things that don't need to be proved."

"I can't *help* showing it –"

She shrugged into her blouse. "You think I'd make love if I don't love you?"

The realization made him breathless with pain. "I'm going to jump a train and come see you."

She bent forward, her forehead against his. "If God wants us to be together –"

"I have no God."

"Oh yes. You do. You just don't know it. God isn't an old man with a beard who cares about each of us. God is the power of good in the universe, the force of life not death. Happiness, not pain. When we do good we're building this power; when we do bad we hurt it, take from it."

He felt he could not breathe. "If only you could stay –"

THE LAST NIGHT the stars were needle-points of ice in a frigid universe as they embraced on the cold back seat of the DeSoto parked among the windy empty army barracks. *Each day I pray for evening,* the radio sang softly, *just to be with you –*

"You have to use a rubber," she said, slim and naked against him under their coats that kept slipping off.

After they'd made love he pulled a coat over her. "If we could only stay like this."

She half-smiled, still breathing fast. "We'd freeze."

"I'll come to Iowa. Soon's I can."

"Even if we see each other again we won't be the same. It won't be like this."

"I could live with you forever."

"We won't. We'll both have other people and life will go on. Whether we like it or not, that's the way life is."

He grew hard again and slid his leg between hers. "The rubber?" she said.

"It's the same one. I don't have another."

It lasted almost forever, the in and out inside her, reaching for her core as she opened more and more to him, her legs up to his shoulders so he could drive deeper, till it seemed that nothing was between them, they touched inside, and finally he came again and fell back gasping, his hand across her sweaty belly in her wet curls, the stars a haze beyond the misted windows. He reached down to remove the rubber; it was torn.

"Oh God I've come inside you."

She sat up fast. "It can't be."

"It tore. I didn't know." *Did I,* he wondered, *at that last moment?* She shoved across him and climbed over the seat, pushed open the door, the dome light blinding.

"Where you going?"

"To pee. I have to wash it out. Somehow I have to wash it out."

He yanked on his clothes in the frigid wind through the open door. She ran back. "We have to go home. Quick quick. I have to wash it out."

He drove savagely through the night, pulled up at her house. She kissed him fast. "Goodbye I love you."

"Can you come back?" he called but she ran up the stairs into the house. The porch light swung in the bitter wind. Driving through the snowy lanes of town he stopped at the Revolution graveyard and walked among the stones whining in the wind. So many young men dead for an idea, a fantasy, the lie that a system is more important than your life. Or than the girl you leave behind. There had to be a key, a way to change this.

Between the bare black boughs the stars were brilliant and grave. Stunned by their cold distance he wondered at all the pain and joy they'd seen. As if they cared.

18

ICE

DAD KNOCKED BACK his whisky, tossed ice cubes in the sink, and stood in the back yard taking a leak and yodeling.

"Quiet!" Ma yelled. "You'll wake the Cormers!"

"Hell," he laughed, "they're a half mile away."

She slammed the door. "Sometimes I'd like to crown your father. With a fryin' pan."

"Maude!" Dad called, "get out here! You can see Saturn plain as day!" He howled like a wolf, a long wavering cry. Rusty joined in, and over on Heartbreak Ridge the Cormer dogs began to bay.

NEARING THE MAILBOX at the end of the road Mick told himself there'd be no letter. And if Tara was with him she'd start singing *"Please Mister Postman wait and see, is there a letter in the box for me,"* real low under her breath to piss him off, but she had piano lesson today.

Inside was a letter for Dad from the Rural Farm Association and two others from Rockland Bank, and a blue envelope with a blue seven-cent airmail stamp, his name and address in Daisy's compact direct writing,

How I miss you in this dreary place. It's rained for days and you can

smell the feedlot for miles. They don't pasture their cattle here like we do, instead they pen them so they can't move and feed them corn to make them fat so they get more money. Out here a one-year heifer gets 14 cents a pound – can you imagine?

Now that we're living with Ma's brother Dan, Pa's leaving us alone better. Not that he's nice or anything, but you know what I mean. My favorite class is current events – how Hawaii and Alaska just became states – and history, the ideas behind the Declaration of Independence, that life, liberty and the pursuit of happiness are inalienable rights, and the purpose of government is solely to secure these inalienable rights.

And – get this – when a government becomes destructive to those rights, then it is the right of the people to alter or abolish it, and make a new one.

They even have a biochemistry class here and I'm going to take it.

Following was more news of classes and new friends, the weather and other stuff. He felt angry she didn't seem to miss him though she said she did. Hungry for her taste he licked the envelope flap where she had licked it, smelling her faint odor on this paper her hands had touched.

He wrote back rarely, feeling he had little to say and would not admit how much he missed her, and after a while her letters trickled to a stop. He'd find a way to go to Iowa soon, that was better than writing.

The day school ended, while Troy stayed working on the farm, Mick started work at the Coke factory in Nyack, feeding dirty bottles onto a conveyor line that ran them through a huge washer then filled them with Coke syrup and carbonated water and capped them. He and Jamie Duclair the second baseman worked side by side, sweat-soaked by the washer's scalding heat, lifting eight dirty bottles every three seconds – four with each hand – from their twenty-four bottle wooden crates and lining them upright in tight lines on the insatiable conveyor belt, some with their caps jammed back on so you had to yank them off, others with cigarette butts and other trash inside you had to dump out or use a wire brush on, the bottles sometimes toppling as the hot steel arms came down to shove them into the washer so you had to reach into the washer and right them, restacking the fast-emptying cases as a forklift roared up with a new pallet of dirties. As soon as a pallet of dirties had been emptied into the washer, the forklift snatched it to the far side of the conveyor belt to be loaded with newly-filled bottles and trucked to stores in New Jersey and New York.

Because the bottles lost pressure over time the machines overpressured them, making some explode and spray hot glass across the factory, people sucking their cuts but no one slowing for fear of losing pace with the machine.

As hot June melted into searing July the conveyor sped up, Mick and Jamie racing to keep it fed. To fight the heat and thirst they drank twenty or more Cokes a day, going outside on break to stand breathless in the shade, the other workers smoking, Jamie wanting to talk about Elston Howard's latest throw from outfield, nobody could say anymore that Negroes can't play as good as us, and just because the Yankees were ten games behind didn't mean they couldn't catch the Indians and White Sox, "Casey Stengel even said so." Jamie swung his arms like a batter doing warmups.

Mick had started chores at four-thirty a.m. and by now felt too weary to talk. Briefly he thought of Daisy, without hope, as a jailed man remembers freedom, or a chained dog the joy of the woods.

"We can't keep the farm much longer," Dad said that day driving home. "The big farms out west produce volume at lower cost. They're not family farms, they're milk factories. And with these new interstate highways it gets trucked from Ohio or Wisconsin at prices we can't match." He coughed, spit out the DeSoto's window.

"Bastards." Mick felt fury that people far away could destroy what his family had built over generations.

"And the county assessor keeps raising the land taxes..."

"How can they raise our taxes when we're feeding people?"

"Because they want us to sell. They have friends who want to build houses out here." Dad nodded at the hills of beeches and oaks rolling like waves into the distance. "You won't want to keep the farm anyways."

Mick thought of the Coke factory's mindless labor. "Better'n what I'm doing."

His father laughed hoarsely. "Me too."

It bothered Mick that Dad's work in the haze and stench of chemicals had him coughing all the time. "If plastic is this bad for people," he said, "we should stop making it. It should be against the law."

"What makes money, son, is never against the law."

"Long ago when we lived in tribes, nobody poisoned himself working for anybody else."

"Yeah the good old days. Till some cave bear grabbed your ass." Dad laughed again, spit. "That's why you go to college. So you don't have to work in a factory all your life."

"I ain't goin to college."

His father glanced at him. "Hell you're not."

"Please, Dad, watch the road."

"You're doing so well, the A's and stuff –" His father banged the steering wheel with his palm. "You think I bust my ass in that goddamn factory so you can jerk off when you finish high school?"

"I'm going in the Marines. Just like you did."

"We'd just been attacked by the Japs. There's no war now."

"If I enlist after high school I'll be twenty-one when I get out and they'll pay for college." Mick glanced up at the hills of Washington's Spring through the bug-spattered windshield. "How am *I* gonna make enough for college? Not working in the Coke plant."

His father looked straight ahead, chewing his lip. "You can get a goddamn scholarship, that's how."

"Troy's smarter'n me. If anyone gets a scholarship he will."

"He's smarter in math. But you got the ability to *see* things. Your brain's like glue, stuff just sticks to it. You understand books, history..." Dad's look was almost tragic and Mick sensed he was speaking of himself too. "You can't let that go to waste."

"It won't go to waste." Mick felt a happy surge of confidence. "After the Marines I'll go to college. If you want, I'll promise you that."

· · ·

"WHERE DID YOU GET that tremolo?" Mrs. Zytomirski asked Tara.

"Get it?" Tara said, confused. "It's just me."

"You need to sing more, girl." Mrs. Zytomirski smacked leathery lips. "Even when you are playing you must sing."

Tara hated it when people praised her singing. Mrs. Zytomirski had bad breath and an old woman's odor. Ma said she'd escaped Warsaw when the Germans killed her husband and kids, but it wasn't Tara's fault that she was alone and had no money and had to do piano lessons.

Maybe that was why Ma made her take lessons, so Mrs. Zytomirski could have money. But everyone kept telling her that her piano playing was good so maybe it was. And it *was* getting better. Pieces that had once seemed impossible now were easy.

But anybody can sing – why make a big deal out of that?

She just sang because she loved it. Not only Negro blues but how these southern white boys charmed it. Elvis and Jerry Lee, who could play a piano with his ass better than a lot of concert dudes with their fingers, that gorgeous Buddy Holly: when music reached right down into your bones and made you whole again.

"Now," Mrs. Zytomirski rasped, "I want you to show me the difference between a tremolo, what you've been doing, and a proper vibrato."

Ma didn't talk much about Mrs. Zytomirski because she hated the World War how Dad was gone and got wounded and wouldn't talk about it. Nothing could be so stupid as wars – what was wrong with people?

But Ma didn't mind talking about girl stuff; even before Tara'd had her periods Ma had told her it was coming, sort of like the rain that falls on the new-cut hay and ruins it so you have to buy hay all winter and go broke. Boys should have periods, they wouldn't be so snotty. Ma bringing the brick warmed on the woodstove and wrapped in a towel to put on Tara's stomach. The first few dark hairs, then more, the warm exciting feeling when you put your finger down there and push back and forth.

"There!" Mrs. Zytomirski enthused. "That's a real vibrato!"

. . .

WITH MICK AND DAD GONE all day and Mom doing the dairy and egg sales and growing all the vegetables, Troy and Tara ran the farm. By the first week of August it was already the third haying, which meant Troy had to bale all forty-two acres of mixed alfalfa hay he'd cut two days ago – Dad had wanted to wait another day for it to dry more but with rain maybe coming tonight it had to be finished today... With twenty-seven cows to milk twice a day, five hundred chickens and over two hundred turkeys being raised for Thanksgiving, plus fields to plow, and the orchard to trim up and keep free of birds and bugs, it was hard to find time for baseball or fishing or anything else.

Friday night they would tow *Bad Dog* to the fairgrounds, Tara riding between him and Mick in the pickup, her thigh against his and her long dark hair down his bare arm. No, he reminded himself as he turned the baler in a wide circle to pick up the next pile, I won't think of her that way.

But now in the barn sometimes she made him kiss her, pushing her lips into his, so exciting and dizzying sometimes afterwards he wondered if it had really happened...

But what would Mick say if he knew I've been kissing his sister? A hot blush crept up his neck over his face and made his underarms sweat. *Why* do I do it?

But Tara liked it, just like she liked it when they did well at the races. Friday night after the race she'd hugged Troy and giggling had shoved his helmet sideways so for a moment he couldn't see, just feel her narrow little pelvis against him... No, he told himself, don't think like that.

A horn hooted from the road. Troy jumped off the baler and ran to the barn as the ice truck backed up to the milking shed. He opened the shed doors and Silas the iceman carried blocks of ice one by one in his metal tongs into the milking shed, the daily twenty-two blocks that would cool the evening's milk till Mom could drive it to the dairy in Rockland in the morning.

"Need one for the house?" Silas said.

Troy ran in and checked the icebox. "A small one," he called.

Silas swung a small block in his tongs up into the ice compartment. Troy signed the receipt, sucking an ice chunk. Tara came down from the barn, jeans speckled with white from painting the back wall. "Give me a taste," she said.

He handed her the ice chunk. She licked it, put it all in her mouth.

"Give that back!" he said.

"Finders keepers," she mumbled, water trickling down her chin.

He glanced at the departing ice truck. "There's some in the milking shed. Go get your own."

She took it out, licked it all over. "Want it back now?"

He grinned. "Sure."

She handed it to him and turned on her heel. He stuck it in his mouth, trying to taste her taste, but could only feel the numbing watery shock of ice. "Aren't you gonna get your own?" he called.

"No," she called back. "I only wanted yours."

He felt his body tingle, didn't know why. Maybe she just wants to get me back, he decided. For not kissing her enough. I want to, but I don't dare.

Sucking on the ice he crossed the stubbled pasture to the baler and sat on the hot metal seat staring at the forest through the heat waves off the engine. It was always cooler under the trees. When you cut down the trees everything got dry and hot. Streams flowed in the forest but dried up when they crossed the fields.

He wished he knew if she was still mad. Whether she was being mean or just teasing. Shame rushed through him. Didn't matter; he had to stop thinking like that.

Maybe life was like stock cars. You get ahead if you build it carefully and learn to drive well and because you've rebuilt the car you understand it and how to make it reach its utmost. And every time you didn't come in first you learned from it and got better. But what did it mean to get ahead? As Mick would put it, didn't you already have one?

That was Mick, always making bad puns. Where did he get them?

A plane droned over against the wind; by the sound of its Continental 300 engine he knew it was a Cessna 170. He glanced up to prove himself right, grinned and started the tractor.

DIRTY DEVIL, a battered fifty-four Buick, cut Mick off on the eleventh lap at the County Fair, smashed him sideways down the track and four cars hit him tumbling *Bad Dog* end over end, the ground coming up and hitting him in the face then lurching over and hitting him again, the door crushed against his arm, the steering wheel snapping off on his chest. *Bad Dog* screeched upside down across the track, roof crunching in, the shoulder belt pinning him to the broken seat.

Stench of acetylene torches through bent metal, hands in white asbestos yanking him onto the grass as with a great whoof *Bad Dog* blew and the ambulance was white and bitter cold inside, full of urgent voices, a howling siren, blackness cascading down.

"He's got a bad concussion, broken ribs and a broken jaw," someone said. He seemed furious as though Mick's injuries were a personal affront. A doctor, maybe. "You're lucky he's alive," meaning *how could you let your son drive a stock car?*

"He loves it," Ma said. "Both these boys do."

"He's the best," Troy said, relieved and angry. "The best driver on the track."

"I'm so glad that damn car's wrecked," Tara clenched Troy's arm, rubbing tears on his shirt. "That you both can't do it anymore."

"He's out of football for the year," Troy said. "Coach Louie's gonna kill him."

19

I DARE YOU

TROY WAS SHIVERING like he always did before a track meet. Not from the cold but fear, from the smell of goose grease liniment and dried sweat, stomach butterflies, why some guys threw up before a race. Keeping his sweat suit on he jogged twice around the indoor track, knees weak, then one semi-fast lap bouncing his queasy stomach, then two slow laps, breathing easy, feet flying over the shiny boards.

"Don't go out so fast at the start," Buck had said. "You're not proving anything in the first quarter. Keep your wind, let the others set the pace, you settle down and find your rhythm."

"I try to," Troy had said, "but I get boxed in."

"So what?" Buck had answered, a serious look on his kind fleshy face. He'd been a shot putter in the 1912 Olympics but was a great running coach too. "Slow down, go around them."

"Bastards break my pace."

Buck slapped a hammy hand on Troy's bicep. "Just run your best race."

In the background people cheering for somebody's long jump. What was the big deal about running then jumping far as you can? Hell we did that back at the orphanage. Trying to get over the fence.

But if he thought about the orphanage it would cut him down like a side stitch.

"Ladies and gentlemen," the loudspeaker crackled. "Next event is the indoor mile. As you know, the high school record here is four minutes and twenty-eight point six-three seconds. But we have four young runners tonight who've done it faster outside –"

Troy's stomach flipped, goose bumps down his thighs; his knees quivered. He trotted to the Nyack High bench and slipped off his sweat suit pants, standing on one leg then the other, knees shaking. He did some stretches, sipped water. Buck glanced over at him and nodded: *You're gonna do it. Don't even worry.*

He shed his sweat suit top and jogged another lap, watching the others. Crawley, the punk from Rockland with the duckass haircut and wicked kick – have to get away from him by the third quarter mile. Steingold, skinny prick from Teaneck with a hairy chest and dark stubble, stretching himself backwards in his yellow shorts. He would go out fast and stay there. O'Neill tall and straggly, bony-kneed – Christ to have his stride.

Jesus I might come in fourth. He glanced round at the other runners beginning to line up. Even some of *them* might beat me...

"One minute, gentlemen," the loudspeaker said.

His stomach heaved. *Why* did he do this? Saturday night, he could be home watching TV – or sitting *up there*. He tried not to look at Tara, Mick, Ma and Dad in the stands.

"That guy Crawley," Tara'd said, "he's kinda neat."

"In five years he's gonna be digging ditches –"

"And you?" she'd pounced.

He shouldn't never have kissed her.

"Thirty seconds, gentlemen."

Deep breathing made him dizzy. He jogged out a few steps, turned round, walked back to the starting line, legs weak.

"Runners, take your marks."

Leaning forward, a hand on one knee, other arm swinging free, he waited for the gun. Silence, echoes through the stands.

"Get set –"

BANG! He was out, sprinting, the others strung out behind him, fleet freedom, tireless perfect speed, remembered what Buck said and eased back gauging the *slapslapslap* of his running shoes on the oak planks, the panting of someone coming up behind – Steingold maybe, remembered to lower his forearms, Buck said *don't run with your arms up, how can you get momentum from that?*, took a fast double-breath and tried to settle in but the pace was too fast, like being pulled by a rope behind a car and you know you can't keep going this fast.

Someone on his shoulder going into the turn, let him take the outside, run the extra steps... Steingold breathing fast, almost sprinting, took the outside on the turn and passed him, skinny hairy legs flying, yellow shorts rippling as he opened up the distance, and another's feet coming up now, *thudthudthudthud* sounded like O'Neill, God am I going to come in last?

Winded, gasping into the third turn he pushed to stay ahead of O'Neill, legs weakening – why so early? – someone coming up, easy long strides, not pushing it, not breathing hard, passed O'Neill, and as Troy sprinted into the straightaway the guy came up beside him, tall kid with flopping black hair, and Troy let him pass, settling down trying to get his breath back –

"Sixty-two five," Buck called his first quarter. Way too fast – Steingold twenty yards ahead – he must've done fifty-eight. Can't keep this pace...

Forget them, run your race, Buck had said, and like a drowning man who grabs at anything, he tried to ignore them, breathing steadily and fast to the cadence *Run your race Run your race*, his stride stretching out, feet hammering the boards, his legs really tired now, half way through the second quarter and maybe this is the Half Mile, I got in it by mistake, have to slow down, if it's the Mile I can't make it all the way...

"Two-twelve," Buck called at the half, Steingold still twenty yards ahead, the dark-haired kid second. I'm third, Troy thought – where's O'Neill? Going into the turn he glanced back, O'Neill then the others bunched up ten and fifteen yards behind.

Half way through the third quarter he could no longer take the pain, past exhaustion, gasping for air that wasn't there, running numbly without the strength to lengthen his stride, pushing to close with Steingold but someone new coming up – Crawley the punk from Rockland with the wicked kick – how would he ever get away from him now?

Crawley like the kid in the orphanage named Ben who always hit you but Father Damon loved him – nights in the dormitory that never ended when you lay there thinking why am I here, what have I done, what will become of me? Steingold fading or am I going faster? How can I be when I can't stand the pain, never run another race, or am I speeding up because Crawley's gaining, and Tara said she likes him and if I'd stayed at the orphanage I'd have never kissed her and breathe deeper faster pushing it down into your belly then quick back out like Buck says and that will stop the side stitch but it's too late I've got it I can stop at three quarters and tell Buck I got the side stitch he won't mind, Buck's warm round red face, Buck who threw the shotput in the Olympics and I don't care if he needs me to win I can't go more...

"Three nineteen!" Buck yelled, and if I do under seventy the last quarter I'll beat the record, don't run with your arms up, breathe from your gut, ahead of him Steingold closer now, Troy's legs wavering, head swinging side to side in total exhaustion, the dark-haired kid beyond him, the steady flutter of Crawley's feet right behind Troy, his steady breathing as he readied to take over.

Go ahead and catch the dark-haired kid, Troy told Crawley, the side stitch a knife in his gut like Father Damon's willow switch, and he could see the Father now, it gave him breath somehow, his legs so far beyond exhaustion they could go faster, beyond pain, fast as Crawley thundering up behind but Crawley never kicks till the last two hundred if I can get away from him now maybe he won't catch me God help me make this distance, passing Steingold on the first curve so Crawley will be slowed or have to go around him but Crawley came now, still on Troy's heels his *thump thump* feet and hoarse gasping spraying spit on Troy's arm as he moved outside on the curve and Troy let him get there then ran faster not knowing how, keeping

Crawley outside, making him eat more distance as they thundered down the back stretch the hazy vision of the dark-haired kid dancing in front and Crawley on the outside choking for air sprinting full speed but still not passing and Troy realized he was sprinting too, was in the death zone where nothing mattered, beyond joy and pain, where if you keep it up much longer you *will* die, the dark-haired kid before him and Crawley surged past blocking Troy behind the dark-haired kid who stumbled and Troy cut around him but was on the outside going into the corner and you won't get away you bastard Crawley just a hundred yards to the end I can't make it, Crawley easing up oh he can't go any faster and Father Damon's whip means nothing and he somehow moved past Crawley on dead flying legs, no breath, no air at all as he snapped the ribbon stumbling gasping sucking air oh God air and walked off the track trying not to fall.

People holding him up and walking him down the track past Crawley vomiting and someone lying on his back gasping and there was so much noise and his heart thundering like he was going to die but it was the crowd roaring and the announcer saying over and over as Tara ran wildly up to him, "Ladies and Gentlemen we have a new mile record!"

THE HOUNDS WERE BAYING up ahead, muffled by night forest. Mick ran toward the sound, stumbling through muck, blinded by the glare of Clem Hays' lantern and trying not to trip on roots or gouge an eye on a branch. "They're runnin one," Clem yelled.

The dogs grew louder, down in the swamp now; the coon had tried to lose them by running in the water. Maybe the coon got away, Mick hoped, maybe he was headed toward the hills while the dogs bayed round a tree he'd already jumped free of.

He slowed to a walk, panting. Clem's brother Carl huffed past trailing cigarette and whisky stink, called, "What you waitin for?" The lantern ahead played on the branches of a big oak, the dogs barking wildly, leaping up it and tumbling back down.

"He's up there!" Clem swung the lantern this way and that, trying to illuminate the branches while Carl pointed a flashlight. "Shut thet down!" Clem yelled, "you'll waste the battry."

"Got to see 'im don't we?" Carl yelled back.

Clem circled the tree kicking the dogs aside, lifted the lantern, shading his eyes as he looked up the tree. "There!" he pointed.

Carl grabbed Mick's shoulder and pointed to a high crotch where two yellow-red eyes gleamed. Clem took out a long-barreled .22 pistol, handed Mick the lantern. "Hold this motherfucker! Shine it right!" He backed away and aimed the pistol high and fired, a cold sharp *Crack*. The bullet twanged through the branches. Still the eyes stared down.

Mick tried not to think how the coon must feel – run for miles through the forest by the baying hounds, in exhaustion and terror finally taking to the tallest tree it could find, thinking it was safe now. *Bang* Clem fired again; the eyes jumped, vanished.

"Got 'im," Carl yelled.

"Fucker hid," Clem countered, grabbed at Mick. "Bring thet lantin!" He yanked a hatchet from his belt and drove a spike part way into the oak trunk, then two above it. "Gimme thet light!" he yelled at Carl, and holding it in his teeth he stepped up the three spikes to reach the lowest bough, pulled himself up and swearing, puffing and spitting began to climb from bough to bough.

"Shine thet light now," he yelled down at Carl.

Its yellow orb played across the trunk, passed a shiny blackness and came back to it. "He's on th'other branch!" Carl yelled. "Up to the right."

Clem gripped a bough left-handed, leaned out from the trunk and fired; the shiny blackness lurched, doubled up on itself and slid off the branch tumbling down and snatched at another bough lower down and dragged itself along it.

"Shoot thet fucker!" Carl yelled, the dogs yapping up the tree and snapping at each other.

"Kin't see 'im," Clem called down. "Goddamit Mick shine thet light will you?"

Watching the dying raccoon Mick slid round more to the right, not wanting to show Clem where it was. Clem fired again, the whap of the bullet loud as the raccoon squealed and dropped from the bough, growing larger in Mick's lantern light till it thumped to the ground, the hounds tearing at it, the raccoon keening as it died, its teeth buried in a dog's neck, the dog screeching suddenly and backing away dragging the coon hanging from its neck, the other dogs ripping it apart.

"Git 'im," Clem roared, "git 'im off my dog!" With Clem and Carl kicking it the coon still gripped the dog's neck, the dog yelping and gurgling and trying to shake free.

Finally it let go; the dog stumbled in a circle, the other hounds ignoring it as they tore the coon apart. The dog fell over and Clem knelt beside it swearing, its throat pulsing great gouts of blood on the dirty leaves.

"He killt Susie," Clem kept yelling, "He killt my dog." He rose and kicked the others away from the coon. "Git thet bag over here!" he said, snatching a burlap bag from Mick. "Killt my dog!"

With the dead Susie and the remains of the raccoon in a burlap bag over his shoulder, blood running down his jacket, Mick followed Clem and Carl all night as they treed and killed four more raccoons, Clem being careful to wound them only so they would fall and be torn to death by the dogs, muttering "Killt my dog will you!"

At daylight Mick stumbled out of the woods carrying one bloody bag with the dog and two raccoons, Carl the other. Clem tossed the bags in the back of his International pickup and dropped Mick at the farm. "You tell yer Dad now, anytime the coons git killin his chickens he lets me know."

Mick washed his hands and bloody jacket at the trough pump and sat with his parents at the kitchen table as they drank their morning coffee.

"Well, now you know," Dad said.

Mick scraped dried blood off his nails. "I near threw up."

"We've got hog wire now," Ma said. "It's not as if the coons can get into the runs and harm the chickens any more. Long as they're locked up at night."

"Seeing that raccoon up there, he knew he was going to die. And then, being torn apart and taking a dog with him... I was rooting for the coon –"

"If you're always thinking for others," Dad said, "you'll have pain all your life." He gently punched Mick's shoulder. "But you'll see the world how it is, won't you?"

"It's evil to kill," Ma said, "when you don't need to."

TROY COULDN'T STOP KISSING TARA, holding her against the straw bales in the back of the barn, her fingernails in his shoulders, her pelvis hard against him. She grasped his prick through his jeans. "So this's what happens to it," she panted.

It made him ache even more. "Jesus don't stop."

She moved his hand over herself, shoving her pelvis up and down his palm. "Christ this feels good –"

He felt her slit wet and hot through her underpants. "I dare you," she gasped, her thighs tight round him, "to put it inside me."

LIVIN' TOO FAST

T ARA RACED BACK from Rockland with a Muddy Waters album and not stopping to take off her coat put it on the Victrola, liking how the record spun so fast she couldn't read the label's blur of yellow and red. She put the arm down slowly but the needle scratched and from the kitchen Mom called, "Careful!"

"Yeah, Mom. It's *my* record."

"Bad for the needle."

She kept singing along with it, trying the ranges,

You just keep on bettin'
The dice won't pass,
Well you know, darling,
You're livin' too fast

Ever since Dad started working at the plastic factory Mom had been getting more and more cranky but nobody talked about it. Said the piano was too loud – as if it had a loudness dial like the Victrola – that the kids were bringing in dirt on their boots – wasn't this a *farm*, Mom? That Dad shouldn't do this, do that...

Dad didn't mind, held her hand and sometimes kissed her and

wouldn't let her do the dishes and took over her chores like she was some New York lady. One time Tara came into the bedroom for knitting wool and Mom was crying and Dad holding her and talking in his low steady voice. Ma, who never cried, not even when that birch log bounced and the axe split her foot. She'd just looked down at all the blood spurting out and said "Tara get the truck keys. I have to drive to the hospital..."

Well I know you're leavin'
Well you call that gone
Well without love
You can't stay long

The same hospital where Mick near died from the appendix but nobody talked about that either. Like if you didn't talk about stuff it hadn't happened. But they sure talked to him plenty about crashing *Bad Dog*. As if it was his fault.

But someday Baby
You ain't gonna trouble
Poor me anymore

"Tara!"

Chewing her lip she went into the kitchen. Ma was pushing wet clothes out of the washer through the ringer. "Can you please hang these out for me? I'm taking the eggs to Orangeburg Market."

Tara wanted to go back to the record but you couldn't be like that. "Sure, Ma."

"You can come with me if you want."

Usually she went with Ma to Orangeburg. She thought of the record waiting on the turntable. "Can I stay?"

Ma laughed, young and golden, caressed Tara's cheek. "Of course." She smiled down at her, called back as she headed for the car. "Don't mind what your brothers say, your singing is beautiful, darling. Don't you ever give it up."

Tara hated hanging the clothes because they were heavy and wet and the line would sag and the clothespins drop and the clothes droop in the dirt and with white things you couldn't shake the dirt off. And who wanted to touch boys' greasy t-shirts anyway?

When she was done hanging clothes she went in and played the record again and again, singing clearer now, *"Don't care how long you gone, Don't care how long you stayin'…"*

The telephone shrilled. "Damn thing could wake the dead," she said to no one, grabbed it. "This the O'Brien residence?" the man said.

"So what?"

"This is Officer Kean, Orangeburg Police. There's been an accident."

Frantically she thought where Mick was, Troy. "What accident?"

"A Maude O'Brien the driver's license says. Are you a member of the family?"

"Is she okay?"

"Are you a member of the family?"

"Is she okay?" Tara screamed.

"They've taken her in an ambulance to Nyack Hospital. You'll have to call there."

She put down the phone and stared out the window at the front pasture, seeing nothing. She ran back to the phone but now Doris Enfield was on the party line. "Mrs. Enfield," Tara said. "I got to call my Dad!"

"My dear whatever for?"

"Get off!"

In the background a scratching noise, the record had finished, the needle grinding on the end track. "Well if that's the way," Mrs. Enfield was saying.

"Hurry!"

Hadn't Mick been saved by getting to the hospital on time? And wasn't Mick fine now?

It was the same waiting room where they'd been when Mick was operated. A woman in a red and black coat sat at the far end, sniffling and looking away. Dad pushed through the doors and a few minutes later came out and took her and the boys outside. It was cold; she sat on a stone step. Dad sat beside her, looking up at the boys. "It was a drunk driver. Your Ma's dead."

THE NORTH WIND drove sleet into their faces and down their coats, freezing their hands as they carried Ma's coffin up the slope under the bare elms to the graveyard on the crest. As Tara gripped one corner of the heavy sluggish casket, the oak handle biting her palm, she thought how many times she'd climbed this path and how innocently doomed life had been, had she known.

Ahead her father slipped on the sleety grass, down on one knee and rose again and pushed onward. He would bear up no matter what. Like Ma said he'd been after Tarawa but a thousand times worse.

She was crying again and wondered where the tears came from – she'd cried for days and nights and couldn't stop. She gritted her teeth, shifted hands. Not for herself. For Ma losing her life.

Troy said once we were cave people hunted all the time by bears and lions. People died all the time and everybody just kept going.

Deer had made long wandering runs through the drifts. Bare boughs brightened the blue sky. Snowdrifts half-covered the lichened headstones and filigreed the eroded long-forgotten names. *Live hard and well*, the names said, *for your eroded unremembered time is coming soon.*

The clearing ringed by white birches with naked boughs reaching down, the newly-dug grave an open dark wound, the hemlocks shaking sleet from their boughs. The family brushing sleet off their coats and kicking it off their boots, Uncle Hal in dark glasses, Aunt Wilma brushing away tears with the back of her hand, Aunt Sylvia motionless with a hand on Johnny's shoulder, Johnny gazing faraway, not here at all.

Ma so cold now in the stiff pine casket into the cold ground. Tara ached to take her mother in her arms and warm her.

"I'm not reading any Bible," Dad called out, face into the sleet. "She wouldn't want that. She wouldn't want anything said. His voice broke. "Thank you, Maude, for every moment."

He glanced up at them, hand on the lowering rope. They gathered round – does anything make people more cooperative than death? – and eased her down.

Snow crinkled under Tara's boots and dashed away on the wind. A jay called, strident. Maybe that's you, Ma, flying away. Tara faced into the sleet to hide tears, waiting for it to end so she could be alone. Ma was dead but she, Tara, would live for her. Talk to her all the time, ask her what to do. Like Dad said, *Even if Ma's dead she still loves you.*

Dad shoveled brown clods onto the sleet-white casket. He handed Mick the shovel, then Tara, its steel shaft stinging her fingers, her dirt dribbling over the casket. Then Troy, silently choking, eyes on the sky.

They walked down the hill toward the house, the wind at their backs. The kitchen smelled warmly of wood smoke. Dad sat at the maple table in his red-checked coat, rough red hands on the wood, looked at each of them. "We're going to soldier on."

She would soldier on. The Marines killing and destroying.

She would never give up singing.

Before now she'd felt shame after doing it with Troy. *But how can there be shame for something you want?* I like having him hot and hard inside me. I wish we could do it more, all the time. Why be ashamed of how you feel? Were others' judgments truer than what *you* felt? How can you ever *be*, if you're ashamed of who you are?

Don't you ever give up singing. That's what Ma said.

TROY CAME IN FROM THE COLD brushing ice off his clothes and inhaling the kitchen's warm woodsmoke air. In the orphanage there was never any warmth. He must always keep the memory of the orphanage in his mind. So he never wondered why he was here. Never stopped thanking God. The God he didn't believe in. The God who killed Ma.

Tara followed him shaking snow off her parka. "Must be ten below," she said.

"Try twenty-two," he admonished.

She stared at him, angry. "What fucking difference does it make?"

"Don't say that word."

"I can say what I want. Asshole."

"When your mother's dead a month –"

She raised fists to her face. "Don't *say* that word."

"*Dead dead dead death death DEATH!* We're all gonna die, even little cheerleaders with pretty faces who think that'll give them everlasting life." Stunned, he ran upstairs and slammed his door, sat on the bed. He couldn't stand it. That Ma was dead.

His fault. If he hadn't come to live with them maybe Ma wouldn't have had to drive to Orangeburg that day. Not at that moment.

He sneered at his face pale and expressionless in the mirror, his jaw aslant, a cowlick hanging down. You always wanted a family. Now look what you've done.

FOR THE GOOD

"**I**'M PREGNANT," Tara whispered, her voice urgent yet low as if wishing to protect him from something, or as if the cows in the barn might hear. "After school today I went to a doctor in Nyack."

Troy felt a numb mix of awe and terror, that at age seventeen he could be a father. The air felt knocked out of him; he snatched at the dumb hope it couldn't be true. "You sure?"

"Don't joke." Her voice was deeper, more assured. Angry and scared. Determined to be responsible for them both. "You can't let on, to anybody. Specially not Mick."

The idea of Mick's knowing terrified him. For a microsecond he'd felt elation at making a child, the sacred gift of life. Then the desolate knowledge that it wouldn't be, would be the murder of his own flesh. "We can get married –"

"What kind of life d'you think we'd have, you with some job you hate, me going to night school, the baby growing up with no money..."

"We could make it, Tara..."

"Stinky diapers and cheap groceries and me going crazy because I can't sing –"

"I'll get a job till you finish high school."

"Then what? More work, more kids, more worries, less time? No freedom to go everywhere and try things and make mistakes and live?"

For a week he wandered numbly. Either choice was evil; there was no way out. "It has to be your decision," he said finally. "I have to do what you want –"

"I don't *want* either of it, Troy. I don't want to kill my baby. And I don't want to have it." She was trying not to cry. He was crushed by this sudden loss of freedom, this anchor of a child. And elated by love for this child, the divine mystery, the flame of life. The wondrous joy of self-replication. A child free of sin, burning with life.

He imagined this child many decades from now, an old man in a leather armchair smiling down at his grandchildren, his rough palms on their heads. No, Troy reminded himself, I'm going to kill him before he's even born. His grandchildren, and theirs, will never be.

Freedom. The secret of life is being carefree. Each day you should be able to wake up and do whatever you want, like Mick says. You won't have that with a baby. "You've got to do what *you* want," he repeated, wanting both.

"You're making *me* decide –"

"I want to keep the baby, get married. But if you don't I can't fight you."

"You don't really want that." Her honesty cut through his lie. What he feared, he realized, was facing the world alone. He wasn't acting out of love for her or this child.

Even if he could tell Dad or Mick, it would just be passing his pain, his problem, to them. And then Dad would face the death of his first grandchild, or the shotgun wedding of his daughter and his adopted son. *Incest.*

White clouds across the blue horizon, the soaring canyons of space. Freedom, not a tiny apartment rancid with diapers, no money and a child, while his friends flew higher and Tara's friends dated and partied, and she and he grew weary and careworn and tried not to hate each other.

Two roads diverged ahead. On one, the antithesis of liberation, he would yoke himself to a woman who drove him crazy, who like a blind person walked always with the white cane of ideas poking her way ahead, and raise an unwanted, beloved child. On the other he'd soar above the icy mountain world, seek freedom in every cloud-topped canyon, like Tantalus who fed the Gods the flesh of his own child.

SHE WOKE NAUSEOUS in the pit of her stomach and had to do chores trying not to throw up this leaden sickness. This child a parasite feeding on her body; her hair dry and wiry, her skin rough. At breakfast she held back the vomit when Dad said *How come you're not eating your eggs and bacon?* and took a cup of coffee out on the back porch breathing steadily and watching the ugly sun rise out of the windblown trees.

Even if Troy wanted the kid it didn't matter; she didn't want to live with Troy forever, just do it with him sometimes when the mood hit but she could live the rest of her life and never do it again if this is what happened when you did.

When the radio sang lugubriously of the girl who died on the railroad tracks because she ran back to get her boyfriend's ring,

Teen Angel, can you hear me...
Are you somewhere up above,
And are you still my own true love?

She thought how stupid, *stupid, stupid* that girl was, how could you give a shit about some guy's ring for Chrissake that you'd die for it, and she wasn't going to ruin her life for some guy's dream either. Even if it was Troy's.

HE DROVE HER to East Harlem to kill the child. For days after, they were locked in sorrow and darkness, seeing nothing, hearing nothing the other said. His sex withered inside him; his voice had a strange breathlessness from a vacuum in the heart. The skin of his hand in the sunlight looked old and leprous. Once more he'd committed a sin that could never be atoned.

"I'm still bleeding a lot," she said. "And I *hate* being weighed down by these huge swollen tits!" He turned away; this cold deep lake of blood divided them; every night it grew larger and they further apart.

TARA HEARD THE SCREECH of brakes and the thud through the kitchen window and knew what it was. Holding a dish towel she went out the door across the dry short grass down the slope to the road. A black sedan was pulling away from a brown and white bundle at the side of the road.

She knelt stroking Rusty's head, her fingers bloody. He seemed to be looking at her and then the light in his eyes died and she felt him shift away. Biting her lip and crying she got the wheel barrow and put Rusty in it and took him to the barn, and when Dad got home from town with Troy and Mick they buried him under the elms by the hammock where he'd often waited for them to come back from school.

"They keep raising the speed limit," Dad had said a week ago. "Nobody wants it, but they're talking about making this a state highway."

She'd looked out at the lovely slope of grass, the little road, the valley with the stream and white church. Why didn't the people who lived in a place have the right to decide what happens to it? Nobody in this part of the county wanted faster roads or more houses. So why was it happening?

Maybe we're not so free, after all.

"I'M SENDING your records to Williams," Mr. Cohen the principal said.

"What's that?" Mick said.

"It's a small men's college in Massachusetts. Probably the best in the country."

"I'm going to Syracuse. They're giving me an athletic scholarship and a car."

"Williams is a better match for you."

Mick shrugged it off. "Why?"

"You like to get by easy, Mick. The only way you respond is challenge. At Williams you'll be up against some of the best brains in your generation."

"I would at Harvard too, but who'd want to go there?"

Mr. Cohen chuckled. "Funny thing is, you're not just saying that." He shut Mick's folder. "Case closed: your records are headed to Williams." He stood extending a long pale hand. "I've got fifty of your peers to find a college for. So get out of here."

NOW THAT THE SHOCK and sorrow of Ma's death had lessened, Tara had turned moody, distant and sometimes weepy and angry. She went to school dances and even had a boyfriend, a pimply creep named Justin that some day Troy would just have to kick the shit out of, teach him that life isn't really about Marcel Proust and T.S. Eliot and all that other crap that she and he worried about, and that living is much more important than reading about living. One night after making love in the barn Troy asked her if she was doing it with Justin too and she laughed, "You nuts?"

But he couldn't understand why Tara would want him so bad some times then snap at him or not talk to him for days. Was he, as she'd once said, a jerk and didn't know it? Or was she ashamed like him about making love but also couldn't stop?

Trouble was, Tara seemed to like Justin's combination of thinking all the time about the troubles of the world and his inability to do anything about it. She bossed the little creep but defended him if you said anything bad about him. But she always came to Troy's track meets and cheered for him, and night before a race she wouldn't let anybody make noise so he could sleep. How could she hate him and want him both?

Maybe she'd love him more if he read all those intellectual books that she and Justin had their noses in all the time. But Proust, for instance, was apparently a homosexual who stayed in bed all his life – what the fuck would he know about anything? And T.S. Eliot, how could you write such unnecessarily complex crap unless you were angling for a Nobel Prize?

It wasn't life. And he wasn't going to pretend he was interested in it just to please Tara.

He squinted across the pasture through the dust of his tilling toward the hazy setting sun. Life was bizarre, even this little rock we lived on, the galaxies racing away from each other – if, as Hubble pointed out, the universe is expanding from one point, what was *that* point, and what had happened before then? If time was infinite, why had the universe started then, at that particular point? It didn't make sense.

The thought of Mick's favorite expression made him grin: *Don't think, you'll hurt the team.* What Coach Louie always said. You have to run a play exactly by the book, each person choreographed like a chess game, but Mick kept arguing that as quarterback he could make decisions in a split second, wanted to pass more but the coach made him hand it off to that lunkhead McCaffrey who piled into people and never got very far.

Isn't that what the Fathers had told them in the orphanage: *Don't think, you'll hurt the team?* What Genesis was all about: God's job is to do the thinking; you're supposed to do what you're told and not try to understand. After Eve gave Adam the apple of knowledge and God kicked their ass out of the Garden, He was still thankful they hadn't found the secret of life. Because then they wouldn't need Him anymore.

Driving the old John Deere back to the barn Troy watched the sun sink into the haze till the western sky blazed with indeterminate light. Why was God always shown as light? A wave that changes frequencies, is slowed by gravity – that's God? He spat dust; people would be better off if instead of spending billions of hours worrying about God they'd put their minds to something positive. Like Mick said: *Show me someone who worries about God and I'll show you someone who don't get laid enough.*

Under that premise Mick sure never worried about God, he and his girlfriend Carol driving off to do it in the DeSoto's back seat or even at home when he didn't have football or baseball and Dad wasn't there and they'd come walking up over the hill holding hands and pretend they were going up to play guitar or study, the bed soon thumping the floor and her little cries driving Troy half crazy till he'd go outside and work on his car or anything, anything...

Carol and I don't love each other, Mick said, *we're just having fun.* How could you just have fun without love? It wasn't like that with Tara – was he going to love her for the rest of his life?

And what good would that do?

THE SUMMER BEFORE COLLEGE Mick drove trucks for the Coke plant, big lumbering GMCs with slide-up side doors from which he pulled down wooden cases of bottles and slung back cases of empties, delivering to corner markets, restaurants and grocery stores in Rockland County.

He loved the hard labor and the changing scenes and people, the sun hot on his face through the GMC's big windshield and on his arm through the open window full of all the scents of summer – spicy fresh-mown alfalfa, sun-warm bark of beeches and birches, black-furrowed soil, the redolent pastures of cattle and sheep, the cool moist air when the road went over a stream.

Wherever he sold, people upped their orders. "What I like," one corner grocer said, "is you never let me down. You always come when you say you will."

Mick shrugged it off but smiled, "Isn't everybody like that?"

"The way you work, you're gonna make somethin' of yourself some day."

He drove on, one arm out the window, shoulder warm in the sun, wind cooling his face, in the friendly grease, diesel and sun-hot plastic smell of the truck. Of course you worked hard, everybody should. It made you happy. How could you not work when your family needed it? Tara waiting tables full-time at Primo's Café on Main Street, Troy running the farm all by himself and delivering papers at four every morning; Dad's salary at the plastic factory had gone up. If only Ma were here.

TROY'S FOCUSED RIGIDITY bothered Mick. Why did he worry so much about meaningless shit? Who cared what space was made of? Maybe he'd done Troy no favor bringing him home long ago, had somehow tainted him. But that orphanage would've crushed anybody. And Troy had given *him* things: Troy's ability to narrow down his interests and energies to just his goal – even if Troy overdid it, Mick had learned it too. All that mattered was that Troy was happy. Was he?

Nor could he understand Tara's capriciousness: helping Troy with chores one night and snapping at him sarcastically the next, hugging him when he won a race and sardonic when he didn't. Anybody can like you when you win, but when you need it is when you're down.

He'd tried to explain to Troy that even though he and Carol weren't ever going to get married they were close friends and loved to make love. Carol was kind and fair and fun to talk to because she was so smart, might be the class valedictorian, and really pretty in a non-showoff way. When they made love she lay back in the DeSoto's seat and sighed *Ah the velvet darkness* and when she came stretched out her long dancer's neck, her eyes half-closed, and giggled.

Her Dad had been shot down in his P-51 over Italy at the end of World War Two, and her Mom then married this guy she'd known before and never wanted. So Carol had grown up in a home where every day her Mom wept for her dead pilot, the new husband regarded Carol with disinterest, and quickly fostered children of his own on Carol's mother.

Driving home one rainy night from Carol's Mick swerved to miss a raccoon and skidded into the ditch, the cutbank smashing the DeSoto's grille. The mud was too deep to back out; he walked the four miles home in the rain and snuck up the stairs past Dad snoring in the big bedroom and shook Troy awake.

"You dumb fuck," Troy mumbled. "How'd you do that?"

"Let's get the pickup and pull me out."

But when they backed out of the barn Dad came out with rain pelting off him. "You ain't hurt?" Dad said.

"No. But I busted the grille."

"Get down there and tow her out. We'll see tomorrow."

The pickup had no windshield so the rain came sheeting in, soaking them and running through cracks in the floor. Mick thought of long ago when Troy had torn the pickup's fender by the woodlot but had owned up to it right away, how Dad had liked that. Nothing was bad as when you lied about it. They pulled the DeSoto out but she wouldn't start so Troy towed her home, Mick steering, and in the morning she started right away and Dad drove off to work with grass and mud stuck in the caved-in grille.

MICK GOT A FOOTBALL scholarship to Williams. He got the one to Syracuse too and to Michigan and wanted to go there but with Troy and Tara going into their senior years at Nyack High and Dad sick, he knew he should stay closer to home. "Williams is the finest small college in the country," Mr. Cohen said. "It will give you opportunities you'd never get elsewhere."

Carol's father had gone to Williams before he joined the Army Air Corps to fight the Germans killing the Jews. Mick would carry on.

With the eight thousand four hundred dollars from selling the farm, Dad paid off all the bank loans and back taxes and rented a little house in Nyack so Tara and Troy could walk to school. The night before the farm was sold, Mick sat on the jack fence between the barn and house watching the sun set over the hills beyond the valley and white church, its red reflected in the house windows, the hammock loose between the oaks, the crows flying home to the forest for the night. He tried to sum up every moment he'd ever lived here, every moment Ma had been here, every furrow of the fields and tree he'd cut and split, the long-dead chickens and absent cows.

It was worse than sorrow. As if your whole insides had been dragged out and spread before you on the ground like one of those medieval torture racks.

Nothing would ever be the same. Like the book said, *you can't go home again.*

He walked heavy-legged down the pasture into the darkening woods, thought of coon hunting with Clem and Carl, that killing raccoons was like losing the farm, thought of cutting school to wander the forest, drink from the streams and track bobcats, climbing trees to avoid bears, losing one of his new shoes in quicksand and Dad coming down with him with a flashlight in the darkness, trying to find the shoe that had cost a day's milk production, patting his son's head on the way home, "That's all right, son, we'll buy you another pair," though wondering where to find the money had stilled Mick's heart.

The house was silent, no lowing of sleepy cows or clucking chickens, no light in the barn where Dad would be working on the John Deere or Ma cleaning out milk cans for the morning. He stood by the kitchen window hearing Ma's strong voice singing – *If you ever go across the sea to Ireland* – the night rustling in the elms, a barn owl swishing past, the wind lightly thunking the screen door – or *light a penny candle from a star* – I've got to fix these holes in the screen, he thought, caught himself.

Maybe it was for the good. Time to be moving on. But that was bullshit.

Maybe he should burn down the house and barn so the builders couldn't have them. But how can you set fire to yourself?

I WILL NOT be some idiot woman out of Jane Austen, Tara told herself. I will not forgive the plastic factory that makes Dad sick, the doctors who write prescriptions knowing he's sick and don't care, the assessor who raised our taxes so Dad had to sell to the developers who walk around our farm as if paying money made it theirs, after two hundred and fifty years of O'Briens working this land.

Men made all the trouble in this world. When they weren't killing each other they bombed cities so women and children died too. When Justin protested he was different she slapped him. "You don't even have the courage," she snapped, "to be who you are."

In May she met a guy with a motorcycle and a black leather jacket. He'd changed his first name to Dean because *Rebel Without a Cause* was the best movie ever. He had quit school, kept a pack of Marlboros rolled up in the sleeve of his t-shirt, had all of Elvis's records, worked at the bus station and had grease under his nails.

He took her for a ride on the bike, the wind flaming her hair, and in the woods she smoked one of his cigarettes and he laid his leather jacket on the ground and yanked off her black tights and white panties and screwed her hard for what seemed to go on forever, then dropped her at the little house in Nyack and never stopped the motorcycle again when he saw her on the sidewalk. *Fuck you.* She tossed her long hair. *I'll get you all.*

A month later she saw the motorcycle parked on Main Street. No sign of Dean. She crossed the street to Dave's Luncheonette. "Can I have some sugar cubes?"

Dave smiled down at her. *"What* are you up to now?"

She pocketed them, smiled. "Sweet tooth." She turned back up Main Street to the motorcycle.

No one seemed to be looking.

She unscrewed the gas cap, took a last glance round, and thrust in the handful of sugar cubes, twisted the cap tight, and walked up Main Street brushing sugar grains from her hands.

She never saw the motorcycle again.

Nor its noisome owner.

Always have the last blow, she told herself. Always.

SHE REFUSED ONE MORNING to stand up for the pledge of allegiance. "It's brainwashing," she told Miss Quinn, who took her to Mr.

Cohen's office. The principal waited till Miss Quinn had left. "But Tara, what's wrong with pledging allegiance to the country that protects you? That pays for this school, for instance?"

"When did I agree to be here?"

He chuckled, tucked his tie inside his coat. "Would you like to leave?"

"This instant."

"Fine." He nodded at the door. "But before you go, can I say a few things? Off the record, as it were?"

She shrugged. "Shoot."

"I've known your Dad for years. A finer man doesn't exist in this fallible world of ours. Your dear mother never finished high school but was the most intelligent person I've ever known; Mick's one of the smartest students this school has ever had the good fortune to have, and a fine young man to boot. Your brother Troy..."

"Adopted."

"– is already an excellent mathematician... He could make a contribution, a major contribution... I wish he'd go to MIT – they want him, you know?"

"I don't care where he goes."

He touched her wrist. "I only say this because you're a remarkable person too. There's nothing in this world you can't do..." His voice trailed off. "Like you, I don't understand why the best die and the useless and evil linger on. In the War, you know..."

He shook his head. "Look, Tara, I believe in you. All of us here do. We want you to have a wonderful life, and to give us all..." he blinked, "give the whole human race, the benefit of your mind, your incredible grace, the sound of your voice..."

Again, almost as if not wanting to, he touched her wrist. "Your voice can move mountains, my dear." He blinked again. "Use it for the good."

22

A GREATER COUNTRY

WILLIAMS WAS JUST three hours up the Taconic Parkway but in another universe. Mick had never had a dime he didn't spend with care or save, but some of his fellow freshmen would blow a hundred bucks in a night and never notice; some kept three vehicles on campus: an Austin Healey or TR3 for girls, a station wagon for traveling with friends, and a jeep or motorcycle for the mountains. Even though freshmen were not supposed to have cars.

He had never known that such wealth existed, never imagined the relaxed attitudes of these young men who would ease through life with more money than they could ever need, and never once fear not having it. For him near-poverty was a norm not only in his family but in his neighbors; in farm country everyone had lived at a level of cautious expenditure.

Set in rolling hills of beech, oaks and pines, Williams was opulent in a conservative New England way. Its old brick buildings, white Colonials, and wide lawns shaded by massive elms and oaks exuded privilege and unruffled competence, a belief that hard work, honor and wisdom were the keys to a good life. But Williams was isolated; there were no girls in classes and thus no incentive to study. The nearest girls were half an hour away at Bennington, an hour at Smith or Mount Holyoke, or three hours away at Wellesley and Radcliffe. And it was boring and unrewarding to spend all your time with other young men, the world of ideas was occasionally interesting but limiting, the mountains too easy to climb, the professors full of the importance of knowledge and thought, which were far less significant than girls.

His roommate, a huge defensive lineman from Nebraska named Link Doolittle, had arrived two weeks earlier for pre-practice, which Mick missed because he drove Coke trucks till the day before classes. Link had taken the bottom bunk and the desk by the window and had filled the closet with his thick jackets, a parka, and three suits. He snorted and mumbled in his sleep and seemed constantly congested. "This air smells like hogshit," he explained.

"I don't know what that's like," Mick said. "Apparently you do."

Link ignored him as someone unlikely to make the football team thus not worth talking to. In Link's few comments about his high school team Mick got a sense of endless parched prairies, long bus journeys, a truculent clannishness. Link seemed to live up to his last name, spending hours locked with *Playboy* in a bathroom stall. "Why don't you try to meet some Smith or Bennington girls?" Mick said.

"Smithies? Shit, think they're smart."

"Maybe because they are."

The first weeks he felt sickeningly lonely, a lesser person than the rich kids in his dorm. "My dad just bought a third plane," one said, "what the *hell's* he going to do with it?" or another's "We own the biggest chunk of *Time Life* but don't have enough voting rights," or, "That bitch, last Christmas in Gstaad we had the whole villa to ourselves but she wouldn't put out." Or others so rich they tried to hide it because their parents feared they'd be kidnapped like the Lindberg kid.

"My Dad coughs up his lungs every night from working at the plastic factory," Mick wanted to say, but felt ashamed. And there was the stigma attached to those who failed. In his occasional letter to Troy he didn't mention it but Troy seemed to sense it. *You won't fail, don't even think it,* Troy answered. *And don't be intimidated by rich assholes who've never done anything in their lives. Because you know how to run a farm and make a living.*

He quickly lost interest in the endless inane dorm arguments about the existence or non-existence of God. It was a waste of time, arguing with guys who didn't understand that religion's sole purpose was to mislead you into imagining death isn't the end. "Virtue is so boring," he told them. "It has no social value. It's just self-abuse."

Classes were intensely difficult – if you missed an hour it was hell to catch up – but the knowledge seemed to fall into his mind as if it had always been there waiting to be rediscovered. "Just read the damn stuff," he told Link, "and pay attention in class."

Some classes were interesting, but they were about things you already knew in your heart. Like *Thanatopsis*, Wordsworth or Camus, or Humboldt who after the French and American Revolutions wrote in *On the Limits of State Action* that individuals, in order to fully develop their potential, should be free to do what they wished as long as it harmed no one else.

It was the same moral question – where's the line between duty to oneself and to the group? In *On Liberty*, Mill criticized the tyranny of the majority, the rules and morals and laws imposed by the group on each individual. Every person, he said, has the right to decide how to live. The caveat was the same, the Harm Principle: providing it doesn't harm others. The question always was, of course, *How do you define harm?*

Because he'd started football late he ended as backup quarterback on the freshman team behind a tall tousle-haired Connecticut kid, Spark Levene, who threw hard and nearly perfect spirals and could sense where his receivers were even in a broken play. Spark's dad was a bigtime lawyer somewhere, testifying in Congress. "I don't know if I can beat Spark for starter," he told Dad the first weekend he hitched home.

"Don't matter," Dad rasped. "You made the team, kept your scholarship. You're there to study."

Glancing round the cramped Nyack kitchenette, Mick thought of the farm's huge kitchen with its black woodstove and the red plaid curtains Ma had made, the cabinets Dad had planed out of storm-downed maples. "I'll never make pro anyways."

"That's no way to live, getting hurt all the time. And no money in it."

"Anyway it would be boring," Troy said, "playing football all the time. You'd miss the world of ideas."

Mick wondered if this was true. "I don't give a damn about ideas..."

"Yes you do," Troy answered. "You're thinking all the time. You just don't show it."

Tara came in late and ignored Mick when he asked where she'd been. She seemed remote as if she didn't like him now he was a man, that alien race hounding her that she'd some day have to make peace with. "School's boring. I wanted to quit, but Mr. Cohen won't let me."

Mick thought of the walkabout with Troy years ago, of Mr. Cohen sending him to Williams. "He can't stop you."

She sucked at her lip. "What else would I do?"

"Go to Julliard?"

She tossed her head. Her hair, Mick noticed, had grown longer, not chopped carelessly around her collar bone. "I like *real* music," she said. "The *blues*. I like it *raw*."

"Like the Kingston Trio?"

She smiled dismissively. "You know Fats Domino – *Walking to New Orleans*, that they're playing on the radio all the time now, right?"

He shrugged. "Sure. And *Blueberry Hill*."

"Well that ain't nothing. You should hear Howlin' Wolf, who you ain't never heard of, he does *Smokestack Lightnin'* and *Little Red Rooster* – that's about sex, by the way – and Blind Lemon Jefferson and Son House, he sings jail music –"

He wondered why she was talking funny. "Tara, you're not a Negro. Why play their music?"

"I don't play it, I *sing* it."

"There's no future in that."

She eyed him darkly. "You always said forget the future, live in the now. Were you lying?"

He thought of Williams lecture halls echoing long-dead thoughts, the sodden bludgeoned football field, bright-eyed Bennington girls sliding tight jeans down long slim thighs. "To live well in the now you have to think sometimes about the future. We always live in what we've already made."

She shook her head, playing with a strand of hair. "Copout."

THE FIRST KENNEDY-NIXON DEBATE was on a Monday night in late September. There was a sense of expectancy: the world was going to change; who would lead it?

Nixon seemed evasive, eyes flitting back and forth like a cornered fox's, face sweaty and pale and seemingly unshaven, trying to sound authoritative but not succeeding. Kennedy was relaxed, upbeat, humorous at times. Nixon kept trying to claim a success of the last eight years, even though everyone knew Ike hated him and had even said he couldn't think of any presidential decisions Nixon had participated in.

The real difference, Troy said, is that Nixon keeps talking about the past and Kennedy about the future. "If we're moving ahead," Kennedy said, "freedom will be secure around the world. If we fail, then freedom fails. Therefore, I think the question before the American people is: Are we doing as much as we can do? Are we as strong as we should be?

"This is a great country," Kennedy went on, clearly in command of the debate. "But I think it could be a greater country. And this is a powerful country, but I think it could be a more powerful country. I'm not satisfied to have fifty percent of our steel-mill capacity unused. I'm not satisfied when the United States had last year the lowest rate of economic growth of any major industrialized society in the world... I'm not satisfied when... four million Americans wait every month for a food package from the government, which averages five cents a day per individual. I saw cases in West Virginia, here in the United States, where children took home part of their school lunch in order to feed their families... I'm not satisfied when the Soviet Union is turning out twice as many scientists and engineers as we are. I'm not satisfied when many of our teachers are inadequately paid... I'm not satisfied when I see men like Jimmy Hoffa – in charge of the largest union in the United States – are still free... I'm not satisfied until every American enjoys his full constitutional rights. If a Negro baby is born – and this is true also of Puerto Ricans and Mexicans in some of our cities – he has about one-half as much chance to get through high school as a white baby... I don't want the talents of any American to go to waste... Seventeen million Americans over sixty-five who live on an average Social Security check of about seventy-eight dollars a month, they're not able to sustain themselves individually, but they can sustain themselves through the social security system. I don't believe in big government, but I believe in effective governmental action. And I think that's the only way that the United States is going to maintain its freedom."

Turning to the viewers, Kennedy summed it up: "Can freedom in the next generation conquer, or are the Communists going to be successful? That's the great issue. And if we meet our responsibilities I think freedom will conquer. If we fail, if we fail to move ahead, if we fail to develop sufficient military and economic and social strength here in this country... the tide could begin to run against us..."

The difference could not have been clearer: Nixon trying to catch up with Kennedy's ideas, mouthing sour criticisms and evasive asides. Kennedy brilliant, cheerful, determined, confident.

Who would you want to lead your country? What astonished Troy was that some people preferred Nixon – is there something deep-grained within them, he wondered, that won't let them *see?*

IN TARA AND TROY'S senior year at Nyack High the classes were easy, but somehow irrelevant. Too much had happened: Ma's death, the child Tara and Troy had killed, the farm sold, the barns empty, weeds high in the hayfields. She and Troy living with Dad in this little house in Nyack that Dad had bought "so they could walk to school" – as if that mattered – it all made her feel tired and confused. Rootless, she thought, that's what I am.

What did matter was Dad was getting sicker and sicker, but the plastics company doctor wouldn't say so. Said it was an allergy due to the new house, something Dad would get over. But night after night she lay in bed trying to sleep, hearing him hack his lungs out downstairs at the kitchen table, a whisky in his hand.

Finally she came down in her bathrobe and fluffy slippers, unable to help but wanting to share his suffering, be with him. At first he'd got crochety and sent her back upstairs, but after several nights she could sit with him past midnight as he fought for breath and, slowly, word at a time, told her about his life and what promise he saw in hers.

"Moment I met your Ma," he waited, suppressing a cough, "I was gone. I'd had no intention of getting serious about any girl – I was a Marine, soon headed overseas. Chances were fifty-fifty I'd come back."

She reached out a small cold hand, clenched his thick hairy wrist. "Thank God you did."

He chuckled, caught his breath. "Don't get religious on me now."

"No, I just use the word God to express thankfulness."

"But then I saw your Ma, one night across a room, with her beautiful eyes and kind, lovely face..." He tried not to choke. "And I was gone." He smiled at her, his eyes shiny. "Gone."

"She was always so beautiful, so kind..."

"Two weeks later we was married. What a great gift..." He smiled. "In no time at all we'd made your brother. Then I went overseas, and when I came back we made you."

She nodded, not liking this detailed confidence, the idea of Ma and Dad doing it, having fun, when for Tara sex was Troy – electric and forbidden.

"So you'll have someone who'll smite you, Darling, don't you worry... You're only seventeen, still in high school. You can't imagine the wonders ahead."

Tara took a breath, glanced at the clock. One-eleven a.m. The very thought of the future made her even more weary.

23

SKULL CAVE

F OR THE SECOND DEBATE a week later, the family gathered round the television at Hal and Sylvia's place, Tara cross-legged on the footstool, Troy on the floor in front of her, Sylvia on a kitchen chair, teacup in her hand, the saucer on her knee, Dad and Uncle Hal standing like they'd only watch a minute. The young Senator from Massachusetts had long dark hair and movie looks, but what he was saying was so true and came from the heart, Tara decided. You couldn't speak like that if it didn't come from the heart.

"Jesus I hope he wins," Dad said when it was over and Howard K. Smith was looking seriously into the camera and you knew he too was rooting for Kennedy because how could anyone like slimy little Nixon with his pushed-up nose and pear-shaped cheeks looking like every time he smiled it hurt.

"This election's important," Dad said. "For the entire future of our country. Whether we can get along with the Russians without blowing up the world –"

"We had an atomic war drill today," Tara said. "Had to squeeze under our desks for five minutes while the sirens went off, like it was a real atomic bomb."

"He's sure got a nice wife," Aunt Sylvia said.

187

"Yeah," Hal added, "she's a piece of ass."

"It's unfortunate, folks don't like people who've had it easy –"

"Kennedy's had it easy? Lost his brother on a secret commando mission against the Krauts, then he was badly wounded fighting the Japs? What more you want?"

"He may find being President," Sylvia said, "is even tougher."

"The people for Nixon," Dad said, "it's like they're afraid of something. They're watchful and don't trust folks. Nixon helped McCarthy's witch hunts that cost so many people their jobs... I wonder if you could know whether somebody's a Democrat or Republican by how happy they were growing up?"

"Every time I see Nixon's pointy little face on that television," Uncle Hal said, "I want to smack him. He's fishy."

"They say even Ike can't stand him," Dad said. "Not that that means much."

"I never was that fond of Ike," Hal said. "But from the Army point of view he was a good general. Tried to win the war without getting half of us killed."

Dad slapped his brother's shoulder. "Hell, you guys were almost good enough to be Marines."

"Anyone can be a Marine. They just have to be stupid and mean."

"You'd have to be stupid to *mean* that –"

"The economy's gone to Hell, unemployment's up – maybe Kennedy can get us moving again –"

"After Eisenhower's eight Jurassic years," Dad added.

"D'you read that *Profiles in Courage* Kennedy wrote? About Senators with guts?"

"He should be in that book himself, for his bravery after his torpedo boat got sunk. And he'll hunt down the Mafia, Hoffa and that crowd –"

"But a lot of people," Sylvia said, "won't vote for a Catholic."

"People change, don't they?"

. . .

1960 ENDED with a sense of hope and dynamism that even the most negative seemed to acknowledge. JFK's inaugural speech the next January 20 was a powerful call to action, a revolutionary appeal for peace and international cooperation.

"Man holds in his mortal hands the power to abolish all forms of human poverty and all forms of human life. And yet the same revolutionary beliefs for which our forebears fought are still at issue around the globe... We dare not forget today that we are the heirs of that first revolution..."

Both the west and east, however, were "overburdened by the cost of modern weapons, both rightly alarmed by the steady spread of the deadly atom, yet both racing to alter that uncertain balance of terror that stays the hand of mankind's final war..."

"He's right," Uncle Hal said. "That's the big tomato."

"Quiet!" Sylvia snapped. "I want to hear."

"Let us never negotiate out of fear," Kennedy was saying. "But let us never fear to negotiate... Let both sides seek to invoke the wonders of science instead of its terrors. Together let us explore the stars, conquer the deserts, eradicate disease, tap the ocean depths, and encourage the arts and commerce..."

"That's a lot of stuff," Hal said.

"Shut *up!*" Sylvia said.

"And so, my fellow Americans," he concluded, "ask not what your country can do for you – ask what you can do for your country. My fellow citizens of the world – ask not what America will do for you, but what together we can do for the freedom of man."

"Holy shit!" Uncle Hal said. "I think he means it."

"Yeah," Dad nodded. "Maybe he can get it done."

ONCE FOOTBALL SEASON ended it was easier to study, because then Mick wasn't exhausted and sore all the time. But the boredom of classes drove him crazy till he discovered cave exploring, going every weekend with two seniors, Tim Rawlings and Avram Spielberg, down one dark constricting cavern after another.

Skull Cave was named because of the people who died trying to reach its end. You climbed down a sinkhole in the middle of a farmer's field deep in the Adirondacks where a stream from the forested hills poured over a waterfall straight into the earth. Most of the year the water in the cave was too high to get through, but in winter it was sometimes accessible. Because of other cavers' deaths the farmer had blocked it and put up *No Trespassing* signs.

They hid the car in the forest and crunched across the midnight snow of the farmer's field. A scant moon lit the snow, shadowing grass stalks bent by the wind. The black sinkhole opened at their feet. They lit their carbide headlamps but the wind blew them out. They rappelled seventy feet down through the waterfall into a thundering frigid pool where the water sucked down a black borehole into the earth with a ghoulish roar.

Knee-deep in the pool they relit their lamps, checked ropes and gear, and one by one squirmed down the borehole into total darkness, trying to keep their faces above the frigid rushing water. After about a quarter mile the borehole ended atop what seemed a tall underground cliff where the water roared over the side, hammering far below into the rocks. They could not see the bottom, only sleek black cliffs descending into darkness. They roped up and rappelled down.

At the bottom was a jumble of slippery icy boulders and chunks of fallen cliff. They could not hear each other over the crashing water. Air whooshing from somewhere put out their lamps; everywhere they stepped they slipped, could not see where was safe and where was the abyss. In the cave less than an hour, they were already soaked and numb and giddy with cold and excitement. Mick had never seen such total darkness, could not imagine it was real.

In a pool under the lower cliff by the light of their lamps they found a grooved tube called by earlier explorers the Rifle Barrel. It was no bigger round than a slender person's chest, so you had to keep your arms at your sides and wriggle down it in darkness, pushed by the water building up behind you. As you slid and banged down the tube you had to keep your mouth up and to the side to reach the sliver of air along the top; in places there was no air, you had to worm forward holding your breath and hoping for an air hole.

After half an hour the Rifle Barrel spit them into a wide subterranean pool. Their gasps and shivers echoed in the tomblike dark. Water was spattering down from everywhere. The pool's current was pulling them along. Avram's wax-covered flashlight showed slab walls soaring into blackness. "This's just the start," he called. "Lots of people get this far."

The current carried them through a long underground canyon, the cliffs vertical and unclimbable on both sides, till a small sandbar opened on the right. Like shipwrecked survivors they crawled up on it, gasping and shivering. Once they had poured fresh carbide into the helmet lamps and relit them Mick felt safer, reassured. This was fun, adventure, nothing really dangerous. They were too smart, too young, to die.

For the next eight hours they worked downward, stopping to eat on a narrow gravel beach under a great rock pillar. With stiff legs they followed it to the end, where the river sank into a hole in the side of a great black cliff. "This's it," Avram said. "Far as anyone's gone."

They stumbled in circles rubbing their bodies, trying to warm up. "Any ideas?" Mick mumbled, "what's beyond?" It was hard to talk without stammering.

"I'll just switch on my X-ray vision," Tim said.

"Fuckin' cold," Avram said. "Carbide's low."

There was no air gap at the top of the hole. The entire river went into it, backing up and roiling to get in. The cliff wall was unclimbable without pitons, and probably led nowhere.

He couldn't bear the idea of getting this far and stopping. "The other tubes, like the Rifle Barrel, there was usually a little air at the top. You belay me down," he added. "Give me twenty feet, if I don't find air I'll come back up."

"You'll come back up," Tim mimicked. "How?"

"I'll give three tugs and you pull me."

"Water's pushing so hard, how we going to know it's you?"

"I'll go down a few feet, then, see what I find." He felt noble, brave, ready to take on the world, to show he was less afraid than they.

Cold blackness sucked him down, hammering his eyes and face, crashing into his mouth, the rope a vise around his waist. He wanted terribly to breathe, have them yank him back up. Wait another few seconds he kept telling himself, suddenly slammed onto a sandy beach. He pulled the rope five times, the signal to come down, and relit his lamp as Avram shot out of the tunnel onto the beach. "Tim's staying," he stuttered. "Too cold. Tied off the rope. So you can come back up."

"Jesus," Mick said, stunned to realize he'd never thought of it, how they were going to get back up this hole unless they left the rope there.

"We're getting goofy," Avram said. "Time to go back."

"What are we, maybe two and a half miles down?"

"Too far."

Across the water Mick could see in the yellowish beam of his lamp a wide valley extending downriver, its soil unmarred. Never before in all time, he realized, had anyone been here. He noticed the gridlike prints of his boots. Never before had a human footstep touched this place. "I'm going further."

"No way."

"I'll wait till you go back up this tube. Then give me half an hour." He didn't dare look at Avram for fear he'd want to come too, knelt and drank a handful from the river. "C'mon, go back up there."

"I'll wait for you here."

"Tim won't know what you're doing. Get going."

"How you gonna tell, a half hour?"

"I'll just go a little ways." Mick was frantic now for Avram to leave. "You're using up my time."

With a shrug Avram swam to the bottom of the tube, found the rope, tugged three times and squirmed into the cascade pouring out of the tube. For a long time his boots thrashed and scraped at the bottom of the tube, then he was gone. Mick looked around himself into the dark wide cavern. He was the only person in the universe.

With a rare joy he wandered downriver, swimming across it each time the cliffs came down to the edge and blocked one side. The sight of the untouched earth was rhapsody, the slick cliffs that had never been seen or touched, the slippery soil unmarred since the beginning of time. It was like being inside a woman, going backwards into birth. Wasn't that what navel-gazing meant, following one's life back up the umbilical cord to the beginning? To when you were a single cell? Before you were a cell?

His lamp sputtered; he added carbide but still it worked poorly. There was a freeness to the air, of never been breathed. Nirvana. It was okay to die if you could die in this place. Sacred here, a seed deep in the womb of the earth.

He saw a woman's belly, Daisy. The lovely place from the navel down into soft fur, the sweet crease beneath. *God I miss you.*

"Hurry up, Mick!" she whispered. "Get back out!"

As he slogged back up the river valley his feet were so numb it felt he was walking on stilts. He got lost repeatedly then remembered to look for his tracks, went back and followed them till his lamp went out. "Hurry up!" she repeated. "Go!"

He kept rasping the flint but got no spark, his fingers too numb to pick a new flint out of the little plastic case. He wanted to cry, kept himself from throwing the flints away, breathed into his hands till the fingers loosened enough to pull out a new one and insert it into the back of the lamp. He added new carbide and water and struck the flint. Still it wouldn't start.

On hands and knees he crawled up the river canyon in total blackness, feeling for his tracks in the soft earth. Each time he swam the river it was hard to find his tracks on the other side. It seemed too good to be true when heard the water rushing out of the tube and minutes later found the rope and tugged it.

"We should have left you," Tim said when Mick climbed out of the tube.

"Got lost," Mick said, couldn't remember anything else.

It took ten more hours before they stood exhausted knee-deep in the pool under the waterfall of the sinkhole. In the dark circle at the top of a few stars shone fiercely. It took every ounce of energy to climb the seventy feet back up the rope to the top of the sinkhole. It was already midnight: they'd spent twenty-four hours underground. Their soaked clothes froze when they crossed the farmer's field. The little car warmed slowly as they drove east through the mountains toward the rising moon.

He'd fallen for the ecstasy of the unknown, he realized as he sat in dull classes remembering Skull Cave. *L'extase de l'inconnu.* Locked inside its chest-constricting tunnels, the weight of the earth crushing you, the thrashing through black rivers and dangling down black unknown cliffs, in a world never seen by any other human, was a metaphor for what life could be. A recognition, non-rational, that this is what joy *is*. *This* is how to live.

24

NEXT TIME YOU'RE OUT

TARA COULDN'T DECIDE about college. Sure, she'd made a couple applications, NYU and Rutgers. But what she really wanted was Berkeley. The music scene out there was *fantastic*, a folksinger who'd played one night in Nyack told her. She'd sent an application, but there was no point. So far away, how would she pay to get there even if she got in?

You had to expect things not to go right. She still felt lost and alone, but she would come out of it. Since Ma's death everything was senseless, barren. But that was normal. It's not about death, she told herself. I've killed enough chickens to know that. Maybe it's just I've got no one to talk to anymore.

Sure, she had friends but they lived in a different universe: with two parents, already at seventeen worrying about husbands and babies, their fathers not crippled with lung disease. She couldn't imagine life with so little to strive for.

Music is your only friend. How it comes up from your gut through your chest and soars into the night. It's free and you're its instrument but you can make it sound what you like. And it makes you *feel* like nothing else. From your throat to the tips of your fingers and toes. *I been gone so long, Lord, I don't know how to get home.* A need that hurts, closer than any friend.

THE FIRST GIRL who stayed overnight in Mick's room was a lissome red-haired Bennington freshman named Tina. Link slept on the living room couch. Next morning Link stared at Mick gravely. "I have to turn you in to the Dean for that."

"For what?"

"That girl spent *all* night in your room. The college rules are girls allowed in the bedrooms only on Sunday afternoons from two to five, and three out of four feet have to be on the floor."

"That sounds like an interesting position," he said to annoy Link. "And sorry about your sleeping on the couch. But any time you have a girl and want the room –"

"What use are rules if we don't live by them?"

"So *who* made them? And for whose benefit?" He shook Link's shoulder as if to wake him. "Why should the College care if we get laid?"

But Link told the Dean and Mick was restricted to campus for a month. He thought of breaking Link's lean unempathetic jaw, but then he'd get expelled.

There was another way to get Link. "Let's go over the Hill," he suggested to Peter Weisman, his best receiver, small, compact and incredibly fast. "I haven't gotten laid since I got restricted," he nodded at Link poring over his math tables, "thanks to the Missing Link, here."

"You know the rules," Link said. "Stop whining."

"I thought of kicking your ass. But then I'd get thrown out."

Link looked up from his book. "You do it again, I do it again."

"I'll go over the Hill with you," Peter said.

"Then let's go." Mick stood. "C'mon, Link."

Link gave them a pained expression. "Where?"

"Albany," Peter said. "Come on, you'll have fun."

Link stood, stretched. "I'll go for the ride. But I don't want to try anything."

An hour later they parked Peter's yellow VW under a working streetlight in the ghetto. The bar on the corner was narrow and dim, a few sullen inebriated men trying to play pool, *Where did our love go?* on the jukebox, the tang of cheap rum, malt liquor, roach spray and cigarettes, the weary odor of people going nowhere.

Several women at the bar who were trying to make customers out of drunken men looked up when the white boys came in. Mick sat on stool and a pretty woman about forty with straight-lacquered hair slid down beside him. They had a beer and she put her hand on his wrist, "C'mon honey, I'll take you upstairs."

He tickled her hand. "Do me a favor?"

"Sweetheart I ain't into nothin too kinky."

"See that guy over there?"

She looked past him at Link. "The one come in with you?"

"Yeah. Can you do him?"

She smiled. "I can do anyone, honey. Who's payin'?"

"If he don't I will."

She gave him a wide smile. "N how bout you?"

"You got a friend?"

Her friend was a teenager who came downstairs tugging irritably at her pigtails and looking sleepy. She took him up to an L-shaped attic with a stained bed and a bald black man passed out on the floor, took his ten bucks, lay down and pulled up her skirt.

"Take everything off," he said, aching with anticipation. Annoyed, she pulled the skirt over her head, and he fell on her, crazed with desire, driving into her then pulling out to lick her crotch, the wiry metallic taste of her hairs on his tongue. "Cool it or you pay extra!" she grunted. He laughed, pinning her thighs to her chest to drive deep inside her. "Hey," she said, "stop pulling out!"

"Otherwise I come too soon –"

The joy of lust was on him, the fire of youth. Then it was spent and he lay on his back on a sticky mattress with a stranger who didn't care if he lived or died as long as he paid, a girl with whom he shared only a common species and language and a recent sex act.

Going downstairs he met Link's woman coming up with another man. "How'd it go, your cherry?" Mick said.

"It didn't. You gotta tell that boy, it's okay to love."

The mountain air felt cool through the car windows as they drove back over the Hoosacs. "It's good to do this," Peter said, "once in a while."

"I always feel funny afterwards," Mick said. "Then a week later, if I haven't had a girl, I'm going crazy till I do it again."

"Lust is life."

"How was it?" Mick called to Link in the back.

"It was fine. No – it was great. Thanks."

"It's very philosophical," Peter said. "You should always do what you want before what you have to. Because you can die the next moment..."

"That's such bullshit," Mick laughed.

Peter geared down as the road twisted higher into the hills. "Think if you had to choose between fucking and doing your homework? Do what you want first, then when you're tired of fucking maybe the homework will look interesting. It certainly won't when all you want to do is fuck. If you live this way, truly and honestly, and being smart about listening to yourself, you'll come out on top."

"I like having the *girl* on top," Mick said.

"NEXT TIME YOU'RE OUT." Dean Brooks peered wearily at Mick over the tops of his reading spectacles. "I don't care how much your coaches beg me to keep you."

"Link is crazy, complaining about me. He wanted to go to Albany."

"You were restricted to campus." Dean Brooks ran a bony hand over his bald pate, slapped it down on his huge hardwood desk. "You're so damn intelligent, Mick, why can't you just watch yourself, study a little sometimes? Leave girls alone for a while?"

"Maybe I'm in the wrong place."

"Here? At Williams?"

"Studying is not my thing. I'm not *philo-sophos*, I'm *philo-bios*: it's not wisdom I love, but life."

"Isn't studying a way to understand life?"

"Living is *my* way to understand life."

Dean Brooks smiled, an elegant, disappointed gesture. "No matter what, next time you're out."

THE LETTER from Berkeley came April 27. Accepted, full scholarship. Tara's tears spotted the page. *I'll hitch out there* – saw herself with a guitar over one shoulder, a ratty suitcase. *On the road.*

Half-blinded she went into the cramped kitchen where Dad sat coughing at the table, whisky in his hand. He stood and held her, her tears dampening his rough shirt. "That's lovely, honey." He kissed the top of her head. "Your Ma'd be so proud –"

She shook her head. "Costs too much to get way out there."

"There'll be money." He pulled back. "They're givin' me a settlement. For the problem in my chest. We can use that."

THERE WERE NO NEGROES on the Williams baseball or football teams, few if any on the teams they played. The few blacks at Williams were mostly sons of wealthy African diplomats and played soccer rather than football, and kept to themselves and a few of the more iconoclastic whites.

Thinking of how he'd viewed Negroes in his mind, hardly ever knowing any except Molly years ago when he and Troy had ridden the rails, Mick realized he'd categorized them as cool but limited to who they were, boxed in by their own image, by his image of them. It was hard to imagine ever being close, discussing one's deepest concerns. It seemed alien.

Sure, Jackie Robinson had broken the baseball color barrier way back in 1947, and since then many had followed – Roy Campanella, Satchel Paige, Willie Mays and others. But there were few Negroes in the National Football League. Some teams, like the Redskins, had to be forced by President Kennedy to open their rosters. But the American Football League was open to all. They were actively recruiting from the black colleges, which the NFL refused to do. For the AFL all you had to do was have talent. Lots and lots of talent. And want to play football more than anything else on earth.

There were so many good black football players out there. Guys like Lionel Taylor and Willie Lanier. Hundreds of young guys nobody'd ever heard of or ever would. Why weren't some of them playing for Williams?

Conversely, at Williams the CIA was over-represented. Williams had more top people at the Agency, it was rumored, than any other school. Except possibly Yale.

The head of the CIA had gone to Williams. And his son had been Mick's biology lab partner. A lot of guys had CIA connections but never talked about it. You couldn't tell, sometimes, who was who.

HE GOT ARRESTED by accident. Susan was a tall sinuous blonde from Sarah Lawrence with a voracious smile, hazel eyes and a blue Austin Healey. He'd made two fake driver's licenses with their ages as twenty-one, and used his to buy a bottle of Jim Beam. They went to a bar in North Adams and he put the bottle in its brown bag on the floor of the booth. They ordered beers and showed the licenses; the bartender brought the beers and when he'd gone Mick poured Jim Beam into each beer and she smiled locking her ankles around his under the table and he felt joyous knowing they were going to make love.

He wanted to leave right then but instead they danced, her body tight against him, and sat in the booth drinking more beers and Jim Beam, listening to Paul Anka, holding hands and looking forward to the night.

A man in a raincoat came in and the bartender nodded at Mick and Susan. The man came to the booth and flashed his badge asking for IDs and then said *Son these are false. You both have to come with me.*

As they stood up in the booth Mick's foot knocked over the Jim Beam on the floor and the cop took that too and Mick and Susan spent the night in jail instead of making love and she would never speak to him again and Dean Brooks said, "We're giving you a year off, Mick, at the end of this semester. I talked to your coaches and they understand. Think of it as being red-shirted. Anyway you're a year young for your class. When you come back you'll be the same age as your peers."

"You'll take me back?"

Dean Brooks grinned, his bald head shining as he leaned forward to shake Mick's hand. "Long as you're not arrested for grand larceny or the like."

Dad tried to hide his disappointment, as if fearing to further undermine Mick's confidence. "I can get through Williams," Mick said. "It's just so damn boring! You sit there with the smell of new grass outside and birds singing and the blue sky and white clouds you can see through the window, and how the hell can anyone stay in there?"

"Shit," Dad answered, for a while said nothing further, as if he'd summed up the problem. "Nobody wants to study when he could be outside in the sun and screwing girls and going fishing and all that good stuff. Nobody but idiots. But you still have to do it."

Mick was caught for an instant wondering how many girls Dad once had screwed, shied away. "Why?"

"Or the people who do stay inside studying will someday enslave you."

"Fuck that," Mick said morosely. "That makes you an idiot too."

Dad knocked back his whisky. "You talk about French literature – Camus this, Sartre that, Saint-Exupéry, that Hemingway book you gave me –"

"*A Moveable Feast.*"

"Christ, and Henry Miller, *Quiet Days in Clichy*? That was quite a book. Hell, Grampy said he shoulda stayed in Paris with those madamaselles after the First War."

"You wouldna been born. Nor me or Tara."

"Why not work this summer and fall for Coke?" Dad leaned forward, hands clasped. "Then do spring semester in France? Then you can work next summer and go back to Williams in the fall?"

25

BURN DOWN THE WORLD

I N THE FALL Troy left for the Air Force Academy and Tara for Berkeley. The Academy's discipline and detail came to Troy automatically, as if he'd always lived it. The rest of the world, the soft undisciplined entertainment-seekers, was insignificant, unreal. Pity we're training to risk our lives to save *them*. But that's what I signed on for.

The Academy was like the Boys' Home, driven by the need to dominate and denigrate. Troy hated the nastiness of the upper classmen who picked on the new ones, made them serfs because once *they* had been picked on, made serfs. "I can't see how it teaches anything military," he said.

"It inculcates numb obedience," a cadet named Throcker said.

"Obedience to your CO," another named Coulton added. "No matter who he is."

But is it always right, Troy wondered, to follow your CO? Suppose he's wrong and leads you into danger?

The principles of war. The science of killing. When you peeled off the image that's what the Academy really was: a place that taught young men how to manage steel machines in the sky to better kill and destroy people and places on the earth.

But he didn't want to kill, had to admit it. Killing a buck every fall hurt his soul but it was food for the family. Yanking a turkey's neck across a pine block and chopping through it was the same: feeding your loved ones. And the kid. The kid he and Tara had killed, who smiled at Troy from his playpen every day, and cooed to him at night.

To drop a steel tube of high explosives on people far down below, people you've never seen, didn't seem what Christ would want. It chilled his spine. He didn't want to kill, he wanted to reach the moon.

President Kennedy wanted to catch the Russians in space. That meant a man on the moon. But with what delivery system, what landing module? How to get fuel for the return? All impossible.

Some cadets didn't like Kennedy because he was a Democrat or because he was a Catholic, even though he was a real war hero not a coward like Nixon. But Troy defended Kennedy because he'd get us into space. It was all part of Kennedy's New Frontier.

After the moon Mars was next. By the time Troy was forty, in 1983, humans could be living on Mars. The Academy was the first step, because wherever NASA went the Air Force was going to be headed. "Test pilots," a professor told him, "NASA's going to use test pilots for astronauts."

I'm going to be a test pilot, Troy had decided.

Soon he'd start flying lessons. Already he'd spent hours on the Link Trainer; every free half-hour running to the classroom off the Parade Loop to leap into the Link, knew the instruments by heart, the commands, could take off and land flawlessly.

Next would be glider school, the sailplanes with the student in the front and the instructor behind. Then you were in the T-28, with an 800-horse Wright that was slow to respond but had plenty of tail-end power. Then the T-37, a twin-engine jet they called The Screamer because of its small engine intakes, a low-down nasty airplane that could take you there and back just like combat.

But it's really hard, he wrote Dad. *This cult of blind obedience – I can see it in warfare, maybe, but not for learning? What are we learning? Not to think for ourselves? That's what they're inculcating and I'm not sure it's good. And there's too much pride in it, in this blindness – "I can be a better automaton than you" – Pride of the enslaved who will one day be enslavers.*

My personal slavemaster is a third-year cadet named Steward Metcalf. A pimple-faced guy from Concrete, Washington. For him I have to run silly errands, polish his boots and shoes, iron his uniform, do pushups and whatever else enters his otherwise vacant mind. "You're going to crash and burn," he told me first day, adding, "I'll be laughing as you go."

So it's a mix of fear and excitement, the worry I've made the wrong choice, that I should've gone to MIT like Mr. Cohen wanted. But I can make it here and I owe this to you. Ever since my earliest memory I've wanted to fly. Without you I never would have been here.

Tough it out, Dad wrote back. *Of course you can make it but don't kill yourself trying to be first. Whatever you do, wherever you go, remember: you're already fine the way you are.*

BERKELEY stunned Tara with its bright clarity of sun and sky glinting off white buildings and voluptuous tan hills. She was intoxicated by the cool, salty wind from the Bay, the warm night breeze down from the hills, the cafés and bistros alive with espresso and wine, the sidewalks thick with young intense people, the sense of easy freedom.

"San Francisco's even groovier," her roommate Juliet said, snapping her gum. "North Beach has all these coffee houses, Italian restaurants, poetry readings, cool bars full of beatnik artists – you can get an ounce for fifteen bucks –"

"An ounce?" Tara said, thinking of recipes.

"Grass, silly!"

"Oh." Tara nodded. That stuff that a junior named Liam had tried to get her to smoke. That made her cough. Would wreck your voice.

Juliet crackled her gum. "They let you into bars sometimes..." She tugged from her purse a California Driver's License coated in plastic, a dim photo. "Says I'm twenty-one'n a half. Randy over in Campbell, he'll make you one if you fuck him."

Here the sun wasn't like back east. It had a dry deep heat sinking into her shoulders as she sat cross-legged on the thick grass reading Goethe, *Du wandelst jetzt wohl still und mild,* chasing the words down one by one in the dictionary, conscious of the raw German and of the sun heating the back of her neck and the sweet crinkly fragrant grass and the dance of light and shadows on the golden hills.

Even classes were fun: there was a purpose to learning. Everything was brighter, more alive, more erotic, as if paradise were closer, beauty of place united with intensity of thought. As if things *could* be understood and it *was* possible to make the world better.

"This's like heaven," she told Juliet. "Not that I think there's such a place."

"Depends on your LOT."

"Your lot in life?"

"Your Life Orgasm Total – the higher it is the further up the wheel of Paradise you go."

TO TROY THE ROCKIES were stunning in their crystalline beauty and dry high air, their peaks snowy even in September, their stark sleek slopes of fir and pine, ragged rocky ridges and red sandstone pinnacles and canyons with icy trout-filled streams.

And there was cross country. The joy of running fleet-footed over the rough piney soil, breathing steady and relaxed, legs stretching out effortlessly, almost flying. For the first weeks the altitude had left him gasping after runs. But once he got in shape, whenever he had a few free hours he ran up the 13-mile Barr Trail to the top of 14,000-foot Pike's Peak, scorning the flabby tourists who had driven cars or taken the cog railway to the top, scorning the doughnut stands and souvenir shops, but entranced by the white-gold prairie so far below, the granite ridges and velvety forests, the sky so blue it was almost black. *Closer to the stars.*

And he liked the wide-streeted Colorado Springs downtown of red sandstone buildings, and to the east the magnificent emerald prairies that when the sun went down behind the Rockies turned the color of blood.

I know I can make it, he wrote Tara. *I love it but I'm afraid... You should come visit. Colorado's a beautiful place.* When he wrote this he almost tore up the page but he'd already filled the other side and didn't want to rewrite. *I've given myself away,* he thought wryly, but didn't know how.

When he could he hid out in the library studying aeronautics texts. Far back in 1915, Robert Goddard had created both the multi-stage and the liquid-fueled rockets, but only now, 45 years later, were they being truly implemented. In 1919 Goddard had written *A Method of Reaching Extreme Altitudes,* full of brilliant ideas ignored for half a century. If you're going to succeed, Troy reminded himself, don't expect the credit.

All Goddard's life people had made fun of him. *The New York Times,* of course, had caustically dismissed his ideas. But while the Americans ridiculed him and the Army Air Corps ignored his designs, the Germans under Werner von Braun used them to create the V2 and other weapons of mass death. That was the problem with advancing the human mind: it could be used to help or to kill.

He was transfixed by Goddard's recollection of climbing a cherry tree in 1893 behind his childhood home, and having a sudden inspiration how to send a rocket to Mars. "I was a very different boy when I descended the tree from when I ascended," Goddard had written. "Existence at last seemed very purposive." And this was ten years before the Wright brothers' first flight.

If you have a task that fulfills you, Troy realized, existence *is* purposive.

By November he had talked his way into aircraft design, stunned by the beauty and simplicity of flight. *It's thrust and lift versus gravity,* he wrote Dad. *Everything comes down to that.*

A week later when Steward Metcalf was decapitated in a glider crash while on approach for the field east of the Academy, Troy felt guilty as though he'd killed him by wishing him gone. In December he broke the freshman indoor mile record at 4:19:32, a stunning time given the 7,200-foot altitude. The older cadets stopped harassing him and those in his class seemed to view him with respectful distance. It rarely occurred to him that he had no friends; perhaps that was what the Academy was all about.

TWO WEEKS BEFORE Christmas vacation, at an Oakland party full of blues and Motown, the air blue with weed smoke, Tara bumped into a tall black man in a lilac jacket, silver slacks and crimson cowboy boots. "Watch your big feet," she said.

"I'm too busy watchin' you."

"Well cut it out."

He took her wrist as she pushed past. "Ain't you the one that sings?"

She pulled away. "Everybody sings."

"You the one. Tara O'Brien."

"So who are you?"

"Blade."

"Shit. Really?"

"Come in here." He nodded at a bedroom door. "I want to hear you sing."

It was a wide room with orange curtains and a kingsize bed in the middle and a wall of guitars. "Sly won't mind," Blade said, "we play one of his." He took down a worn Martin with a scratched top, sat on the bed. "What you wanna sing?"

The wall of gleaming guitars made her nervous and unsure. "*Black Cat Blues*? The way you do it?"

He led into it gently, the soft notes and the deep chords giving her a platform to throw her voice on, and she watched his eyes glisten and that made her sing even freer, brighter, till suddenly the room was full of people in rapt silence and she broke down for an instant in this communion with them and the core of song and life, caught herself and cleared her voice.

"Whoa," Blade shook his head. "You something, girl."

"Sing another one," someone said. "Yeah," others urged, and soon she no longer felt fear but lust, lust to pour life into them, the *fire* of life. To burn down the world with song.

. . .

IT FELT STRANGE to Troy to leave the Air Force Academy and be back in Nyack for Christmas. At once, he realized, he missed the Academy. The reassurance of its bright straight hallways, the pure discipline, how you greeted someone, how you lived. How you see yourself. What you demand of yourself. Demand of yourself without shirking or complaint. Because the military gives you the confidence, the power, to believe you can do so.

Even the posture – how you'd got used to your back being absolutely straight at all time, shoulders back, until any other bearing felt unreal. And the bitter dry December Rockies wind so much cleaner than this swamp-like, lowland chill.

The little house in Nyack felt out of place, and Mick and Dad foreign there, as if they too didn't belong. Which of course, he told himself, they didn't.

And Tara hovering there like a St. Elmo fire blazing at the tip of his wing. To divert him into death. To watch the ground reach up for you and not care.

Yet seeing her in the living room when he came in and dropped his duffle on the carpet she looked so lovely and kind he had to hold her, inhale her long ravelly hair incensed with tobacco – didn't matter – her heady scent. As if nothing had changed.

"How are you?" he gasped, stepping back.

She gave him a lovely smile, eyes flashing. "Good to see you."

"And you." He pulled away. "Where's Dad?"

"In the kitchen." She kissed him, hard. "Go see him."

He looked at her. "You're thin."

Dad was sitting in a wooden chair by the woodstove, in a blue plaid shirt and khaki wool pants, work boots unlaced; he turned and saw Troy and stood quickly, "Well where the hell *you* come from?" reaching out to embrace him and almost falling.

"It's okay, Dad." Troy took him in his arms and sat him back down. He turned another chair backwards and sat facing Dad, his hand on Dad's wrist which felt cold and thin.

"Tara told me you were coming," Dad said. "I thought tomorrow."

"I'm here now." Troy looked at him closer. "How are you doing?"

"Doing fine." Dad shrugged. "Just old age."

Troy went to the door. "Tara! Mick!" he called, "get in here. I want to catch up with both of you."

CHRISTMAS EVE was somber despite everyone's attempts to have fun. The family gathered at Hal and Sylvia's small brick colonial tucked into a back street behind the 1776 House. Grampy in a chair by the fire with his whisky neat, Uncle Howard stuttering and glancing at the gold watch he kept tugging from his pocket, as if he had somewhere to go, Uncle Ted who had once fought off a black bear and now seemed old and stooped, lonely and disoriented after his wife Cordelia's sudden death from an aneurism last year. Even Uncle Phil's wife, Aunt Wilma, she of the small dangerous fists, seemed less intimidating.

Johnny sat in the background gazing at the fire as if it held some explanation for how and why everything had changed, but would not tell them. Troy thought of saying hi and decided *wait till later*, turned to look for Tara or Mick but couldn't see them.

Maybe it's just I'm older, Troy thought, remembering back to his and Mick's thirteenth birthday party, the first time he'd met most of this close-knit farm family now slowly being disjointed by time and the new suburban world devouring the land they had worked and loved. No, it's time, time itself, which destroys us all eventually.

He wanted to help them, fight for them, defend them. How?

And Dad – he owed him his life, his happiness, the Academy, everything. How to help him? Ever since Ma had died Dad had retreated further and further into himself, and the illness made it worse because Dad wouldn't admit it. For Dad, Troy realized, all that counted now was the happiness of his three children. Even me, he thought, suddenly near tears.

He went out on the rickety back deck where Tara stood looking at the dark, rambling sky. "At the farm we saw thousands of stars," she said. "Here there's nothing."

"That's civilization for you," he joked, wondering how she'd known it was he. He put an arm around her waist and pulled her close, her slender hard hip against his thigh.

She turned into him, hugged him hard, pulled back. "I can't wait to get out of here, back to Berkeley. This whole place drives me crazy. The whole deal."

"Dad?"

"Not him. But I feel I can't leave him."

"We all feel that. But we *are* leaving him." He smiled. "I told him I'd take a year off from the Academy and come back to be with him, and he said *If you do I'll shoot you.* I think he meant it."

She hugged him again and pulled away. "I'm sure he did."

He wanted to kiss her more, knew she'd let him, that she wanted him, but it wasn't possible, not here with the family gathered round, not possible now that he'd gone to the Academy and she was his sister again.

Everything we do to get free, he thought, only binds us tighter.

FROM THE STERN of the *S.S. Statendam* Mick watched the Statue of Liberty shrink into the darkening sea. The strangeness of this wild ocean, of leaving America, the cold salty wind and frothing waves, the lunge, rumble and roll of the ship, all gave him a sense of fearful solitude, ecstatic communion, and the rupture of an ancient chain.

He was leaving it all behind: Williams, the family after Christmas Eve, and all the subterranean sorrow invested there, Dad, Tara and Troy... Dad in weary pain, Troy's distance and rigid formality, Tara's craziness about music – as if that were going to be a way to live her life... And all the time he'd hoped Berkeley would give her some sense.

Driving Coke trucks all summer and fall he'd saved nine hundred dollars. This round-trip voyage had cost two hundred forty for a tiny third class cabin with four bunks deep in the hull. He had six hundred sixty dollars to last four months in France.

Years ago, he and Troy had wandered the rails and begun a new life. It had been fun and lonely and very scary and there'd been a lot of pain at the end. Now he was on a new walkabout and it was going to be scary sometimes too. But he was older now, and what he felt, he realized, was elation.

How can one always be free? Was it possible? Being free made him think of Daisy, and his mind shied from the pain. Why had he not written her more often? And now, was he leaving her behind? He imagined her standing at the rail beside him, the wind in her hair, her gladdened eyes and wide smile, their unspoken, invincible togetherness. Why had he stopped writing her?

Because it was over, he told himself. Had to put it behind me.

In the semi-darkness laughing gulls rose and fell screaming over the ship's wake. The other passengers went in one by one and he was alone, palms on the wet rail, watching the darkening wake and sky. His ancestors had once passed here going the other way, excited, nervous, and solitary. Was he closing some circle?

Seeking the Holy Grail was the quest for the meaning of life. Tonight it was *here*, just beyond reach, beyond a wave's glistening crest, the starry horizon, ready to appear.

26

DOOR TO NIRVANA

A FIERCE STORM HIT that night. The ship shuddered and rolled crazily through huge waves, tall seas thundering over its decks, the crew nauseous, vomit on the floors and walls, even on the ceiling of the stairway when Mick came down for dinner.

"You're not sick?" a waiter inquired wanly.

"Doesn't seem to bother me."

He ordered a beer called Heineken; just ten cents a bottle. He grinned to think how adult-like it felt to order it, as if it were something at age eighteen he often did. After a few more he finished his chicken cordon bleu and went outside to watch the waves crashing on the decks. With each huge wave the ship's prow buried itself in the roiling sea as if going straight to the bottom, could never pull out, then it came shuddering up with the seas cascading off it like multiple Niagaras.

Grabbing a handhold on the main deck he waited for a gap between the waves and dashed forward through the near-horizontal sleet to the prow and grabbed its inside rail. The ship dropped into thundering seas that came crashing above his head across the prow and exploded down the deck like a river, a huge fish flopping across the deck then sliced apart on the rails.

For hours he crouched there at one with the wind and storm and winter sea, barely conscious of danger. Later in his airless bunk with three snoring roommates he felt terror at how easily the sea could have smashed him overboard into the frigid waves, thinking *how lucky I've been. Why do I taunt fate?*

It was raining five days later when they docked in Le Havre. Rain blurred the train window's view of pale winter landscapes, bare-limbed forests, stone farms and barns and stone-walled fields, thin winding roads and strange small cars, slate-roofed towns of narrow alleys, church towers and ruined battlements.

Paris felt busy but uneasy; President DeGaulle had nearly been assassinated in August by a paramilitary group called the OAS. They had wanted to kill him because he'd agreed to give Algeria its independence after the military had brought him to power precisely because he promised Algeria would always stay French. The attempt had been named the *Opération Charlotte Corday,* after the young woman who had killed the revolutionary Jean-Paul Marat in 1793 during the French Revolution, when it had become difficult to know what was revolutionary and what counter-revolutionary.

Two years after France had lost Vietnam to the Viet Minh in 1954, armed revolution had broken out in its colony of Algeria, a quick trip across the Mediterranean from Marseilles. The ensuing war had claimed nearly fifty thousand lives; by 1961 Algerian revolutionaries were killing police in Paris; in October 1961, the police responded by attacking a large Algerian protest march, killing nearly a hundred, many of whom died after being tied and thrown in the Seine.

Three months later, cold-footed in the chilled expensive streets of Paris he tried not to spend money, tormented by the cakes and croissants in *patisserie* windows, envious of the well-dressed people going in and out. The restaurant aromas of stews and steaks and fish cooked in butter, and liqueurs and coffee made him cross the street to avoid them. He thought regretfully of the vast tables of food in the *Statendam*'s third class dining room, when any time he could have had another steak, another chocolate cake.

Chased by police from the Arc de Triumph for warming his

numbed feet on the Unknown Soldier's Eternal Flame, he wondered who this soldier was and what had been his life. What had he died for? Might have even been a German – in the horror of exploded trenches who could tell the nationality of some blistered chunk of flesh?

On the train south to Aix the countryside warmed and greened, the air through the open window scented with sage from the hunched red hills. Everything was new, had meaning: the fossil-like backbones of the limestone peaks, the rambling farms and vineyards, the pale blue streams, the white cows on the rutted green hills, once a Sherman tank rusting by the tracks, gun barrel down, its white American star rusted. He wondered what had happened to the crew eighteen years ago. It was ancient, nearly old as he.

Five others occupied the compartment, a gray-haired woman in a blue wool coat, a gangling elderly man in black with a silver mustache and a black hat who kept checking his fingernails, a small priest in a black cassock silently speaking the words of a black prayer book in his pale hands, a couple in their forties – a blonde woman with a wide sensual mouth and a tall irritated man who kept shoving steel-rim glasses up the bridge of his nose – sat rigidly beside each other not speaking.

The countryside drifting by outside was one he'd never seen, white jagged rocks and hunching scrub, fields of vines in perfect rows, big white cows and now and then the tall white walls of the distant Alps.

For nineteen dollars a month he rented a small apartment in Aix on the sixth and top floor of a medieval stone structure tilting toward another across a twisted cobbled street. Two mullioned windows looked over ancient terracotta rooftops to the bony green hills. White cats and pigeons sunned on the red tiles. Voices and the smells of pastries, onions, garlic, coffee, cherries and tangerines rose to the windows; at night the town was dark and silent and the stars grew bright.

The classes at the Université d'Aix were boring to the point of meaninglessness. In huge lecture halls of steep rows of seats the professor would walk to the podium and for forty-five minutes read a chapter of his book that the students had had to buy. The professor then left the room; no discussion, no questions. I'll just read the damn books, Mick decided. Spring was coming to Provence.

He wandered the cobbled alleys and fountained boulevards of Aix and the countryside of Cézanne, the chunky whites, greens, browns and blues of its rubbled ancient landscape over which the great limestone spine of Mont Sainte-Victoire rose like avenging angel, belying the peaceful landscape with its threat of vertical death that called him like a lover.

Everything fired a sense of the past – all the lives that had been here over hundreds of thousands of years, the dreams, the words said and thought and written, the loves and hatreds, the *mystery* of it – he ached to enter these past lives, live them then come back to tell about it.

He climbed the cathedral roof from the convent roof beside it, stone by stone up the Gothic tower to the belfry and up to a tiny platform atop it to look down between grinning gargoyles at the tiny humans crossing the cobblestones far below. His back to the sun-warm stone, he read *Sisyphus* and *La Condition Humaine*, liking how the meanings locked together, that life must be understood and lived in truth. More importantly, that asking these deep questions about life and how to live was not only right but *essential*.

Serious and hardworking, the French students were also curious, cheery and pro-American. "Everyone in France likes the USA," Gérard said at a café table one night.

"Everybody loves Kennedy," somebody put in.

"Two wars you saved us. Saved the world," Gérard added. "But why does a great country like America try to destroy a little poor place like Cuba?"

"Because the American Mafia ran it," a Norwegian student named Katya snapped. "Till Castro threw them out. They want it back."

"*No, no,*" Gérard riposted. "Because all of Latin America is poor, America is afraid if Cuba wins, everyone from Mexico south will go Communist –"

"*No,*" Mick smiled at his naiveté. "Cuba's only a hundred fifty kilometers from Florida, and Castro will bring in Soviet nuclear missiles that can destroy our country –"

"So?" Katya turned on him, speaking English. "America has missiles in Turkey and Germany and all around pointing at Russia – it's the same."

Trapped in her lilting accent and flashing blue eyes, her chiseled face framed in tawny coils, her elegant innocent smile and dimpled cheeks, he fought for an answer. "That's different."

"Ah?" She smiled, her chin on folded fingers, elbows on the table. "How?"

He was first surprised then angry that anyone could imagine America wrong, but began to realize that many people did, and slowly began to wonder himself. There was a heady freedom, as one reclined in a café chair in a warm night on a jasmine-perfumed terrace at a table of friends from France, Africa, South America and Britain, lightly drunk on Côtes de Provence, to see the world as *they* did, if only briefly. And when his thoughts returned to his world it was with a new objectivity, as one might see a cherished lover after a long absence.

IN WARM SPRING DAYS he explored the green hills, finding ruins of old houses and fortified towers, abandoned mills where Cézanne had painted, climbed Sainte-Victoire's sharp cliffs, alone and without ropes, always promising himself to avoid danger, the pitiless white precipices so far and vertical below. But an easy climb would grow difficult, or he'd choose it, scanning routes up every steepening wall, sometimes caught halfway up, fingertips in a tiny crack that unexpectedly vanished above, trembling in terror against the flat warm vertical limestone, no toehold, no way back, aching to fall into the white-green abyss below just to end the terror.

I will not do this again he told himself as he clambered gasping over a sharp crest and collapsed trembling and nauseous on the top, then hiked down the easy side, panting with exhilarated terror, knees quaking, toward the green valley he'd left two hours before.

But days later he'd find himself halfway up an overhung wall, more afraid than ever. "Why do you risk your *life?*" Katya said. "What if you *die?* How stupid is that?"

"I'm careful." He heard it ring false. "I always have a way out."

"Someday you won't." She shrugged as if he were a hopeless case. "I think you have a love affair with death."

"That's Kazantzakis' question: is it better to live never thinking of death, like Zorba? Or to be aware of it every moment?"

"Maybe it's the same."

That night she came with him up the six twisting flights to his crooked little room under the eaves. He lit a candle whose ardent light danced across the pitted limestone walls. On the wooden table a bottle of red wine, a chunk of bread and hunk of cheese, Katya waving her cigarette like a semaphore while her words fell like autumn petals, lovely and free. Her lips were warm and wet, her kisses avaricious, her body hot, her underwear crumpled on the cold tiles, her body arching under his on the narrow squeaking bed as if relinquishing her center to him, they could reach it together and never have to return. All night she wanted to make love and in the morning also, and the next afternoon after class, her thighs round his waist as he pinned her to the door.

But she wouldn't stop sleeping with Gérard too. "I don't see why it bothers you. He is my boyfriend also – back in Norway I have both Nils and Sven – *they* don't seem to bother you..."

"They're not here."

"It's not as if we are going to marry someday, you and me. We're just kids! It's fun to make love with *lots* of people." She tugged at a lock of golden hair, twisted it round her finger under her chin. "When I'm older and have children I will be a one-man woman." She grinned. "Maybe."

But there were lonely nights also, racked with the terror of finding himself beyond the known. Homesickness so bad that even jobs and classes became good memories. Seeing himself unable to change, impotent before the easiest tasks, afraid his future would be a failure.

When he felt down and lonely he reread *Catch 22*, its sardonic laughter and sharp sorrow depicting the total insanity of war and the bureaucracy and ignorance that made it inevitable. Catch 22 was the military's circular logic: if you were crazy you wouldn't have to fly incredibly dangerous bombing missions, but if you were sane you had to. The *catch* was that if you *did* fly them you were crazy and therefore didn't have to; but if you *didn't* want to fly them you were obviously sane and therefore had to.

The book's manifold characters from generals to hookers gave a truer picture of war than movies of milksops like John Wayne and Ronald Reagan who'd never fought but filled the screen with pablum about easy courage. In an American culture that glorified war, the book's honesty had the clarity of lightning through clouds of lies, reminding him that books are written to keep us from burying the truth.

"It's ironic," Jules said one night, "that America was born from revolution but tries to stop revolutions everywhere. Even Vietnam – it was our colony till fifty-four, but we lost it after Dien Bien Phu... My older brother Serge was wounded there. The Vietnamese said they wanted to be like America, to stop being a colony. But Eisenhower split their country after he promised not to, and the southern half is run by military stooges supported by America."

"That's crap," Mick said angrily.

"You think so?" Jules snapped. "You know what else Eisenhower did? He had Patrice Lumumba killed. Him and the Belgians, they had him arrested and killed. Because he spoke too honestly of colonialism and for all African nations to free themselves, unite. It was the CIA –"

"You *must* read Frantz Fanon," Katya said, *"Les Damnés de la Terre.* He's a black who grew up in Martinique, joined the Free French to fight the Nazis and was wounded in Alsace –"

"He got the *Croix de Guerre* for bravery under fire," Gérard said.

"He's a doctor and psychiatrist," she went on, "a philosopher who studies how colonization affects people, how a colonizer's language influences their consciousness, how it alienates them, how every colonizer's power is based on military force."

"He's in Algeria now," Jules said, "they say he's joined the revolutionaries."

"*Les Damnés de la Terre* reveals the torture of Algerians by the French Army, what that lawyer in Paris, Gisèle Halimi, wrote about. So it's censored here in France –"

"*Liberté, égalité, fraternité,*" Mick grinned.

"You think it's funny? Wait till *you* have to do military service!"

"We're not in any war," Mick retorted. Though Katya's aggressive opinions annoyed him she seemed to care for him, at least when he was with her. She expounded often on his faults and how he could become a more successful, happy person. She condemned his diet – too many pastries, far too much wine – wanted him to bathe more frequently, thought his view of people too negative and pessimistic, urged him to be happier. She herself was happy all the time in the erotic intensity of a young woman who saw herself and others clearly, spoke the truth and set no limits to her enjoyment.

Contrary to her disputations he found his faults far easier to keep than change. There was no proof they were faults anyway. He did not consider himself happy nor expected to be happy or successful in the future. As for his diet, it was a basic merger of budget and lifestyle. Regarding cleanliness, there was only one bathtub in the building, on the ground floor at the bottom of the lightwell; you had to push seven five-centime pieces into its gas meter to heat enough water to fill the bottom two inches.

Plus an American girl had died in it last month when the flame went out and the gas filled up the room and poisoned her.

Even though he'd never met her, her loss emptied him with sorrow. And for the parents, coming here to collect the body of their beloved daughter. They hadn't wanted to let her come, but she'd insisted...

A COLD MISTRAL hit Provence; he decided to go south.

"What will you find in the Sahara?" Katya said the last night, pressing her lovely little breasts against his chest. "That you don't have here?"

He ran his fingertips down her spine, liking her silky skin and the hard vertebrae beneath, how she arched the small of her back and tightened her pelvis against him. "It's different. New."

"Already I am *old* to you?"

He snickered against her shoulder. "An old crone, *une vieille bique.*"

She pinched him, raised up on an elbow. "Always you are doing these dangerous things. The Algerian War isn't over. They are still killing anyone who's not Arab..."

He scratched his back into the sheet. "I'm American. They won't bother me."

"*Acch* such a fool!"

Side by side facing each other he could only enter her a little, excited by the brushy softness and hot tight stickiness of her crotch. *Door to Nirvana,* the words came unbidden. "I've always wanted to go to Timbuktu –"

She rolled atop him. "That's not a real place, it's fairy tales."

"It's in Mali, was once on the caravan route for the gold and salt trade. There's no roads to it, just trails. You take the overnight ferry from Marseilles to Algiers, then it's two thousand miles across the Sahara, there's trucks to hitch rides with –"

"*Across* the Sahara? Now I *know* you are crazy!" She closed her thighs.

Laughing, he kissed her ear, down the lobe and behind it, his palm roughing her taut body, the girlish breasts and smooth little belly. "I'll come back."

She opened her thighs, reaching for him. "Who's to say," she sighed as he drove into her, tightened her legs round him, "that I'll still be here? Even if you do?"

TIMBUKTU

A LGIERS AT DAWN had a downtrodden miserable air. The Revolution was ending but no one seemed to care. The French had left and the soul of Algeria had gone with them. All was filth, overcrowding and poverty, a continual din of Islamic rants from mosque towers and tinny radios, rats and sewage underfoot and Koran slogans sprayed across bullet-pitted walls. Women veiled in black trod the soiled streets barefoot.

Hiking out of the filthy reeking city he caught a ride on a farm truck seventy kilometers through the Atlas Mountains to Médéa, a dusty timeworn crossroads of drab houses and brown barren earth. After two hours he caught another ride to Djelfa, equally dusty, barren and dispirited. He spent a few centimes on bread and a fly-bitten piece of meat that he cooked out on the desert at nightfall using thorn scrub twigs for fuel, and slept in the bushes by the side of the road, listening for snakes and possible rides, hating himself for leaving Katya and Aix.

The sparsely bearded young man who picked him up next morning was headed across the desolate foothills of the Ouled Naïl Mountains to work on a gas pipeline west of Laghouat, but did not seem excited by it nor about what would happen in Algeria after the

Revolution. He kept the radio tuned to a succession of Arabic laments, sometimes singing along, getting out every fifty km to piss or pray on the roadside.

"You're not happy," Mick asked him, "that the Revolution's almost over?"

A grim smile. "It's not yet. We're still fighting the OAS, the French generals who have murdered thousands of Algerians, even tried to kill DeGaulle."

"But wasn't it those generals who brought DeGaulle to power because he promised Algeria would always stay French? Didn't they feel betrayed when he signed the Evian Accords separating Algeria from France?"

The young man glanced at him then faced the road. "You ask many questions."

"My real question is: was it worth it, the Revolution? The million killed?"

"And tortured –"

"Both sides did that, no?"

"We tortured them because they tortured us."

"We?"

"The FLN, the *Front de Libération Nationale,* tortured French soldiers and *pieds noirs* – French who lived here – and Algerians who worked for them. But the French tortured *us...*" Again the grim smile. "Humanity's very good at blaming after the fact. But it is careful never to interfere while it's happening."

"Like what happened to the Jews in concentration camps?"

"That's a myth. It never happened." The young man raised his right hand from the steering wheel. "You see these scars? I too was tortured." The back of his hand was spotted with round dark red gouges. "Cigarettes. I was a student at the University in Oran, majoring in economics. I believed if we could improve economic conditions we could avoid revolution, have a peaceful transition. One night in fifty-six, March twenty-nine –"

"That's my birthday. And my half-brother's."

Again a smile like the Devil's when another innocent steps into

Hell. "They came while I was studying, the French police. They said I was *PAM, Pris avec les Armes à la Main* – taken with weapons in my hand – My only weapon was an economics text."

"That can be very dangerous."

"They took me to the torture center at Constantine where hundreds of people were held, mostly young men, some even boys, but also women and old men, all waiting to be tortured, many to be killed." He stared down the empty road blazing in the sun. "Many people there were tortured to insanity then dropped from helicopters into the sea, legs and arms tied. Some floated ashore; the police called them *crevettes Bigeard,* shrimps of the infamous paratroop commander Marcel Bigeard."

For a while he said nothing, then, "I was lucky. For eight days they kept me in a cell too small to lie down. No food. Then I was taken to a concrete room, the floor sticky with blood. They made me take off my clothes and for a whole day, I think it was a whole day, they beat me with *matraques,* the leather-covered steel clubs... See this?"

He raised his left arm. "Broken in three places, that's why it's all bent. When I still had nothing to tell them they hung me upside down putting my head under water. Then came the telephone –"

"After all that they let you *call* someone?"

Again the grim smile. "They attach a wire to your private places, give horrible electric shocks. Then the cigarettes, more beatings, but there was still nothing I could tell them. So finally they let me go. 'Go back to your studies,' they said. 'If you ever speak of this we'll kill you.'"

"I wonder if torture only hardens people."

"As I said, we did it too, the FLN, tortured many people, disemboweled them, cut their families' throats in front of them... War *is* torture, my friend."

"It's safe now, to speak of it?"

"Perhaps. But what will come now? What will the Revolution bring? And where will we be without the French? There's a million *pieds noirs* going back to France, because we're still killing them. But didn't they build this country too?"

South of Laghouat Mick got out and stood waiting for a long time in the desiccating sun, but no vehicles passed. Then a shabby truck with rattling fenders took him south across the flat wastes of the Sahara to Ghardaia, the fat driver expostulating on the glory of Allah. "Christians lead morally despicable lives. You must see that, no? Like porks in swill."

"Pigs. Pork is the meat of pigs."

"Condemned by God!" The driver waved at desert mirages. "The women go about half-naked –"

Mick grinned. "Often *completely* naked."

The man's eyes gleamed. "Unforgivable sin!"

"Who said?"

He snorted as if the answer were obvious: why does this truck exist, this road?

Mick watched the wind-scoured dunes. "Does religion make you happy?"

"*I* am nothing. Allah tells me what to do, to think, how to live. What matters if I am happy?"

AFTER TWO DAYS of more truck rides he reached the oasis of In-Salah, where he was told the track to Timbuktu was closed. "Too many rebel attacks," the captain at the Foreign Legion In-Salah garrison said in German-accented French. "I will give you one of our maps... You must stay on the main road to Tamanrasset."

"How far is that?"

The captain tugged at his moustache, thinking. "Seven hundred kilometers perhaps. But there should be trucks, at least one a day. After that you take the desert track another four hundred kilometers across the Tassili du Hoggar into Mali..."

It was getting dark; the north wind frigid. "Is there a hotel here, or something?"

"Here?" the captain laughed. He stepped into a back room, called "Hey!" at an ancient Arab crouched against the western wall. "Who can this guy stay with?"

The old man came forward clutching his *djellabah*. He shook Mick's hand and held his own over his heart. "Travelers sometimes stay with old Ben Younès –" He led Mick through narrow alleys between low huts, the dusk wind gnawing their eaves, and rapped at a green door. After a few moments an even older man dressed in a worn blue robe opened. They spoke briefly in Arabic and the older man swung the door wide and smiled at Mick, *"Entrez, mon ami."*

It was one room of whitewashed clay walls, a rough-plastered low ceiling, an uneven red-tiled floor with a woolen carpet, a fireplace in one corner, a low-slung bed with a coarse blanket in another. "You have not eaten," the old man said.

"I'm fine."

"You are not French."

"American."

"We Algerians love Americans, because of Kennedy. You may put your sleeping bag there, by the fire. I have some camel yogurt; we will share it." He poured two cups of tea and set them on the carpet. "Sit now, and tell me all the places you've been."

He had a gnarly inscrutable face half-masked by a tangled white beard, his long white hair surmounted by a Muslim skullcap. "Why do you take in travelers?" Mick said.

"For many years I was a Koranic scholar and taught in Oran. I no longer believe in the supremacy of the Koran but still I'm happy to exchange ideas with anyone. That's why I offer my humble floor to passersby; you see, most people in this world are quite boring and haven't done much in their lives, but those who travel the Sahara are nearly always interesting."

At first it felt strange to recount to this old man the vagaries of his own short life, his hatred of school, about his family and how Troy came to live with them, of being thrown out of college, the fear he might never find a woman to love.

"Women and war," Ben Younès said, "are the troubles of men. In the Koran are many instructions on how to live wisely with women, to use them as a tilled field, take no more than four in marriage at one time, all that. But also it is said that a woman's eyes are the Devil's well in which a man drowns." Crosslegged on the carpet, Ben Younès changed position. "Ah my knee, was hit by shrapnel, a French bomb."

He crossed his legs again. "Think of Adam and Eve, even the Christians believe what the Koran teaches, that woman led man into evil by seeking knowledge, and so people fell from paradise, feel shame and wear clothing to cover their bodies – is that not how we live today?"

"I think women are the joy of men, and that war is the trouble."

"War, the Koran says, must only be undertaken to destroy infidels, people who do not believe in Islam, but all religions recommend this, to increase their followers –"

"And *this* revolution?"

"Ah, the Revolution." Ben Younès leaned back. "When it began nobody wanted it, nobody believed it would happen. Nobody wanted the French to leave, there were just a few crazies, young men who were mostly criminals and who found in the Koran incitement to kill and torture. Life was good with the French, everyone had plenty to eat, there were schools and doctors and roads and jobs. We were French citizens, voted in French elections. But the Koran says no Muslim should be beholden to an infidel, befriend an infidel, or they'll go to the same Hell that infidels are fated to."

He shrugged. "But of course that's how revolutions work: the crazies began shooting the French, setting off bombs everywhere, killing hundreds of women and children and old people, people who'd never done any harm... Naturally the French started hunting the crazies, attacked them with soldiers and helicopters, accidentally killing other people too, that's how war is, the crazies were hiding behind all the people who didn't want a revolution. And people who liked the French, worked with them, the crazies tortured and killed them and blamed it on the French... Soon we had mobs of ululating women, lots of people hating the French and saying we need a revolution... forgetting that the French had brought us jobs and modern life and education and medicine and all these other things. People don't think, you know. They get carried away, they don't think."

"It took years," Mick said, "for all that to happen?"

"It began in November, 1954, the crazies, the *fellaghas*. We all thought it would end at once, the French would quickly finish them. But the crazies hit and ran, the Mao doctrine of a rebel as a fish and the people as the water he swims in... By 1956 the French had thousands of soldiers in Algeria, electrified barbed wire on our borders, napalm and torture, and the crazies were making reprisals, atrocities, disemboweling people, throat-cutting, killing children because their parents were pro-French, the French who'd been here a hundred thirty years, they owned the farms you see, farms that were just empty fields before they came..."

"Is there such a thing as a good revolution?"

"We humans love to kill but want an excuse so we don't feel guilty for killing. So we make up reasons like religion, getting rid of colonialism, the evil Europeans. But without colonialism countries like Algeria, Morocco, Egypt, India and all of Africa, we'd still be illiterates eating off the ground and living in stick huts, dying of ancient diseases. Nobody wants to admit that. Ah, me..."

For a while Ben Younès watched the fire. "Over time the few hundred crazies became thousands of FLN, the *Front de Libération Nationale*... But nobody understood the only path to liberation is inside yourself. A group, a government, a religion – they can't do it for you. What they give you is the pretense of liberation, but you're only changing one master for another. Revolutions are caused by men who love only power. They don't care about women, families, nothing that deters them from that perfect place where the sorrows of their childhood will finally be avenged." He raised a finger. "I'll tell you all you need to know about revolutionaries: they don't have children."

"You're saying it never works?"

"Ours was a nightmare. A million French people have to move back to France, leaving Algeria without technical competence or objectivity. We've all lost, except the idiots who began it. And I fear years to come of murdering each other in the name of Islamic perfection."

"But it will be a democracy?"

"Democracy is not possible under Islam. Islam means *I surrender;*

the Koran does not allow independent thought. Once you give your reason over to religion, you cannot think independently. Look at the world: there is not one Islamic democracy."

Ben Younès scratched his beard, thinking. "We must avoid idealisms. We must never substitute ideas, words, for life. Never kill. And we must be particularly careful of this word humane, for only humans are evil. No animal is evil, so when we say *humane* we mean *evil.*"

He broke a piece of camel dung and put it on the fire. "So, you really want to go to Timbuktu?"

"I like to go where I've never been, see new things."

"That's the old argument, isn't it: is it better to know one place deeply or many places superficially? I for one have lived in Algeria all my life but for one trip to Paris... In any case, we all have the great journey of death."

Mick glanced round the little whitewashed clay-walled room, the small apsed window, the clay corner fireplace sending out its trickle of sallow warmth against the frigid night. "Death is an abomination, an atrocity, a murder no different from any other. I want to live hard as I can till then."

"When I was a boy I believed that by following the Koran's precepts I'd have eternal life, better than this one..."

"All religions say that. It's how they sell themselves."

"Of course now I know this is the only life, there's nothing after, nothing that's better. The virtue to crossing the desert is you are reborn, that's the only heaven. Be reborn as many times as you can in your life... Ah, and the young always have hope... That's their great deception."

FOR TWO MORE DAYS Mick hitched across the bleak Mouydir Mountains to the turnoff at the palm-studded oasis of Tit just north of Tamanrasset. "The Timbuktu trail is gone," an old Bedouin said when Mick reached Tamanrasset. "The desert covered it."

Mick bent closer, not understanding his harsh French. "Must be another way."

"There is a track to Ti'n-Zaouâten. Sometimes a car goes there."

Next afternoon a car did come, a rusty tan Peugeot 403 with no windshield, a chubby, cheery mining geologist named Fayeed who was driving ninety km southwest to the oasis at Silet. "But you'll have another three hundred kilometers to the Timbuktu road," Fayeed said. "If someone comes, gives you a ride... But if no one comes..."

Sun burning his neck, Mick glanced at the bleak huts of Tit. "I'll wait. Or walk."

"Three hundred kilometers? In this heat?"

On the Foreign Legion map the track from Silet turned southwest through desert, canyons and mountains. "It's high there," Mick said. "Perhaps it'll be cooler."

"Not in day. In night very cold."

"Do many cars come?" Mick said.

"Sometimes as many as one or two a week. Many times none."

Diligently the Peugeot clambered up the ragged hills, a mix of windblown gravel and jagged outcrops, great boulders strewn under gleaming cliffs. The wind through the empty windshield was superheated. The track narrowed to two ruts with an abyss alongside, then snaked across a stony waste between bare black mountains. "You have water?" Fayeed said.

"Five liters."

"Not enough. There is no water till the oasis of In-Tedeini, three hundred kilometers. But I have two more I can give you. That's still not enough..."

Mick felt embarrassed by the offer. "No, you might need it."

The track steepened toward a huge stony bowl in the cliffs and turned left. "Here I go north," Fayeed said. He motioned at a fainter pair of ruts heading right. "The way to Timbuktu."

Mick felt a terrifying loneliness, wanted to stay with Fayeed. But then where would he go? "I'll be fine."

Fayeed gave a quick nod of good luck, crunched into second then rattled to a halt. "Watch out for vipers. At night sleep in the cliffs, for the sake of hyenas."

Mick watched the Peugeot pick its way down the northern slope, its rusty roof sun-reddened, its rear window flashing like a diamond. It crawled over the downrolling dunes into the vast golden-red desert trailing a tiny kerchief of khaki dust, its shadow stretching far beyond it as the sun set. He felt a moment's exaltation to be alone in this vast emptiness.

Then he felt horribly bereft. The breeze down the cliffs had turned frigid. The desert had darkened, endless and cold to the edges of the earth.

"This is what you wanted to do," he said aloud. "Don't back out now. Don't undercut yourself. This is a challenge you gave yourself, so go ahead and do it and shut up. You've done tougher things before."

He wondered what those tougher things had been, dismissed the thought, shouldered his pack and climbed the track to a rocky shelf twenty feet up the cliff. It tilted outward and he feared falling in his sleep, so brought up small boulders to line the edge and keep himself in. This is great, he told himself. This is what I wanted.

The hyenas came as Fayeed had promised, their demented laughter echoing through the canyons, one panting at his scent below, starlit yellow eyes glinting up. The icy night ate through his thin sleeping bag, the jagged shelf impossible to sleep on. Rubbing himself to stay warm he waited for day.

At first light he studied the map, ate a chunk of bread and cheese and drank a little water. He scanned his back track; there was no sign of a car. The wise thing was to start up the trail rather than wait; if a car came fine, if not he could later backtrack to Silet. The steep rocky track snaked through jumbled shattered boulders and scars of windcut sand. Again he felt elation to be in this magnificent solitary place, and pride that he'd dared.

After sunrise the air turned searing hot. A flock of sparrows darted over the cliff; their song vanished down a raw deep canyon. He wanted more water but didn't drink till midmorning when his throat was burning, then only a sip that evaporated in his throat before he could swallow.

Higher up it grew cool and windy. He sat on a cliff edge, liking this strange endless place where he was the only person. It reminded him of Skull Cave, where he'd gone where no human had ever been since the beginning of time.

He felt a warm connection to this immensity of rock and sand devoid of humans. But the wind burned his face; his lips were swelling and his tongue blocked his throat. He realized his first water canteen was empty. Should have brought more, he told himself. Maybe should've stayed in France.

The trail dropped into a cauldron of sun-shattered rocks over which a molten wind lisped anxiously. The light hurt his eyes but when he closed them he stumbled and fell, burning his hands on the rocks. Night fell like a stone; he found a perch high on the cliff but could not sleep for fear of falling. The air turned frigid, the stars pitiless and bright. No hyenas came.

Had to admit this was lonely. At dawn he took a sip of his second canteen and went on, knees weakening. He could turn back to Silet now but still had four liters so there was no reason. For what seemed hours he followed the trail across a blazing plateau, twice losing then finding it. He sat down on a rock but it was too hot, tried the sand but that burned too.

He could die here. Didn't seem likely. Just three hundred klicks. Barely two hundred miles – how many had he done today? He looked at his watch – twenty after four. How could that be? The sun was straight overhead, too fierce to look at.

The second hand wasn't moving. He'd forgot to wind his watch. Now he wouldn't know what time it was. How far had he come? He tried to remember yesterday's hike. Maybe two hours. Ten km. Today he'd done at least four hours. Maybe thirty km total. Only twenty miles. Was it yesterday he'd started, or some other day?

He made himself think. Only two hundred seventy klicks to go. A hundred eighty miles. Back home he could do that in five days. But he was supposed to wait for something. What was it? Why wait, in this sun?

He pushed to his feet and followed the track toward great black shimmering peaks. Ti'n-Zaouâten was beyond them, the map said, but how could anything be so far? Maybe the map was wrong.

It was easier to walk after his rest; he felt tall and buoyant, light-footed. He raised his thumbs to his shoulder straps but they weren't there.

He had no pack.

He'd left it when he'd stopped. How far was that? He should have a drink of water, clear his head. But the water was in his pack.

Going back he lost the track. Perhaps he'd already gone too far. He turned and went another way but could not find the pack, or where he'd stopped.

If he didn't find the water soon he'd die. He stared up and down the windy desolate rocks but had seen none of this before. He'd rest a while then find the pack. When it was cooler. But here there was no shade. He peered over the cliff edge; vast desolation danced in the heat below.

He backed away, imagined falling and smashing into the rocks so far down. He stumbled on something weird and fell backward into a cactus that stung and burned terribly. Before him lay the pack. He'd stumbled over it.

He snatched a water canteen. Empty. In another a little water sloshed in the bottom. He drained it, threw it away, looked around. Who'd stolen his water?

The third liter was full. He only drank a quarter wishing he'd taken Fayeed's extra two liters. So thirsty.

All afternoon he walked eastward through scorching canyons empty of all but wind. Hell, but he didn't care, didn't think, kept walking. That night in the infinite bitter desert under the vicious stars he felt a crazy loneliness, pure terror, seeing the eternal cold pit at the end of life, told himself it was just thirst, wondered if he was dying, and why he didn't care.

28

I TOLD YOU

SOMEONE HAD STOLEN his water, the last canteen empty; its rim burned his lip. For the hundredth time he spread the map on the searing earth, pushing a track along it with a dizzy finger, tried to see but the map kept shivering with heat, would not stay still.

How far had he come? Maybe another twenty. Twenty from what? There had been a place but he couldn't remember. Maybe he should turn around, go back to where he'd started. Where was that? Who would come? He felt self-hatred that he'd done this to himself. Calm down, he told himself. Once you get scared you're done for.

No place to hide from the sun. No matter how many times he opened them the canteens were empty. No matter how many times he looked back down the track no one came. Each breath burnt his throat, his lips cracked and bloody. Thirst pounding in his veins made him nauseous and afraid.

He'd killed himself, like firing a bullet into his brain. When he hadn't wanted to. Or had he? A fool to have squandered his life.

Not giving himself time to think he shouldered the pack and moved on.

After an hour his last energy began to flag, legs trembling with thirst, the air a furnace. He climbed a crest of sand and looked back;

where he'd started this morning was a stone's throw away. He sat for a moment, leaned back against the pack. His hand bumped a rock, caught fire. A hot spike drove through it, he writhed on the ground gripping his hand to his chest.

The pain roared up his arm. On his palm a spreading red welt. On the rock a scorpion backed away, tail raised.

He thrashed in agony wanting to die, anything to stop this pain. After a while he stumbled to his feet, gasping through his swollen lips and tongue, his arm hanging. He couldn't remember why he was here, why he was doing this, just that it had to be done.

By afternoon the heat grew truly unbearable. He tried not to breathe because it seared his lungs, and walked with eyes closed to keep them from burning up, tripped and fell.

Vague shapes beckoned through dancing light. Cool delicious water sparkled before him, turned to molten sand when he touched it. He got up and went on.

Finally the sun touched the peaks. The rocks and sand screamed with heat. His arm and shoulder ached horribly; the world spun queasily, his brain throbbed. He fell down beside a stone outcrop, pulled the map from his pack. The wind took it and he watched it go, a white bird soaring over the cliff. So this is it, he thought.

Tara and Troy would never know. For an instant he was in the old farm kitchen with everyone. Food on the table, water, milk. "It's okay, son," Ma said.

Okay to die. The terror faded into a delightful peace. He lay on the hot sand waiting for death, surprised to not fear it. He'd come here to die, it was fate.

This brought a weird confidence. Maybe if he wasn't afraid of death he wouldn't do anything wrong, could find a way through a crack in time back to life.

Over his rattling breath came a strange singing. So this was death. The singing tailed off. Something called. Another answered. Then a huffing grunt. A boy in white and two men in white and three camels. Another mirage. Maybe angels. He tried to call, a whisper. The boy saw him, called the others. One of them picked up a rifle and came toward him.

His narrow face was blue, his hands blue, his long hair curly and black. His mouth was thin and sharp. Mick could not understand, answered in French at which the blue-faced man tossed his head angrily.

Again the blue-faced man spoke, a question, glanced behind Mick. His meaning was clear: you're alone? And behind it a deeper meaning: *We'll kill you.*

The blue-faced man called to the boy, who said something Mick could almost understand, realized it was French. The boy ran back to the camels, returned with a brown rock that Mick saw was not a rock but a canteen. The boy wore a Foreign Legion kepi. "Who are you?" he said in accented French. "Where do you come from?"

In the cooling dusk they brought him more water, sour warm yoghurt and dates that stuck to his fingers. When it grew cold they built a fire of camel dung and placed him beside it. At dawn they made tea, mounted him on a camel with a goatskin over him to keep out the sun, and set out westward, their shadows rising and falling before them across the crimson dunes.

"Where are you going?" Mick asked.

"Tamanrasset," the boy said. "In three days you will be there." He nodded his chin at the old man. "He's buying a new wife. He already has three that do him no good, but he has stolen a new young camel so he'll trade it for a fourth."

Three days later they turned south outside Tamanrasset and Mick walked into town alone. It had a grim forlorn air. It seemed unreal to have left here in Fayeed's car barely a week before, to have nearly died, and now to return on foot a lifetime later. He wanted to kneel down on the sand and pray thanks but didn't know to what. Maybe this was what Ben Younès meant by being reborn. Not only given back life but taught how to live better.

Light-headed and serene, he waited for a ride, drinking canteen after canteen of Tamanrasset's bilious water. As in Skull Cave, in the storm on the *Statendam* and on the cliffs of Sainte-Victoire, he'd challenged death and lived. Why?

Not all quests left you alive. The line between life and death was razor-thin, could be cut at any moment, with the tiniest mistake, the simplest illusion. As in Skull Cave he'd pushed the unknown too far, lucky to get out before it struck back.

"How was Timbuktu?" the old Bedouin said.

"Couldn't get there."

The old man spat. "I told you."

"AMERICAN-LOOKING STUDENTS With Sailing Experience Wanted" appeared one day in the *International Herald Tribune*. "I can get this." Jules slapped the newspaper on the café table.

"You're not even American –"

Jules straightened. "I *look* American –"

"Hell you do. You have a big French nose."

"Hah – you don't have any sailing experience."

"Sure I do," Mick lied.

It had been a month since he'd returned from the Sahara. While he'd been gone Katya had moved in with Gérard. After the vast gleaming desert his tiny apartment felt cramped and dark. He walked the streets seeking work, finally found a job *en noir* – under the table – as a masonry laborer. "You're not French," the foreman had said.

"American."

"Long as you're not Arab."

They were repairing the top floor of a twelfth-century townhouse. All day he carried a hundred-twenty-pound trough of wet concrete up five stories of the building's narrow stone stairs, then brought down the same weight in broken plaster and stone debris to dump in the bin outside.

By noon he had made forty trips. Weary but hardened, sticky with drying sweat, he ate *steak frites* at a café on the Cour Mirabeau in the breezy shadows of the plane trees. One must imagine Sisyphus happy, Camus had said. But of course Sisyphus was happy, in the simple physical joy of strength and action. Each concrete trough lunged to the top, each pile of rubble brought down and thrown into the truck, was a victory. But he was only doing this a few weeks, not forever. Didn't anything done forever turn to Hell?

Watching those around him, other laborers, people in the streets and cafés, it had seemed they cared for little, went about their repetitive tasks worrying about their irrelevant preoccupations, eyes resolutely shut to the magnificence of existence and its impending loss in death. Even the news in *The Herald Trib* was all fury and fuss, people believing in leaders, ideas, promises, anything to avoid personal freedom.

In the Sahara he'd been to death and back; now wasting even an hour of this precious life seemed insane. If others enslaved themselves that didn't mean he had to. Not even out of guilt or sympathy.

As in the Sahara he often now sensed the meaning of life, could nearly reach its immanent immanence. Enticing, like a girl nearly naked who slips away leaving a dull numb perception, a bad memory, the trace of a dream, the haze of normal life.

But no matter what he did he couldn't induce it, this sense of being in touch with the life force of universal truth, the being *alive*. Then it would come when he wasn't thinking, a sudden deepening of perception, a connectedness, a union. As if he did not know what life is, but could almost sense it.

When his laborer's job was done he bought a Moto Guzzi, a fast Italian motorcycle. The day of the *Herald Trib* ad he took the *route nationale* to Nice, Jules tippy on the seat behind him. He parked the bike on the *Promenade des Anglais* before the august white façade of the Negresco Hotel. They changed into clean clothes in the gilded marble-floored "Gentlemen's" under the baleful smirks of liveried attendants, and rode a gleaming elevator to a ninth floor suite to wait for two fast-talking polyestered Americans in sunglasses to interview them and take their photos. "Come tomorrow at ten," one said.

They slept on the rocky beach in the sibilant rush of the waves under shimmering stars. Next morning he got the job, a thirty-second TV commercial for Canada Dry's new Grapefruit Drink, to be shown in the States. The three others chosen, a Frenchman about twenty-two and two French girls, spoke no English and hardly looked American.

According to the plot two young couples have a sailboat race then sit at a table on the beach celebrating with Canada Dry Grapefruit Drink. It was shot in reverse, the beach part first. All morning the crew milled round them shooting and yelling for quiet and adjusting reflectors and refilling their glasses with more Grapefruit Drink. But at each good shot the sun faded behind a cloud, wind tousled the tablecloth or a girl's hair, or a fly landed on someone's nose.

Endlessly they chatted animated nonsense and raised their glasses of Grapefruit Drink as if it were the elixir of life. Out of boredom Mick kept downing his, which was immediately refilled. It seemed insane to be creating this false picture of life after having lived so deeply in the Sahara. His supposed fiancée was deliciously pretty, narrow-hipped with high cheekbones and long chestnut hair. But she was distant and unfriendly; all three were evasive as if caught slumming, and seemed to view him as outlandish, a primitive.

After hours of Grapefruit Drink they began the race, one couple in each dinghy while the crew circled in two speedboats filming. Mick had no idea how to sail, his erratic course compounded by a stiff wind and chop. Each time the boat tipped his partner hissed at him, readjusted her bikini over her scant tits and stared furiously away. Twice to his dismay he hit her with the boom, further reducing chances of on-location romance.

Eventually he discovered how to use the tiller and control the boom, and could keep a decent course. Back and forth they ran down the bay of Nice while the film crews circled waving and shouting, trying to shoot the sailboats side by side, but each time a wake would cross, or another cloud, or Mick would accidentally yaw to starboard.

He regretted the gallons of Grapefruit Drink he'd drunk, for now he had to piss. Each thumping ride over the waves in the cold wet wind, his bare feet sloshing in the hull, aggravated the problem. But he couldn't just stand on the stern and do it, he'd have to jump over. They were on a long tack, the film boats circling madly, when he could wait no longer and leaped into the water holding the stern rope.

It was shockingly frigid; the boat yanked him along as his partner shrilled down at him. The film boat roared up. "What the fuck you doin?" the assistant producer yelled.

"Fell off," Mick sputtered, dragged under.

"Fuck you did. You jumped off already."

He still had to piss terribly but couldn't because of the icy water and the girl and producer yelling at him, the waves smacking his face. He pulled himself to the boat and climbed in, snatched up the rope and sat on the cold wet stern ignoring his partner's sharp-toothed glare. Oh my God, he moaned silently, do I have to piss.

Finally they sailed to shore and he swam out into the bay, thinking as he finally let go, never have I had such bliss. One of the sharp-talking polyestered men gave them each twenty-five dollars for the day's work; "I should charge you a hundred bucks," he said to Mick. "You ruined the day's best shot."

"You should market this shit as a diuretic."

Headed toward Italy on the *Promenade des Anglais* Mick swung the Moto Guzzi out to pass an ancient Renault signaling a right turn with the little hand lever that popped up between the front and back doors. But the woman in the Renault turned left not right, the Moto Guzzi hit the back door and Mick sailed over the roof and came down face first on the asphalt, sliding to a stop as Jules landed on his back.

The bike was wrecked; he had no insurance and had not changed the registration when he bought it, so the only sensible thing was to wheel it into an alley and leave it, its smashed headlight dangling miserably. "Sorry, old girl," he said, wiping his blood off the handle bar, reminded of a World War Two Bill Mauldin cartoon of a soldier sorrowfully shooting his busted jeep in the engine as if it were a broken-legged horse.

"Life's too dangerous when I'm around you," Jules said, and took the next train back to Aix. Seventeen stitches later as dusk was falling Mick stood hitchhiking in a spring rain on the Italian border. After an hour a battered green Panhard pulled up, a young man and girl in front, another man in the back. "Thought you might be American," the driver said. He looked vaguely familiar, a bright skinny face, rimless glasses on a long nose and short blond hair.

"Where you going?" Mick said.

"Wherever the road takes us."

Mick sat in the back trying not to get rain on the seat. "You look like you can use this," the girl said, handing him a jug of wine. "What happened to your face?"

"Wow," the driver said when Mick told them.

"I know you," Mick said. "You went to Williams."

"Amazing!" the driver said, staring back at him.

"Watch the road," the girl said.

The driver, Dave Singer, had been a senior Mick's first year. Even more unlikely, Mick had repeatedly gotten in random meaningless fist fights with Dave's roommate. "You were a punk," Dave grinned. "An obnoxious punk."

"I got kicked out," Mick said. "If I'm good they'll let me back in this fall."

"I'm going to write Dean Brooks," Dave said, "tell him keep you out."

For five days they wandered through Tuscany, eating and sleeping in the straw-deep barns of Albergo, drinking rough red wine from cool clay jugs tasting of the stony hills, eating juicy black olives, hard pale cheese and sauces of fresh tomatoes, oregano and basil, sang and argued and played Boccaccio.

It wasn't really arguing but passionate discussion, reaching for the truth, for the absence of falsehood. For the first time in his life Mick found his every statement challenged, his every idea plumbed for meaning. No idea or sentiment was sacred; over the passing days he realized that most of his opinions were self-contradictory, based on false premises, or complete mistakes, and there seemed little to take their place.

No subject was too arcane or embarrassing; it was lovely to talk openly and honestly about things he'd never said. Joel was headed to Harvard Law, Penny to Oxford and Dave for a PhD in Russian at Yale. Filled with patience and a gentle compassion for the unwise, the unlucky and unfit, they spoke of individual freedom from governments, a universal code of behavior, where the rights of one merge with those of the many.

"People don't always act in self-interest," Joel said one night they lay in sleeping bags on the fresh straw of a rustic barn. "A fireman who dies trying to save a child –"

"You can argue that my father fought in the World War Two because he was Jewish," Dave said. "But Mick, why did yours fight? Why risk his life for people thousands of miles away?"

"Dad went to war, I think, because of the injustice. Even back in nineteen forty, when he joined up, he said everybody already knew what Germans were doing to the Jews. Then we had Pearl Harbor, so he ended up fighting the Japs instead."

"What would have happened if he hadn't? If no Americans had fought?"

"People protect themselves and their children first. Then their relations and neighbors, their tribes or religions or races, then their countries. We'll never unite the world till we're attacked from outer space."

"But if we're all one tribe we have to care for each other, treat each other fairly. Not attack and steal and cheat others... There's not a single idea in existentialist philosophy that equals *Do unto others as you would have them do unto you.*"

Mick snickered. "So you guys killed him."

"We had to make him famous so you goys would listen to him."

His companions were living at a higher income level than he, though they wanted to pay his share, and after a week in Rome he'd run out of money. They were heading to Pescara and up the Adriatic coast to Venice; one cool rainy morning he hugged them goodbye and hitched north toward France.

Immediately a Fiat 850 stopped, the driver a black-cassocked priest. Set into the middle of the Fiat's dashboard was a little record player that could be pulled out to change records. The priest played it constantly as he drove at high speed, dodging between trucks and other cars as he scrabbled through a pile of 45 rpm disks looking for something he hadn't played, singing vociferously with the arias from the record player. "Don't worry," he smiled black teeth. "God is with us."

A day later a truck dropped him on the coast road north of La Spezia under dark cliffs crested with black firs. It had turned gray and misty and night was falling. He walked uphill on the shoulder, trucks spraying him as they roared past. There was no place to hitch and no one could see him in the driving rain. It ran through his hair down his chest through his crotch and legs and sloshed in his shoes. By midnight he gave up and squirmed into his soaked sleeping bag in the scrub at the edge of the highway.

Trucks thundered up the hill all night, tires hissing. At dawn two businessmen picked him up. He sat shivering and steaming in the back seat of their Lancia, trying not to drip on the glossy leather. They gave him twenty lire and dropped him at a town with a café where he huddled over a bowl of coffee and milk and flat dry pastries.

Rides were too few, the waits too long. Unceasing frigid rain sawed through the trees, swept the glistening road and rumbled in rivulets and rivers down the mountains. Everything he had was soaked: there were puddles in his pockets and inside the sleeping bag; his last chunk of bread was pudding.

That evening he slogged into Genoa. In chandeliered restaurants men and women dined at plush tables on white china. His stomach seared with hunger, an acid emptiness, a dizzy weakness, a sense of defeat. He was furious with himself for being alone and cold and miserable while these handsome people lived warm contented lives. They had fixed themselves a secure niche in life and he had failed.

A train ticket to Menton took the last fifteen lire of the twenty the businessman had given him. The train compartment was warm and lighted and he could look out the shiny window and wonder at the lights of homes and farms as they flitted past. A woman came into the compartment and sat by the window across from him. She took out a half-done sweater and began to knit. Occasionally she smiled at him. She left the train at a small town where wind riffled the puddles under the weak platform lights. As it left the station he noticed her purse in the corner of her seat.

The train screamed and shivered through the night. He thought of the sandwiches in the restaurant car. After a while he closed the curtains and opened her purse. A handkerchief, lipstick, and fifty-three lire. He took the money, put the purse back in the corner and opened the curtains. A passing conductor saw the purse and took it.

The conductor returned with two carabinieri. One explained in French that it was obvious Mick had taken some money, there was none. They made him empty his pockets, counted his money and asked how much was hers.

He said it was all his, feeling horrible, pretending to be angry but was sure they could see into the back of his eyes, his guilt. The train stopped at a small station; while it steamed and idled in the rain he could see the carabinieri telephoning. Trying to seem calm he walked quickly from car to car, pneumatic doors hissing, and at an open coupling slid down between the wheels and out into the darkness.

Back in Aix he was hounded by guilt. There was no way he could send her the money for he didn't know her name or address. As soon as he got another laboring job he put twice the amount in the poor box at St. Sauveur but felt no better. He stepped out of the cathedral into the Provençal sun resolving to never steal again, knowing that would not absolve him either.

29

THE LIVING DEAD

TARA DIDN'T GO HOME to Nyack in June after her freshman year, instead took her two suitcases of books and clothes and her battered guitar and moved in with Blade in his Oakland pad, and two weeks later went with him on his next tour, bar gigs first in Oakland then Fillmore Street in San Francisco, then San Jose and all over the Bay Area, belting out the blues to mostly black audiences who were hostile at first but soon cheered her wildly, assaulting her with hugs and free beer. "You the one!" a big man squeezed her to his sweaty belly. "You sing like an angel, girl. A white angel."

"You got Odetta *down*, Baby," Blade said.

"I'm not Odetta. I'm me."

It was entrancing to be alive, deep in the joy of song and freedom. Music sweet music for hours, from morning through day and night into morning again. When then they didn't tour they practiced in the chilly back room of a south Oakland warehouse. When she thought about university it was like a boring dream. Blade on the piano and vocals, his deep voice like an oak tree in the middle of the song, Sybil the drummer so understated, so clean, Tiny the huge bass player, so black his skin shone like ebony in the sweat of concerts, and Luis, Luis the fiery guitarist, doctor and priest of the sweetest most beautiful soul-moving solos, his blue Telecaster reaching for the infinite of perfect truth and beauty, touching it and falling again – it was the greatest human achievement: going beyond. Touching God.

Once in a flash she understood music for the first time, discovered what she'd been living. That music is talking to God. Sometimes even touching God, when the artist reaches perfection.

"This, what we're having now, like it's the most amazing musical renaissance since the eighteenth century," Luis said. "A return to Mozart, like for instance. And *we* are right in the *middle* of it!"

Even mainline music was moving. The stuff white kids listened to. Sure there were tons of adenoidal love songs, *You're the Reason I'm Living* – how silly could that be, to base your existence on another person – *Can't Get Used to Losing You,* or the misnamed *End of the World* – can a guy actually imagine his world ending just because some teenage girl tells him goodbye?

Did all love music have to be saccharine? Not in the blues. Not Johnny Cash,

Bound by wild desire
I fell into a ring of fire...

Then there were the meaningless songs, *Puff the Magic Dragon,* that the Pentagon had used to name a C-130 gunship that could riddle a football-field sized piece of Vietnam with 50 Caliber bullets, or *Da Doo Ron Ron, Everybody's gone surfin', Surfin' U.S.A.*

Most people didn't surf. They fought every day just to be alive. Where was *that* music? There was this raunchy skinny kid with a voice like a coffee grinder and a beat-up guitar. Peter Paul and Mary sang one of his songs,

How many years must one man have
Before he can hear people cry?

Out of the syrupy morass of commercial music, where did this come from? It went on...

Yes and how many years can some people exist
Before they're allowed to be free?

Enough to blow your fuckin' mind. Maybe there was some hope, after all.

MICK RETURNED in June to Nyack, happy to be back but already missing Provence, the girls and wine and food, and worried about Dad who seemed even more frail and alone. Rather than drive Coke trucks Mick got a better-paying job digging ditches for Rockland Construction, sweaty hard work that left him every evening feeling weary but productive: unlike school, what he did created something, even if it was just a hole in the ground.

ALL SUMMER Troy worked at the Air Force Academy on a physics project – "learning how to fool radar," he told Dad cryptically in a two-minute call from Colorado Springs. He came home for just a week in August, thin and muscled with his sandy hair buzz-cut, freckles darkened by high-altitude sun, sleeves rolled down and buttoned, and with a taut aloofness Mick remembered from their first day in the deserted army barracks.

They got a sixpack of Blue Ribbon at Hal's, took it up to Washington's Spring and sat on the knoll as the orange sun set behind Lafayette's house, turning the pasture a golden haze. "Dad's afraid you're going to fuck up Williams again," Troy said.

"I hate it, the sitting in an airless room learning about the composition of some molecule, while outside the sun's pouring down over the leaves, the birds are singing, the air's warm – or it's a beautiful winter day with blue sky and sun sparkling on the snow – you'd have to be crazy."

Troy leaned forward. "But that's how you get ahead."

"Ahead? Where to?"

"To do some good in the world, dammit. You know what I'm talking about."

"You shouldn't have to cut off your nuts to make the world a better place."

The mosquitoes began to bite so they went down to Hal's for another six-pack and went back to Nyack where Dad was sitting at the kitchen table doing a crossword puzzle.

"You should stay longer," Dad said to Troy.

"He must have a girl out there," Mick said.

"No." Troy's face was serious. "When I meet a girl I get all worried, can't be myself. I try so hard to relax I can't relax at all."

"You'll find somebody to love." Dad coughed, covered it. "Then when you look back on these years you'll wonder why you ever worried. Or forget you did."

"Sometimes at night I walk across the snow, every flake glinting like a star, and I feel I'm walking out there, in that universe, that my time on earth is tiny, and forever after I'll be wandering the stars. And not having a girl doesn't matter."

"What does matter?" Dad said, trying not to cough.

"To be a pilot. Take care of my country."

Mick grinned. "Your country's doing just fine."

"We're surrounded by dangers." Troy's face strained with explaining the obvious to someone who won't understand. "The Communists are even in Cuba now."

"That was a revolution, for Christ's sake!" Dad growled. "Got rid of Batista and the Mafia, the casinos and whorehouses and heroin, gave the people back their country. And now we have all these Cuban Mafiosos in Florida begging Kennedy to attack Castro, put them back in power. It's nauseating."

Troy gazed at him with distant hazel eyes. "Kennedy screwed the Bay of Pigs."

"The CIA was supposed to do it," Dad snapped. "On their own without the military. They double-crossed him, got stuck and begged him to send in troops and air cover, tried to take him down when he stood firm."

Troy looked away, not speaking. "You don't leave men on the beach."

"I got left on the beach," Dad said softly. "At Tarawa a lot of good Marines got left on the beach. The brass said the beach was clear and it was an easy wade. But they dropped us a mile offshore – lots of Marines drowned before they ever reached that goddamn beach. Then the Japs opened up. We got shredded. You can't know what it's like to be pinned on a beach with machine guns working you over and all you hear is the whack of bullets killing your friends." He cleared his throat. "Then our planes bombed us and dropped our supplies on the Japs."

"I know what it's like. War."

"Hell you do. Not till you been in it." Dad stifled a cough. "But the Bay of Pigs? We had no right to be there. That's what revolution means: people have a right to have their own country."

"Vietnam," Mick said.

"Vietnam?" Troy snickered. "We're just pissing around in the jungle, getting a little practice. Nobody'd be so stupid as to get into a war there."

"We shouldn't be there, either."

"We're not," Troy smiled.

"Don't joke," Dad said.

Mick stared at his Blue Ribbon can as if it might contain the key to Troy's hostile distance. "Buddhist monks are setting themselves on fire in Saigon. To tell the world how bad things are..."

"We're supporting a Catholic dictatorship," Dad said, "in a country that's ninety-eight percent Buddhist. They're killing hundreds of people, peaceful folks worshiping in temples, gunning nuns down in the street, trashing pagodas, Christ, they kill praying monks for Chrissake. Coup after coup of murdering generals, all supported by the good old USA – where do they think that'll lead to?"

"They don't value life," Troy said. "Those people."

"Don't say that, son." Dad looked at Troy. "Don't even pretend that's true. Not about anyone."

. . .

TARA WATCHED BLADE drop his clothes to the floor. Behind him the closet mirror door showed his back, long and sinewed, the slender muscled shoulders, the hard buttocks and chiseled legs. Naked under her silk kimono on the waterbed she felt hot and trembly. He came toward her, the thick prick in its black nest already swelling and she knelt up and kissed it, rose up and took him in her arms, loving the hardness of him.

"God, Baby," he whispered, rough fingers up her spine, "I love to fuck you."

"I love it too. I love you inside me."

"I love how you sing, how you walk, you talk. But most of all I love to fuck you."

She caressed his prick. He sighed; she squeezed. "That why you're fucking Melanie too, and that groupie Ginger?" She squeezed harder "– don't say you didn't –"

"Ginger I just did once, Baby. Had to, poor girl was in a nervous breakdown."

"You don't stop fucking Melanie," she squeezed tighter, "you're gonna have a dick breakdown –"

He took away her hand, raised her up and slid her down on top of him, deep inside her. "Oh Jesus this is so good," she bit his neck, raked his back. "Fill me up, you bastard, you prick. Fuck me to death."

PLAYING BASEBALL in the warm August evenings made the so-called trouble in Vietnam seem unreal. To Mick the only reality was the lowering sun through the tall oaks and elms, the cooling breeze, the chatter of crows strutting at the edge of the outfield, the magic whack of a wooden bat against a speeding ball, a lovely twisting line drive down the third base line and its satisfying smack into his glove – these things were true, the instant fusion of perception and reality, joy and understanding.

Generals and politicians were without joy or caring. Spent their lives hunched over the fine details of murder, to the exclusion of the heartbeat, the song of birds, the fire of love. Mick and his friends were young and alive, the generals old and long dead. Nothing those old men could do would hurt them.

Every evening after work he'd go back to the little house in Nyack to have a whisky with Dad and cook dinner, then head out to the ball-field to meet up with whoever wanted to play ball. These days it seemed it was the adults teaching baseball to the kids. Back then we learned not from adults but from our friends, from other kids. It made us a tribe.

By mid-August he'd done enough overtime with Rockland Construction to go to Williams for early practice. The summer of digging ditches had turned his arm into what Coach Kaminski happily called The Big Gun; he was throwing flat hard passes thirty and forty yards, nailing his receivers. After each full day of practice he and Peter Weisman ran routes till the falling dusk made it hard to see the fast-moving ball and you risked breaking fingers. Two weeks later he'd beaten Spark Levene for starter. "You were on television all summer," Peter said. "Some grapefruit drink."

Mick snickered. Lovely Katya, then near-death in the Sahara, Dave, Penny and Joel in the battered green Panhard wandering Italy, the preposterous polyestered Hollywood men with their fake soda pop script, creating illusions on television to make people buy things they didn't need. Or that weren't even good for them.

Like war.

AND WAR WAS ALWAYS WAITING. Fearing the silos of American missiles ringing its western borders, the Soviet Union had secretly shipped missiles to Cuba in the fall of 1962. When Kennedy learned of it, his military advisors argued for an Air Force attack on the silos. Fearing nuclear war, Kennedy instead ordered a quarantine of all ships entering Cuban waters. Soviet Premier Khrushchev termed this quarantine "an act of aggression propelling humankind into the abyss of a world nuclear-missile war."

While the world waited, the two sides negotiated. Kennedy won:

the Soviets removed the missiles in return for an American promise to never invade Cuba.

But once again, Mick realized, we've been warned.

THE COMMUNISTS had built a wall through the middle of Berlin, encircling the zone governed by the US, France and Britain. Before this thousands of Eastern Europeans had escaped to the West via Berlin.

Once again, Kennedy met them with strength, going to Berlin to promise its surrounded citizens that they would be protected. "Freedom has many difficulties and democracy is not perfect," he told them, "but we have never had to put a wall up to keep our people in, to prevent them from leaving us."

"When one man is enslaved," he said, "all are not free. When all are free, then we can look forward to that day when this city will be joined as one and this country and this great continent of Europe in a peaceful and hopeful globe."

AFTER THE BAND TOUR Tara worked afternoons as a grocery checker and practiced with the band at night, the supermarket's daily boredom and exhaustion tempered by the fun of seeing people she knew and liked from their Oakland neighborhood, catching up on their stories, their daily lives. Then the burning excitement of music at night.

Wherever they played live, the bars filled, the broken-down old movie theaters where they stood up on the stage and hammered out the blues to cheering clapping crowds, lots of white faces now under the bug-stained fluorescent lights, the music a lovely snake up and down her spine as she sang out its glory to the crowd.

Blade had stopped fucking Melanie and Ginger but now was doing a half dozen other women at the same time, every chance he got, up against a wall in the women's bathroom, in the back of the band bus rolling through peaceful San Luis Obispo farmlands, in a closet behind the stage before a concert, in a potato field in the rain.

She didn't care, she told herself. She and he weren't going to last a lifetime. And doing it with him every fuck was precious, none to be lost. Look at it that way. And she was still fucking him twice a day – so who cared about these other chicks?

And like he said, any time she wanted she could fuck someone else. Luis maybe; one night drunk and stoned she'd almost come just kissing him. Be fun to fuck him, see what Blade did.

But Blade was a little crazy these days, his little cousin dying in that church dynamite bombing in Birmingham. Beyond sickening, the Klan killing four little girls and injuring a lot of others, in the middle of a sermon, Blade said, about loving and forgiving. You could see why Malcolm X called us white devils.

JUST A RUN-THROUGH, Coach Kaminsky said, no pads. Thursday practice, a week before the Thanksgiving Game at Amherst. Mick dropped back to check off his receivers, drew back to gun one to Peter on a slant as Link Doolittle broke through the line and smashed him to the ground knocking the ball loose and ripping his arm out of the socket. He writhed under Link's huge weight, crushed by pain. "Get off me you asshole!"

Link pushed himself up, smiled down. "Sorry, man. Got carried away."

Mick sat up choking with agony. Bolts of white-hot pain shot through his shoulder. The arm would not go back in the socket. He walked bent over in circles gasping. The arm hung uselessly, the shoulder afire. Coach Kaminsky ran up. "Oh Christ," he said. "Oh Jesus Christ."

At the hospital it took an hour to get the arm back in the socket. He lay sleepless all night in a shoulder cast and no matter how much morphine they gave him the pain never eased. In the morning he went to classes wracked with pain and nauseous with codeine, because if he cut another class Dean Brooks would throw him out. He threw up in a toilet and came out into a strange silence. A professor ran by weeping. A student sat on the front steps with his face in his hands. "Oh no," someone was crying, "Oh no."

"What's your fucking problem?" Mick said.

The kid looked up at him, astonished. "They just shot Kennedy."

No. It wasn't possible. Nothing could be that bad. No one would do this. He wandered across a lawn, wind sighing in bare elms. The sun gleamed. Tears ran down his face. "I loved him so much," he cried. "We all did. Who could do this?"

The shoulder pain was forgotten. He didn't care if he ever played football. He didn't care about Williams. No one cared about anything except to huddle round somber televisions as the blood-stained widow wept beside the ugly schemer from Texas, the state where the President had been murdered and America's future poisoned for good.

This nation of 180 million had crossed an irrevocable divide and would never trust or value itself as it had. Americans would never think of themselves with the same innocent pride. A nation that kills its leaders is not worthy of pride.

Where could this happen but in a totalitarian state, a fascist dictatorship? Is that what we were? America was dead, but like a walking cadaver would carry on. The living dead.

30

EVERY TRUTH

L IKE A WALKING CADAVER America carried on, in a stunned, hollow and bereaved world. Even in the far reaches of the Soviet Union and the depths of Africa millions wept; around the world stores sold millions of long-playing albums of JFK's speeches and photo books of this handsome man, beautiful woman and their pretty children.

The mourning did not cease, just slowly diminished the way an amputation never goes away. Some people even exulted: Kennedy was too handsome, too smart. The people loved him too much. Johnson was a Democrat too but at least he was from Texas. To Mick it was a sickening metaphor: the bright, caring president and his lovely wife usurped by the nation's ugliest man and woman, their homely daughters fawning toothily in the background.

Sorrow remained but fury grew. America wanted payback. To find the killers and make them suffer for the nation they had bereaved and disenfranchised.

Oswald had been killed in the Dallas jail by a Mafia hit man tied to the CIA, but there was no connection, the government said. A week after Kennedy's assassination Johnson appointed a committee led by Chief Justice Earl Warren, one Republican and one Democrat

Senator and Congressman, the former CIA director Allen Dulles, and the former head of the World Bank. "It's the fox in the chicken coop," Peter Weisman said. "The CIA was probably involved in killing Kennedy and you have its former director on the Commission?"

"And four right-wing politicians. Three southerners and some guy from Michigan named Ford."

"Probably an Edsel," someone chuckled.

"Gonna be a coverup," Peter said. "Just wait."

As months passed it became clear the truth would not be told. America wasn't going to face that it had murdered itself. Mick's grades slid, but why bother if a degree meant entry to a culture you had no desire to join? A rat race where you had to be a rat to get in the race?

The ripped nerves in his arm came back, a steady agony from hand to shoulder. But he would never play football again, never throw a baseball. "You can keep your scholarship," Dean Brooks said. "We owe you that. But you have to study."

"I don't give a damn about studying."

Dean Brooks glanced at his long fingers folded on his mahogany desk. "None of us gives a damn sometimes. Since last November I don't either. But the measure of a man is he soldiers on. That's what Jack Kennedy would want you to do."

"You don't soldier on," Mick answered, "if you're in the wrong war."

"NEGROES GET KILLED if they register to vote in Mississippi. Some almost entirely Negro counties don't have a single registered Negro voter. Most folks can't get an education, they're not allowed it. And the white police, most of whom are equally illiterate, are incredibly brutal."

Daisy Moran sat jammed into a crowded Kent State lounge with rust-red curtains, its night windows streaked with rain. A muscular, dynamic man in his mid-thirties, wearing a blue pinstripe button-down shirt, Al Lowenstein was speaking to nearly a hundred students about helping to register Negro voters in Mississippi.

He paced the low smoky room talking fast, his hands chopping off words, a man with so much in his mind he couldn't get it out fast enough, wanting so hard to reach these young people squeezed onto sofas, the girls in plaid skirts sitting on the carpet with their knees tucked sideways, the guys in tan chinos with their backs against the wall.

"Mississippi's the poorest state in our nation," he said. "Most Negroes live far below the poverty line." His black-rimmed glasses kept sliding down his nose and he pushed them up as he spoke, his black tie askew, a wiry powerful man bent forward by the strength of his shoulders. He turned to Daisy. "Where you from?"

"Jefferson County, Iowa."

He grinned. "Farm country."

She smiled back. "*Hog* country."

He pretended to hold his nose, pushed up his thick glasses. "How many of your neighbors don't vote?"

"Nobody don't," she said, slipping into Iowa twang, corrected herself. "Everybody votes."

He faced the others. A warm, expectant kindness seemed to emanate from him, yet he seemed always on the attack, seeking the right solution, the just answer. "Ask yourselves the same question."

The room fell silent. "So we want to send the best of America to Mississippi," he called loudly. "As many of you as possible. To give other Americans the chance take part in this remarkable democracy of ours..." He pushed at his glasses. "But I have to warn you: some people who come down are getting arrested and beaten..."

To Daisy, caught in the ecstasy of giving, being beaten seemed a small price to pay for these people's freedom. Her heart warmed to think of herself standing bravely at the bars of a cell. After all, her mother had been beaten, hadn't she? Many times? And me too, she remembered. With shame.

"We need you for many things. For this summer's SNCC voter registration drive. That's the Student Nonviolent Coordinating

Committee – I want you to remember that its most important word is *Non-violent*... We need you to help register people to vote, help them fill out the forms so they can't be turned down by the registrar. To teach in our Freedom Schools, give kids the basic education they're not allowed in public schools."

Last year, he said, NAACP and SNCC had started the Freedom Vote, Yale and Stanford students came to Mississippi to set up mock elections showing how to vote. "And now we're creating a whole new party, the Freedom Democratic Party, because Negroes have always been shut out of the Democratic Party. We're going to challenge the traditional Democrats for seats at this year's Democratic presidential convention..."

Daisy felt him reaching out to her personally; it gave her a warm flush up the back of her neck, tingling the hairs. "Expect it to be difficult," he said. "Expect it to be dangerous. Negroes have been lynched simply for going to meetings..."

He let that sink in. "If you want to join us you have to apply by April 15. By May 15 we'll tell you if you're accepted and where you'll be assigned. Bring a hundred and fifty dollars to orientation, and proof of a source of bail money."

The choice was almost funny. She could help poor people in Mississippi or take two summer graduate classes there at Kent State. One was advertising sociology, the other on *The Lonely Crowd*, Reisman's analysis of how Americans had become other-directed, living in a desert of suburban superficiality, driven more by their peers' values than their own.

Anyway Mississippi couldn't be that bad – this was America. Mr. Lowenstein was just weeding out the uncommitted. "I'm going," she told her roommate Bethany.

"Sounds scary to me. Even Mr. Lowenstein said you could go to jail."

"There'll be so many of us... We can change our country!"

Back in her room, full of excitement and energy, she switched on her radio. There it was again, that amazing Dylan song that made you weep, how a drunken tobacco farmer named William Zanzinger caned to death a 51-year old black waitress with ten children because she was slow in bringing his next whisky, and the judge, after lengthy contemplation, had given him a six-month sentence.

It didn't seem possible. Everybody needed to get together and change things. We could do it; it wasn't impossible.

NEW YORK CITY was an animal. Alive, breathing, moving, passion and danger. An animal that devoured people, Mick realized every time he went there. It left their mutilated bodies in the East River, under elevated subways, in Central Park, in Harlem, and all the finest funeral parlors and cemeteries. There was no sentimentality involved. New York merely hunted you down.

If you were young and strong, you stupidly did not fear it. You watched in the subways at night and kept your distance on the sidewalks. You were careful in traffic, or thought you were. But no matter what you did, if New York wanted it would kill you.

It was killing Cousin Johnny. Johnny who had never belonged, an alien parachuted into the family – too gentle, too unconcerned – couldn't get along with Uncle Hal coming home late from running the bar, smelling of tobacco smoke and sweat, and Johnny in bed dreaming of ways to leave home.

The easiest way was reform school. At fifteen Johnny'd gone there. A few minor thefts and they yanked you from your alleged home and isolated you with other guys who'd done things far worse than you, so you had good teachers. It was a school for crime, and when you did two years, as Johnny did, you'd learned a lot.

What Johnny learned most was heroin. "Sitting in that cell, man, day after day." He paced his dirt-poor Harlem apartment as he always did, facing downward as if in a cage too small, speaking in clauses conjuncted with "man", a rhythm, a beat. "Sitting in that cell, man, nothing to do. Going crazy, man. Guy offers you the needle. That's grace, man." Pacing, waving his cigarette, short and scrawny, handsome peaked features and lanky blond hair.

And every time Mick talked to Johnny about going straight he promised he would. Nodded and agreed, waving his Viceroy in smoky circles, how Horse had ruined him. But he had to take care of his dealers. Or they'd kill him.

Mick had stopped to see him on his way to meet Tara in the West Village. She was in town for a concert and staying as usual at the Chelsea Hotel. "So go away," Mick told Johnny. "Come to Williamstown in the fall and stay with me."

Johnny grinned yellow teeth at Mick's innocence. "They'd find me, man."

But maybe some people just wanted to ruin themselves. You tried and tried to help them and it didn't work. So after a while you tried not to care – did that make it worse?

After leaving Johnny's place he'd taken the Seventh Avenue Express downtown to the West Village and walked Christopher Street to the White Horse.

Tara waved from a table in the corner and nearly knocked over her glass as she jumped up to hug him. He felt the ribs in her back; her hair was frayed, and she smelled of patchouli and Lucky Strikes.

"You are such a hunk!" she smiled. "Wish you weren't my brother."

He felt an instant as if a stranger had become his sister, thought of Ma. "So you're playing at Crossroads?"

"Tuesday and Friday nights." She lit a Lucky, squinting through smoke. "You've been there?"

"For Peter, Paul, and Mary. They were amazing. Put you in another place."

"Yeah?" she grinned, eyes sparkling with affection. "So how's Dad?"

"He likes having me home, I think. He's getting around, coughs a lot. Drinks a lot of whisky, but then he always has."

"Us O'Briens –" She smiled into his eyes. "What about you?"

"Uncle Hal got me a job working construction... Good money. Most of it goes to Dad, his pension's not enough to live on."

She nodded, looked away, back at him. "I'm sending money too. He paid my year at Berkelely out of his plastics factory settlement..." Her eyes dampened. "And he was so unhappy when I didn't go back..."

Mick shrugged: what could he tell her? Give up this music foolishness, get a real life? Oh yeah? What kind of "real" life did *he* have?

"What you drinking?" he said, to stop thinking.

"Benedictine. Gives a nice roughness to my voice. That and the cigs."

He said nothing, so as to hide his disapproval of her smoking. Or was he angry she'd left school? Then annoyed at himself for being such a hypocrite? "Heard from Troy?"

"Last month we did a gig in Denver, I called him. He said he'd come up from Colorado Springs but never did."

"He thinks it's right, Vietnam –"

"We've got a new agent, Barney Dilson – you heard of him? Anyway he's talking to RCA, sent them our tapes."

How many bands, Mick wondered, were trying to make it? In how many garages and basements around the country? "How's your love life?" It was easy to ask, but he didn't want to think about her fucking.

"Still with Blade." She shrugged. "We're traveling all the time... Sometimes it's good, sometimes not." She lit another Lucky Strike. "You know how it goes –"

"No I don't."

"He's laying all these other chicks. Sometimes three or four a night, I never know if I'm sleeping with him or down the hall." She smiled resignation; he saw through it to the sorrow inside. "He tells me to screw anybody I want." She tipped her Lucky into the ashtray. "But I'm not that interested." She tried a perky smile. "I just want to make music. Be with Blade... We got a little black cat. He calls her Onya because she's on ya all the time."

"I still think about Rusty –"

"Yeah." Her eyes sparkled. "I'm gonna have a farm some day, a dog like him."

"How much you miss when there's no animals in your life."

"Onya sleeps on me. Sits on the floor and listens while I practice. Christ she even climbs on us when we're fucking –"

His flinch was noticeable. "So how's *your* love life?" she asked.

It surprised him, the question. "Don't have one."

"Since when have you not been getting laid –"

"Yeah, that – sure. But I want to be with somebody I love. Want to come home at night and she's there, be there when she comes home..." He couldn't explain it, this hunger for warmth and affection, the closeness of another's beloved body.

"You can never be alone yet be real lonely," she said.

"It's not that, I love my solitude. It's –"

She lit another Lucky, slowly shook out the match. "Yeah?"

He shrugged, thought of Daisy Moran, from back in Nyack High. Why had that been different? Or was he just imagining it, as a way to avoid commitment now? Memory's a lie, anyway.

"What do you think they'll say," she asked. "This Warren Commission?"

"That Oswald was the only shooter."

"They think they can fool an entire country?"

"We're easy to fool. Just tell us salute the flag and recite the pledge of allegiance, pay our taxes and keep our heads in the trough –"

Two couples came in laughing and hugging. "How out of tune the world is," Tara said. "Look at them all happy while our President's been killed and the government lies to us about who did it. While Vietnam is being destroyed, and nobody cares... All over the world good and evil, happy and unhappy people, and no harmony, no connection."

"The farmer busy plowing?"

"So many people dying to supposedly make a better world."

The idea was disgusting. "Every lie just causes more evil."

She smiled over the rim of her glass. "And every truth?"

31

FREEDOM SUMMER

MALCOLM X HAD EVERY RIGHT to hate whites, Mick concluded, once you understood what he'd lived through, what so many black people had gone through. Though Malcolm didn't stress it.

Speaking in the basement of a worn, mildewy Harlem church, he was less fiery than gentle, leading his listeners inexorably from point to point, from reason to resolution. Mick was at once transfixed by Malcolm's simple logic: if something is wrong, we can learn what it is and fix it.

When Malcolm had been a child his family had been threatened and chased from state to state by the Ku Klux Klan; they burned down the family home and killed his father, drove his mother crazy. For years he bounced from one foster home to another, remaining however a brilliant student till a teacher told him that niggers couldn't go to law school.

He wandered, worked odd jobs, moved to Harlem and slipped into a life of crime, got arrested and sentenced to eight years in jail, where he converted to the Nation of Islam. Once paroled he became a major spokesman and minister for the group, teaching that white people originated from devils and would soon vanish, that blacks were the first people and superior to whites. Better than integration, he preached, was total separation of blacks and whites till blacks could go home to Africa.

He scorned black civil rights leaders for embracing non-violence, because violence was sometimes necessary for self-protection, as he had learned growing up. In return the civil rights leaders feared and disliked him, and worried he would hurt their image.

But with his impetus the Nation of Islam grew fast, pulling in well-known people like Cassius Clay. When Castro had come to the United Nations he'd met with Malcolm and invited him to Cuba. But Malcolm was parting ways with the Nation of Islam over its too-intensive religious doctrine and hostility to the white world. The way to progress, he was learning, was to work with other black leaders, speak on campuses, forge a dialogue. Change the world.

As Malcolm spoke, Mick eyed the weary old church, the rust stains down the plaster walls and the holes in the linoleum floor; the varnish had worn from the pews. Malcolm spoke brilliantly, earnestly, his hands and fingers stressing his points. "We do not believe in the accommodation of the so-called civil rights movement with corporate, racist America," he said. "And you out there doing the peaceful thing, the non-confrontational thing, you're not helping change our servitude. You're not changing the whites." He stared round the room. "You can forget freedom, unless you're ready to fight and die for it. You can't be civil if you want your civil rights."

People clapped and cheered, the young guys excited. Faces turned toward Mick and Johnny, the only whites in a thick crowd of blacks; a few scowled but most smiled: *we don't mind you being here.* "Please remember, all of you," Malcolm pleaded, "no one but you can guarantee your freedom. No one but you can make you feel equal or give you justice. You have to take it on your own –"

Mick turned to a man named Smiley, one of Malcolm's bodyguards. "He says it like it is."

"And like he says," Smiley answered. "Non-violence is cool, long as it works."

· · ·

DAISY'S ORIENTATION FOR MISSISSIPPI lasted a week at the Western College for Women in Oxford, Ohio. "Many Negro people don't even know they can vote," a young soft-spoken man named Bob Moses told them. "Many are sharecroppers scraping out tiny incomes for endless hours in other people's fields, and don't know what rights they have or if they have any at all –"

He halted mid-phrase, letting it sink in. "Because they get so little school many are illiterate. Yet to register to vote they must pass a literacy test given by a white registrar who will fail them anyway no matter how well they do."

Slender and intense, he radiated both a calm clarity about what was wrong and right, that as a black man he'd seen the only way to change things was to live what was right. "When other folks and I first came to Mississippi in 1960," he told them, "we realized that change will come only for Negroes when they can vote."

He'd said when other folks and I, yet he'd been the one who ran the SNCC voter registration drive, had left a safe life in New York to risk death every day. The first man he'd registered, Herbert Lee, had been shot. He'd been threatened so many times, beaten and jailed, but it didn't seem to diminish his quiet determination.

"When we first came to Mississippi," he added in his mild, careful voice, "many Negroes were afraid to talk or meet with us. They knew the whites hated us and wanted to kill us. They expected we'd get them in trouble then leave. It was only when they realized we were there to stay, that the Negroes began to come around."

Passing him that evening in a corridor she ached to wrap his slender frame in warm protective arms, imagined making love with him, his thin agility, his hard ribs. She swallowed. "I'm happy doing this. But I'm a little scared."

"We're all scared," he smiled, and she felt instant shame to have spoken of fear to one who faced death so constantly. "Part of the deal," he added. "Free of charge." He squeezed her arm. "Consider it a growth experience. And the good you do will keep on growing." He turned to a man tugging earnestly at his arm. "Sure," he told him, "we can handle that," then glanced at Daisy. "I thank you."

"And I you," she said fervently, eyes glistening, a catch in her throat.

How symbolic his name was Moses, for wasn't he was leading them out of the desert of not thinking? Of not knowing what happened in their own country? The desert of not caring?

"THREE VOLUNTEERS ARE MISSING," Bob Moses told them the last morning of orientation. "They went down yesterday to Neshoba because Mount Zion Church was firebombed by the Klan. Our volunteers were taken by the police then released last night and somebody's kidnapped them. We don't know if they're dead or alive. But we don't expect they're alive..."

All three had been at the first days of orientation: Andrew Goodman an intense, brilliant, and kindly guy Daisy had had a moment's crush on; James Chaney, an easy-going, lankish black man with a quick smile; Michael Schwerner, also brilliant and quietly determined. Daisy glanced around for Schwerner's wife Rita but she wasn't there.

The room had fallen so still she could hear her heart beat, felt a nauseous fear for the three men, herself. "I must ask you all," Moses called out, "do you still want to go? If you don't, we understand."

She saw the others' agitated faces, the fear in their eyes – who would back out? The tall, slim kid in a long-sleeved red shirt, dark tousled hair down over his brow? The blonde girl with the tough, pretty face – was she really not afraid? The red-haired guy in chinos and loafers? Maybe they'd all back out and she wouldn't go, this was telling her to get those credits in social psychology, finish her thesis on the lonely crowd.

If things were this difficult it meant you really shouldn't do them. If these people are so backward maybe there's a reason. You can't dominate the strong...

Bob Moses was still talking but she couldn't hear over the roaring in her ears. Were these three guys already dead? She felt darkness, thudding sticks and pain.

No, they'd soon reappear. Some simple explanation. When you don't know, it's easy to imagine the worst.

MISSISSIPPI was unending ragged jungle and wide undulating fields where women in brightly colored headscarfs bent working in the sun, white plantation mansions with tall fluted pillars and vast lawns, sharecropper cabins of tilted wooden slats and plastic sheets over the roof, tin chimneys, broken front steps and barefoot kids, a black boy chewing sugar cane and staring out of sightless white eyes.

In the sweltering mosquito-thick swamps where the poor held on in penury and squalor, every dream was forbidden. The poverty and aimlessness of it hollowed her soul. These people would never break their chains. As in Sartre they had no exit. Locked in a room called Absolute Poverty with no door, no window, no way out.

Try to give your children a better life was all you could do. But most of the time you knew it wasn't going to happen. "My Pa and Ma were slaves on the Anderson place," an ancient woman said. "Now you tellin' me I can *vote?*"

A white man in a rusted fifty-nine Dodge, unshaven grin, double-barreled shotgun in her face. "Goddamn Nigger Lover I can shoot you any time I want and call it a hunting accident." He smiled goodbye. "Remember, it's always coon season in Mississippi."

"Look, kid," a white farmer told her kindly, "I've lived here all my life, forty-four years. These people know their place. We know ours. Nobody wants to cross the line."

"They do."

"Most of 'em's devious and crooked and lazy. Drunks, when they can afford it. Stupid as rocks. Why we have to let them into our world?"

"They're not like that and you know it. And they didn't ask to come here."

"We also brought pigs'n chickens to America. You want them to vote too?"

. . .

A PLYWOOD KITCHEN TABLE lashed with baling wire to four pine log legs, a jar of chicory coffee in his hand, a forty-year old man with three teeth and eighteen grandchildren, a man who baled cotton and walked everywhere on bare feet, who had no car, could neither read nor write. "We appreciate you young folks comin' down here," he looked at them kindly. "But this's somethin' we got to do on our own." He clasped long sinewy fingers. "And those three volunteers? We prayin' they still alive."

The tropical air was a sweatbath of filth and decay, mosquitoes eating them alive, fireflies like omens beyond the open windows. They sat on crates around the plywood table – she, Bethany, a volunteer named Simon, the farmer and his wife. Line by line she and Simon were showing them how to fill out the State of Mississippi Voter Registration Form. Six or seven children were playing beneath the table or on the scrap of carpet or going out the screen door that had no screen and slapped against the frame. A rusted Coleman lantern with a burnt-down wick flickered in the corner. Great moths flew in and out, hissing into the lantern and into the single candle on the table.

Daisy rubbed her feet up and down her calves to slay mosquitoes. She'd been here three weeks and felt weary and heartsick. So much poverty, powerlessness, ignorance, despair. To not know what the outside world is, to understand nothing beyond the land you walk barefoot and the rent you pay.

She'd been a fool to dream that there was such a thing as justice. A right or wrong you can easily determine. The whites were caught between being racist or opening their world to dangers beyond their comprehension – it was easy to call them bigoted but many seemed just unaware or disengaged. When you too are living far below poverty, walking the earth you rent with bare feet, trying to find enough whisky to keep you going, it's so easy to go under, you've got so much to fear.

They left the cabin swatting at mosquitoes. The car was thick with them. Simon drove past the chicken coop out the mud road to the blacktop. "I'll drop you off at the Emersons' place. Like always, don't go anywhere tonight."

"What about you?"

He glanced at headlights coming up behind them in the mirror. "I'll take this old crate home. And pick you up tomorrow –"

The narrow blacktopped road curved left uphill under thick magnolia branches throwing black shadows against the dark jungle. The car behind them neared; the road curved at the crest and dropped down a long valley but there was another car across it. The lights behind them popped over the crest. "Hold on!" Simon braked and spun the car around but two more cars cut it off.

"Omigod," Bethany wailed. "They're going to rape us."

With all the headlights in their eyes Daisy couldn't see. "Don't get out," Simon said. "Whatever you do don't get out."

Big burly men blocked the lights, axe handles and ropes in their hands. "What you're doing is against the law," Simon said.

"The law!" one thunked an axe handle on the Buick's open windowsill. "We are the law, and we're arrestin you –"

"We've done nothing!" Daisy yelled.

"Shut up!" Simon hissed.

"Yes you have you stupid bitch, comin down to start a riot. That's a felony –"

"Get em out," another said. "Le's see the two cunts." He yanked her out; she punched him, smashed at his beard and rough face and stink of tobacco juice, tried to writhe loose but he held her easily, one great paw handcuffing her wrists, the other crushing her breasts as he yelled, "Hey Joonya cum get some a this!"

Joonya loomed near, huge against the lights. "Let them other ones go. This one's a keeper."

32

TONKIN

DAISY BEAT BLOODIED FISTS against the jail bars, paced the mucky floor, fists throbbing with pain, kicked the rusty steel door, stood on the bedframe trying to reach the tiny air hole in the ceiling, sat and ran a finger along the bed's corroded edge. *They will rape you,* she told herself. *Then* they kill you. That's how they do things in Mississippi.

Why had she come here? Was it worth dying for? What a fool she'd been, imagining she and other students could come down here and help these black people. Even SNCC warned you, didn't they, girl, you could be killed.

Like they killed the other three volunteers.

No, she wouldn't leave this cell till SNCC came and got her.

A cell six steps long, four across. A flop-down metal bed, a rotten blanket. The stinking hole in the floor with its chunks of shit and toilet paper made her almost vomit. *Cell.* One cell in the great body of prisoners all over the world.

She wouldn't leave till SNCC came.

Her lock yowled open and a heavyset man in a yellow shirt with tobacco teeth and a rusty beard yanked her down the corridor to an office where an immensely fat man in a gray police shirt with a gold badge watched her as imperturbably as Buddha.

"Hey Missy!" a girl called from the cells. "Watch where they takin you!"

"Shut up you!" the Buddha rumbled, turned back to Daisy. "I'm releasin' you to the custody of Hiram here."

"I won't go. I want to make a call. Please, sir. I have a right... *Help me!*" she called. "*Help! My name's Daisy Moran and they're taking me out to kill me and –*"

Hiram's great hand came down on her mouth, his other arm around her breasts as he dragged her out to a pickup truck, pinned her in beside the driver who slipped it into gear and the truck lurched away,

The night was thick and hot; she couldn't breathe. "Stop!" she screamed, kicking and fighting but couldn't break free, shaking with terror.

Still clamping her mouth Hiram jammed his tobacco beard against her ear and whispered, "When we crost them brook in them trees we slow down'n you jump out'n run up them dirt trail there 'long side the brook –" He let go her mouth. "–'n it goes to a tar street'n you go left maybe half a mile'n someone'll call your people come get you."

The idea was horrifying. "Somebody's not waiting to kill me up there?"

"Nobody ain't. I promise you thet."

"Why? Why you doing this?"

He touched her cheek, the fist that had numbed her wrist gentle now. "Go home, girly. Go back up North, 'n leave us folks alone."

She ran up the dirt trail stumbling over roots in moon-shadowed darkness. Her panting terrified her because she couldn't hear. The trail ended at a clapboard hut and a tar street glinting in moonlight. Cicadas rattled, a bird called. Somewhere a radio was singing *dancin' in the street*. Running down the street she kicked a bottle she hadn't seen that went clattering and clanging and a dog barked and then several more but no one came. After a long while she slowed, gasping and gripping her sides. Like two suns a pair of headlights came over the rise, Simon yelling in his nasal Brooklyn voice, "Daisy! *Daisy!*"

TROY CAME to Nyack for a week, taut and distant, as if Mick had offended him in some unspoken way. "If all goes well I'll be over there soon, flying F-16s."

"If all goes *well?*" Mick said, keeping the sarcasm out of his voice.

"I mean, if Vietnam lasts."

"We should get out. Now." Mick popped another beer, slid the tab into the can and offered it to Troy.

Troy waved it off. "Better Red than dead?"

"Don't give me that."

"One by one these countries 're going Communist –"

"I'd be Communist if I was them. You would be too."

"– because their legitimate governments –"

"*Whose* fucking legitimate government? Like our puppet generals in Saigon?"

"– are being undermined by the Chinese and Russians. It'll take ten years and thousands of casualties. But we'll win."

"Vietnam's nothing but rice paddies and water buffaloes!" Mick stormed. "A stone age country! It's not a fucking pawn or domino. Christ, their hero's Abraham Lincoln because he freed the slaves. But they don't tolerate invaders, so they're fighting us now just like they fought the Chinese and Japanese and French. Just like you and I would if we were them."

In the dim light of the back porch Mick saw Troy tuck in his chin and sensed he couldn't reach him, that Troy had immersed himself in a belief system, a religion safe from analysis. "It's so sad to think President Kennedy would've had us out by now."

Troy shook his head no. "And you think that's why they killed him?"

"If that's true the Warren Commission isn't going to tell us. Or they'll get off like the guy who killed Medgar Evers last year."

"Who's Medgar Evers?"

"You idiot, he was the top NAACP leader in Mississippi killed by the Ku Klux Klan. He left a wife and kids. Bastard who killed him just got off."

"Shouldn'a stuck his head in in the first place."

"Who, the Klan guy?"

"This guy Evans. If I had a wife and kids I wouldn't make such a fuss."

"Maybe he cared more about them than himself."

"So what kind of life are they going to have now? A woman and kids with no husband or father?"

True, Mick realized; I'd thought the same thing. But how do you draw the line on who or what you'll die for? "They're widening Main Street, so we have to dig new water and sewer trenches, cut down these old oaks that've been here since the Revolution. Just to have more cars."

"You used to climb those trees and wait for Daisy Moran."

It stung, the memory of Daisy in a red cardigan, strong slender hands and lovely, open face, her smile without restraint. Why did Troy always bring her up? "When she and I were kids it was like we'd always known each other."

"Ever hear from her?"

"Couple years ago. She got a National Merit scholarship to some college in Ohio."

"You should go see her."

"I thought of it." Mick rolled his shoulders against the night chill. "But who's to say what she's up to right now? Maybe has another guy..."

"You're better. She'd want you back."

Mick looked out at the growing darkness, shook his head. "Not likely." He turned to Troy. "What do *you* do, out in Colorado, to get laid?"

Troy forced a chuckle. "It happens."

"You seem so uptight I worry are you getting any. Sex is better'n war."

"You know what is history's longest-lasting republic?"

Mick sucked down the cold, delicious beer. "Shit I don't know. Rome?"

"Sparta. Seven hundred years. Because they stayed tough. Offense is the best defense."

"Not in football." Mick stood and pissed off the porch. "This new general, Westmoreland – can you *believe* that name? Exactly what we did to the Indians."

"I remember your Dad pissing off the back porch at the farm and your Ma yelling at him he was killing the pansies."

"She was *your* Ma too."

"I sometimes wonder what it'd been like. If I'd stayed in that orphanage."

"Nah, you'd of got out somehow."

Troy stood dusting his knees. "You're gonna have to go in too."

Mick popped another beer, glanced at the dusk, the house. "Ain't no skeeters."

"I mean *The War:* you're going to have fight too."

Mick shook his head. "You know I always wanted to be a Marine like Dad, fight anybody who attacked our country. But these poor rice farmers in Vietnam... I won't kill somebody who's done me no harm, my country no harm."

Troy shrugged, not listening. "The Generals are saying it'll be easy, but they know it's going to be a big one. A long war."

"I have no interest in dying. I intend to live for fucking ever."

Troy nodded at the sky. "Venus is twenty-five million miles away but it seems so close. Remember *Perelandra?* I always wanted to swim in that warm sea."

"Plenty of nice warm seas right here on earth."

"Yeah, but the ones that interest me," Troy stepped back, "are all far away."

THE BRUTALIZED BODIES of Andrew Goodman, James Chaney and Michael Schwerner were found in a Mississippi dam. The bodies of three young Negroes who had earlier been kidnapped had also been found, but the news made less mention of them.

"They're not white and Jewish," Simon said savagely that night as they sat at a scarred aluminum table drinking cold coffee and going over the next day's plans.

It was all so despicable. Daisy could not stop imagining what it had been like to watch Chaney beaten to a pulp and shot, and then be shot yourself.

And the men who did it would never be prosecuted.

To keep from going crazy you had to give up any hope of justice. Then why fight for what you have no hope of? Just to not give up. Patient and determined to the end of time.

"Fucking tragic," Simon went on, "that it'll take their deaths to get the Freedom Party into the Convention. Johnson can't turn them down now." In three weeks the Mississippi Freedom Democratic Party was sending a slate of delegates to the Democratic Convention in Atlantic City to replace the Jim Crow racist slate of the regular Democratic Party. Now Johnson had no choice.

"Here's to the state of Mississippi," Phil Ochs, on the radio everywhere,

If you drag her muddy rivers,
nameless bodies you will find.
And the fat trees of the forest
have hid a thousand crimes...
Mississippi find yourself
another country to be part of.

THE SAME DAY in August a US destroyer claimed it had been attacked by three North Vietnamese torpedo boats. And six days later Congress passed the Tonkin Gulf Resolution giving Lyndon Johnson the right to wage war anywhere in Southeast Asia without further Congressional approval.

Mick stood leaning on his shovel in bright sun waiting for the excavator to finish wrenching the roots of the last great Tappan oak from the trench he and three others were digging. For half an hour the huge machine had fought the roots; finally it ripped the last of them free and dropped them into a dump truck.

"You lazy fuckers get to work," Brent the foreman yelled. "In one hour I want this trench six feet deep and flat." He unbuttoned his jeans and pissed into the trench; it spattered near where Mick and the others stood. Mick almost climbed out and smashed him in the mouth, but then Uncle Hal would be in trouble for getting him the job.

Like Johnson, Brent thought he was in charge and could do what he wanted. Tonkin Gulf was no different; even in the newspapers it was clear North Vietnam had not attacked; why would they, with nothing to gain and so much to lose?

"No little fucker's gonna volu-intarily take on a big fucker," reasoned Max, another laborer, as they stood at Hal's Bar after work. "Johnson wants war. But it ain't him what's going to die in it."

"If we're going to war," Uncle Hal said, slapping the bar for emphasis, "goddamit let's not lie about it."

"Sometimes we need to be led into things," the cop Ray said. "Like Roosevelt in World War Two. He snuck all that Lend Lease stuff to England, waiting for us to be attacked. He knew it'd take a Pearl Harbor to get us off our ass."

"Yeah," Hal chuckled. "And it got yours nearly shot off, too, didn't it –"

"This shit happens all the time," Barney the painter said. "Remember how Hitler made up stories about attacks on Germans in Czechoslovakia so he could invade them?"

"Our ships was in neutral waters," said a small peaked man in a gray fedora.

"Lookin for trouble," Hal answered. "Who says they was fired on anyway? Even the papers don't believe it –"

"You got to believe your country," the small man said. "No matter what it says."

"I knew a guy," Hal said, "went through terrible battles all the way from North Africa up Italy then into France and Germany and survived them all. Went through Hell. First day home he slips on an icy curb and fractures his skull and dies. I knew the guy." He swiped at the bar with a rag. "That's what war's like. Fuckin' stupid."

"When your country calls," the little man persisted.

"I don't see you doin it, Sam. How come you're not lining up to fight?"

THE TONKIN GULF Resolution was the template on which the War would be built. And it turned a president who had never been elected into a military dictator beyond the control of the people. Not that they seemed to care.

"That Resolution is immoral," Peter Weisman said, when Mick went one Friday night to meet him and a City College girl named Lois at the White Horse in the Village, "for it posits the slaughter and maiming of uncountable human beings as legitimate government policy, and so teaches us not to expect morality from our government."

"Linguistically," Lois said, "it teaches us to use words falsely." Dancer-slim with a wide mouth and long golden hair, she seemed old beyond her years, as if some dark experience had aged her. "So *our* intrusion into their territory becomes *their* aggression. A person is no longer a father, brother, or son, a teenager dreaming of college or his own farm and family or a better world. Now he's *gook*, a *commie*, a little yellow thing in black pajamas to be riddled with bullets, bombed and incinerated with napalm. Thus words lose their meaning and become political symbols, and we lose understanding of reality. Why can't everybody *see* this?"

Mick shrugged. "And if you ask someone are they free, they'll say America's the freest country in the world, but it turns out they've *never been* to another country, have no idea about anything except what they're fed and taught to regurgitate when the bell rings. Some Pavlovian politician says *'Communist!'* and our fierce ignorant patriot stands up, salutes, sends other people off to die and curses anyone who disagrees with him."

"Speaking of freedom," Lois said, "this Mississippi Freedom Democratic Party may take over the state delegation in the Democratic Convention. Wouldn't *that* be something?"

"I give you Nietzsche." Peter said. *"To the extent an ideal has been falsely worshipped, reality has been robbed of its value, its meaning and its truth."*

"No shit," Mick laughed. Fat, happy, and disinterested, most people seemed ready to rob reality, to avoid an honest reckoning of the path their leaders had chosen, to numb the truth of slaughter by worshipping false freedom. Just as good Germans had disconnected concentration camps from their love of country, as Spanish priests had taught that killing an Indian was the only way to save his soul. And nothing, he realized, would change them.

ATLANTIC CITY was windy and damp; the ocean frothing under the boardwalks smelled cold and rank. The Democratic Presidential Convention was opening, but Daisy had a premonition that nothing good could happen here.

"You just got home from Mississippi," her mother had complained when she'd left Iowa for Atlantic City. "Now you're going again?"

"Mom! I worked all summer to help make this happen! We're going to get the Mississippi delegation's seats!"

"We?"

"The Freedom Democratic Party. It's going to change the country."

"Child, you can't make a difference in what politicians do."

"But if a whole bunch of us work together we *do* make a difference. Look what *we* just did in six weeks – just a bunch of scared young Negroes and white college kids – we signed up eighty thousand people –"

Her mother had turned away, folding laundry. "I'm real proud of you, dear."

It *was* exciting to be here. The MFDP delegation was led by Fannie

Lou Hamer, one of twenty children of Mississippi sharecroppers. The word was that the regular delegation was going to be denied. "The California Democratic Council's come in behind us," Bob Moses told Daisy. "And the Americans for Democratic Action."

Martin Luther King spoke to the Convention with the photos of Goodman, Chaney and Schwerner behind him. "The Party says they'll give us half the seats," Bob Moses said.

"*No!* We should get them all! Those racists, they..." she stomped in frustration.

He smiled at her affectionately. He seemed thinner and older than two months ago, before the deaths; something had gone from his eyes. "A worst case scenario."

"What about President Johnson? He *can't* let it happen!"

"If the regular Mississippi delegation isn't seated other southern states will walk out too. Johnson's afraid he might lose the south to Goldwater."

"But Goldwater doesn't stand a chance!"

"In this country, as we've seen, Daisy, anything can happen."

"They *have* to seat us! The regular Democratic delegation is tied to the people who killed Andrew, James and Michael! They're Nazis! The Democrats can't seat *them!*"

He gave her a fleeting smile. "We're not at liberty to define who seats who."

When Fanny Lou Hamer sang everyone linked hands and thoughts and dreams, you could feel the blood of your fellows coursing through your veins. "Man, this is shit," Stokely Carmichael said, leaning back under his broad-brimmed hat to stare down at her. "We're getting nowhere here. The whole situation needs a more radical approach. People only change things when there's a threat to the way things are."

"That's very cynical," Daisy said. "And I don't think it's true."

"You wait, they won't give us any seats. Or a token. Such a lovely word, *token* –"

"I think you're being faithless," she'd snapped and walked away.

Fannie Lou Hamer gave a rousing speech to the Credentials Committee that was carried on the news: "If the Freedom Democratic

Party is not seated now, I question America. Is *this* America? The land of the free and the home of the brave? Where we have to sleep with our telephones off the hook, because our *lives* be threatened daily?"

It did no good. Lyndon Johnson was nominated for four more years with flabby-lipped, sycophantic Hubert Humphrey as Vice President. The Freedom Democrats got only two seats. Goodman, Chaney, and Schwerner and so many black people had died in vain.

"It can't be!" she said.

"It's what King agreed to," Stokely said. "Him'n all the reasonable niggers."

Impossible that only nine months ago Jack Kennedy was President.

SHE TOOK THE TRAIN from Altlantic City back to Iowa, watching out the window as the flatlands of lower New York gave way to hills and lovely valleys of sparkling farms and oak forests, and she couldn't decide whether she was crazy or the world was.

The first time she'd taken a train had been when Pa uprooted them from Nyack because he'd lost his job and took them to Mom's brother in Iowa… the first time she'd taken any train. This made her think of Mick, the trains he and Troy had taken so long ago. Here she was sitting on a plush seat, and they'd been riding in boxcars.

But why did Mick stop writing her? After Pa took her and Mom from Nyack she'd written Mick for months, almost every day, and he seldom wrote back, then didn't at all.

He must've found somebody. A tall blonde, a dark-haired willowy anti-war activist. Women would go crazy for Mick. Strong, kind, loving, and honest… he really *was* like that. And funny too. And really cared for people.

Seven years, she realized with a shock, since she'd seen him. Since she'd gone away in a train with her stolid mother and silent, red-faced father. Her heart clenched, her eyes blurred with tears, a hollow ache in her throat.

The ache of sudden loss of friends and homeland. The loss of Mick.

Traveling into the painful unknown. The ache of no money. Salvation Army dresses till she'd learned to make her own. The wide emptiness of the Iowa farmfields, horizons of distant barns and seas of bare dirt and corn. The lonely roads strung together by telephone lines.

No one was sitting in the seat opposite her so she took off her sandals and put her feet up on it, skirt loose on her hips. In the seven years since Mick she'd had other guys but they weren't the same. Maybe because Mick was the first, it was so intense – sometimes twice a day but always having to hide it, do it fast somewhere... With the guys since then it just hadn't been as hot, as deep. A couple of guys in high school, more in college – that had been fun – then doing it with Simon at three a.m. on the floor of a Baptist church in Mississippi, mosquitoes howling at the window screens.

Sex with Simon was heightened, she'd known even then, by the danger and excitement. When you're at risk your body wants desperately to breed. And because of fear and watchfulness you're living at a very deep level, which makes sex extraordinary.

But once Mississippi was over the excitement had faded – Simon's nasal breathing and endless questioning. His lack of hope had bored her, killed her desire.

He hadn't come with her to the Democratic Convention. Said beforehand that the Mississippi Freedom Democratic Party would not be seated, and she was a fool to think it would.

She let the breeze through the half-opened window cool her thighs under the cotton skirt. The loveliness of flesh. The farmfields rolling by so peaceably – hard to realize this was once deep forest, huge ancient trees.

There'd be plenty of men where she was going next.

But would any of them be like Mick?

SHE AND HER MOTHER watched the last night of the Democratic Convention on her mother's flickering Zenith. At the end Bobby Kennedy came to the podium to introduce a film about his brother.

The crowed erupted with a roar of cheers and thunderous clapping. Slightly embarrassed, Bobby stood at the mike nodding his thanks and waiting for it to end.

The cheering loudened, banners and placards waving for Oklahoma, South Dakota, Arkansas, Wisconsin, every state, the whole nation. Minute after minute it went on, louder and louder. Five minutes, ten minutes; Bobby was stunned, wasn't sure what to do, kept trying to talk and the crowd roared and screamed and clapped louder, His wife Ethel smiling from the side, stunned by it too.

"Jesus their hands must hurt," her mother said.

Tears gleamed in Bobby's eyes. *He thinks this is for Jack,* Daisy realized. But it's not. It's also for him. Our giant killer. Come to take back our world.

He stepped from the mike but they didn't calm. *Six thousand people cheering,* Walter Cronkite intoned, the thunder of voices drowning his words. The chairman pounded a gavel; the cheering grew louder. "We want Bobby! *We want Bobby!"*

In the TV's cascading frames Bobby's shy smile and reluctant grin, his sad watchful eyes. The heart of the Democratic Party, of the nation, he was realizing, was his. The people's man, the man of hardworking honest caring Americans who loved their families and their country; only he could bring back what they'd lost.

"He's got my vote," her mother said.

"He's not running, Mom –"

"Don't matter. He's got my vote. Whenever and wherever he needs it."

After twenty minutes the crowd quieted enough to let him speak. In his Boston twang he thanked them for what they'd done for Jack, how Jack had been sustained by their principles and ideals. That this Democratic Party founded by Thomas Jefferson and James Madison, the world's oldest political party, must carry on to make the world a better place for coming generations.

The television picture started to flutter. "Fix that damn thing, will you!" her mother snapped. Daisy knelt before it turning the dial but then the frames started flitting back the other way, Bobby speaking of Jack, quoting Romeo and Juliet,

And when he shall die
Take him and cut him out in little stars,
And he will make the face of heav'n so fine
That all the world will be in love with night.

Aren't we all, Daisy wondered, in love with night?

In a week she'd be leaving Mom again, heading to Seattle for Peace Corps training. Then, if she was chosen, off to Kenya for two years to teach. Strange to think she'd been fighting for the freedom of people whose ancestors had been brought as slaves from Africa. Now she was going to Africa itself. Were the people the same?

Into the heart of darkness, she thought. Could that be true?

For a moment she had the impression that Mick was there beside her. Don't be afraid, he whispered. Embrace the world.

33

THE GIFT OF LIFE

GUNFIRE AND GRENADE BLASTS roared from the TV in the Williams dorm lounge. Bombs flickered; tiny figures dashed across a flare-lit field, tracers darting after them; the camera panned on American soldiers lying in pools of blood.

"Communists," said a pimpled kid. "Attacked our base."

Bodies sprawled like sleeping children on the grass. Mick stared at the screen, horrified by the useless deaths of young Americans who could have been his friends, by the courage of these small half-clad Vietnamese attacking a fortified base with their ancient rifles. "It isn't worth this."

His friend Seth Calhoun smiled ironically that anyone should challenge what the country did. "We have to stop them here. Or Indonesia's next."

"We're the invaders, not them." Mick said no more, sensing Seth's conflict between his natural humanity and his family's hardcore patriotism. Maybe Seth knew something from his Dad being so high up in the CIA. Maybe it was okay to relax into this belief – *To trust, when you know it's wrong.* Wasn't that *faith?*

Or just plain stupid. And immoral.

The camera zeroed in on a bloody beaten face, wide Asian cheeks and smashed lips, black hair splayed across a forehead, a dead stare of fatal resignation as if he'd always known he'd die here, now.

Mick went outside into the dark forest and lay on the cool moss, thinking about these new dead – young Americans and Vietnamese – and what it had felt like to die and what they'd done on this last day of their lives. Would they agree their deaths were worth it? Would their loved ones?

We couldn't keep killing and dying for nothing, he reasoned. Seth's father and the people like him who ran the country were basically good; they'd stop this War.

Through the bare November boughs he watched the myriad stars. Lying there he could imagine himself from above, looking down through the branches. Then he could rise higher, seeing the naked crowns of the trees below him, then the night-dark tawny landscape, the hills and valleys rolling away on all sides. He rose higher, seeing the edge of the earth with its gauze of blue air. Even higher till the earth vanished and the sun shrank to nothing in skeins of galaxies where he swam like a dolphin in a starlit sea.

In this vast space he felt no time or fear or loneliness, only joy in its indifferent immensity. At will, he returned to the distant bright dot that became his galaxy of gleaming synapses down long nerves of light to his own tiny whirling pinwheel, his own miniscule sun and earth, this cold moss beneath the early winter trees.

In such vast mystery how could people waste the gift of life? Kill each other?

FOR THE FIRST TIME in her life Daisy took a plane, a Boeing 707 from Des Moines to Seattle, barely a week after she'd arrived at Mom's from the Democratic Convention.

They'd driven to the Des Moines Airport in Mom's sun-faded '57 two-tone blue Chevy. Daisy felt like a criminal for leaving her mother now that her father had gone somewhere and hopefully wasn't coming back. But she felt a stubborn determination that the best way to help her mother was to go to the other side of the earth and teach school. Or maybe, she wondered, I'm like my father: running away?

From the first day, however, Kenya Peace Corps training at the University of Washington could only be described as intense. From day one the language was Swahili, 12 hours every day of Swahili, East African history, the top twenty most dangerous snakes, political unrest, the twenty most dangerous insects, black-white anthropology, other dangerous creatures including hippopotami, lions, elephants, rhinos, leopards, hyenas, politicians and many more.

Swahili came easily, as if she'd known it long ago, its roots deep in Bantu and the region including Tanzania, Kenya, and five other countries. She wondered where the Bantu had come from, and the languages before that, all the way back to the Africans who headed north a half million years ago to create the modern world.

A metaphor for East African history, she decided, could be the boundary between Kenya and Tanzania, supposedly drawn by Queen Victoria in 1886 to give Mount Kilimanjaro as a gift to her grandson Wilhelm, the German Emperor. Though the story might be untrue, she smiled to think at the irony of it, it was adopted as anti-colonial rhetoric for the offhand way European monarchs traded their African "possessions." As if it were a board game.

The truth was the British gave up Kilimanjaro for Mombasa. And the Germans gave up Mombasa to get Kilimanjaro. Guess who won?

Who lost were the Maasai and other tribes whose territories were suddenly cut in half and now subject to differing groups of white men in London and Berlin.

She was sent to Kilifi in January after finishing training. What a cool place, she thought. On the Indian Ocean, it was flat, treed country with a taste of sea in the air, near the equator, very hot in summer and even hotter in winter. There were palm trees and a sandy beach and the water of the Indian Ocean felt even warmer than the air.

Many of the people had built shacks on poles above the ground to avoid snakes, centipedes, and scorpions. Most had no screens so they burned green wood all night as a partial defense against the howling hordes of biting mosquitoes that killed many people every year with malaria.

Her students were skinny, cheerful, bright, very strong, and fast.

Most everyone was poor, many in pain, but most seemed happy. As if indifferent to their fates.

REFUSING TO LIVE any longer in a dorm, Mick rented an abandoned dentist's office at 50 Spring Street in Williamstown for fifty dollars a month, half the second floor of a three-story late Victorian with an abandoned storefront on the main floor, one other apartment on the second, and two apartments on the third inhabited by other seniors like himself who wouldn't live in dorms.

His apartment had a large pine-floored living room with tall windows on the main street and in its middle a two-foot hole where the dentist's chair had been. It had a desk and a flip-out couch. To one side was a small narrow room that had been the dentist's laboratory. It had a slate-sided sink, a two-foot-square window and a single bed. Down the corridor was a sunny little privy overlooking a wild garden.

He loved to lie on the couch at night watching the car lights flit along the ceiling, hearing voices from the sidewalk, a distant radio, a dog barking. He was free – at least from the asphyxiating social life of dorms – and though you couldn't define freedom you sure knew it when you had it.

Herm and Flossie Gooding lived with their cocker spaniel Buster in the other apartment on this floor. In their eighties, Herm and Flossie drank and fought night and day. They threw dishes and yelled and stamped the floor and broke bottles and plates till Buster would whine and one of them kicked him, at which he would howl and bay and the fighting would stop and the house grow silent again. Buster's head and back were naked with mange, for which Mick renamed him Fester. Herm, Flossie, and Fester soon came to represent *No Exit's* fated trio, a proof that Hell *is* other people.

The three other seniors upstairs were poly sci majors. One, Leo Cummings, was likely to be class valedictorian and rumored soon to be a Rhodes Scholar. If he studied at all Mick could never ascertain, as his Vassar girlfriend Wendy was always there and her erotic vocalizations very frequent as they set repeated records for sex marathons.

But as a student of American government Leo was growing worried about Vietnam. He came down grim-faced to Mick's dentist's office one February morning with James Reston's column in the *Times*. *"This country,"* Reston wrote, *"is in an undeclared and unexplained war in Vietnam. Our masters have a lot of long and fancy names for it, like escalation and retaliation, but it is a war just the same."*

"What did you expect?" Mick asked sententiously, grateful that his darker view of humanity had won out over Leo's habitual optimism.

"It's not force of law, this war! There's been no congressional declaration! Johnson doesn't have the legal right!"

"Law's just an instrument of power, Leo, you know that –"

Leo leaned forward, pointing the rolled *Times* like a sword. "There *is* a place in international politics for war. When other methods break down..."

"As long as there's war other methods always break down."

"Kosygin's been in Hanoi, working on the North Vietnamese, to make them negotiate... Now we've bombed them they *can't* back down. We've made a fool of Kosygin and the Soviets when they were trying to make peace! We've blown a fantastic chance..." Leo stood up, angry and dispirited. All his life, Mick knew, he'd aspired to public service, and now he feared he could not work for the country he loved.

I should be more sympathetic, Mick thought, but Leo's views had always seemed irrationally positive. Where, Mick wanted to ask, is your awareness of the gaping maw of Hell?

"They're going to wreck it all," Leo said as he threw down the *Times* and left, leaving Mick to wonder who and what he meant. Through the open window came warm sun and a car radio's *"Stop! In the Name of Love"* fading as it drove away.

Late at night Mick often hid out in the math library attic reading – *Germinal*, which asks what do we do in the face of others' misery? *La Condition Humaine* – is another's search for justice our responsibility as well? *The Tragic Sense of Life* – "man's highest pleasure consists in acquiring and intensifying consciousness," and Frankl – "the striving to find a meaning in one's life is the primary motivational force in man."

Though he didn't like the word "man." It recognized only half the human race, and by far the less interesting and more evil half. When speaking of people you should call them *people*. Or *humans*.

What possible "meaning in one's life" could there be? To live as most people seemed to – blindly accepting life without trying to understand and live it in the wisest and most responsible fashion – was insane, the squandering of a unique and priceless gift. And if, which he did not believe, life did not end with death, to have wasted it on trivialities seemed a crime worthy of any Hell.

MALCOLM X DIED in a hail of bullets and shotgun pellets one February evening while speaking at the Audubon Ballroom in Harlem. His killers were three members of the Nation of Islam, the group he had renounced in the last two years. To Mick what made it so ironically sad, beyond losing this incredible man with such an extraordinary mind and the willingness to speak the truth, was that he was killed not because he was radical but because he wasn't radical enough.

Killed because he didn't hate enough, not enough to survive under the rules of the Nation of Islam. How could blacks get free if they fought each other as much as the whites?

Was there some unwritten rule that only the good shall be killed?

WITH SLIM SHARP TEETH Miranda Lodge tore into an apple. "Ideas like freedom just keep you poor. For instance you could decide not to work in order to be free today, then starve tomorrow."

"You have to take a longer view," Mick said. "That's why dumb people aren't free – they can't imagine the future."

She smiled appreciatively, as her pet ocelot might at a rabbit dropped suddenly into his cage. Enjoying the irony of Mick fancying himself free, not one of the dumb ones.

She'd brought her ocelot to Mount Holyoke, walked him on a leash and all the dogs kept far away. He pissed on their hydrants and tried to rip out their throats through fences. She often carried him with his front paws over her right shoulder, back legs and tail over her left, his head high and yellow eyes staring. But now he lay sleepy-eyed across the floor of Mick's apartment, spotted tawny pure muscle.

"But freedom *is* limited," she said. "I might want to sleep with you tonight, but I have a duty to Cynthia that limits my freedom. She *is* my sister. So I can't be as free as I want to be –" she smiled, "if I *wanted* to be."

Her sister Cynthia was a sensual, dark-minded Smith sophomore with a throaty laugh, Asian eyes, a vicious sense of humor and a deep, innocent hunger to love. Her kisses lit up pinball machines behind Mick's eyes, her mouth shocked him, addictive as a drug you can never get enough of. "Cynthia doesn't mind," he said. "We've talked about it."

Miranda hissed softly, almost under her breath, and the ocelot padded over, slid into her lap and faced him. "Never was a woman born," she said, "who didn't care. If you're ever *my* lover and you cheat on me I'll claw your eyes out. Promise."

Grinning he went into the former dental lab that served as his kitchen and brought out more wine. "You wouldn't dare," he raised his glass to hers, "to sleep with me."

She flickered him a feral smile. "Why should I want to?"

34

THE OCELOT'S CLAWS

HE WOMEN IN KILIFI did most of the work, Daisy realized within days of being there. The men sat around the baobab trees and drank palm wine and swapped daughters – "you need a fourth wife? Well I do too" – while the women bore and nourished the children, worked in the fields with hoe and machete in the blazing sun, then walked often for miles to a water hole and back with a huge plastic jug of water on their heads, or walked for miles to the last standing trees that could be cut down and carried home as logs on top of their heads, and they cooked the meals and watched over the children and satisfied the men's needs and on and on and on...

What did this say about men and women in Kenya, she wondered. Or all of Africa, for that matter? And what about the future? Could the women take over and save the place? Or was there something ancient in this denigration?

She wanted to tell them that we have only a few years to live and no guarantee of anything after. This is probably our only life. After this, we cease to exist. And we're surrounded by mystery. We understand little of this universe, of time, of life.

How can we all do better?

. . .

THE TWO SISTERS frazzled Mick's days and inflamed his nights. With Miranda he felt cautious and predatory as her cat. She was too beautiful and lean under her Levis and madras. Her every act and intonation seemed to focus on the magic place between her thighs that would drive him crazy if he ever got into it.

She kept him leashed, saying he was Cynthia's. The sisters had agreed, perhaps without ever discussing it, that neither would hunt the other's prey. But she could tease all she wanted. And maybe take it further. Anytime she wanted. *To Hell with Cynthia,* anyway.

Like their illustrious Republican family both sisters were a mad mix of sophistication and rigid Catholicism. Both had spent long periods in Europe and could be equally ruthless in French, German or English. They were infernally complicated beyond his understanding – one minute wanting to ride cows in a field, the next weeping over a toy lost years ago. He could not decode what made them so similar and far apart.

He felt an insecure superiority over them because they had led pampered lives. When they'd first met, Cynthia was innocent, guilt-obsessed, afire with lust. They spent Thanksgiving weekend alone in her family's vast estate on the beach at Fire Island, writhing for hours in clothed coitus on dusty couches, antimacassared chairs and slippery silk carpets while the radio chanted *She Loves You Yeah Yeah Yeah* in the background, but never would she undress completely and make love.

Mornings they drank coffee with her father's 35-year-old cognac while she played a black Bösendorfer, filling the huge grim rooms with the rich thunder of Saint-Saëns, Scriabin, Couperin and Bach. Afternoons they barefooted the beach, played sex, Schubert sonatas and blues guitar, talking like children who have just discovered their voices, their separateness.

Like the sand and wind, the star reflections rising and falling on black waves, like unfulfilled desire, infinity was everywhere. Everything could stand for something else – was a grain of sand only a grain of sand, a star just a star? Everywhere they looked they were lost in the infinity of infinite infinities, worlds without end. "Yearning for joy," she whispered, half-naked, "for understanding – desiring, nearly demanding it – will only make it more inaccessible."

"The things I worry about are *all* insoluble. So why do I worry about them?" He'd been sketching a pebble and unsatisfied with the sketch had dropped the pebble. Now he looked but could not find it amid the sea of pebbles at his feet.

"Maybe it's just coping with the knowledge of defeat. That no matter how we try we'll never understand things."

Back at Smith she sent him long letters almost daily from her "nunnery", full of frustration, desire, argument, and explanation. Long passages about Hopkins and Greek tragedy and the *Pathétique* hid brief confessions of lust and love. *"Darling boy,"* she'd start, or *"Charming Prince"* or *"Chou chou"* – "cabbage cabbage", meaning darling in French, *"my new decision is not to think about the blackness – the horrid obscurity with a thousand thrashing beasts –"*

The poems she sent, like the one by Wen-Che'en Meng-chia, only irritated him with their non-directness.

A soft breeze issued from your mouth: I felt
It pass through my body and my heart;
I yearned to keep that moment forever,
But it fled without pause.

Why couldn't she just *say* what she felt?

But she did that too, in a way that drove him crazy with teasing promises,

"Dearest boy were I there I would put my hands on your shoulders and look at you. Probably I would blush. Then, should you fail to kiss me within 7 seconds, I would kiss you myself, very gently, barely touching your lips, merely whispering over them. Then I should take your face in my hands, molding my cupped palms to your cheekbones and after looking again, after searching your eyes, I would run my hands through your hair. You should know the sensation of running one's fingers through short hair – a few

seconds of warm contact, a titillating break and coolness of the air slipping
under the fingers first and rushing then to the palm..."

Her letters annoyed him, too romantic and literary. And if she felt such physical affection why didn't she let herself go? He wrote occasional short answers trying to cut through her mind games. "You seem far too preoccupied with your own state of mind – like a hypochondriac with a self-induced illness – it annoys me when there's so much real grief in the world. Think of Vietnam –"

"Mick, I'm trying to pierce *all* the veils. Right down to raw life."

"Vietnam *is* raw life."

She came up from Smith every weekend. They fought and sometimes fucked and threw things at each other and took long walks in the forest. They'd reached, he realized, the point where love and hate, need and disrespect, weighed equally. Sex sowed intimacy and dissension, desire and guilt, a poisonous balm that glued them and from which they tried to tear apart. She feared it and could not live without it, hid her nakedness and vaunted it, wanted to be filled and loved her emptiness.

Sin and *Thea* he thought of her: Goddess of Sin, or *Syn* and *Thea*: a synthesis of goddesses, and in this duality between the Goddess of Sin and the union of the divine burned his need for her.

"Darling boy I hate you for what you've done to me," she said, taking him inside her, clawing and biting—*It's only love, and that is all; but it's so hard loving you.* Then she'd go for long lone walks in the rain coming back to lay wet hair against his cheek, "Darling I love you so. I'm so young still. I just don't understand. My *needing* to talk makes me say silly things..."

She called one Thursday that she couldn't come this weekend because of a Chaucer paper. "But Miranda's going up to Williams to see some preppie. You finally may be able to sleep with her, as she and I've agreed it's okay."

"I have no say in this?"

"She's so much more sensual than I. Still I wish you'd come down here. Not that I grudge you a good lay but I should like to see your blue eyes that can look so deeply into mine."

When he came back from rock climbing Saturday afternoon, intending to hitch to Smith, Miranda was sitting on his sofa in a Red Sox t-shirt and white underpants, her fiery lioness hair spread out like a fan in the sunlight. "I've fucked the guys upstairs," she said. "It was boring."

"Where's your goddamn cat?"

"Back at Holyoke. I only recently discovered sex, you know. I had no idea..."

"Cynthia told me," he started to say but didn't want to risk Miranda feeling guilty. Her kiss was powerful, her lips wide and strong, her deep warm throat sucking him in. She pulled off her t-shirt and underpants and they made love on the dusty couch and on the floor beside the hole of the dentist's chair and in his narrow dental lab bedroom on its squealing single bed. "I love this," she gasped. "Jesus don't you?"

Afterwards she lit a cigarette. "I don't see what all the trouble is."

"About what?"

"About sex, silly." She leaned up on elbows, breasts drooping, put out her cigarette on the floor. "It's *so* lovely, such *fun*. Why do they castigate it?"

He felt sated, sleepy. "Who?"

"We're not supposed to make love till we marry, can't make love in the Holyoke dorms. Why can't we just be free, enjoy each other's bodies like God created us? Why's sex a sin? When it's what gives us life? Is *life* a sin?"

Sitting up she banged her head on the low ceiling. "You park with a boy and a cop shines his light in. Your parents don't want you to do it when *it's* what that keeps them together, that caused them and you to exist – why? Even *they* call it *making* love!"

"You're an ideologue." He kissed her breast. "A Leninist of love."

"I'm eighteen and I've just discovered sex." She gripped his tired prick. "Four years I've wasted... could've started at fourteen." She kissed the muscles of his stomach. "It's the single best feeling in the world..."

He woke with her long body cooling against him. The setting sun through the small square window reddened his hand against her pale shoulder. His skin looked like the sun-cracked surface of a desert lake, as if he were already old or dead. He got up, dressed not looking at her, and hitched to Smith, crushed by guilt that poisoned every sense of goodness, happiness, self-trust or aspiration. Why, he wondered watching the dark looming trees slide past, am I already so ensnared in the morality of marriage?

He walked with Cynthia through the Northampton woods. They stopped on a wooden bridge across a stream that reflected distant streetlights. "So did you?" she whispered.

"Did I what?"

"Sleep with my sister?"

How could he tell her, give her the pain of knowing her sister had offered freely what Cynthia gave so rarely and with such restraint? "No."

"I thought you would."

"I didn't."

"I thought you would."

He'd betrayed Cynthia for cheap sex. But he'd also deserted Miranda without goodbye, a girl who'd shared her lust and life openly. Was *that* love?

Cynthia's letter arrived Tuesday. "I called Miranda today," she wrote. "We were remembering riding school in Ireland at Colonel Bryce Mountbourne's – our mother rode his horses for the Dublin show when she was twenty. Miranda seems very guarded toward me. I think she's jealous of my relationship with you. Or perhaps she's guilty?"

The trap had been Cynthia's. When he finally admitted it to her, beyond the guilt of sleeping with her sister was the greater guilt of lying. "I told you I didn't care," she seethed sweetly, "but I asked you to tell me the truth. I *trusted* you –"

. . .

I TRUSTED YOU. What every American could have said to Lyndon Johnson, who had campaigned for his 1964 reelection on the promise to send no American soldiers to Vietnam. But on March 8, 1965 he sent the Marines ashore at Danang, the first U.S. regular combat troops in Vietnam, and what everyone had feared of Barry Goldwater was being done by his opponent.

People watched stunned as Washington became *Animal Farm.* Perhaps it always had been but they'd never realized. PhD technocrats shilled the War with doublespeak, and to doubt them was a thought crime. It was as T.S. Eliot had described, thirty-five years ago.

And I pray that I may forget
These matters that with myself I too much discuss
Too much explain...
Suffer us not to mock ourselves with falsehood

Between dark-haired medieval Cynthia and fiery red-haired catlike Miranda soon erupted an undeclared war. As wars are often fought over ground not very different from any other, he realized, so they were fighting over him. Silently and fiercely in the deadly covert spirit of their wealthy reclusive family, neither admitting their war even existed, acting as dear sisters and allies but each baring whatever claws and skin were needed to snare him. Cynthia was a year older and felt she had him, but Miranda's craving was stronger; she was more jealous, hungrier, wilier, more ruthless in bed, as if by sated flesh alone she could win him.

With Cynthia he was slipping into a ruthless attraction. With Miranda he was a male tiger – hungry for this female but wary of her claws. Neither sister was enough; the two drove him wild, his back raked with fingernails, loins weak with exhaustion. Every hour with Cynthia was intensified by guilt over Miranda; every moment with Miranda burned hotter because it was so evil and uncontrollable.

.   .   .

"**EVOLUTION IS PREFERABLE** to revolution, no?" Thierry Gascon knocked his pipe into the waste basket beside his desk. "Look at what happened in the French Revolution."

"What's the difference?" Peter Weisman said, sitting on the edge of the desk.

"Evolution, is the natural flow of events, no? But Revolution is an *intellectual* decision, *forcing* change. Not just letting it happen. Perhaps replacing change with its semblance?"

A visiting Williams professor from Paris, Thierry was 26 and brilliant, with a wild sense of humor. "For those who think," he quoted Walpole, "life is a comedy. For those who feel, it's a tragedy. So it's better to think than feel, no?"

"But the French Revolution was essential to the founding of modern France," said Tom Barnhardt, sitting on a backwards chair at the front of the desk. A co-founder of the Williams chapter Students for a Democratic Society, he was determined to find alternatives to an existing American sociopolitical structure that did not seem to work.

"No, no, no!" Gascon riposted. "Before the French Revolution, everything was already changing. The aristocracy was leading many of these changes, in land reform, education, banking, elections. Then the radicals took over and tore it all down, the good and the bad, destroyed some of the world's most beautiful architecture, executed thousands of good and thoughtful people... It took years for France to recover. Then we had Napoleon who set out to conquer the world to prove he wasn't a little man, and beggared and murdered us all again."

He stopped to fill his pipe. "Political structures must evolve, not be destroyed, no? Look at the Soviet Union, the same thing was happening then the Leninists unseated Kerensky and created the most repressive regime in modern history. A shame, no?"

IT WAS THE BEATLES' YEAR. They succeeded because they made people happy, but they could not have touched people as they did without the death of JFK, for there was an undertone, a subconscious sadness overcome, in their magnificent music.

And they reinstated the long-lost legitimacy of honest love and sex, after generations of anodyne music and denial. The days of singing nuns, mindless crooners, and meaningless ditties had vanished; nothing could be plainer than *"Can't Buy Me Love"* and nothing more complex.

And they were so astonishingly creative they could write and record ten or fifteen excellent, unique songs in the time other musicians trickled out one "hit", which was perhaps as fast as their songwriters could write them. And the rock album as a single piece of art, as a concerto or symphony, was born.

Late into the night Mick played Beatles on his beat-up Fender Mustang that he'd named Black Beauty till his fingers were raw, till the words ran like mantras through his mind; he woke with them flowing effortlessly through him.

Music concised the world. So much happening simultaneously, billions of people living their lives – how do you say it all in a few lines, sum it up? Music.

This last semester he cut over half his classes, wandering the forests, playing music, playing soccer with the Africans Williams had imported to upgrade their team.

He was on the verge of flunking out again, this time really for good. He locked himself in his room and tried to study, but after an hour it became too boring, the soft breeze outside the window too enticing. "Please try," Cynthia would plead. "Just study for the next hour, then when that hour's done do it again. Like the Chinese say, the journey of a thousand miles is just a succession of single steps."

Truth was he'd rather walk a thousand miles than study one more hour.

TROY BANKED THE GLIDER hard to line up on the long black line of the Academy airfield. Blinking to clear his eyes he scanned the sky once more for other aircraft but saw none. It was a bright blue afternoon with the sun a hand's width above the conifered western hills.

Cool mountain air whistled past the canopy giving him a feeling of peace and seclusion. He checked again that the field was clear; banking a final ten degrees he straightened course and dropped toward it. "Verify your approach," Lieutenant Scanlon said laconically from the instructor's seat.

"Verified, Sir."

"Verify again."

Irritated, Troy scanned the skies but could see nothing but the hazy western hills, the Academy stretching to the west, the Chapel's shiny spires blurred by the glider's plastic canopy. He eased back on the stick and let the glider settle into its final approach.

Suddenly the glider jerked hard starboard and dropped like a stone; he fought with the stick but it didn't respond, the ground coming up sideways; from nowhere another glider twisted past him and dropped fast toward the field. "Jesus, Cadet," Lieutenant Scanlon yelled. "You blind? You didn't see that goddamn aircraft?"

Scanlon had taken over the controls. Troy felt fury and fear. "He came from nowhere, Sir."

"Hell he did! He was at eleven o'clock and two hundred feet below you. He had landing precedence and you damn near tore off his wing!"

Troy toggled the stick but it didn't respond. "I'm taking her in," Scanlon said. "And I'm taking you off flight classes till further notice."

I didn't see him, Sir, Troy started to respond, but didn't. *I never saw him at all.*

35

ROLLING THUNDER

TARA CHECKED HERSELF in the bathroom mirror, adjusted her fake pearl necklace and earrings. A stall door clanged; a muscular crewcut woman in a black t-shirt came out. "My, Honey," she smiled, "don't *we* look hot tonight."

"Thanks Sybil."

"Nervous again ain't you Honey?" Sybil gave her a quick hug. "All those people out there, remember – they're *all* family. *Our* family." She patted Tara's jaw. "Let yourself go. Let your love pour into them."

"I get so terrified sometimes, I'm shaking so hard I can't sing."

Sybil gripped her arm. "You're the very best blues singer most of these folks're *ever* gonna hear. You remember that." She held open the door. "So let's go *do* it!"

Tara tucked back her hair, tugged her thin top away from her breasts, gulped some Benedictine and strutted onto the dark stage, waiting for the light.

Jesus, I promise. I will never do this again.

THE LETTERS on the eye chart were too small. It wasn't fair; last year Troy could've seen them easily.

"Don't squint," the doctor said.

"I can see fine. It's just my allergies."

"This isn't allergy season, Cadet."

"It's an A, an E, a D. Next line is an F – no, that's an E..."

The doctor flipped on the light. "Sit down, son." Troy sat. No one at the Academy had ever called him "son" before. "It's a common problem," the doctor added, "young men your age..." the doctor put a hand on Troy's knee, and Troy thought of long-ago Father Loudy at the Boys' Home, but it wasn't like that now – this man just wanted to help him – "at the end of adolescence their eyes go bad."

Troy took a breath. The worst was over once you admitted it. "Last month, I nearly had a mid-air."

The doctor nodded. "That's why you're here."

Troy swallowed. The worst's over, once you admit it. "I'll never fly?"

"Never."

"Ever since I was a kid I wanted to fly. Explore space..." Tears rushed from the corners of his eyes; he couldn't stop them.

"There's plenty to do in the Air Force without flying. The wars of the future'll be fought with missiles. With your engineering skills you can lead the way."

"I want combat."

"Then you should cross-commission into the Army or Marines or Navy, get some time in Vietnam. Whatever you do you'll always be a fine fighting man."

THE INTENSIVE BOMBING of North Vietnam began March 2, 1965, named Operation Rolling Thunder, from the Christian hymn, *How Great Thou Art,*

> *O Lord my God, When I in awesome wonder,*
> *Consider all the worlds Thy Hands have made;*
> *I see the stars, I hear the rolling thunder,*
> *Thy power throughout the universe displayed.*

Then sings my soul, My Savior God, to Thee.

Mick could not stop thinking of the thousands of tons of explosive steel raining down on villages, farmers' rice paddies, schools, hospitals, stores, roads, and the rest of that poor little country, could not help but imagine himself in thin cotton clothing in the dark night, the earth-shuddering explosives, the hailing death and wrenching agony thundering out of the skies.

When the rolling thunder of the bombs fell on the thousands of Vietnamese families, did *their* souls sing *My Savior God, to Thee?*

What right did he have to be careless, happy, and free when his government was killing half a million people? There was no answer, no possible solution.

Guys at Berkeley had started burning their draft cards. Was that the answer?

He'd been brought up to see the country as good, as a positive caring force in the world. But now how could Americans consider their country good? Yet they seemed to believe the lies they were told in a blind intentional stupidity, a numb obedience. "Do not kill," Christ had said. "We can kill millions," the Americans answered, "and still be good Christians."

BEAR CREEK SPARKLED fast and cold. Troy sat on a sun-warm boulder watching yet barely seeing the silvery flowing water caress the rocks and ledges and downed aspens along the banks. Cutthroats flashed speckled bellies in a cobalt pool, dippers waded the shallows and towhees pecked along the edges; the tracks of a mother black bear and the diminutive prints of her twin cubs mottled the sand; wind sighed in the pines and hissed through the tighter needles of the Douglas firs; cotton cumulus chased each other nose to tail across a bitter sky he would never rise above.

Impossible, hateful, that his eyes had gone bad. He felt betrayed, despised his body, his eyes, the eternity of things gone wrong. What had he done, to cause this?

Tomorrow he'd return to the Academy med office and stare at the eye chart and see everything sharp as always down to the sixth row, his vision like a razor. "Twenty-ten," the doctor would smile. "You'll make a fine pilot."

He had always seen clearly not just with eyes but the mind. Could separate shit from truth, see the nexus within, focus on what he wanted and *get* it. Now his eyes had betrayed him and space was beyond his grasp. When it had been so goddamn close.

Goddamn: that was *it*. God threw us out of the Goddamn Garden because we wanted to *see*. Wanted to understand the *secret* of life. What was so Goddamn wrong with that? Didn't God need all the help He could get? Didn't He need allies not slaves?

Fuck God. He blinded me so I'll walk the night on my own.

Dad was a Marine. I can't call him Dad but I will anyway. My real Dad was a Marine too. He would've wanted me to be a Marine. But what if my real Dad had hated the Marines, wanted not to be killed but to be home with his wife and baby boy?

Couldn't think that way. Mick's Dad had brought him home, told the Fathers go fuck themselves. What they'd been doing all along.

He watched the water curl and flow, the bubbles join and separate like galaxies. In the four years he'd been at the Academy, Bear Creek had always been his refuge, at first to escape the upper cadets, then the pointless rigors of the Academy itself: if this is how we're making warriors we'll never win the next war.

And now these cheating scandals – how could Air Force cadets change the world when they couldn't even change their own hearts? Didn't we all swear to follow the Honor Code, *"We will not lie, steal, or cheat, nor tolerate among us anyone who does."*

Had all the 109 cadets who resigned for cheating thought it didn't matter?

As a member of the Honor Board he'd had to decide how many cadets to throw out and how many to discipline but let stay. Two cadets had broken into an office and stolen the exam papers, then sold them to most of the football team and a lot of other cadets. How could you discriminate between stealing and cheating?

Over the sparkling creek a dragonfly snatched a mayfly as a cutthroat rose to catch it and as the dragonfly flew away a towhee snatched it from the sky. What better message: to live is to kill. Life is death.

Fucking Vietnam. Wimps like Mick not wanting to go. Troy stood brushing sand from his jeans, spit into the creek. Marines you motherfuckers here I come. Hope it don't end before I get there.

I want blood.

I TRIED TO CALL YOU, Troy wrote Tara, *but you never answer – is it the right number? Is something wrong?*

She sat in the warm sun on the back deck of her Berkeley one-bedroom with his letter on her knee. It made her want to choke, this strange mix of wanting and not wanting him. To know he existed. And now he was telling her he couldn't fly, that all those years of hoping and planning had come to nothing. His bedroom at the farmhouse, the shiny airplane models hanging from transparent leaders, him sitting at the kitchen table late at night calculating physics problems, eyes gleaming with plans to navigate the stars.

That first night in the barn three years ago – she'd taunted him till he did it to her, up against a wooden post then down on the straw. He'd wanted it, too – then the times in the woods, upstairs in Lafayette's house. It wasn't sex like she had now with Blade, it had a heartbroken hunger that couldn't be satisfied. Then they killed the baby and Ma died and she was a tree cut off at the roots.

She imagined Troy in his uniform standing at attention, saluting. She giggled. How funny, this skinny bucktoothed boy so seriously training – now for what?

She went back in the kitchen to refill her coffee. Strong and black, warming the cup in her hands, the sun warm on her back through her denim shirt. She moved a chair into the shade of the lemon tree, and another chair for her feet, lit a joint and savored the coffee and the weed together in the fragrance of lemon flowers. *I love Troy*, she realized suddenly. *I don't love Blade.*

If she lived with Troy he wouldn't have other women. She cleared her throat, rough and hoarse, took another swallow of coffee. "Too much weed," Sybil had said. "Deadens the throat. Gonna hurt your singing."

Fuck my singing. The thought of touring made her stomach contract, her arms feel weak. Maybe she'd tell Blade, no more touring. Tell him tonight.

She felt the sun on her back, looked around the kitchen, bright and homey, the lovely back deck with its lemon and lime trees – *Then who'd pay for this? And for the yellow XKE and the coke she did sometimes? The pleasurable knowing that you don't have to worry, you have enough?*

A female hummingbird hovered over a lemon blossom, the tip of its tiny tongue darting from its long beak as it drank. The morning air was scented with the dry grassy heat of the hills and the far tang of the sea. *Take what you can, girl,* she told the hummingbird. *While you can.*

TO ESCAPE KILIFI, Daisy sometimes borrowed her neighbor Jeremiah's tan Datsun pickup on weekends and drove all the way to the Tsavo, hungry for its vast dusty emptiness and gray-green scrub, for some echo of the past, she realized, of our four-million-year journey from these deadly savannas to the verge of space.

At night she slept doubled up in the front seat of the Datsun, a makeshift mosquito net hung from the half-open windows, listening with shivering fear and delight to the roars of lions and snarls of leopards, the thunderous shrill of elephants, the mad cackle of hyenas, the songs and sorrows of a hundred other species, the slow rumble of the stars overhead, stars so thick they made the night like day, a vast milky luminescence.

In the blistering days she climbed a tree to be safe from lions and watched the wildlife, or drove slowly along the ancient potholed roads looking for cheetahs, for any place where bones might hint at a distant past.

Jeremiah was a machinist and could fix anything, made new vehicles from parts of others. In his fifties, white-stubbled, he lived with three wives and nineteen children in a rondavel on the hill above her hut in the village. He was tall and slender but muscular with strong hands, and sometimes he came with her to Tsavo and stretched a hammock between two thorn trees, and they made love all night rocking the hammock and listening to the animals and laughing and watching the stars.

In Kilifi they could not do this because as a teacher she could not visit men alone, and to live with her he'd have to take her as his wife… *None of that,* she'd told him, *don't you even think it.*

Yet he came to her hut whenever he could evade her nosy neighbors, slipping through the darkness out of the rain, his shoulders glossy wet as he lifted her and set her upon him, her body afire.

One night in Tsavo an elephant herd came through the acacia grove where they were sleeping. They lay not daring to breathe in the hammock under the mosquito net as the huge creatures rumbled around them, ripping branches and munching down the leaves. A mammoth female bumped their hammock with a columnar leg; her black silhouette blotted out the stars. Then she began to pee, sighing as it spattered down on the hard earth beside their hammock.

"She must've peed for twenty minutes," Daisy whispered when the elephants had gone, settling against Jeremiah now the danger was over.

"Don't put your feet down," he said. "Not till morning."

"Even then…"

From the neighboring hills a lion roared disconsolately, a few hyenas chattered back, and the wilderness grew quiet again.

But she couldn't sleep in the aftermath of fear and the lingering, warm stench of elephant pee. Once in this place people lived in trees and climbed down to wander with the elephants. How strong and safe the elephants, and how puny we are, and they didn't mind us traveling with them. That's how we first went out into the world, after all. Wandering with the elephants.

Lying in the hammock she could practically reach that time, *touch* it, the way *it* was back then. Coming down from the trees, then wandering the savanna clothed in skins, then fire. What made us different, more canny, than everyone else? Why did we progress and our brothers and sisters, bonobos and chimps, did not? What lethal cue in the brain made us so dangerously different?

Were our paleolithic ancestors more peaceful than we?

What if the so-called "nuclear" family is just that – an explosion that destroys millennia of tribal connections, of being one with others? No other primate lives a nuclear life; no other primate except a single species of lemur is monogamous.

Would we be better off as a clan?

Would that have stopped my father from becoming what he was?

In daylight she drove the ancient, potholed dirt roads, scanning for wildlife, the flowing herds of wildebeest, gazelles, impalas, zebras, buffalos and kudus, the clouds of birds rising from the marshes, the languorous crocodiles dozing on riverbeds, ready to attack at race-horse speed anyone foolish enough to come near, to take that person down and spin them underwater till they drowned, then bury them in the bottom mud for delectation weeks later.

No, she grinned, hands easy over the steering wheel, she didn't want that. Life is full of crocodiles wanting to spin you down into the depths, to store your corpse for later.

Then back to Kilifi, boring and flat, the children gregarious and unchanging, the schoolroom superheated, simple words and numbers in a humid furnace. The Indian Ocean so hot she sometimes got out of it to cool off in the blistering air.

Life in the hot swamplands of coastal Africa.

THE GRASS had a tangy pleasant odor. Mick took a hit and drew in slowly, fearing he'd cough, lungs balking at the hot smoke, and passed it to Cynthia who waved it away. He fingertipped it to Seth who inhaled, chuckled, and handed it to Miranda who sucked it into her lungs, eyes bright, fingertips caressing Hugh's as she gave it to him.

Delightful warmth rose up the back of Mick's brain. He smiled at how fascinating everything was – Hugh's living room with the German poetry books stacked up the wall, dead flowers in dirty water, dark shiny floorboards, a stained coffee pot, an open bag of English muffins, a dusty chunk of fluted marble, the candlelight on Miranda's forearm, her tawny ocelot watching them with feline scorn from the Victorian couch.

The back of Miranda's hand grazed his. Her cool electric heat flowed into him; he felt the shock of her body, her animal vitality and tingling excitement, her hot invisible sex. The wine caught fire in his glass. Another joint came around; a fragrance of chestnut fires and burning cane straight down his throat into his brain.

Cynthia's black hair brushed his cheek. Across her shoulder Miranda's azure eyes watched him. She turned to the light showing her body through her white silk dress with nothing beneath it, her perfect breasts, small waist and indented navel, the shadow of her crotch.

They sat cross-legged on the rug, Miranda opposite him with Seth on one side and Hugh on the other, Cynthia and Mick. Miranda crossed her legs letting him see up her long pale thighs. They smoked and drank more Beaujolais, arguing about Nietzsche and Vietnam and rock 'n roll and freedom. Mick lay back with his glass watching the darkness of Miranda's cunt.

Hugh took off the medieval German organ music. "Put it back on, creep!" Miranda hissed. He put on Muddy Waters, a hand on Miranda's shoulder as he sat beside her.

Mick stood on the porch watching the stars, sucking in the cool Williamstown night air that smelled of damp soil, young leaves, and the breeze from the forest. Miranda came out with a bottle and refilled his glass. Drops ran down his fingers. She put the bottle on the porch rail and leaned beside the door, half-shadowed.

"You better go back in there," he said. "Seth'll miss you."

"Tant pis." She lifted her dress past her knees and thighs to her belly's fiery curls and slim waist and up over her high pink-nippled breasts. Suffused in her golden glow he reached for her, but she dropped the dress and ducked back inside the screen door and smiled. "Just wanted you to remember. What you're missing."

Walking home to his apartment Cynthia turned to him laughing

313

about Montaigne and her face turned green, her flesh dripped from the bone; eye sockets merry and red. "Love is death," she whispered.

Later they lay naked on the sofa beside the dentist's hole. "I didn't say that," she said. "I don't think that."

"I can see the heart of things. Hot and red and beating. The truth under the skin."

She took up his Mustang and began to play *Malagueñas*, four fingers and thumb, faster, then faster so it became a rhythmic trance, a key to life. He could feel the gypsy guitarists in Granada, their scratched voices, the brandy and garlic olives, their music throbbing like the stars.

36

WE CAN GO PLACES

A GIRL NAMED GLORIA CAME down from Bennington for the week before Mick's final exams. She was tall and rangy with a gap between her upper front teeth that showed when she smiled. Mick gave up studying; they sat on his mattress beside the dentist's hole and smoked grass and she sang, low and hoarse, while he played the blues.

"It's silly," she unbuttoned her blouse and pulled it over her head and shook her hair loose, "that the most important, mysterious, wonderful thing we can do, the creation of life, is seen as dirty, disgusting, shameful! Sex is *so* beautiful – I *love* having you inside me," she unhooked her bra and slid it down her arms, "it makes me feel so good – why is it hated and denigrated and feared?"

"Not by me."

"You have guilt too." She unbuckled her jeans and wriggled them down her hips. "I do too, it's in our culture – how do we get rid of it?"

"By making love." He kissed her belly button and down into her fragrant red cotton underpants, the downy hair. Stooping over the HiFi she put on a new group called the Rolling Stones, grinding her hips to the beat.

She had finished Bennington early and was leaving for Peace

Corps training and Thailand. The last night he saw her, she was in her room, all packed, and crying.

"You sad to leave?" he said.

Wordless, she handed him a letter. "It's from my Mom."

I'm sorry to tell you Dear but it was in the paper last week Tim Dugan was killed in Vietnam. We want to call his folks but don't know what to say. As you know he was their only child. And yesterday Carl Sanborn's death was in the paper, from your high school class. Did you know him? Please stay safe, dear girl, watch your health. We miss you.

"Tim Dugan,..." she said. "He was a red-haired kid with a short round nose, blue eyes and freckles. Lots of girls liked him, but he asked this homely, overweight girl named Debbie Schneider to Junior Prom because he liked her and didn't want her sitting it out. And found he liked her more and more and they'd kept dating and she'd lost weight and turned out kind of pretty and they both went to U Mass. Where's Debbie now? Oh my God what's she feeling?"

She shook her head, denying the undeniable. "Carl Sanborn played linebacker and hated Latin and brushed the front of his crew cut with a wax stick. He always wore tan chinos and black loafers. His dad ran Sanborn's Pharmacy. We used to sit on the red vinyl stools at the counter and drink chocolate malts. His father got sick so Carl quit college to help run the pharmacy. Who's going to help now? Where are Carl's soft laugh, his big knobby hands? What do you suppose *he* thought it was, this life?"

"He was your boyfriend?"

"Not at all." She started to cry. "I just *liked* him."

TROY SMASHED HIS RIFLE down on the soldier's helmet and drove him deep into the mud. The soldier clawed at him; he pushed him deeper, mud closing over his face.

"Good!" Sergeant Aikens screamed. "That's a kill!"

Troy yanked up the other Marine, a tall black kid. *"You!"* the black kid gasped, "you fuck'n *crazy!*"

Sergeant Aikens shook him. "This's how you win wars," he yelled.

"I don't want you to die, in Vietnam!" He shoved the kid back into the mud. "You're stuck there till you beat somebody." He spit into the mud, stared round at the squad of recruits. "Now who's gonna kick this guy's ass?"

Troy sat on a tree trunk wiping mud from his rifle. "That's good," the Sergeant smiled down. "I like that –"

"What's that?"

"Cleaning your rifle right away... Someday it's gonna save your life." He turned to the others, "Hey you assholes! We got a real Marine here, not one a you piss*ant* cowards who don't remember to clean his rifle!"

Troy stared down, furious and ashamed, thought of Father Loudy reaching for him in the orphanage cell, then, strangely, of the Ten Commandments.

The others started cleaning their guns. The black kid won his next match, stood wiping mud from his face with the back of a forearm. "Sorry," Troy nodded at him.

"Asslick!" he muttered.

"What?" Troy yelled, *"what* did you say?"

The kid faced him. "Go fuck youself."

"*Hey!*" the Sergeant called at Troy, "Y'ain gonna take that?"

Troy looked at the kid. "I beat you fair –"

"Yeah?" the kid nodded. "You still a asslick."

Troy snatched him by the shirt and the kid punched him and Troy threw him into the mudpit. Breath knocked out, the kid lay choking. Troy pulled him out, held out his hand. "No point to fight. We're on the same side."

The kid bent over, gasping. "Hell no we ain't."

WHY ARE WE HUMANS like we are? When we don't need to be? Or *do* we?

No matter how much Daisy thought about it, every answer led nowhere. She lay on her rope bed in her pole and bamboo hut in the starlit smoky stillness of a Kenyan town in jungle night, banana leaves rasping on the rusted metal roof, an aggrieved birdcall, the far whisper of sea on sand.

Why do we plunder and rape and burn and slaughter and love and cherish, protect, nourish and engender? There *had* to be a reason.

Something deep in the brain. DNA?

The answer was research. And for that she needed a damn PhD. When being out on the Tsavo could teach her so much more...

The idea of a PhD made her think of Jeremiah's big throbbing cock. How she loved to grip it as he stuck it into her. She giggled, *Oh girl, you* have *to get more serious.*

This made her giggle again, and she decided maybe she should look into the link between big cocks and peaceful nations.

When they're that big you don't have the energy to do anything else.

How funny that here in East Africa they actually tie stones to the boys' cocks when they're little. So they run around, stretching them out.

No kidding, she imagined telling Mom. *They really do...*

Each day she wrote her mother a letter, and each week she sent them all in one envelope from the Kilifi post office to Iowa. Six weeks later, she would get one letter in return.

"I want to do research," she told Mom. "There's something out there I want to understand."

"Something out there?" her Mom wrote back. "What?"

"I'm not sure," Daisy answered, "But it's out there and I want it."

Your brain, her brain told her. *You and me, we want to understand each other.*

Then we can go places.

MICK FELT LONELY and unprepared. His own classes were nearly over and he was behind in every one. The worst burden was *Ulysses,* sole subject of a senior double seminar, and astronomy, which required actual work.

He'd majored in English because it was easiest. Good books were fun; boring ones could be skimmed. But six hours a week for ten weeks the class had droned through *Ulysses* like sheep eating their way up an endless mountain.

Hard as he tried he couldn't force himself to read it. After a few pages he'd fall asleep on the couch, at a table in the snack bar or in class. Or he'd postpone it, feeling guilty and dumb. "You're screwing yourself," he raged. "You're going to flunk."

Professor Hunt was a kindly old man, a world authority on Joyce. So enamored was he of this book he'd extemporize for hours on a tiny phrase, how its meaning rippled through the pages, give twenty interpretations of the symbolism of one word.

Joyce had thrown in five thousand word games, Hunt said, little riddles to delight the critics. To us what purpose, Mick wondered, with the beauty and fragrance of spring exploding all around, the nectar of creation rising in the air? Why read about life when it's everywhere crashing into our lives? Unable to tolerate the rattle of words inside the barren classroom while the world turned green and warm outside, he started cutting classes, never went back.

Now final exams loomed. "You're totally fucked," he told himself.

He and Seth took their rifles and hiked into the mountains. They shot cans in a quarry and blew insulators off a power line. The afternoon was hot and smelled of new grass. A freight train rattled through the valley below. Mick fired at a letter *a* in *Erie & Lackawanna* on a boxcar. White splinters flashed; a man stuck his head out the door and shook his fist; his hat fell out and bounced down the tracks. "Oh shit," Mick said, wanting to run down, grab the hat and chase the train to give the man his hat back, stunned he could have shot him, someone like Molly's Joe.

There were new Vietcong attacks on TV that night, more burning villages and more bodies in pools of blood. In what agony and horror had each person died?

"What we French learned from Vietnam," said Thierry Gascon as they drank cheap California wine in a bar downtown, "was that we were not righteous, as we thought, but evil. It took us thirty thousand dead to learn that. And a million dead Vietnamese."

On the flickering gray screen President Johnson had been serious, resolute. "I have agreed with General Westmoreland's request for forty thousand more troops. The brave South Vietnamese people are turning the tide against these aggressors. With a little more help from us they'll win."

"In World War Two," Peter Weisman said, "Lyndon Johnson stayed home as a Congressman. Then because he was afraid he'd lose his seat to a returning veteran, he went to the Philippines after the fighting was over, and took a ride on a B-26. General MacArthur needed Johnson to write a positive report about him, so he gave Johnson a Silver Star in return... Can you imagine – while guys who died after twenty brutal and terrifying missions got nothing?"

Were we the Home of the Brave or the Nation of Sheep? "We're killing a thousand Vietnamese a day," Johnson said – and the sheep ate it like spring clover. "We're napalming these children to save their souls" – and the virtuous worms squirmed happily through their burrows, eating their own shit and calling it delicious. "So jes' shut up," came the Texas smile. "Jes' carry on yer normal, wormlike, sheep-like lives. And pay yer gol-dang taxes. So we can pay for killing all these folks. And you young guys, you die when I tell ya."

And how they obeyed, the multitudes of virtuous worms and *baaing* sheep. They kept their heads down, didn't look around at what their country – thus they – were doing, climbed voluntarily onto the livestock truck and rode straight to the slaughterhouse. The slaughter of others, of their own souls.

While *The New York Times* and other newspapers allowed themselves occasionally to criticize gently, it was always in good form. "It's essential to see both sides," chorused the *Times* and other liberal papers, while carrying photos of piled corpses, helicopters spitting fire, and the irregular acne of bomb craters dispensed from the safety of thirty thousand feet.

"In 1939 Germany," Mick said, "would they have tried to see both sides?"

"I'm a Jew," Peter said. "Don't ask me that."

"That's what I'm saying: what if there aren't two sides? What if one is clearly right and the other an abomination?"

There seemed no way to stop this headlong rush to slaughter, but one could refuse to join. But if he didn't want this, what *did* he want?

The question was so confusing he could not even elucidate it. He wanted to live, but that wasn't enough. You had to commemorate life somehow, the passing moments in all their mystery and excitement. *Enthusiasm* meant *to be possessed by a god*, and that god was freedom.

But there could be no freedom till Williams was done. He had a majors final on *Ulysses* but had read few of its eight hundred pages. An upstairs classmate, Victor Forman, had obtained a case of sherry; the night before the final exam they divided *Ulysses* down the middle. Mick would scan the first half and Victor the second. The each took a bottle of sherry and began reading. After an hour they would give each other a verbal summary of what they'd read.

Soon it was time to open another bottle. This sherry must be low in alcohol, Mick decided, for Victor had opened another one too.

Through the wall came Flossie's tinny shrill. Herm's squeaky quaver rose to meet it, and like a tortured chicken Fester chimed in till he choked on his own spit. "I'd go pound on the door," Mick said, "but I'm sincerely drunk." Victor was asleep.

When Mick did bang on the door it lurched open instantly. Herm teetered gasping, head tilted, white-eyed. Inconceivably, he held a cooked lobster by the tail. An upside-down pail lay in a pool of water on the floor. Flossie sat grinning scant teeth behind the table, gin bottle in hand. From between her feet Fester risked a soft snarl.

Herm's wild white hair was haloed by the bulb hanging from the ceiling. Yellow-gray plaque coated his teeth. "Can't an old man," he hissed, "have some peace?"

"I sympathize," Mick said. "But –"

Herm's arm came down like a fastball pitcher's. Mick ducked as the lobster flew past, skidded across the hallway and clattered down the stairs. Herm slammed the door, their voices raging anew behind it.

"The ocean's straight east," Mick called to the lobster, and went back to his room.

He woke a half hour after the exam had begun. Sticky-mouthed, he ran upstairs to wake Victor and they dashed nauseously across campus to the exam room. Everyone was scribbling earnestly in blue books. Wordlessly Professor Hunt handed Mick and Victor a mimeographed page. Mick slunk to the rear feeling ashamed and worthless.

Knowing he'd fail, feeling stupidly unaware and cursing himself, he scanned the questions, heart plunging at suggestions that he quote passages from memory and cite examples. He glanced at Victor, who was writing relentlessly. Mick cursed himself again, and Victor for deserting him.

Why, he wondered, do I hate this book so much? That I would risk my future by refusing to study it?

Because, he began writing, novels are not made to be studied. They are made to give joy and understanding. Life truly described adds to the reader's experience, to the total of human awareness, helps us grow. Novels are not intellectual peaks to be summited, mental constructs to be dismantled and discussed among lifeless intellectuals. Novels are not a replacement for sex, joy, nature, fresh air, music, or love, and any writer who cannot live and celebrate those things is a fraud. Literature is not a game of chess between writer and reader, it is story telling. It ramifies our understanding of life.

Demonically he poured out his frustrations with *Ulysses*, with education, the neuter world of thought, and left the exam room shriven, as after wild sex, a tough game, a terrifying climb.

The next grim reaper was astronomy. He hadn't studied or gone to class. What right did he have to pass? After years in the woods he knew his constellations – Dad had taught them to him, out in Lafayette's pasture at night – *but you can't bullshit science and math.* Stepping from the exam room into the bright sunlight he knew he'd failed.

I was right all along, he told himself. *Should've been a Marine.*

The next day he met Professor Hunt on a campus sidewalk. "You made it," Hunt said a little breathlessly.

"*Ulysses?*"

"Of course *that*. Your exam was *brilliant!* I mean you passed astronomy."

Giddily Mick thanked him, understanding that the kindly professor had somehow convinced the astronomy department to pass him. Silently he went back to his dental office room and sat in the window bathed in sunshine and happiness. Life was suddenly open again: somehow he'd passed and could put Williams behind him and go out into the world.

Beaming in the sunlight he added up the days he'd spent in a school's indenture, now finally done. Seventeen years of nine months a year made about two thousand nine hundred days – nearly eight solid years out of his life taken for servitude in the guise of education.

That night Cynthia came up from Smith and they sat round the dentist's hole with Victor and another girl drinking the last of the sherry, singing and playing guitar. Later, for the first time, Cynthia made love gladly, almost openly as if she wanted to. In the morning they made love again, and he dressed for graduation.

They gathered for the ceremony under the sunlit elms and oaks. The commencement speaker, Adlai Stevenson, told of America's wonderful future, but Mick barely heard the words of the man for whom at age thirteen back in the 1956 presidential campaign he'd passed out leaflets all over Tappan. The statesman who had first given him hope for politics, a vision for democracy, a trust that humans can improve on the life they share.

I'm glad it's over he realized, as he took his place in line.

THE END

FREEDOM

FIRST PAGES OF AMERICA BOOK 2

HOTEL KALI

THE 1776 HOUSE lights sparkled through diamond-paned windows onto the lawns and juniper hedges and the bough of the oak where the British spy Major André had been hung.

Mick went into the bar. Troy wasn't there yet, and it was Hal's night off. Mick ordered a beer and stood with his back to the bar, trying to imagine this room crowded with General Washington's officers that last desperate winter, the rushed meetings, the urgent planning of battles and resupply and provisions. The room was long and low, a ceiling of thick square oak beams with ancient plaster between them, oak-beamed walls, the maple floor shiny and worn, the creaking ancient irregular rooms and old mullioned windows, the massive fireplace, gray river granite from floor to ceiling. Was it in this room Major André was sentenced to death? How had this brilliant young English aristocrat ended up murdered in an American village? Should any man die for something as abstract as a king or nation? Mick's ancestor who had stood guard over André the last night had later written, *The prisoner was quiet except for a frequent need to micturate.*

The door slammed but it was a man with wavy dark hair and a woman with a bleached bouffant and thick lipstick.

When I'm watchin' my TV, Mick Jagger snarled,
and a man comes on and tells me
how white my shirts can be

There was an old oil painting over the stone mantel, a pastoral scene, in the foreground a man with a straw hat and a wooden staff walking along a dirt road beside a split rail fence, beyond it a river easing through soft hills with a farmhouse atop one. He felt a terrible surge of envy and loneliness, wanting to walk that dirt road, back in the time before cars when the air was free and open, there was no separation between you and the world, and everything moved at a walking pace.

He racked the pool balls and broke, sinking them in order. How unlike Troy to be late; he thought of him in a Marine uniform like Dad's, of meeting him that first day in the deserted barracks, riding the rails, growing up together. How Troy had become the Marine that Mick had always thought he himself would be. But this was the wrong war. Like Sun Tzu said, you get to choose.

But weren't all wars evil? That was the goddamn problem.

Troy came in wearing a snap-button cowboy shirt and jeans. "Sorry." He shook Mick's hand, then hugged him. "Was there with Dad, he just kept talking."

Mick nodded. "Did he talk about my leaving?"

"Said you're driving him crazy, can't wait for you to go..."

"Old bastard," Mick grinned. "I hate to leave him."

"C'mon, you've worked all summer and fall driving that Coke truck. It's time."

Mick smiled, thinking about it, that this eased his guilt for leaving. "What *you* drive up here in?"

"Fifty-seven Chevy with racing slicks, a two fifty-seven with two four-barrels and a four-speed. Lays rubber in every gear. Made it from Quantico in seven hours."

"And you're going back tonight?"

"Be there by five a.m., if I leave soon." Troy's face seemed harder, his reddish hair drained of color under the weak lights, his eyes pale gray.

"And then?"

"Next Wednesday. LA, Guam, Okinawa, Danang," Troy recited, as if off a map, out of a book.

"And then?"

"Up country somewhere, replace some other second loot."

Who's been killed, Mick thought.

"Some guy who finished his tour, probably," Troy said in that way they'd always had of knowing each other's thoughts.

It was unbearable that he'd saved Troy from the orphanage only to lead him to possible death a decade later. "What you going to do with that hot Chevy?" he said, to fill the silence.

"Leave it at Quantico."

Again it seemed to Mick that every thought was heavy with omens: what would happen to the car if Troy didn't come back? *Don't think like that.*

Mick brought four beers to the table while Troy chalked his cue and waited for Mick to break. "When *you* leavin?"

"Monday. Like I said on the phone, Seattle to Calcutta, then Katmandu."

"Who ever heard of it? Like that place, where was it, you went in the Sahara?"

Mick sank the six but drove the seven wide. "Timbuktu –"

"Notice they all end in 'u' –"

Like Pleiku, Mick wanted to say. "Wish you weren't going."

Troy snickered. "Climbing in the Himalayas you'll be in more danger than me."

Mick raised his cue, watching Troy. "It's horrible what we're doing in Vietnam. I wish you weren't part of it."

Troy glanced up, annoyed. "Can't you fuckin' understand? It's what I *want* to do."

Mick realized the Marines had been taught how to deal with such issues by patient repetitive explanation. "You don't like the War either."

Troy let his cue slide down through his hands; the butt thumped the floor. "I can't back out on my country."

"Because I haven't joined up you think I am?"

Troy tipped his head back, looked Mick in the eyes. "Yes."

"But if this War is wrong, don't you hurt your country by doing it? If you'd been a German in 1938 what would've you done?"

Troy's ball skewed sideways. "You always make things sound so simple."

"Remember riding the rails with Molly'n Joe? What Joe said – freedom means not lying to yourself about what you do?"

"Oh yeah? Well, Joe was a Marine in Korea –"

"And he said it was insane, remember? That the soldier is the ultimate lemming, because no one else'd be stupid enough to run toward a machine gun, or die in some other horrible way, just because someone told him to! Is that what you want to be?"

Troy placed his beer carefully on the edge of the pool table. "You were always one for easy answers, Mick..."

"This War's making me hate our country. And *that* makes me even angrier. I want us to be a good country, to back freedom not military dictators, to spread wealth not steal it, to give life not kill people –"

"You know how many guys *we've* lost already? Guys like you and me who loved their families and cared about their friends and tried to do what's right?"

"And *who* put them there in the first place? It's sickening to think of the lives they would've had. It's criminal we sent them there –"

"So their deaths were for nothing?"

"Yes, if we're wrong to be there. And more killing won't bring them back."

"And loyalty?"

"Is it more loyal to do wrong because your country tells you to, like the Germans in World War Two? Or is it more loyal to your country to insist that it do right?"

Troy took a breath, nodded. "When I look at Dien Bien Phu," he said finally, "how the French lost Vietnam in fifty-four, I'm not sure we *can* win this." Hands in pockets he looked at the floor. "Just like the French, we're underestimating Giap, their ability to resupply, their morale. You'd think we'd study how France lost, but instead we're saying, 'Oh those dumb French, who cares why they lost? We know how to fight wars better than they do –'"

"So don't go."

Troy snickered. "I'm a Marine. I don't get to say what I want."

"Can't you be a conscientious objector?"

Troy laughed. "Dope-smoking draft dodgers – you want me to be like them? Johnson just signed the law outlawing draft card burning – you want me to do that?" He shook his head as if all conversation were useless. "Hear from Tara lately?"

"Last week. I was planning to fly through San Francisco to see her, but they're on tour in Texas."

"Touring all the time, what I hear."

"They've got a record out, but I can't find it."

"I write her but she don't write back."

"Last summer they did a show at the Crossroads, this famous place in New York. She said you were going to see her in Denver but you didn't come."

"Yeah, the Academy, it was during that cheating scandal. I was on an Honor Board judging those assholes. Can you imagine swearing not to cheat, then doing it?"

"Not everybody's like you, Troy."

Surprisingly Troy squeezed Mick's arm. "Or you."

They left the 1776 House and walked to separate cars. "Okay, man," Troy said. "G'bye." They hugged; it felt meaningless, mechanical. Troy gunned the Chevy, backed out fast and roared away, carbs snarling. Mick felt empty, alone.

He drove the old pickup the other way, along the River Road toward Dad's place in Nyack, thinking how when they argued Troy's face had reddened, a flush up his neck under the red-gold hairs as he laid the cue along the edge for a side shot. Mick had sensed a new hostility, an anger he'd never seen in Troy before – the passion of someone defending the only thing he'd ever dared to love.

It was not the risk of death that made the War so bad, but the abdication of all rights to one's own life. To place oneself in the total power of someone else – whether it be an ignorant sergeant or the men in Washington, DC – seemed insane. And doing it in obedience to an unjust, meaningless and ferociously brutal invasion of a faraway peasant country was so spiritually and morally damning that his body revolted from it.

I can't reach him, Mick thought. *He believes absolutely.* Maybe it was the only way Troy could deal with uncertainty. And anything that countered his belief had to be instantly rejected. Even Troy's letters displayed a certain attitude, nonchalance mixed with irony, a conscious distance. Hadn't he always been that way, though, from that first day in the deserted army barracks?

That first day Troy had wanted to fight because he'd been scared. Was that how we got into Vietnam? If so, what were we afraid of? Afraid of being taken over by Communists? Of losing to them, being forced to live their way? That some flaw in ourselves, our system, would cause us to fail? That the world's starving billions would not choose our way?

This was the real fear: that we weren't as good as we thought we were. The world he and Troy had grown up in had vanished, replaced by something cold and fatal. He suddenly feared he'd never see Troy again.

He thought of the Himalayas, cold, deadly, beautiful. *Maybe I'll be the one who dies.*

ABOUT THE AUTHOR

MIKE BOND is the author of nearly a dozen best-selling novels, a war and human rights journalist, ecologist, international energy expert and award-winning poet. He has been called *"the master of the existential thriller"* (BBC), *"one of America's best thriller writers"* (Culture Buzz), *"a nature writer of the caliber of Matthiessen"* (WordDreams), and *"one of the 21st century's most exciting authors"* (Washington Times).

He has covered wars, revolutions, terrorism, military dictatorships and death squads in the Middle East, Latin America, Asia and Africa, and environmental issues including elephant poaching, habitat loss, wilderness survival, whales, wolves and many other endangered species.

His novels place the reader in intense experiences in the world's most perilous places, in dangerous liaisons, political and corporate conspiracies, wars and revolutions, making *"readers sweat with [their] relentless pace"* (Kirkus) *"*in that fatalistic margin where life and death are one and the existential reality leaves one caring only to survive." (Sunday Oregonian).

He has climbed mountains on every continent and trekked more than 50,000 miles in the Himalayas, Mongolia, Russia, Europe, New Zealand, North and South America, and Africa.

Website for Mike Bond: mikebondbooks.com

For film, translation or publication rights,
or for interviews contact:
Meryl Moss Media
meryl@merylmossmedia.com or 203-226-0199

MIKE BOND BOOKS

GOODBYE PARIS

Special Forces veteran Pono Hawkins races from Tahiti to France when a terrorist he'd thought was dead has a nuclear weapon to destroy Paris. Joining allies from US and French intelligence, Pono faces impossible odds to save the most beautiful city on earth. Alive with covert action and insider details from the war against terrorism, *Goodbye Paris* is a hallmark Mike Bond thriller: tense, exciting, and full of real places, and that will keep you up all night. "A rip-roaring page-turner." —*Culture Buzz*

SNOW

Three hunters find a crashed plane of cocaine in the Montana wilderness. Two steal the cocaine and are soon hunted by the Mexican cartel, the DEA, Las Vegas killers, and the police of several states. From the frozen peaks of Montana to the heights of Wall Street, the Denver slums and million-dollar Vegas tables, *Snow* is an electric portrait of today's America, the invisible line between good and evil, and what people will do in their frantic search for love and freedom. "Action-packed adventure." —*Denver Post*

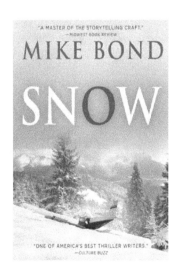

ASSASSINS

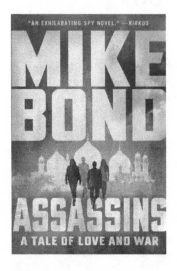

From its terrifying start in the night skies over Afghanistan to its stunning end in the Paris terrorist attacks, *Assassins* is an insider's thriller of the last 30 years of war between Islam and the West. A US commando, an Afghani warlord, a French woman doctor, a Russian major, a top CIA operator, and a British woman journalist fight for their lives and loves in the deadly streets and lethal deserts of the Middle East. "An epic spy story." —*Honolulu Star-Advertiser*

KILLING MAINE

Surfer and Special Forces veteran Pono Hawkins quits sunny Hawaii for Maine's brutal winter to help a former SF buddy beat a murder rap and fight the state's rampant political corruption. "A gripping tale of murders, manhunts and other crimes set amidst today's dirty politics and corporate graft, an unforgettable hero facing enormous dangers as he tries to save a friend, protect the women he loves, and defend a beautiful, endangered place." —*First Prize for Fiction, New England Book Festival*

SAVING PARADISE

When Special Forces veteran Pono Hawkins finds a beautiful journalist drowned off Waikiki he is caught in a web of murder and political corruption. Hunting her killers, he soon finds them hunting him, and blamed for her death. A relentless thriller of politics, sex, and murder, "an action-packed, must read novel ... taking readers behind the alluring façade of Hawaii's pristine beaches and tourist traps into a festering underworld of murder, intrigue and corruption." —*Washington Times*

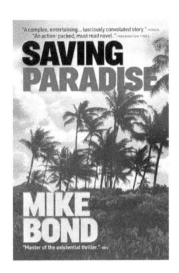

THE LAST SAVANNA

An intense memoir of humanity's ancient heartland, its people, wildlife, deserts and jungles, and the deep, abiding power of love. "One of the best books yet on Africa, a stunning tale of love and loss amid a magnificent wilderness and its myriad animals, and a deadly manhunt through savage jungles, steep mountains and fierce deserts as an SAS commando tries to save the elephants, the woman he loves and the soul of Africa itself." —*First Prize for Fiction, Los Angeles Book Festival*

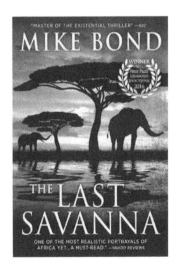

HOLY WAR

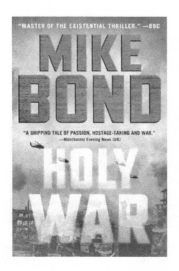

Based on the author's experiences in Middle East conflicts, *Holy War* is the story of the battle of Beirut, of implacable hatreds and frantic love affairs, of explosions, betrayals, assassinations, snipers and ambushes. An American spy, a French commando, a Hezbollah terrorist and a Palestinian woman guerrilla all cross paths on the deadly streets and fierce deserts of the Middle East. "A profound tale of war ... Impossible to stop reading." —*British Armed Forces Broadcasting*

HOUSE OF JAGUAR

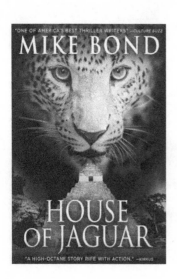

A stunning thriller of CIA operations in Latin America, guerrilla wars, drug flights, military dictatorships, and genocides, based on the author's experiences as as one of the last foreign journalists left alive in Guatemala after over 150 journalists had been killed by Army death squads. "An extraordinary story that speaks from and to the heart. And a terrifying description of one man's battle against the CIA and Latin American death squads." —*BBC*

TIBETAN CROSS

An exciting international manhunt and stunning love story. An American climber in the Himalayas stumbles on a shipment of nuclear weapons headed into Tibet for use against China. Pursued by spy agencies and other killers across Asia, Africa, Europe and the US, he is captured then rescued by a beautiful woman with whom he forms a deadly liaison. They escape, are captured and escape again, death always at their heels. "Grips the reader from the opening chapter and never lets go." —*Miami Herald*

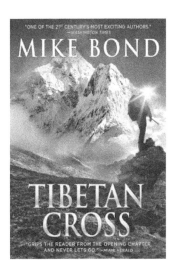

THE DRUM THAT BEATS WITHIN US

The tradition of the poet warrior endures throughout human history, from our Stone Age ancestors to the Bible's King David, the Vikings of Iceland, Japan's Samurai, the Shambhala teachings of Tibet, the ancient Greeks and medieval knights. Initially published by Lawrence Ferlinghetti in City Lights Books, Mike Bond has won multiple prizes for his poetry and prose. "Passionately felt emotional connections, particularly to Western landscapes and Native American culture." —*Kirkus*

9 781949 751208